TO ASMARA

Thomas Keneally

WARNER BOOKS

A Warner Communications Company

Warner Books, Inc., 666 Fifth Avenue, New York, NY 10103

W A Warner Communications Company

Printed in the United States of America
First printing: October 1989
10 9 8 7 6 5 4 3 2 1

Library of Congress Cataloging-in-Publication Data

Keneally, Thomas.
    To Asmara / Thomas Keneally.
      p. cm.
    ISBN 0-446-51542-6
    1. Eritrea (Ethiopia)—History—Revolution, 1962– —Fiction.
I. Title.
PR9619.3.K46T6 1989   89-40035
823—dc20   CIP

Designed by Giorgetta Bell McRee

*To my family
who allowed me for a time to travel
with the compassionate Eritrean Relief Association
and
the brave Eritrean People's Liberation Front*

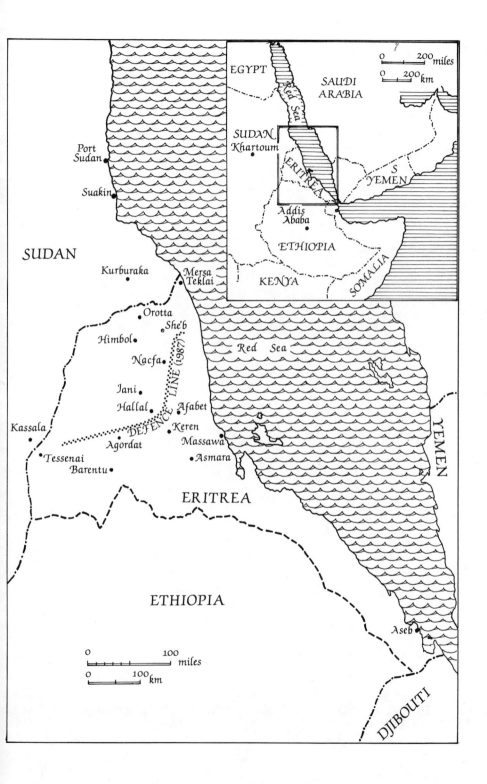

EGYPT

SAUDI
ARABIA

Red Sea

SUDAN
Khartoum

ERITREA

S
YEMEN

Addis
Ababa

ETHIOPIA

KENYA

SOMALIA

0   200 miles

0   200 km

SUDAN

Port
Sudan

Suakin

Kurburaka

Mersa
Teklai

Orotta

She'b

Himbol

Nacfa

Red   Sea

DEFENCE LINE (1987)

Jani

Hallal

Afabet

Kassala

Keren

Agordat

Massawa

Tessenai

Asmara

Barentu

ERITREA

YEMEN

ETHIOPIA

Aseb

0   100 miles

0   100 km

DJIBOUTI

The Author's Note

This is an attempt at fiction. There are nonetheless references to Eritrean events of 1987 and early 1988, though these have sometimes been compressed or relocated for fiction's sake.

As for the normal disclaimers about character, I hope the reader will accept the following: If there is a BBC correspondent in Khartoum, Stella Harries is not intended to represent that person. If there are a number of Ethiopian officers held prisoner by the Eritrean rebels, there is no evidence that—though disowned by their government—any of them ever collaborated with the Eritreans in the way Major Fida does in this account. If there is a cinematographer who has chronicled the struggle of the Eritreans, Masihi is not intended to resemble him either in person or family history. Similar reservations could be expressed about Darcy, Lady Julia, Christine and Henry. They merely stand as the author's poor simulacra for those folk, Africans and Europeans, who are drawn to Eritrea and find there all the horrors and all the extraordinary hopes.

Thomas Keneally
May 1989

Editor's Introduction

Recently, Stella Harries went back into the mountains of Eritrea, to the great rebel Eritrean base cantonment of Orotta, by the same route as that taken by Darcy and Henry, Lady Julia and the "child" Christine some months past. Ms. Harries traveled briefly to the front line as well, and even beyond it, but she was not able to visit the area to the west of the city of Asmara where Darcy was last seen. Not only is this region of high plateau a battlefield, now more than ever, but there are rumors too that, with most of its military credit gone, the Ethiopian regime, which is fighting the Eritreans, will resort to unleashing chemical weapons against the rebels.

There are other factors which inhibited Ms. Harries' travel. One was that in Eritrean villages high behind the Nacfa Front and in the dust bowls of Barka province, famine—always there in waiting behind the corner of the next erratic season—has come down harder still. Yet again, the so-called *late* rains have not appeared in what they call the Sahel, the sub-Sahara. Ms. Harries was conscious that the space she might have taken up in vehicles could have been better devoted to a couple of bags of sorghum.

The second factor which limited her movements was the scale of what's been happening there since the time of Darcy's disappearance. In the mountains, and all along the old Italian road where Darcy was last seen, there have been since March massive battles in which thousands of men and women were engaged and which, for all the world heard and hears of them, might as well take place on the moon's dark side. Again, Stella found space on trucks, coming and going, reserved for the wounded, and traveling to any timetable was impossible.

On top of that, she was delayed in Orotta by a recurrence of the malaria she originally caught in the Sudan some time back. The exhaustion of the trip and the weakness caused by continuous diarrhea left her wide open to the malarial infection in her blood. At first sweating and ranting, then helpless and somnolent, she lay in Orotta ten days. On getting up to go on with her inquiries, she collapsed again and had to be trucked back to the Sudan in a weakened state.

We know from Ms. Harries' inquiries, and the mass of taped and written material, including interviews, which Darcy left behind in his pack and which Stella brought back to the Sudan with her, a great amount about Darcy's time with the Eritrean rebels.

With a few exceptions which will become obvious to the reader, we therefore present the story of Darcy's journey into Eritrea with the "child" Christine, with Henry, and with Lady Julia, the elderly English "female affairs" warrior we shall meet later. Among the exceptions, however, are certain events to do with the Ethiopian p.o.w. Major Fida and incidents of which Darcy either could not have had knowledge or else, even given his energy for writing and recording, did not have time to note down.

The Rock Singer

I suppose my connection with the Eritreans, brave and starved creatures of the Horn, began not with my first visit to Africa but a little later, with something I and half the world saw on television. In my case, the television was located in an airshaft-facing room at the Hotel Warwick in New York.

I had just been to Colorado on a cheap flight to do an article for *The Times*, the London not the New York version, on the plight of the Ute Indians. These days getting by on a portion of arid mesa in the southwest of the state, the Ute once owned all that land which is now occupied by a string of glittering ski resorts west of Denver.

On my way back to London, while I ate my breakfast in my hotel room in New York, I saw the rock star appear on the screen, saw that solemn, youngish, straw-hatted man with dark, lanky hair, that face so familiar to people in the West, so drawn down by the weight of its own humanity.

The news segment we all saw that day went like this: The rock star stands by a small tor of bagged wheat. The wheat itself, the rock star tells us, lies outside a famished town called Mekale, in the Ethiopian province of Tigre. Behind him and beyond the wheat pyramid rises a great cliff of primal rock, and beneath the brow of this escarpment sits a crowd of villagers, their wives, their children. The men all carry wands in their hands: They are goat herders, though as the rock star soon tells us, most of their goats have died. They crouch on their haunches. Their free hands are cupped over the skulls of girl or boy children with hair cropped in an African manner, only a forelock growing freely.

These gestures of the fathers in the newsclip, this framing of the children's shaven heads with the fathers' hands, seems to be a statement: "Here is my child, precious above all others." Nonetheless the viewer is aware that a frightful patience and etiquette restrains the peasants from being vocal. They are stoical people. They deserve—you feel—a benign prince, even a benign God.

Still in the television clip, the famous singer in the straw hat shows us a particular child. Ethiopian officials seated at a table in the open are measuring it for height. Next, through an editorial cut, he makes some comments on the measurement of the same child's arms and legs. The sad dimensions of the child's hunger are marked down in a book by the Ethiopians at the table. The singer remarks that these meager centimeters shame the world.

Then, shaking his head at the camera, he begins to display more than a mere editorial outrage. His authority to be angry in an ancient, prophetic way arises—as I know—not only from what he sings to the world's young. Because the truth is, his songs aren't particularly well known. His authority comes from this: that the last time Ethiopia starved, he persuaded the big groups—Heaven Sez, The Judge, Messiah, and so on—into a performing consortium called Worldbeat, to sing on behalf of the stricken peasants of Ethiopia. Money was raised from records, tapes, and performances. Western governments were shamed into matching gestures of goodwill. Foods and medicines were packed into donated Hercules aircraft and flown to Ethiopian provinces where the greatest need lay. The Ethiopian government had been able to restrict and dominate the movements of most aid bodies, even of the Red Cross. But the singer and the Worldbeaters were too famous for Ethiopia's handsome dictator Mengistu to hamper and tyrannize. Hence the rock groups' grain went wherever the famed singer on good advice—on somewhat better advice than the sort of advice you get from dictators—wanted it to go. *Worldbeat* was a song, a surge of rock and of goodwill, to end all famine.

And yet now again, the rock star in the film clip tells me in my hotel room and the world in all its diverse locations, the catastrophe has repeated itself.

You could gauge from the suppressed anger in his voice that he is wondering how he will find the strength to do it all again, to appeal to the groups and to the youth of the West, who believe they've already dealt with the problem last time and for good. A genuine fury enters his face and makes his mouth taut. People still remember now, a year or more afterward, what the rock singer says then: Despite the cries of these children, a food convoy of some thirty trucks, on its way to an area just as stricken as this one, has been attacked by rebels and destroyed with grenades. These rebels are the Eritreans from the north, he says. They have fallen on a line of vehicles on its merciful way from the city of Tessenai and have obliterated hundreds of thousands of dollars of aid. The trucks in question, the singer assures us all, bore the insignia of the UN, the Red Cross, Worldbeat, other humanitarian groups. The Ethiopian drivers of the trucks have been harassed, and one was killed as his truck exploded.

These Eritrean rebels then, whose name the rock singer uttered so tightly, a little like a curse, were fighting against the central Ethiopian government, and had been for more than a quarter of a century. The rock singer had little patience for the willfulness which made them fight. There is no pity from them, said the rock singer. There is no pity. There is only the ancient lunacy of politics.

As captivated as I was by the rock singer's authentic grief, I had a sense of the man's knowledge of the television medium working under the surface of the footage. He knew how long he would get on network news. He knew there was time for him merely to state a scenario: a disaster and a cause, a crime and a culprit. Forty-five seconds. Given this rigid scale, and his genuine outrage, he knew that you didn't muddy the prime-time water by suggesting that the story might be complex, that there might be more than one evildoer.

So, as we all saw on our television screens, apart from the in-human drought at which no one could be personally outraged, the rock star blamed above all the rebel Eritrean attack for the just fears of these stark-eyed Tigrean farmers, of their wives swathed in the eternal patience of many-dyed cloth, and for the unsatisfactory thickness of the limbs of the pot-bellied children. It was in these Eritrean rebels that the human malice of famine was found.

At that time, I knew very little about this satanic rebel movement in the Eritrean highlands of the Horn of Africa. During my earlier assignment in the Sudan, and throughout my friendship with the generous Stella Harries, the BBC's official correspondent in Khartoum, I'd met a journalist or two who had been over the Red Sea border into Eritrea. I'd been impressed by a French cameraman who worked for the rebels, an exotic, turban-wearing figure called Masihi, who brought a few rough-cut film documentaries out of Eritrea to show to interested people in Khartoum. There could be found in Eritrea, according to the few journalists who knew, a massive war which went largely unrecorded, except of course by the French cameraman. Even in Khartoum, this war in progress in the Eritrean mountains, on the flank of the Sudan—this war which had now begotten a string of burned-out aid trucks—seemed to rouse only occasional interest.

About the same time as the rock singer's broadcast, Stella herself visited these rebels for a few weeks and came out very thin but—if you could judge from her letters and the radio programs she made—very partisan about the Eritreans. The situation she described was a complex one, and her programs were broadcast in Britain late at night, when I'd been drinking, and when the chains of political causation Stella describes were a little hard to follow.

Just the same, I began to seek out a little literature concerning these Eritrean vandals. One night, in a church hall in London, I attended a lecture by a Labour member of Parliament on the topic "Free Eritrea Now!" The event was one of those dismal, ill-attended, cold, damp, but lively sessions of the type you often see advertised in *The Times*. The politician's remarks were punctuated by plumbing noises from the nineteenth-century walls.

Drinking coffee in the lobby of the hall after the lecture ended, I was aware of the reserved presence of half a dozen Eritrean men and women. Two of the women wore padded jackets of military origin, as if they'd recently been engaged in the sort of attack the rock singer had denounced. The men wore sportscoats and watched me calmly over their mugs of steaming coffee. They were old soldiers of the Eritrean cause, these men and women—I'd heard from Stella Harries that only the most brilliant of the veterans of the Eritrean war with Ethiopia got these overseas postings, representing their rebel movement in Europe as once Benjamin Franklin and John Adams had represented the American revolutionaries.

I considered their well-made African faces and their limpid eyes. I tried to envisage them destroying with grenades the food of the nine-centimeter-arm-diameter children of the Horn of Africa.

A French Girl in the Sudan

It is four months since I saw the rock singer's newsclip, and three of us are waiting on the Red Sea coast of the Sudan in heat so downright it's best to ignore it. Besides myself there is a lean, Nordic-looking American aid worker called Mark Henry, and the French girl. We are in an old barracks from the days of General Kitchener, a barracks—it seems to me—built for Rudyard Kipling and his *h*-dropping Cockney redcoats. It is time to begin writing things down and muttering things into my tape recorder. Because at the start of such a journey I'm frankly apprehensive of what I will perceive and meet, because perhaps of what my wife, Bernadette, would call my primness, I'll work in the past tense. It's a good way to put a distance between myself and the rawness of events.

First though: An outsider going into the rebel-held parts of Eritrea for whatever purpose can travel only by way of the Sudan. You fly to Khartoum and then to Port Sudan and then come south on the back of a truck to a town of ruins called Suakin—this town with its barracks. The Eritreans run a clinic here for their maimed.

Is it too fanciful to say that my companions and I are suspended between states? Between the Sudan and the unfulfilled Republic of Eritrea; between the desert coast we still inhabit and the mountains we're bound for? Even our passports are behind us, deposited with the intellectual veteran who manages the Eritrean guest house in Port Sudan.

My marriage is somewhere behind, too, but inadequately dis-
carded, and the other two carry the same sort of freight—the girl
Christine carries her peculiar childhood, and Henry his oddly noble
attachment to his Somali woman.

Enough heat-induced portentousness, though!

The eastern gate of the barracks at Suakin opened directly onto
the Red Sea; it was only a step or two from the lintel to the fever-
blue water. Latrines for the damaged veterans of Eritrea hung
rakishly out over the sea. With the consent of the Sudanese government, the rebels brought their maimed up here to the coast, to
Suakin and Port Sudan, because there was nowhere farther south,
in Eritrea itself, where the limbless or crippled could wheel their
chairs safely by daylight.

The three of us stood by this gate and inspected the richly blue
Red Sea. It hurt the eye, yet Christine held its gaze, lifting her chin
and mopping her neck—which like the rest of her stopped just
short of being bony—with a brown bandanna we'd bought together
in Khartoum. She turned to me and arched her eyes in a way that
said, "Well, the Red Sea. Close up!" Then she turned back to the
courtyard, and Henry the American and I followed.

A young Eritrean man missing a leg sat there in a wheelchair
surrounded by a fence of Eritrean false limbs. On the foot of each
prosthetic leg sat a black, lace-up shoe. He held one such leg-and-
shoe combination in his hands and rubbed black polish onto the
leather. This fresh-faced shoe shiner had already carried on a conversation with us in excellent English, telling us in its course that
he'd trodden on a Russian mine down near Asmara.

"We saw them in Port Sudan," Christine had said in her flat
yet quite exact English. "All the young Eritreans at the clinic.
They shined their shoes, too, and went out for a walk in the
afternoon."

Though I remembered sharply they hadn't walked—they'd
wheeled their chairs and lurched along on crutches.

"Walking is very good for those in the clinic," the shoe shiner
told us, closing the subject.

Now he was still preparing the boots on all these disembodied
legs so that at sunset his brothers and sisters in the clinic could don
them and set out on their crutches or in their wheelchairs for an

evening promenade. They would flash their dazzling toecaps around the little bay where the scrawniest of Mecca pilgrims bathed—the ones who couldn't afford anything better than the old steamer between Suakin and Jeddah.

As the three of us could hear just at the moment, in a ward by the second gateway, the one into the lane, less proficient English speakers than the shoe polisher were holding class. "Hamud lives in the city of Asmara," they called from their beds and their wheelchairs, "but his cousin Osman is a farmer in a village in Barka."

The shoe polisher told us, "Yes, I know Masihi well. There is no one in the Liberation Front who does not know Masihi."

I noticed that the shoe polish had turned nearly to oil in the heat, but he scooped it all up deftly with his cloth. There were no drips. I looked at the girl. She was agog for news of Masihi the cameraman.

"I remember," said the polisher, "when we took the town of Barentu. I was in the infantry then, the Hallal Guards. At dawn we were already all around the enemy, the soldiers of Ethiopia. We sealed the road to the east. Then we came forward over a plain of stone and we saw the buildings of the town, naked in front of us. As we went, I heard a noise behind me, and I thought, *Tanks!* for the noise was the noise of a machine. But instead it is Masihi and he is carrying his big churning camera, sixteen millimeter, which makes the same noise as a Russian bus, and he follows us, right behind! The stones in front of us, in front of the buildings on the edge of the city, are bouncing with bullets. For still Ethiopians remain there, and their officers have told them we will cut their arms off if they become prisoners, cut off their feet and stuff them in their mouths. And then Masihi and his camera and his sound machinist . . . they pass right through our line of infantry, they move faster than us, and they seize the town. They step over the outer trenches. Ethiopians are running away all around Masihi—he could reach his hand out and touch them. He has taken their spirit though. He has conquered them with his camera lens. They think he is a weapon. Masihi, who wants to capture only the morning light! He turns around in those houses on the outskirts and photographs us as we arrive . . ."

The boy laughed at this extreme cinematic style of Masihi's. The girl, Christine Malmédy, even in that solid heat raised her right hand over her eyes to cover her delight, which was deadpan in her normal style and yet fierce. With her other hand she caressed her right shoulder. Pulling forward until she was stooped. Making the story her own. A tale of her lost father.

I had once, in Khartoum, met Masihi—or Roland Malmédy, as he'd still been when Christine had last seen him. I knew that deadpan wasn't his style. I felt a pulse of anxiety for her. If we found him, what would he make of her? Would he look at her noncommittal face and wrongly think she was stupid?

I'd met her first a week before in the Hotel Akropole in Khartoum, the capital of the Sudan. It was a Thursday evening, a few days before I was supposed to leave the capital for Port Sudan and cross the border into rebel Eritrea. I was dining with two Norwegian acquaintances, both of them army officers and friends of my own friend Stella. Half the Norwegian army seemed to be involved in the aid business in Africa.

The Akropole is renowned among European travelers in the Sudan. It is an old-fashioned place, the doors of whose rooms, which are generally booked out, open directly onto the lounges and the dining room. In the dining room, a sweet-fleshed variety of Nile perch is served superbly every evening.

The Akropole is, of course, owned by a Greek family—the Nile, from the Delta in Egypt up through all its cataracts and courses to Lake Tana and Lake Victoria, has always been a Greek highway. It is exciting to think of those relentless Greek traders climbing the cataracts, coming to this elephant-trunk-shaped meeting place of the White and Blue Nile, doing deals with the nomads of the Gezira before there was even a city here or a rumor either of Christ or of the Prophet.

The Sudan had, until a few years before the night I went to dinner there, a Marxist president, Numeiri, and during his time all the aid agencies had been expelled from the country. The Greek family which runs the Akropole had, however, kept all aid running, arranging for the clearance of customs documents, for the delivery of goods which arrived at sandy Khartoum airport or by way of the great harbor of Port Sudan. My friend Stella swore by this family of experienced African operators, these two youngish Greek men and their wives, and an elegant mother in her sixties.

And in the evening, the Akropole's turbanned Sudanese waiters moved around the dining room with the calm style of men who have canny and spirited employers. I loved to sit and watch them do their stuff, bringing soup and fish to the tables full of journalists, aid and medical workers, engineers, and businessmen of the city.

On Thursday evenings, after the cry to prayer from the El Kabir Mosque brought on the clear Nilotic night, dinner was followed by a late-release movie shown on a video machine on the roof.

We'd finished the meal and were talking over coffee when we noticed a young European girl waiting some five steps from the table for a chance to interrupt and introduce herself.

I thought there was something infallibly French about her. Young Canadian, American, British, and Australian aid volunteers were plentiful in the region, but I knew this girl was not one of them. She had that slightly underfed European look, though she was not abnormally short. Her face was an untidy, European one, full of planes. It lacked blandness. I could imagine it in time coming to express a middle-aged existential despair.

She'd made herself up in a careless but vivid sort of way to come to the Akropole. Her hair was brunette and was heavily and sensibly cropped for travel in this dusty republic. She wore a halter-neck sleeveless top which would have earned her corporal punishment under President Numeiri and could even land her in trouble under the present law of the Sudan. This unwisely chosen garment suggested that she was a recent arrival in the country.

I went through a sort of dumbshow, raising my eyebrows to let her know it was all right to intrude if she wanted to. She saw the signal, stepped forward, and began speaking in accented English. "Mr. Dar-cy! You are a friend of my father's, I think. I am Christine Malmédy."

The army officers and I ran through the list of our African acquaintances, which in my case wasn't very extensive. Before we'd finished she said, "They nickname him Masihi. You may know that name. But his true name is Roland Malmédy. Do you know him now?"

"Masihi?" I asked. "The cameraman?"

She nodded.

In fact I knew him, the filmmaker called Masihi. But one of the Norwegian officers had even been into Eritrea, and announced now to the girl that he'd seen Masihi working "in the field," as the Eritreans referred to their besieged nation.

As if we wanted to flatter her, we began telling her all at once about her father. How he was a legend in the region, a sort of cinematic Lawrence of Arabia who came over the mountains into Sudan every few years with appalling footage of the war, footage of napalm raids by the Ethiopian air force from which the sizzled flesh had not been cut out. Polemic film, as Masihi liked to call that stuff. He would show it to the journalists and the aid workers in Khartoum. I had seen his footage during my first visit to Sudan.

"I saw him a year ago," I told the girl. "My friend Stella Harries knows him much better than I do and introduced me to him right here, in a villa in Khartoum."

The girl looked away and laughed softly and to herself. "Does he wear a turban?"

"Yes," I confirmed. "He certainly wears a turban. Speaking of that—of clothes, I mean—I hope you'll forgive me for saying that the sort of blouse you're wearing doesn't go down well with the local authorities."

She shook her head. "It was the only thing I had time to pack," she said, as if she expected that an answer like that should satisfy the Sudanese police. Saying it, she had the pinpoint eyes and the air of a woman who had packed in a hurry and didn't want to be delayed by local nit-picking.

One of the Norwegians laughed. "You are as brave, mademoiselle, as your father."

"And perhaps as foolhardy," said the other correctively.

But then their eyes shifted away from her in embarrassment. Because she was still palpably a child belonging to someone, and we weren't sure whether it could plausibly be a man with such an odd history as Masihi. She was a bit of a rare case—she'd lost her father to a revolution, rather than to some woman who was a stranger to her and her mother.

"The Eritreans are my stepmother," she said suddenly, reading our tentativeness. We blinked at that. She was as aware of the ironies of her situation as we were, and that routed and bemused us. "I am on my way to see him if I can," she announced. "The manager is telling me that you too are going to Eritrea, Mr. Darcy."

"To Eritrea, to Eritrea," muttered one of the army officers in a sing-song Scandinavian voice. He was wistful at the memory of the heroic Eritreans, even though his journey there had been harsh and marred by illness.

She did not take her eyes off me. "You are a journalist, the Greek family say."

I still wasn't used to that description. But I said I was. I said I was writing for *The Times*. Even these days that generally headed off further questions. It was a name which seemed to sedate the inquirer's itch to ask more.

"So you will write about the war or the hunger?" she asked.

"About anything I find," I said. I did not tell her about the Eritrean Colonel Tessfaha and his more specific invitation to do with an ambush in the direction of Asmara.

"My father was a journalist. A camera journalist."

"He still is," one of the Norwegians insisted.

"No," she said, barely shaking her head. "When I was fifteen he wrote to me and said he wasn't a journalist any more. That he kept the film diary for the rebels."

"Well, that too," I admitted.

"My mother," said Christine Malmédy, "says he was a very strict maker of films. He wanted to win awards. She says that the rough ground and the bad equipment in Eritrea should make him mad. She said anything like that made him mad when he was married to her. Anything that was . . . at all . . . not up to the mark. Anything . . . *unprofessional*."

We said nothing. The unspoken truism lay between the three of us men like an embarrassment: What drove someone mad in a marriage is not necessarily what will drive him mad when he's left it.

But I knew her father must have always been an imperfect and occasional parent. He had been, he'd told me, a cameraman for the French government network in Beirut, where he acquired his Arabic nickname. So that even before he left Lebanon for Eritrea, he already must have been no more than a visitor in her life.

I found I remembered pretty sharply the sun-tanned, tired-eyed

Roland Malmédy, and how, during a night we sat up illicitly drinking, he'd explained that the Palestinians had disappointed him as a man seeking the revolutionary essence. He used a phrase, *"La Révolution, la femme particulière!"* The Palestinians didn't have it, they were faction-ridden. Some of their factions blew up planes and threw grenades into airline queues peopled by blank-faced innocents. Besides that, there were always Syrian and Israeli intrusions to muddy the image Masihi saw through his viewfinder in Beirut.

The Eritreans, he said, were different.

In 1975, at a time this halter-necked girl who now sat at table with the two Norwegians and me was perhaps not yet seven, Malmédy-alias-Masihi heard news of the pure and highly focused revolution in Eritrea. Financed by his television network, he had flown south to Baladiyat Adan—which the British had once called Aden—in South Yemen. He had caught a Red Sea ferry which did a circular route to pick up the poorest of hadjis, or pilgrims, returning from Mecca.

He'd landed at last in the Ethiopian-held port of Massawa on the Red Sea coast of Eritrea. Led by a young Eritrean rebel who carried the sound gear, he marched ten days, toting his own 16-millimeter camera, to reach the Eritrean rebel positions just north of the great highland capital of Asmara. There he had found the people of his heart.

In Fryer River, at the center of another continent, I had sacrificed my wife for a people I could not belong to. If Bernadette came looking for me now, what new disappointments would I have ready for her? I felt—it's almost embarrassing to say it—a fatherly pulse of fear for this scrawny, serious French girl. Was there room for this child under the peculiar umbrella of Masihi's *femme particulière*?

I think it was Masihi's company that night we all met him in Khartoum which ultimately persuaded Stella that she had to go to Eritrea. I believe she was very taken with Masihi. But briefly, since Masihi was always moving.

I knew, too, that Roland Malmédy had filmed three famines in the lowlands and highlands of Eritrea, had recorded the great Eritrean advances of 1977, when the Ethiopians seemed for all purposes defeated and finally expelled. Arriving in the hills outside the port of Massawa with the Eritrean vanguard in the predawn of a September morning of 1977, he had filmed the bombardment which the Soviet navy out in the Red Sea was laying down on the Eritrean positions. This was all famous footage among journalists and aid workers.

The Russians, of course, had a historic desire for ports like Massawa—ice free, tranquil, screened by islands. Here they poured into the fight, in support of their Ethiopian allies, all the tanks and MIGs and Antonovs they could supply; called in also the East German security forces, the tank drivers and artillerymen of the South Yemeni Republic; called or invited in ten thousand Cubans, avid for African experience. And in the face of such force, Masihi had filmed the Eritrean retreat to a long high trench line north of the city of Asmara, and then the rebel repulse of the eight offensives the Ethiopians threw at them.

He had recorded also the educational passion of the Eritreans, the skills I hoped to see exercised in caves and bunkers and brush shelters. He had filmed their surgery performed in holes in mountains, their fervent dances, all their celebrations.

His daughter's present urgency had made her a very unrealistic traveler. When I asked her was she staying there, at the hotel, she told me that the Greeks had no room.

Then she said without any concern, "I have my sleeping bag. I can stay in that park by the Blue Nile."

My friends the Norwegian officers both raised their eyes in a way which imagined the worst. Dangerous little Nile urchins and disgruntled Sudanese soldiers moved at night through that park beside the river.

I told her that she could stay at Stella Harries' place. This was the top half of a villa in North Khartoum. Downstairs was rented by a surgeon, upstairs by Stella. The garden was always full, during the morning, of women wearing masks, sitting patiently on stone benches and waiting for gynecological advice.

Since Stella was in England visiting her parents, two rooms were free in her half villa, Stella's own bedroom and the small one out the back which everyone called "the pit."

Stella has stories of people, aid workers and journalists, coming back from the battle fronts and the refugee camps of Sudan and sleeping off their fevers and mystery viruses there. I decided Stella would probably want the girl to use her bedroom.

"You must accept Darcy's offer," one of the Norwegian officers told the girl. "The park is far too dangerous."

"Very well," said the girl, glancing away. I could see it didn't worry her one way or the other. She just wanted to be on her way. I was both amused and a little chagrined that she showed no gratitude. But then she surprised me by staring into my eyes. "Too kind," she said with emphasis. It sounded like a phrase she had picked up from reading English novels.

A little later, we all took our dinner chairs up to the roof and watched a Paul Newman film set in the snows of Philadelphia. Above our heads the dry, enormous sky produced a full moon so bright that it was hard to appreciate the artful umbers of the camerawork. The girl sat with us, watching without complaint but without apparent interest. As the credits began to roll and the hotel guests began to talk and light cigarettes, she said, "It's curious—don't you think, Mr. Darcy?—to see Paul Newman in the open."

"It's the way a lot of Africans see him," I said, covering a grin. I was disarmed by her metropolitan French innocence, the fact that lots of Frenchmen throughout France's wide African empire would have watched movies in roofless cinemas. I was, of course, working round to the vanity of telling her that that was how I had seen my childhood films, too, as an infant of another empire. In cinemas wide open in summer, a roof of canvas flung over in winter.

So I began to tell her, in an *old bore* sort of way I couldn't stop myself falling into, about the remoter towns in Australia where my father had managed banks. Years past, as a student, I'd liked to talk about these distant wheat and wool towns, about cinemas open to the sky, about wide-verandahed pubs and stolid Victorian banks dressed up in yellow or blue paint, about whole towns dazzled to inertia by recurrent, glaring noons.

Memories of my student orations make me cringe a little now. Those Australian villages, I would say, were dominated by drought, the memory of it and the prospect of its rolling around again. That much was true. And then I would start badmouthing the graziers and wheat-growers for thinking they could be farmers on the European model. I wrote a poem once in which I said, "They did not get the sun's long message." I liked to say that what the sun brought to these little bush shires was news of that other great and absolute continent it had left half a day past and would soon return to—Africa, that is. I admitted the farmers loved the earth. I'd seen too many of them weeping in the bank, or turning up with tormented faces at our front door asking for audiences with my father. They would certainly suffer to hold to their ground through all the fairly unyielding demands of the big banks, demands my father could only soften to a certain degree and not in essence. But, again, they didn't get the sun's long message.

Which was, of course, that Australia and Africa were sisters. "Two gangling and dark sisters from the one black dam of Pangaea." (Me, in one of the speeches!) This was long before the time my wife, Bernadette, and I received our fierce enlightenment in Fryer River, in Australia's Western Desert. Before, that is, I'd woken up to the fact the world wouldn't go to much trouble to fit itself into my smart-aleck theories. So I was capable of standing, pale but cocksure, for shameful lengths of time at the bar of squalid Melbourne student pubs and talking about this dark relationship.

I'd heard from some science undergraduate, for example, that the botany of the two continents was related, always allowing for the fact that the Indonesian deep-sea trenches protected Australia's eccentric plants for millennia from outside influence.

So, armed with half-truths, I'd say, "Just look at the plants of the two places!"

I knew I was on safe ground. Very few of the student boozers had looked at the plants.

I wasn't seriously interested in whether Australia and Africa were sisters, half-sisters, cousins. I was just a colonial boy trying to explain that Europe wasn't the only model, might in fact be a misleading model. "A pale though fertile mother stricken with low blood count and sated with all the frantic passions of culture." (Me again, in a speech.) It was a common enough Australian argument, say twenty years ago: "We're not just a poor relation, you know. We've got rich and unexpected kinships!"

I hasten to say that the drinking student Darcy had no real boyhood obsession with Africa as such. That wasn't what brought me to the Sudan and to the roof of the Akropole, this night twenty years after all my student fervors had been well and truly quenched by the absolutely grotesque business of my marriage.

When I finished talking to the girl about open-air cinemas in the Australian bush, the Norwegians started in on fantastical stories of their own sub-Arctic childhoods, tales of astounding lengths of darkness and of daylight, and what that did to folk. The girl listened politely—I watched her and was touched because I realized she must have listened to me exactly the same way. For behind the politeness, I could see, these tales of climatic quirks didn't capture her or have application. Again, she just wanted to get going to Port Sudan and then into the mountains across the Eritrean border, where Masihi could be found.

At last it was time to go. I said good-night. The Norwegians gave me plenty of advice on Eritrean diarrhea and promised I'd lose some of my London flabbiness. I led the French girl downstairs at last, out under the wide arcade at ground level, where a dozen child beggars slept at night.

Khartoum is full of child refugees, sucked into the city by need. Some of them lost their parents to thirst or hunger on treks up along the railway line from the south. They are tough, spare, fierce children. The gentle ones are dust across the railway line in Kordofan province.

Their demeanor toward someone dressed as I was, in the paramilitary gear of the aid worker or the journalist, is usually pretty passive. They understand that people such as we are uninformed by any Islamic tradition of alms. For us the gift of fifty piastres, even a Sudanese pound, to a given child isn't the answer to the question. The child beggars seem to know that we world-beaters from the outside think we're engaged in larger and more mysterious alms: the doing-away with beggary through as clever a scheme as we can devise, not through the rewarding of it as a trade.

But a large-eyed thin girl like Christine, wearing a halter-neck as well, was worth putting out your hand to. Someone uninformed enough to dress like that was probably also uninformed enough to give them gifts. And certainly, as I automatically called *"Imshi!"* to the kids, she stopped and began to search her pockets for coins. She did not drop them into their palms—she didn't try to avoid their flesh. The flinch of the hand and face which characterizes most almsgivers, whether in Manhattan or Cairo, wasn't seen in her. Surrounded by them, she almost looked one of them.

I'd been using Stella Harries' four-wheel-drive truck, and while we were driving back toward Stella's half villa in North Khartoum, I found that the girl hadn't any Sudanese papers at all, except for the visa which had got her into the country. Nor did she have any invitation from the Eritreans to go through into their embattled region. Just to get as far as Port Sudan on the Red Sea, where an Eritrean truck could fetch her, she would need an ornate movement permit from the Sudanese.

I tried to swallow the irritation I felt. I knew that all the next day would be spent in the offices of Sudanese immigration, in police offices as well, waiting on benches with an Islamic patience which isn't really my character, while officials took their mysterious time, not wishing to offend God by working faster than they knew He did.

"Did you come on an impulse?" I asked her.

"No. But I wanted to come here as quick as I could."

I wanted to ask her whether her mother knew she was here. But though she looked like a child, she had a woman's presence, and it was her business. I asked her if she had any passport pictures, and she searched languidly inside the large leather bag she carried and dropped perhaps a dozen tiny straight-faced photographs on the seat beside me.

"That's good," I said. "You need photographs for everything. You'll need half a dozen documents. Even a permit to take scenic photographs."

"But I don't have a camera," she told me.

"Wouldn't your family want you to bring home a photograph of Masihi?"

She waved this possibility aside. "The rebels have a camera section. They can give me a photograph."

But she sounded as if she half expected to stay in Eritrea for good.

The route to Stella Harries' place goes up Zubeir Phasher Street, a typically broad Khartoum thoroughfare. That night its pavements were silted up with sand from a *habub* of a few days past. But there was also a detritus of garbage and rubble which might easily prove to be, on closer inspection, some huddled child shipped up from the south as a house slave by a pederastic Sudanese officer and now used up and thrown onto the streets. For that was another way the poor of the provinces made it to the big city.

"You speak English so well," I remarked to the girl, making conversation in this sad city.

"My mother managed a French hotel in London."

"After Masihi . . . ?"

"Yes. I went to school there for six years." I was going to make some conventional noise about her disrupted childhood, but she nodded toward the road ahead. "Look, there's a policeman."

We were nearing the great circle of road which runs around the outskirts of the market named Suq Two, always still brightly lit late at night, a great swath of canvas under which peaches, oranges, and dates are displayed. At the stem of the Suq Two roundabout a Sudanese policeman walked into the street armed with an ancient British rifle and waved at me to stop. I obeyed.

The policeman leaned in at the cabin window. I cursed the infidel halter-neck the girl was wearing.

"*Salaam!*" I told the man, and since he seemed to be a Nuba and the Nuba often spoke English, asked, "Is there any problem, sir?"

I knew even as an occasional visitor that the man wanted to test me, to work out in what degree I harbored the most treasured Sudanese virtues—politeness, composure, that patience which is in fact a kind of humility in the face of time's great circle. I handed over my papers, the ones which had smiling from them a slightly plumper, slightly younger, not quite as bald Darcy. A photograph in fact taken before the tribal disaster hit Bernadette and me.

The Nuba handed back my papers and inspected the girl, asking only for her passport. He stared with particular emphasis at her shoulders, as if he was punishing her with desire.

"Do you have any Scotch with you?" he asked.

I told him I didn't drink. That wasn't exactly true—I drank with Stella when she was at home. But she knew the ropes and had a reliable supplier. She spoke Arabic well, too. For anyone who didn't, the dangers of being found with a black-market bottle were considerable enough to make you hesitate—jailing and flogging and public humiliation. Besides, the stuff cost two hundred Sudanese pounds a bottle, and as a freelance I wasn't well enough off to dispose lightly of that amount of money.

"Do you want some *khat*?" the Nuba policeman then asked me.

The girl was ignorant of the subtlety of this question, I was pleased to note. For it implied I was taking her home for sex, and the axiom even among the aid workers was that sex was mightily enhanced by *khat*. I knew, too, that my buying the *khat* would be the policeman's price for overlooking Christine Malmédy's bare arms. I had been very happy until now behaving paternally toward the girl. Now the Nuba had offended me with the other possibility. I had no desire, and the question was why, and the answer was only partially Christine's childlike scrawniness.

Stella had told me the going price for a wad of *khat* was about twenty-five Sudanese pounds. I took out a collection of five-pound notes. The Nuba languidly placed a heavy wad of the drug on my lap.

"The lady should know that *Sharia'h* is the strict law in the Sudan," he said. "The law of Islam is the law of the land."

This was—and I could have said this if I had been bold or stupid enough—the exact cause of conflict between the Islamic north and the Christian south, a conflict I'd written about last time I was here. But not this time. I suspected the Eritrean war, far to the southeast in the Ethiopian highlands, would occupy me wholly.

I said the politest good-night to the Nuba.

"I will burn this damned shirt," murmured Christine.

"No, you can store it as Stella Harries'."

"I bought it for the film festival last year. It didn't cause any trouble at all in Cannes."

In the market the next morning, before we went to the police and Interior offices, I helped Christine buy three khaki shirts, for the Eritreans suggested that color—it did not show up against the ochres of the Eritrean landscape and did not attract the eyes of bomber pilots.

Christine handled the shirts with the bewildered reverence of a recruit receiving her uniform. A brown shirt buttoned to the neck, with the sleeves buttoned at the wrist or even rolled up one or two turns, did not offend against the *Sharia'h*. Nor attract the attention of big Nubian cops with *khat* for sale.

Since she hardly had any more money than she needed to fly to Port Sudan, I bought her a water bottle, too—she hadn't thought to bring that particular item with her.

I enjoyed steering Christine around the town; I was restored to a flush of paternity as we consulted each other over the question of her shirts.

"They don't even like short sleeves?" she asked me, astonished in her mute way.

"Not even short sleeves. Only people in temperate zones find it's decent to flirt with the sun. Here, a bare arm is like a buttock."

"That's ridiculous," she murmured, but a truck went by and in a second she was brushing dust off the front of her new khaki as if the hedonism of film festivals on the Cote d'Azur were well lost.

The Eritreans also kept an office in Khartoum. Driving to it, I asked her if she wanted to visit Omdurman later in the day? It was, after all, the city's chief tourist attraction, the site of the tomb of the Mahdi, the great Sudanese unifier whose Dervishes had captured Khartoum and killed General Gordon a century before. There had then been a great battle over there in Omdurman, where General Kitchener had mown down the Mahdi's troops.

As I spoke of Mahdi the Avenger and of the Battle of Omdurman, she looked at me as if I were naming rock groups too esoteric for a normal, busy girl to take an interest in. To hell with Omdurman! She had come to Africa to see one sight—Masihi the filmmaker.

An old-fashioned and no doubt racist print of brave General Gordon at the head of a staircase in Khartoum and facing the first of a tide of Dervishes advancing up the stairs with a spear had hung on the walls of one of the number of bush schools I'd gone to in Australia. The memory of it caused me to ask about Christine's education.

When I asked, she let me know that she'd been studying graphic arts at some polytechnic near Fontainebleau.

"Do you like it?"

"I would prefer to study film, but that makes my mother nervous. She says filmmakers have no proper life." The girl shrugged and smiled briefly. "With graphic arts you can make a living and still pretend you're doing proper, serious work."

"You might be able to help your father," I remarked. But I wasn't sure whether it was right to start such hopes in her.

In any case, she didn't seem to have any unrealistic yearnings. "I can do sound," she said. "I've done sound for some of the students in the film course."

Tessfaha

When I first came to London, I was equipped to take Fleet Street or Wapping by storm. I gravitated toward the aid newspapers in Covent Garden. I attended press briefings by prominent African exiles or by African foreign ministers visiting the old imperial capital. After the vast electricity of the Australian sky, England's low horizon suited me as well as the unchallenging work. I lived poorly in one-room-with-kitchenette in southwest London. Bernadette did not call me. I used half my earnings telephoning Australia, talking to those who now knew where and how she was.

Having been at one time very nearly, though unofficially, the *Times* correspondent on matters of remote Australia, I was invited by an adventurous editor to travel to the Sudan, a republic tormented by tribalism, and to write about the civil war in the south. For a time there I traveled with a water drilling crew under the protection of a Sudanese army escort. I sent my stories back from the Akropole in Khartoum. That sprawling, annoying, and engrossing capital delayed me for some time. In the Sudan Club I met Stella Harries, the BBC correspondent in Khartoum.

Given that the cost of living in Khartoum was so much cheaper than England, I stayed on for some months, operating on the basis of a loose brief from *The Times*, selling some taped material to Australian and Canadian radio, living in Stella Harries' villa. She soothed my pride by accepting a token rent. Despite Stella's urging, I resisted learning Arabic. Stella accused me of behaving as if learning Pitjantjara had been dangerous enough. The loss of Bernadette had made me suspicious of languages.

I lacked the confidence, too, to set myself up in my own right in the Sudan. At last I headed back to the misty and squalid comforts of England. I took the cheap flights through Saudi Arabia, not the more fashionable British Airways or Austrian Airlines, the ones on which high Sudanese officials flew.

When, at Stella's urging, I contacted the Eritrean office in London, to put myself on their mailing list for press releases, I was flattered to find that they knew about me, had read my work in *The Times*. They sometimes invited me to go with them to an Eritrean restaurant in London.

On a grim February day earlier this year, after my visit to Colorado, they called me and invited me to meet one of the visiting leaders from "the field," a man named Tessfaha. They did not comment on Tessfaha's exact status and function in the Eritrean struggle. They referred to him as "the Colonel," but I didn't know whether that was a rank or a nickname. The meeting place was an Eritrean restaurant in Kilburn.

I'd half expected the other Eritreans would be included in the dinner party. So my eyes flickered around the restaurant looking for a group but picked up only one shape, very tall and thin, leaning by one of the tables in the darker reaches of the place.

"Is this an O.K. table?" asked Tessfaha, indolently intent, absolutely at home in a world where people chose not only what food to eat but also the spot of all spots to eat it in. "My colleagues tell me they always bring you here, but they suspect you might prefer Indian food."

"No," I insisted. "This food is good for me."

"You might well prefer French cuisine, though it's generally too much for our people, even if they live in the West for years. If you grow up on millet and lentils, the stomach simply cannot believe in French cuisine. It's a sort of gastronomical nirvana which leaves the stomach gasping. I suppose I am used to it because of the EEC politicians who speak to me over dinner in Strasbourg. Anyhow, please say if you would prefer another restaurant . . ."

Again I denied it, so at long last we sat. Waiting for our food, we both drank beer. I remarked I'd thought that perhaps some of the others from the Eritrean office might have been with him.

Normally they would have been, said Tessfaha. But they were busy; they had a lot of what was called in the West "fence-mending" to do in view of our friend the rock singer's broadcast.

"The tyrant," Tessfaha told me, "moves people by the million from ancestral ground to concentration camps of his choosing, where they starve in sight of well-fed officials. Yet it is not the tyrant who bears the blame, but somehow it is we the Eritreans. Because we attacked thirty trucks and brought the rock singer close to tears on television! In fact the number of trucks was not thirty but twenty-three . . . but even so. What brutes would deliberately anger such a nice young rocker, make him shed tears for the nature of man? What brutes would throw grenades at aid trucks? My colleagues have to answer questions of that nature, and they find it dispiriting."

I confessed I thought people were entitled to ask that sort of question.

"Especially," agreed Tessfaha languidly, "since some of the trucks we load our own supplies on from Port Sudan actually carry the generous rock singer's slogan: *With Love from Worldbeat*. Especially since also we are grateful to him for the impartiality with which he gave help to us as well as to the Ethiopians. And so, the world asks, *What manner of ingrates are these Eritrean bandits?*"

Tessfaha smiled subtly behind a double moustache of hair and beer froth.

"I suspect that you aren't ingrates," I conceded. "So perhaps there has to be a reason which evades the understanding of both the singer and myself."

Tessfaha took from the pocket of his sports jacket a brown paper envelope marked *Do Not Bend*. From it he slid out a color photograph. It was like some which Stella Harries herself had taken during her journey to Eritrea. In it three Eritrean rebels sat on stones. Two girls and a boy, none of them much more than, say, twenty years of age. One of the girls looked ironically, frankly at the camera. She wore khaki shirt and shorts. Her long legs were knees-up to the lens. And on her feet were the standard plastic sandals. Beside her sat a tall young boy, not as skeletal as Tessfaha. He, too, was bare-legged, but his ankles were encased in old-fashioned military gaiters. The third rebel did not look at the camera at all. She was writing something in an exercise book. Her hair, like that of the other two, was exactly barbered. She wore long khaki pants bleached to paleness, and a crisp white shirt under her khaki jacket. A thorn bush cast a shadow over her.

The photograph thus expressed from left to right a gradation—from frank girlish interest in the lens through an equal degree of boyish curiosity in the middle to quiet young scholarship on the right.

A caption, typed on flimsy paper, was glued to the photograph. It said, *"Three young EPLF rebels, fifty meters from the Nacfa frontline trenches."*

Tessfaha pointed indolently to the figures in this photograph. "Those are the ones who so distressed the rock singer. And if not them, children like them, children younger than the war itself. Remember the Vietnam war? I was at Georgetown University when Saigon fell. The relief and the shame of that! Students held placards which said, *No More Babies Need Burn!* But these three I show you were babies then, and still in their way they burn. Do these two girls and this boy assault aid trucks, believing perhaps that it is better for the people to perish than to be fed by the enemy?"

A woman came to take our orders. Without answering the questions he'd posed, Tessfaha ordered heartily—salad, spinach lasagna, a new beer apiece. As if he had not just now been talking about food and the burning of food, he gave due weight to choosing from the menu, discussing ingredients with the English waitress.

At last, the order settled, he returned to me and to his argument. I was to remember, he said, what these children younger than the war had seen. In the towns and the pastoral villages where they had grown up, they had often watched convoys of aid pass, never stopping, ignoring a famished landscape, moving toward the great granaries of the army, of the oppressor. Walking pot-bellied behind their father's goats, they had seen the grain of America, Canada, Australia, benign New World grain, bypassing them always, traveling in the same string of trucks as the artillery shells. Food, after all, must not be put into the hands of the troublesome, of the seditious Eritreans and Tigreans. "Unless, of course, the presence of foreign observers and monitors of aid makes a certain sharing necessary."

Such were the causes which had made these children rebels, which had, on top of other experiences, raids, confiscations, massacres, caused them to go to the mountains and join the rebels. For in the

remotest villages, Tessfaha argued further, the children had ob-
served worse perversions still than the ones he'd just detailed. They
had seen Arab caravans moving from the south, across the starving
grounds of Eritrea, into the Sudan. Camels loaded with grain and
cheese and powdered milk, consigned to the markets of the Sudan
by Ethiopian generals and officials on the make.

"And so now that they have arms in their hands," Tessfaha murmured, gesturing with the hand which didn't hold his beer, "the
children look from the ravines down onto the roads where the
convoys move, and history, all they know of it, does not dispose
them to accept the lines of trucks at their face value. For even if
the vehicles carry the flag of the Red Cross, even if they say *With
Love from Worldbeat*, these children believe the convoys move under
military command, that they are driven by the military or else by
conscripted drivers. And now one of our regional commanders,
leading our young and maddened by the hypocrisy, has at last made
an error of judgment and burned a string of trucks."

He paused, and then, as if out of transcontinental solidarity, he
turned his eyes and mine to older turpitudes still. "Did Stalin try
to feed the Ukrainians? Did he wish to behold in his dreams a
countryside of plump Ukrainians? Did he weep when he discovered
that he and the generous Westerners had failed between them to
keep life in some ten or fifteen million of his enemies? Or did he
sleep better for seeing them vanish? Was, indeed, their going his
purpose? Ai, the politics of food . . ."

The spinach lasagna arrived. My appetite had been blunted by
the colonel's intense picture-making, but Tessfaha began working
on the food functionally, quickly. I could see strands of spinach on
the man's tongue as he continued to speak. Now the EPLF had
offered to negotiate truces and safe conduct for convoys of *bona
fide* aid, but the Ethiopian Dergue did not want safe conduct, wished
to go on mixing the food and the armaments, wished to have the
benefit of any Eritrean mistake in attacking those convoys which
for once hauled nothing but food. From that occasional error a
gracious benefit came to the regime. Namely, that the impeccable
young rock star stood amid the desolation and was moved to tears.

"The rock singer," said Tessfaha, chewing fiercely, "whom I love
like a brother, does not weep for the complexity of the question.
The rock singer stands near smoking vehicles and burning grain"

—though my memory of the newsclip was that it was among hungry children that the rock singer stood—"and merely says, *Oh the blindness of the rebels!*"

"You're telling me," I asked, by now a little irked by Tessfaha's spate of rhetoric, "that the Ethiopians dress up their military convoys as convoys of aid? That they carry the insignia of the Red Cross, say, but are in fact convoys of armaments and supplies?"

Tessfaha agreed. That was exactly the accusation. I was engrossed by the way that, while he spoke, he still went on deftly and studiously cutting up sectors of spinach and cheese with his fork.

"This is a hefty sort of accusation," I told him. "I can't see why the aid bodies who work with the Ethiopians would let it happen?"

Tessfaha nodded toward the photograph that still lay by the salad. "It's not extraordinary news if you come from Africa. Those three know it. Every soldier in their sector knows it. Every Ethiopian soldier in the opposing trench line knows it. Every Ethiopian in every garrison in Eritrea knows it. Every Somali and Oromo knows it. It is not so extraordinary, it is not startling. It is the daily traffic of the hunger zone."

He cut up the last of his lasagna.

"There isn't much I can do," I found myself saying. "I could talk to the editor about it, but I lack objective information. I don't think, with respect, that we could consider you objective information."

Tessfaha smiled. "No, I am not objective," he admitted pedantically. "I confess to being in some ways subjective, or at least to not being able to demonstrate my objectivity."

Nonetheless I knew at once Tessfaha had something to suggest. We ate and drank a while longer, though. The something did not emerge.

And then, when we were down to the lees of our second beer, it presented itself. If I were there at an attack on a convoy! If I could report *that*! Would *The Times* perhaps fly me as far as Port Sudan, after which the Eritreans would look after me? As well as they looked after Stella Harries, Tessfaha promised, smiling. In a cashless society, since south of Port Sudan cash did not operate!

I did my best to seem calm and qualified and dubious, but in fact I felt a great giddiness. I'd had little to drink, but nonetheless I took ecstatically to the idea of a rehabilitative journey. I found at moments of promise like this one that I thought about rehabilitation in terms of impressing my wife. I knew that she was no longer interested in any penance I might do, but I couldn't convince myself of it.

As well, there seemed to be all at once a strange acrid smell above the table—the dusty smell you got in the streets of Khartoum in the minutes before the *khamsin* struck. I realized then that it was the odor of my own fear and excitation. And to be frank, the stench of simple ambition as well. Not just the primitive hope of arresting Bernadette's attention, but straightforward ambition: to be *there*, at the point where the crucial things happen, the things which— when adequately witnessed—change the opinion of the world.

"I'll have to think about it," I told him. Knowing I'd already thought of everything.

Mark Henry

The Eritreans at their office in the city had warned me that our
—Christine's and my—date of departure for Port Sudan coincided
with the third anniversary of Numeiri's overthrow. Flights out of
the city's mud brick barracks of an airport to Port Sudan might be
canceled without explanation. The army might, for purposes of their
own, seize the few aircraft of Air Sudan.

Indeed, Christine and I found the blue wooden doors, beyond
which tickets to Port Sudan were to be issued, locked and barred.
I already had my ticket and at least therefore a notional seat on the
Air Sudan flight, whenever it left. I'd been prepared to have to
compete for a ticket for Christine. I'd not expected these bolted
doors, though. I might have once vapored on about the kinship of
Africa and Australia, but I found I had a pretty European taste for
exact timetables.

The barring of the domestic airport could mean anything, but
no one in front of the doors seemed to have been flustered into
voicing loud speculations about it. Passengers conversed in polite
and discreet Arabic. Public servants and businessmen stood around
in their exquisite white jellabas. Family men urged their masked
wives into the shade of the terminal's side wall, since the temperature
was far over forty degrees centigrade. Nuba, even Zande tribespeople from the south, carrying tribal slashes on their cheeks and
crusader swords in their belts, kept their counsel, their faces shad-
owed beneath swirls of dazzling white linen. But no one wandered

around asking whether southern rebels had brought down another Boeing with a Stinger ground-to-air, or whether the military had commandeered the domestic aircraft as an early move in a coup. People here knew how dangerous idle opining could be.

Amid the Muslim women shone the face of an exquisite girl whom I guessed to be Shilluk or Nuer—I'm not informed enough to tell infallibly the difference between tribes—swathed in diaphanous green cloth. A starched headpiece gave an elevation, a nunlike peak, to the fabric across her forehead. The cloth framed a face which was sensual in an ancient way, a face at once innocent and concupiscent. Like most of the men, she carried a highly polished attaché case with tumbler locks. Air Sudan—nicknamed Sudden Death Air by Western journalists—were notorious for being overbooked even when they did fly. In the battle to board the aircraft, the attaché case with its metaled corners might become a weapon.

Waiting by the wall, too, was a certain blond American I'd seen in the dining room at the Akropole. He lolled against a wall, his head back against the retained night coolness. One of his hips was leaning against a massive duffel bag, and he was riffling through a diary and journal stuffed with photographs, loose pages, grimy business cards. He wore the washed-out browns and duns of an old African cat and had that unfussed look of a frequent flyer on erratic airlines.

An official opened a judas window in the door and called out some genial information in Arabic. My Arabic is of the phrasebook variety, but I heard the recurrence of the phrase *b-it-tayyara*, plane. The American seemed to get more of the speech than I did, however. He raised his head, took stock of the crowd, and so caught my eye. It was pretty much that point in a bemusing wait where Europeans in an alien crowd begin to be drawn together anyhow. A primal gathering of skin unto skin.

The man hitched his enormous duffel bag and strolled toward us.

"Ladies and gentlemen," he said with a midwestern drawl, "if my Arabic serves me right, there are certainly no planes flying. Tickets may be even more speculative."

Christine Malmédy groaned and shook her head.

The American told us the rumor at the Akropole was that the government might relax the *Sharia'h*, the Islamic law, today, as a gesture toward the southern Sudanese. "In which case," said the man, "we can all roll round to the old Sudan Club and get tanked, a prospect which doesn't dismay me in the slightest." He squinted as if from the first sting of Scotch on the palate.

Ahead of us, the doors now swung wide. A wedge of people, led by the Nuer-Shilluk woman, surged over the doorstep and into the dimness inside. "I think this is where we do it, ladies and gentlemen," the American told us. "*Inshallah*. God willing."

In the scrum indoors, he would occasionally stroll up and down chatting in Arabic to one nomad or another, or to a portly businessman. Gradually I began to see that his Arabic wasn't much better than my own, but he flourished it with greater confidence. The words which emerged most commonly from the American's discussions with the other Sudanese passengers always included *Malesh*—too bad!—and *Inshallah*—if God wills it.

He took special care of Christine. He knew how to work an African airport scrimmage, how to make openings into which he deftly and unselfishly inserted the French girl. Soon we all had tickets and confirmed seats for a plane which was rumored to be leaving the next day. We did not bother to tell the girl that if there was trouble it was unlikely to leave for two weeks.

Happily, I'd asked Stella's Eritrean assistant Ibrahim to wait with the truck. I offered the American a lift into town. He accepted and climbed into the cabin. He reached across the front seat to shake my hand. There were four of us crammed there when he closed the door against his ribs. "My name's Mark Henry," he told me. "I'm with Southern Unitarian Aid, but I'm not a southerner and I'm not a Unitarian. I've been marking time down in a refugee camp at Wadi Belidayah. Lots of southern Sudanese down there. Great people, sad cases."

I introduced Ibrahim, the girl, myself to the American and returned to something he'd said.

"Marking time?"

Henry shrugged as well as he could in the room he had. "We were thrown out of Ethiopia. I mean, I was, Southern Unitarian Aid was. Punished for complaining, for stating the obvious. That God doesn't make famines, governments do. But as you know, Ethiopia is the focus, the glamour post for the aid people. They all want to be there. That's where they have the really big-time famines.

They've got lots of prestige invested in staying there. Well, friend, no longer. We've been cast out!"

He shook his head. I'd noticed this sense of exile in other Westerners who'd been expelled from Ethiopia.

We sweated shoulder to shoulder for a while, talking about the Gezira refugee camps. I didn't mention that the girl and I were going to Eritrea. Because of my contacts with the Eritrean "colonel" Tessfaha in London, it seemed best to keep that a private matter. But then the American said, "So I got an invitation to travel elsewhere. Eritrea."

"Invitation?" I asked.

"From the Eritreans, the aid people here in Khartoum. I thought I'd go and see the other side of the equation. That's what they say of Eritrea. It's the other side of the whole business. You can't know Ethiopia until you've seen Eritrea. Just like you can't know the U.S. until you've seen Mexico."

I asked him if he was going to Eritrea *right now*, as soon as he could get a Port Sudan plane.

"Exactly right," said Henry. "And so are you and Miss Malmédy here. The Greeks at the hotel told me."

The arrangements I was now stuck with—delayed flights, the girl, the American—had even more thoroughly punctured any of those fantasies about a secret trust which my recent interview with Tessfaha might have raised in me.

The girl said, with her normal fixity, "I'm going to see my father in Eritrea. He is the filmmaker in that country. His name is Masihi."

Henry whistled.

"He who expects the Messiah," said Henry. "That's what it is in Arabic. Does your father expect the Messiah, missie?"

He laughed without any malice, and the girl shrugged and said, "My mother says he is an atheist and a kind of Marxist. But she thinks all rebels are Marxists. His real name isn't Masihi. It's Roland."

With the name of Roland hanging over us—the name of that virginal French knight and trumpeter, who burst a cerebral valve while blowing a warning of the coming of the Muslims in the vale of Roncesvalles—we entered upon a small incident, an adventure which—to use a cant term from the social sciences—*bonded* us as fellow pilgrims. As Ibrahim turned the truck into El Kabir Avenue, we found ourselves facing a broad wave of Sudanese, tightly packed from the walls on one side of the street right across to the sanded-up paving on the other side.

"Islamic Brotherhood," said Henry. "Dead on cue."

The crowd facing us included devout women as well, apparently chanting and wailing behind their veils. Banners as wide as the avenue carried a legend I'd become familiar with, under the tuition of Stella, during my earlier visit to the Sudan. "Islam is our religion, Allah is our ideology, the *Sharia'h* is our politics!"

The marchers, it seemed, were on their way to the Nile banks to dissuade the President from repealing "the law." They wanted to keep their nation safe from halter-necks and drunkards.

The truck seemed to back not so much because of Ibrahim's engaging reverse and expending a little quantity of fuel, but on the gusts of energy from all these fundamentalist folk. In any case we found a quiet laneway, and from there made our way into town by narrower streets. There, at institutions such as the Golden Elephant Panel Beating Company or the Nile Crocodile Electric Repairs Company, less frantic Sudanese had ignored the holiday and got a morning's work done.

We seemed to understand that the three of us were fellow travelers now and would not easily escape each other's company.

Something About Henry

The day the girl and I first met Mark Henry in Khartoum, at the desert fort/airport, Islamic law was not lifted. Nor had the military by dusk taken over the city. In what felt like a normal evening, Henry asked the two of us to dinner at the Sudan Club, a European meeting place which—thanks to the lobbying of the Islamic Brotherhood—was still dry.

The club stood in what must have been once the best garden in town. It had been laid out, and the bar, mess, and residence built, in the early twentieth century, in the years after Kitchener's triumph across the river at Omdurman, that bare stretch of hilly ground which Christine Malmédy had shown no interest in visiting.

Now that the people who built it and the purpose they built it for had both vanished, the club seemed a strange irrelevance. There was a villa on the grounds where British officers and their memsahibs once stayed while in transit. I imagined them resting on the verandahs while their peach-skinned children, now old age pensioners in a new Britain, went hiding and seeking among the date palms.

In the bar and dining room, officers must have found a continuation of the luxuries of Indian messes. These days, though, the bar where such finicky gentlemen once drank real liquor was full of skin-and-bone aid workers attenuated by malaria, hepatitis, by the so-called "mystery viruses" which rise up out of the Nile, or else by a taste for *khat* and hashish, which somehow suppress the appetite.

Having come through the day intact, the *Sharia'h* was preserved at the bar that night by a turbanned and jacketed barman who had no intention of learning how to pour cocktails. Over a meal of the Sudanese specialty called twisted fish, accompanied by *karkedeh* juice and soda water, Henry began to talk a little about his history.

He told us he came from near the Canadian-American border, from the industrial city of Sault Ste. Marie. This coal and steel town sits astride a neck of the Great Lakes, some of its bitter suburbs in Canada, the other half in the United States. As he described it, geographically and in terms of culture, it was its own state. His parents died when he was ten, and he was raised by an uncle for whom he felt some affection. But he disliked the shameful squalor of his home city. He liked what he called "the honest squalor of other parts."

"I studied agriculture at a cow college in northern Michigan," he said.

"Cow college?" asked Christine.

"Sorry, missie," said Henry. "Agriculture."

He had an agricultural ranginess, was tall to the point of stooping, with a thatch of hair which had once been golden but had now turned a fairly flaccid nicotine. And he was an old cat in more than African terms—he told us he'd worked for the Peace Corps and for Southern Unitarian Aid in Sumatra, India, Bangladesh, Ethiopia, and now Sudan. His specialties included soil conservation, deep water holes, small community dams. "I have in my time seen the light enter thousands of faces as the water flowed, friends!"

He had been put in charge of his organization's Khartoum office just recently. "But it's a tough business. Listen, you just can't get medicine or grain or water drills into the parts that need them most. Into the Southern Sudan, I mean, into Darfur and Kordofan, let alone into the Bahr Al-Ghazal or Equatoria. It's the civil war. Last month, for example, some rebels handcuffed two of our drivers to the steering wheels of their trucks and then incinerated the trucks! How's that for a death!"

The French girl blinked. Then she asked with her usual suddenness, "Are you married?"

Henry paused in a way which made me suspect inexactly that he had a wife somewhere. "I have a fiancée," he told us. "She's a Somali and her name is Petra. She's under house arrest in Addis. I'm still negotiating her visa."

I seemed to remember Stella mentioning a particular American who went around lobbying people, wanting pressure put on the Dergue to give his girlfriend a pardon and an exit visa. I wondered had Stella been talking about this man, Henry? I hoped not, because I believe she said also, "Everyone knows the woman's probably dead."

"I'm bad at languages," he confessed a little irrelevantly. "I let Petra do most of the talking for me, even though I know a little Amharic. I get by on gestures and bullshit. My only talent, though, is sketching."

And he took a few minutes to do us a passable sketch of the waiter.

Mellowed by the twisted fish, he returned to Petra's story later in the meal. "I knew her for nine years," he said, "and I thought I could look forward to knowing her forever. That is, till the big expulsion."

I wondered why he hadn't married her and given her the protection of his passport. But there could have been trouble with her family, who probably didn't approve of the liaison.

In any case, in the year he was thrown out, the good rains of July and August had ended a famine in Showa province. It was a point of history at which Henry could congratulate himself that his small wells and dams had saved some hundreds of lives, if not thousands, and might make the future return of cyclical famine less likely in at least a few villages. And then, with little warning, the Ethiopian government, the Dergue, its premier the army officer Haile Mariam Mengistu, successor since 1975 of the Emperor Haile Selassie and displaying the same autocratic habits, expelled SUA from Ethiopia.

"He chose us to make an example," Henry forlornly told us in the Sudan Club. "He was gearing up for this eighth great offensive against the Eritreans. He told governments and aid bodies not to give any food or other materials of any kind to the Eritreans. Most of us continued to. And some of the SUA officials, guys more senior than me and more full of opinions, said this and that about his shitty policies. That landed SUA and me on Mengistu's list of hostile bodies. And the boys at the Ministry of the Interior in Addis didn't like me having a Somali girl. So I was on the hit roster in any case. Mengistu threw us out with his real enemies, the French crowd *Médecins sans Frontières*. That's who he really wanted to get." He stared into the lees of purple juice in his glass. "But all this goddam expelling didn't extend to Petra. She stayed! Oh yes, she stayed."

The girl leaned forward. "How old is she?"

Henry waved a hand. He took out a wadded diary, extracted a photograph from it, and waved it in front of us. It showed a woman as tall and thin as the people of Somalia generally are. "Graduate of the University of Addis Ababa," said Henry. "No cow college for her, a real seat of learning where it was hard for Somalis to get admission."

Her father, the American told us, was a surgeon from the Somali city of Mogadishu, and she had worked with the Red Cross in that region called the Ogaden, the great plain in the southeast of Ethiopia which the Somalis consider their own but which was—by decree of the UN—part of Ethiopia. Somalis still persist in calling the Ogaden "Western Somalia," but—Henry said—Petra avoided even in private such emotional and dangerous terms as that. She was very careful in case anyone mistook her for a Somali rebel. "The Amhara are a great tribe, friends, but you wouldn't believe how antsy they can be about the others, about the Oromo, the Somalis down in the Ogaden, the Tigreans in the north. Above all, of course, of the Eritreans. If you're Somali, you don't have to go around using terms like *Western Somalia* to get into trouble. On some days they were likely to arrest you just on the basis of your face and your background!"

I don't think Henry meant to give us Petra's full history. He was drawn out by the girl's dogged questions: "How old is she?" "What is her family?" etc., etc.

I wondered if my story and Bernadette's ran as close to the surface of the skin as Henry's did, whether it could be so easily started running?

Petra was already working in the Addis office of SUA when Henry first arrived there. "But it was *Fetasha* that made us friends," said Henry.

I'd heard of the period known as the *Fetasha*, the Search. When the Emperor had first been overthrown by the Dergue, there had been excitement among the robust minorities in the capital: the Somalis, even the small group of Eritreans who were students at the university, and all the others. But Mengistu and the Dergue had by the time of *Fetasha* disabused them of all hopes. The regime armed gangs of unemployed youths with leftover American weapons from the Emperor's day and sent them into the streets as vigilantes to keep order, to demand orthodox revolutionary behavior, to take vengeance on those who showed a flicker of fear—fear being misread as false politics.

Anyhow, Henry used to escort Petra home to her small walled house behind St. George's Cathedral through the impromptu roadblocks of the *Fetasha*. He would at one time, he said, stay there for more than a week, keeping guard over her in her tiny rooms.

I imagined them holding to each other behind shuttered windows, listening to the armed and feckless children scurrying by in sandals, M-16s in their hands. The shouts, the threats of the armed children, and the screams and whimpers of frightened adults were sometimes less than half a block away.

Whenever he used the word *fiancée*, the girl and I would find ourselves exchanging glances. She pitied him in her wide-eyed, stark, economical way, and I both pitied and envied him. He was still active in the question, after all; he was still working and angling away for the liberation of the Somali. Over the *karkedeh* juice and soda in the Sudan Club I was all at once conscious, in a superheated sort of way which cried out to be treated with strong liquor, that I was by contrast outside Bernadette's affairs, that the time when I could even have pretended to be taking part in them was gone even by the night she ran off in the center of Australia with the jailbird Burraptiti.

What is obvious—apart from the pity of it—when Henry uses the term *fiancée*, is that he wants the listener to know that his affair with the Somali woman is a matter of honor and not of mere convenience. During his period of exile from Ethiopia, Henry spent three months with relatives in New York, chivvying U.S. Immigration officials to let Petra into the United States and—more than that—demand that Mengistu issue her with an exit visa. He made the rounds of offices in New York and Washington.

"I said to them, 'You fight to get goddam Refuseniks out of Russia. Well, Petra's a Refusenik.' When Mengistu sent in that '85 offensive against the Eritreans—you know, the one they call the Silent Offensive—I frankly hoped it would work, that the whole thing would be settled and Mengistu would smile and issue exit visas to everyone who wanted to leave. But the Eritreans held and Petra stayed home under house arrest."

Henry himself went home to Sault Ste. Marie for Christmas after Mengistu had expelled him. Over the punch, he records, his uncle said to him, "Why didn't you tell that Mengistu to go fuck himself? He needs *you*, that monkey!"

"But the fact is," Henry told us in the Sudan Club, "I needed my villages. I got these dreams of silt washing off the hillsides, clogging the dam walls, turning them to these shallow ridges. Nightmare stuff. Genuine nightmares! And my uncle—he was just like the rest of the public in the rich world. You couldn't speak to any of them. They couldn't understand what drives an aid worker any more than they could understand Himalayan monks. And you can't explain anything to them; the words in your mouth don't mean the same as the words in theirs.

"New Year's Eve, I drove to this park I knew from my high school days, right above the dirty waterway between Huron and Michigan. I drank a bottle of vodka and ended up in the hospital with hypothermia! See, I wasn't equipped any more to live in the West."

Waiting on the Coast

The Eritrean-run villa in Port Sudan where Henry and the girl and I waited for our transportation south to Suakin and Eritrea stood in a broad alley by the Red Sea salt pans. It had its own high-walled garden of sand, a little echo of the Sahara. Scattered about this garden were piles of plastic bottles with the label of a West German brand of bottled water. Port Sudan's water supply was, according to Eritrean analysis, unfit to drink.

The house was run by wounded veterans of the Eritrean war. One by one they approached us during our first hours there and shook our hands with that solemn thoroughness characteristic of handshakes in the Sudan and Eritrea.

A young man who edged forward on crutches seemed to have nothing inside the legs of his pants except thin metal substitute limbs. He was nonetheless able to wring our hands. He sat with us at a small table in the hallway.

"You brought no wood?" he asked, winking at one of his fellow veterans. He was the villa wag.

Not knowing what was coming, we admitted we'd brought no wood.

"You should have brought wood. It costs like gold in Port Sudan." He grinned at us. "I need wood. All the trees are gone from the Red Sea shore."

I watched Christine greet this news with an old-fashioned, prim solemnity.

This young man, it turned out, designed prosthetic arms and legs

43

out of steel and plastic and leather and wood in the yellow garage in the corner of the garden. And the wood was—as he said—expensive.

Both Henry and the girl seemed to be able to take this strange household as it came. But in a way I'd begun my time in Port Sudan badly. On the afternoon we'd arrived, we'd seen the "therapy cases" returning to the Eritrean clinic from their afternoon walk: emerging from the tracks and small hillocks around the salt pans, those square lakes of Red Sea brine stewing under the last of the sun; from the donkey and camel tracks; from the wastelands around the airport where nomads waited to do business in the city the next day. They came on in long lines, on crutches with crooked determination, in old-fashioned wheelchairs passed down to them from an earlier generation of American or European maimed. Last light from the Red Sea hills lit them. We'd all been awed to see them, but neither Christine nor Henry seemed to have been reduced to the same useless, mawkish fear and reverence which overcame me.

Both Christine and Henry were able to go off to the garage and watch the young amputee, the one who'd teased us about wood, fitting limbs to legless young men and women. I admired the way Henry and Christine talked there, asking the limb maker prosaic questions about resins and wood and padding. I was meant to be the questioner, the journalist, but I couldn't achieve a conversational tone. I lost my breath in the middle of sentences. At that stage I thought what a steady, functional companion Henry was going to be.

Through a gateway across the alley you could enter the much larger blue house which was the Eritrean clinic. It was a fancier institution than the clinic we would later see in Suakin.

Here, on a stairwell, when I was coming down from the roof, from a visit to a boy who had been cut off at the buttocks by an explosion and who, supported on his strong forearms, had been doing algebra in an exercise book, I saw a thin one-legged girl come to despair. Not yet fitted out with a substitute limb in the yellow garage, not yet familiar with her crutches, she let herself slump sideways in an angle of the stairs. She did not know I was above her, watching. Defeated, she let her shoulders slacken as she considered the blue wall. She wasn't substantial—she could have been a coat hung there—wishing, I suppose, that the mine or bullet which had taken her limb had also attended to her life. I could tell, as if from the angle of resignation of her dark, braided head seen from above, that she dreaded the rough, cheery rehabilitation her fellow rebels were offering.

My concern was not to be seen by her, and while I waited there Henry appeared through the same door the girl had. "What's the trouble, missy?" he asked, brushing by her, reviving her—it seemed to me—with the friction of his joviality. She began to move. I was stuck meanwhile, two flights up, at the far end of the axis of her misery.

Henry and I hung our rinsed shirts on the wire line in the garden, careful lest they fall on the sand and need a rewash. He looked at home in the withering light, mumbling his way through a series of jazz tunes.

He'd been just as solid and accepting a man as that when in Khartoum we'd fought our way aboard Air Sudan's eccentric flight to Port Sudan. The flight engineer had prepared for the takeoff by collecting all the nomads' crusader swords—they would be in his care until touchdown at Port Sudan. But the second officer wasn't able to get the forward hatch closed. A mêlée of Sudanese gathered, helping the pilots apply their shoulders, and Henry left his aisle seat and fraternally joined other passengers in trying to force the thing shut.

They fought with it for three quarters of an hour, and whenever his suggestions, compounded of snatches of Arabic plus some gestures, were discounted by the group, he would wink down the plane at us.

Throughout, I assured myself fairly impotently that in closing the hatch mere force wouldn't count for anything, and that if two Sudanese pilots, an old hand like Henry, and several senior Sudanese public servants were all not adequate to get the thing closed by cunning, then neither was I. Though I admired Henry's neighborly pushing and shouting, I believed that in another few minutes this flight would be canceled. There would be no spare parts. The Sudan's foreign exchange holdings, greater these days—under the bullying of the International Monetary Fund—were still not adequate to afford spares.

At last the door closed simply in any case, with one heave of many shoulders and then a deft turn of the handle by the pilot. The group of strugglers laughed together, the vindicated Henry among them. A practical man and a doer.

Within that villa where I developed my early admiration of Henry, we encountered besides the manager and the maker of limbs a sort of Eritrean elite—even though *élite* seemed to be a word forbidden among the rebels. We met men and women going to or returning from foreign missions. A pharmacist from the great Eritrean base camp of Orotta was waiting in the villa for a flight to Khartoum and thence to West Germany, where he would take delivery of a new demineralizing machine he needed for the manufacture of surgical drips. Also there that first night were two veterans, each of about forty years, one on his way to open a political lobbying office in Washington, the other the Eritrean representative in Bonn. They were lean intellectuals. They discussed Milton Friedman and John Kenneth Galbraith. The Emperor Haile Selassie had educated them, taken them grudgingly into his great university at Addis which, in their youths, like the Polish universities in the thirties with Jews, accepted only the smallest number of Eritreans, a *numerus clausus* of which they were members. They had postgraduate degrees from Cornell and Northwestern. They wore lightly the marks of another sort of education, the scar tissue of shrapnel wounds on their bare arms and neck and, in one case, forehead.

Sitting with Henry and the girl and me at a minute table in the fly- and mosquito-ridden front hallway, they ate with a sort of military voracity. The meals were pasta, canned Italian mackerel, and the excellent tomatoes of the Red Sea coast.

In view of the events which later seemed to turn Henry sour, it's worth saying that on either side of this hallway were two great dormitories where the men slept on whatever bed was free—the envoys, the rebel pharmacist, the maimed prosthetic-limb maker, the veteran who managed the house, Henry, and me. Fans churned, but even the Eritreans found it too hot to sleep beneath a mosquito net.

These beds at the guest house were considered luxurious by all old campaigners. The envoys lay on them, modest suitcases packed and ready to go beside them on the floor, and consumed copies of

Time, Der Spiegel, tissuey editions of *The Guardian Weekly*. Wolfing the newsprint as they'd earlier wolfed the pasta.

Upstairs was the women's dormitory, which Christine Malmédy shared with Bufta, the cook. Christine had become fascinated by Bufta's hair, teased out along the scalp into lines and dressed with oil or—as Bufta would confess to the girl—rancid butter. I don't know why it didn't smell bad. In fact, the few times I came near Bufta it smelled of robust maternity. The girl seemed fascinated by Bufta's face altogether, the slits at the side of her forehead where some sort of primitive medicine had been practiced on her in her childhood. Some of the double-degree envoys also wore such markings on their eyebrows or temples, but in Bufta's case the effect was compounded by a tattooed Coptic cross in the middle of her forehead.

"The cook is very beautiful," Christine told me. It seemed that for the first time since she'd arrived in Africa, she was taking serious notice of the African visage, of Bufta's visage and that of the amputees and cripples. And none of the discomforts of that humid seaport seemed to give her any trouble. She didn't complain about the heat, the uncertain trickles in the shower room, or the fetor of the cloaca. Correctly and calmly, she guessed that there was worse to come. Obviously she was preparing herself for her meeting with her father.

Her only confession of discomfort was that she bought too much sweet Malinta cola from the street stall behind the clinic. It was a sort of addiction, this storing up of sugar, even though sugar was—if Stella could be believed—the one luxury the Eritreans made sure they had "in the field."

I often went with Christine across the open dusty ground by the salt pans. My excuse was that in this area of town the police sometimes showed their suspicion of foreigners by seizing them for questioning. Rightly or wrongly, I thought I could talk them around, or at least give her some companionship in custody.

The street stall always closed in the early afternoon. Then, just as the prosthetic works in the garage was opening for its evening fittings, the stall would open again and she would set forth to visit it.

One afternoon when I was with her on this short journey, she pointed out an Eritrean boy and girl from the clinic. They were on their compulsory afternoon walk, he in his wheelchair and she on crutches, one of her pants legs empty, as if she had yet to be fitted up by the crippled veteran at the garage. She was not, however, the slumped insubstantial girl I'd earlier seen despairing on the stairs.

The two veterans had paused a moment by the salt pans and were talking, the girl leaning over the head of the young man.

Again, Christine did not seem to indulge any easy emotions about these cases. Under the awning of the stall, she bought four Malinta bottles from the Arab boy she always dealt with, left two with me, and took the other two across to the engrossed boy and girl. Half-embarrassedly they accepted the drinks, both of them offering her a solemn handshake.

When she came back I put her own drink into her hands. She applied herself reflectively to sucking the oversweet cola.

"They are very lucky," she said.

"You don't envy them their wounds, do you?" I asked.

She said of course not.

And for the rest of the drink, belching softly on the carbonation, she discussed in what sense the two were fortunate. They were maimed, but she knew the maimed had great honor among the Eritreans. They felt their sacrifice meant something, whereas she knew from films that Vietnam veterans from America did not feel that way, felt their injuries as obscene accidents.

And thirdly, these two did not have to fight any more.

Right at the end of the list of blessings, she said with a half-embarrassed authority, "And they have each other for friends."

I suppose I date the problems I had with Henry from the night we went into the port with the veteran-manager of the guest house for a meal of sweet-fleshed Red Sea fish on a rundown terrace above the oily port. After dinner, the man walked us through the British-style administration section, among barracks and customs houses in their gardens of dust, past botanic gardens in which grew trees but no grass. He talked to us about *Malesh*, the whimsical tolerance of imperfection which had stopped the gardens growing, filled the bay with perilous oil slick, made plane timetables a matter of guessing, and rendered the people too tolerant of bad governments.

"There is no *Malesh* in the Eritrean soul," he told us. "We have not fought for a quarter of a century to be happy with *Malesh*."

Suddenly, Christine had taken hold of my hand. It didn't worry the guest house manager—in Africa the holding of hands is a far less sexual gesture than it probably is in the West. I knew there was no desire there and suspected she was claiming me the way a girl does who shows tenderness to A to frighten B off. But who was B? Henry hadn't given any sign of pushing himself at Christine.

"What does this mean?" I couldn't stop myself asking in a low voice. But the question might have sounded to Henry like a smug rhetorical one, from the man who has been admitted into possession. Christine did not answer it. I thought I saw a strange, angry flicker of Henry's eyebrows.

We drank sweet tea at the Red Sea Hotel in an environment of mosquitos, and Henry and the veteran discussed their brushes with that fever. But there was an edge of grim boast to Henry's voice now.

The veteran-manager did not seem to notice it. "I get malaria because of my wounds," he told us, looking up at the old photographs on the walls, snaps of British women, wives of officers, resting in oases between legs of journeys.

The man wasn't going to state what those wounds were. When everyone had their scars, it was taken as ungracious to speak about that except in objective terms. For they wanted you to know they *had* been wounded, but they didn't want to talk about it in the Western subjective way. So, no reminiscences of shock, of awakening from anesthesia, of what the doctor said, *of how it felt*!

Back at the villa afterward, I was hunched on my bed beneath the fans when Henry came in, picked up his packed and aged diary-journal and the sketch pad in which he had been sketching some of the Eritreans in the guest house, and made room for himself to sit on his own bed.

"Well," he said confidingly. "We know what the trouble with Mademoiselle Malmédy is now!"

"Trouble?" I asked him.

"You know what I mean. How spaced out the kid is!"

I wondered if his idea of *spaced out* covered also her grabbing my hand during the promenade through Port Sudan.

"Seems she's had an abortion," he told me. "Last month in Paris."

I disliked above all the adolescent lack of finesse in Henry, the way he conveyed the gossip, diminishing himself, diminishing the enthusiastic prosthetic-garage conversationalist and closer of plane hatches that he'd been until now. Just the same, it struck me that here was an explanation for the girl's fey detachment toward nearly everything but finding her father.

Next I began to wonder how this information of Henry's was got? Henry didn't seem embarrassed to have it. But, after the sweet fish flesh and the tea, and the false signal of Christine clasping my hand, could he have been driven up to the roof to make a frantic try for the girl? And could Christine have then passed on the news of the abortion as a sort of rebuff, a curse on all men?

Anyhow, I couldn't stop myself asking, "How do you know?"

"I went up on the roof to check things out. She and Bufta sleep up there. For the cool, you know. I walked in on Bufta braiding her hair by kerosene lamp, and you'd think I'd walked into a ladies' room somewhere. Bufta gathered up all her combs and covered her head with a shawl. And the girl wasn't very friendly. *Thees ees the womeen's sec-shyern*, the little mam'selle told me. I told her I hadn't heard the roof was off-limits and asked her why she was hostile, and she came out with this! She yelled it. *Why sherd I want to see murn when becurse of wurn I hev hed an abur-shurn?*"

I didn't like his mimicry. Nor the way that, having a few seconds before seemed like a high school boy loosely giving away a girl's secrets, he now shook his head like a middle-aged man who didn't know if the future should be entrusted to the young.

"She mightn't be telling the truth," I suggested.

"Sounds credible to me," he said, shaking his head. "I've seen a lot of her. I mean, over at the clinic."

Perhaps he thought he was punishing me by describing the girl's behavior in the Eritrean clinic. She watched videos of British and American educational television programs with the maimed. She didn't seem to have a Florence Nightingale complex, said Henry. It was the young Eritreans who looked after *her*, rather than the opposite. They would scoot off in their wheelchairs and fetch glasses of water for her. He'd seen her working with a musical group—the *kirir* (a sort of banjo made out of the back of a chair), a thick pipe and a thin pipe both peculiar to the region, and of course the

universal instrument of the music of the young, the Japanese key-
board.

Henry confused me now by becoming suddenly disarming. "She
doesn't seem to want to cry," he said, "like I do when I go over
there. But she likes their company. She's likeable herself when she's
over there. There's no *womeen's sec-shyern* bullshit from her over
there. If you offered to take her legs off tomorrow and put her in
a wheelchair beside them, I think she might just go for it."

I turned down the light. We lay on our beds. I soon found that
Henry wasn't reconciled to all that had happened tonight.

"It's up to her to tell her father, don't you think? That is, if it's
the truth."

"I'm not a barbarian," Henry told me. "Anyhow," he asked with
a frank contempt, something I hadn't seen in him before, "were
you ever married?"

To my surprise, I said, "Yes."

I was surprised afterward that I told him a little, the simplest
version: My wife was living with another man.

Yet sitting on the patio at the villa the next day, I found myself
confiding to my tape recorder, the little inbuilt mike close to my
lips, some details about Bernadette.

In my home city, I believe it's honest to say, friends of Bernadette
and mine still use old-fashioned terms like *unlucky* and *ill-fated* as
they pass on what they know of us and what's become of us. One
thing that's become of me is that I won't be able to be reached in
Eritrea. I told Bernadette when I met her the last time that she
could always reach me if she chose. There was a side of me which
considered this a generous offer. In any case, the promise clearly
meant little to her but much to me. And it was valid whenever I
was in England, or even in Poland and the Sudan, where the newspaper had at various times sent me. It was valid for Colorado while
I was there—there were always friends Bernadette knew how to
find who could tell her where I could be found.

But it wouldn't be true of Eritrea. Eritrea was anything but
contactable by the existing technology. There were ways in which
Eritrea was not the present. It was the future in terms of the
theories—military and revolutionary—which hung in its fiery air.
But there was no telephone system. Even if Bernadette made an

unlikely appeal to me, the news wouldn't reach me there. In a world where our most banal inquiries—"Are you missing me?" "What time is it there?" "Has it been hot?" "Has it been cold?" "Has it been wet?" "Has it been dry?"—whistle around the globe in an instant, people cannot wait months for answers any more.

At the time I graduated as a lawyer, there was a fashion in the law faculty of my university: advocacy on behalf of the Australian indigenous peoples. That is, on behalf of those native Australian tribes which had been lumped together under the classicist's name, *Aborigines*—people who'd occupied Australia *from the beginning*.

I'd been averagely enraged to find that there had never been any treaty between the European Australians and the Aboriginal peoples. The tribes had been deprived of their earth without even the benefit of a compact, however flawed. Young law graduates like me might therefore spend their days working for long-established firms of solicitors, conveyancing wealth in cash or kind from one company to another, and then give their spare time free to the Aboriginal Legal Service. Work was a shadow. The two or three hours a night we spent in the airless shopfront offices of the service were the real business of the lawyer.

My clients in the Legal Service were those who'd fled from Aboriginal reservations to the city. They lacked the profound contact their grandfathers had had with the tribal earth. They bore as well the shame of being the first generation of uninitiated men and women. They had, that is, lost their faith. The elders judged them too vitiated by booze and cars, by rock and television, by the blood of whites. The genial mysteries had not been extended to them. The old men preferred to die with those rites and procedures, that tribal physics, locked up in their brains for good.

The dispossessed children I dealt with in the Aboriginal Legal Service courted their own deaths. They flayed themselves with the European scorpion, liquor. They hadn't known it at all for the thousand tribal generations which came before. Now they knew it as closely as their own blood. They were frequently charged with breaking and entering and armed holdup. They were guilty of assault, generally against their own.

I noticed a young woman with an Asian face and a workaday

Australian accent coming and going in the offices of the Legal Service. She had her own office with one word—*Bernadette*— scrawled in black lettering across its glass door. I would hear her competent no-nonsense voice rising from discussions she held with clients or their young lawyers, who didn't seem as clever as she was. She dressed in dutifully dowdy social worker gear: handknit black sweaters and patchwork denim coats. But she had a sumptuous air about her.

As I got to know her I was enchanted by her history—I have a weakness for that. Her great-grandfather had been brought to Australia by a Melbourne Chinese merchant in the nineteenth century—along with thousands of other peasants from Fukien and Canton—as an indentured digger and washer of gold-bearing soil. Bernadette liked to tell of how, as a child, she had been taken by her grandfather to a basalt-covered hill in the Castlemaine gold fields and shown a perfectly dug tunnel, wide enough for two small men standing side by side to walk for a mile and a half beneath the earth. From this sap, the Chinese had plundered the hill of all its lodes.

Bernadette's parents were property owners and importers of cloi- sonné and other Asian wares. Her family, though not European like the Australian majority, had followed the pattern characteristic of new worlds—a laborer great-grandfather; a small merchant grandfather, owner of real estate in Melbourne's Chinatown; a pros- perous father, owner of real estate throughout the general com- munity; a socially concerned, noncommercial *next* generation— Bernadette in this case—working for small pay in a cause more worthy to her than mere clan aggrandizement.

We appalled our parents by living together for two years, and then maybe more so by marrying. At the wedding party in my back garden in South Melbourne, the four parents to the union had to share the feast with fourteen habitual housebreakers, seven grievous- bodily-harms, and five multiple-automobile-thefts. The Yang and Darcy parents both looked out at their foreign child-in-law with brave incomprehension.

At the time of the marriage, I hadn't yet thought in more than a notional sort of way about giving up my work at the well-known legal firm; about going into remoter Australia; about working ex-

clusively with people who were not so far down the road as the
city blacks, with people who were still in large part tribal, who had
not been denied access to their own mysteries.

Tribal councils, particularly in the desert, had advertised for people like Bernadette Yang and me to work as community advisers.
There was some debate among our friends about whether this demand had been artificially created—had been suggested by white
officials in a way which left the tribal councils no option—or
whether the need was objective and obvious to everyone.

But the bulk of opinion, particularly the forthright Bernadette's,
was that the tribes *needed* subtle mediators. For in the desert there
existed two wildly different systems of law, the tribal and the European; two systems of health; and two species of education. Few
people were equipped or willing to make a bridge, and if Bernadette
and I thought we might be among that number, maybe it was a
very venial sort of self-delusion. It would attract a heavy punishment, just the same.

Our friends later confessed to being amused by the adroit way
Bernadette moved me, more skeptical and congenitally cautious—
after all, I had a bank manager's genes—toward the idea that we
were fitted for this cultural liaison work. Over late, after-dinner
glasses of wine, at dinners at the Darcy-Yang flat, or in restaurants,
she could make it seem like one of the few challenges left to hu-
mankind. Not just a work of interpretation between two sullen
camps, but the making of a span between two planets. And how I
loved and relished her persuasive force, the mysterious face and the
practical voice, the voice Australians had picked up from Cockneys
and the harsh-tongued birds of their country and which now
emerged from perfect Cantonese lips.

We were employed in the end by the tribal council at Fryer River,
three hundred miles west of Alice Springs, close to the continent's
geographic center of isolation. The tribespeople were members of
two large tribal groups: the Pitjantjara and the Pintubi people. The
Pintubi were among the last on the continent to have had contact
with outsiders. These two sets of related people lived on an immensity of esthetically pleasing but very barren country. They knew
how to *read* it, though, and had come to terms with it millennia
past. This traditional earth of theirs, so remote from cities, had been

granted to them, freehold title, by the federal government only a few years before Bernadette and I were posted there.

Bernadette hoped to be particularly useful to the women, who —she knew—had different secrets and mysteries than the men. The women were believed to be the most powerful influence behind the tribal council, even though none of them were members.

The Yang and Darcy parents faced another shock therefore when they saw their expensively educated children board a jet plane bound for the tribal milieu.

From the start, I loved the Fryer River country. It took me by surprise. The balance of enthusiasm for my new task and this new locale shifted almost at once away from Bernadette to me. It was here that my old half-serious bar talk about the sisterhood of Africa and Australia seemed to take on visible form. For, whether you knew it or not, you *did* see Kenya there; you saw the Sudan, you saw the mountains of Ethiopia—or of Eritrea for that matter. Here was a fruitful desert where wild honey dripped from the fronds of the grevillea. Desert oaks, said to grow an inch in a century yet three times as tall as a human, populated the plains. And arcing away from the settlement, to the north and the south, were two great ranges of apparently sterile mountains, brazen at noon, purple at other times, home nonetheless to a million flowerings of desert botany, as also to antique clans of euro, kangaroo, wallaby, and dingo.

Fryer River itself, one of the earth's most ancient watercourses, also mimicked Africa by being a ghost of a river. It ran only in rain time, perhaps once in three years or even once in ten. From its warm bed she-oaks and eucalyptus trees grew, drawing on a secret river deep beneath the geographic one.

On the empty banks, Bernadette and I lived in a trailer partitioned into bedroom at one end and kitchen–living room at the other. Friends from Melbourne slept in that living room during visits. Air conditioning came from the settlement's diesel generator. But the Pitjantjara and Pintubi did not always want the government's light or artificial breezes. Few of the Pintubi had a taste for air conditioning. Bernadette and I both saw that the people were more concerned with the night cold than the blaze of noon. There seemed to be a connection between the cold nights and the ceaseless activity of spirits, who, during the hours of sleep, might steal the crucial coating of fat from around the kidneys of a man or a woman.

I believe I'd never done better work or had more of it to do than in Fryer River. I was so zealous; I had encountered a fresh way of looking at the earth. The tribal council brought me to the view that houses in the European sense were not always a mercy, for the Pintubi in particular but even for the often more "worldly" Pitjantjara. These people were attached to the earth in a literal sense. There were stories of Pintubi who, when arrested and imprisoned on floors of cement or planking, died in the night of pining for the mother-breast of earth. Housing seemed to the Pintubi a ridiculous closet into which to crowd a human soul.

The other large claim on my attention in Fryer River was the strange desert addiction to petrol sniffing. Pintubis and Pitjantjara, nomads in their hearts, looked upon everything as equally a product of nature. I liked to expatiate on this fact to visitors. In European societies, I'd say, the disposable—tissues, pens, packaging—declares itself. The collection and hoarding of the merely disposable is always looked upon as an illness, and collectors of garbage and wrappings and newspapers have been certified and locked away for seeing permanent value in the throwaway.

The desert nomad, however, takes the aberrant view that everything is equally disposable, that everything has a limited and a merely vegetable life—except the spirit itself, which is eternal and which endlessly returns!

The end products of this nomadic view were in fact littered all over the desert. Tribespeople who went to Alice Springs would spend too much of their mineral royalty money on secondhand automobiles—bombs, lemons, clankers. When these cars gave out on the way back to Fryer River, in the dry river beds or the red foothills, the Pitjantjara and Pintubi driver didn't feel orphaned by a failure of technology, as a European traveler would. Sometimes he would push the vehicle onto its side to see if any obvious fault declared itself from beneath. But if nothing could be done with the thing, he walked away from it without too much regret. For its cycle was finished.

The desert west of Ayers Rock was littered with vehicles which —in the dry atmosphere—never decayed.

And an unhappy conjunction existed between the vehicles and the Fryer River children. These boys would have been, in a traditional and untouched tribal setup, going through the lessons, making the long journeys to particular sites, training in ritual enactments; would have been desert seminarians. But the old men looked upon them as rendered partially unfit through white education and rock 'n' roll.

Because of their unworthiness, their initiations were delayed. They treated the painful gap by siphoning petrol from the desert wrecks and inhaling it for a high. During my stay at Fryer River, Freddy Numati, a man of about forty-five years who headed the tribal council and was a trained mechanic, one day led me to a tree under which lay a dead fourteen-year-old Pitjantjara boy, his face jammed into a peach tin half full of petrol.

The elders had no tribal precedent for dealing with this strange addiction. They looked to me because they knew my spirit was more akin to petrol than theirs. They looked to the police, too, who came through on patrols. The council were more willing than I would have liked to use the police as a means of ejecting some petrol-obsessed youth from the Fryer River settlement to the reform school outside Alice Springs. For there clinical psychologists and social workers, their souls also more akin to petroleum products, could deal with him. To the council, this petrol-sniffing disease had arrived at Fryer River like an unscannable virus from another planet.

The idea that one should thrash a child for its addiction, or kick it in the arse, again had no history among the desert people. In fact, the tradition was the opposite, and for every blow you landed on a child the members of his clan had to strike you back.

Unequipped, I found myself speaking to the sniffers, negotiating between the police and the tribal elders.

In a normal suburb of tormented people, Bernadette would have been superb and compassionate. But it was against the tribal order for the elders to ask Bernadette Yang to counsel young men. I didn't particularly resent this. I believed that Bernadette was busy enough with the women.

The women had begun painting in acrylics, using the designs which had for thousands of years been employed for painting in ochres on sand. The Pitjantjara and Pintubi symbols adapted to this method were circular patterns for the waterhole spirit places and dots signifying the plenteous spirits themselves. These paintings were maps to the core of Australia, but they were esthetically pleasing as well, and a good one could sell for $10,000 in the United States or Europe.

Bernadette was learning to use this painting technique, though she did not understand the patterns as a tribal person would. As far as I knew at this stage, she had found among the women the same perfect place I enjoyed among the tribal council.

But, according to what visitors told me afterward, Bernadette Yang was already unhappy. She had begun to complain of the desert women, of how they avoided her eyes and fell silent as she approached. I barely noticed it though. Like Masihi, I was besotted with a people I could not belong to; I was engrossed in their scheme. When that happens, it's too easy for a certain type of human to sacrifice the usual attachments of blood, of what you'd call—even though our trailer didn't have one—the hearth.

I didn't notice. I would need it explained and ultimately demonstrated to me. Henry had had the *Fetasha* to alert him to the threat to his Somali. I needed something of that weight and obviousness to grab my attention. I wouldn't be getting it.

Trucking the Paraplegic

In the shimmering wreckage of Suakin, a town which had been left to decay after the Turks departed this coast and yet looked as if it had been bombarded, the vehicle which would take us down the Red Sea coast and into the Eritrean mountains arrived. It halted among the rubble in the laneway outside the Eritrean barracks and clinic where we had been waiting. It was small and, in theory, faster than the big Mercedes trucks. Sand bogs would reduce that advantage though. *Deutsche Arbeiter Bund*, it declared in rainbow colors on its green side—a gift of the West Germans. The muscular young driver wore military fatigues and a bandanna round his neck. His name, he said, was Tecleh. He loped and was casual. He called to us in subdued English. "Ready to join the mountain bandits?" It was what their enemies called them. *Mountain bandits*.

In that heat, the three of us were bewildered children. We watched Tecleh lift our luggage, including Henry's massive duffel, onto the roof. He tethered it all there, covering it with a tarpaulin to keep the sand out. But he would not let us board yet. He was waiting for someone but did not know how to explain that to us. "A sick man," he said. I imagined a leprous figure staggering toward us across the town's rubble heaps.

While we waited, four Eritrean nurses—two male, two female —appeared in the courtyard carrying a stretcher with a wasted shape on it. They eased it out of the gate into the laneway. The shape had the face of a young man, another Eritrean hero. A further two nurses—paramedics, aides—followed the litter, one bearing surgical infusion bags, the other a metal box with a red cross painted on it.

I watched Tecleh stretch a foam rubber mattress along the floor in the rear of the truck. The stretcher bearers loaded the young man onto this, two of them boarding backwards and then stooping to keep the stretcher level. When the sick man was in place, the two women bearers at his feet also boarded the truck and exchanged mumbled wishes and handshakes with him. Then all four dismounted and made room for the lean young men carrying the drip bags and the box of medicines. These two, apparently, were to travel with us. One of them, seeing the lanky American Henry about to take a photograph, called "No!" and held up a preventive hand. Perhaps they feared their Sudanese friends might be affronted to see, turning up in some international magazine, a photograph which showed that if one of the injured rebels at Suakin got ill, the Eritreans trucked him back over the mountains for surgery by their own doctors, their own team.

The two young men aboard began connecting a drip to a vein in the patient's arm. One of them opened the metal box and took out a syringe, some pain-killer already drawn up into it.

"Barefoot doctors," Tecleh said. But they weren't barefoot. They wore the Eritrean plastic sandal which, it would soon become apparent, was one of the dress icons of the rebels.

"Trucking a paraplegic?" Henry asked me.

In the vehicle as packed, Tecleh, the girl, and Henry took the front. I was a little surprised that Christine let Henry ride at her side, in view of what had happened between them in Port Sudan. Perhaps she was letting me know now that the clasped hands in the streets of Port Sudan hadn't meant anything more than similar gestures between schoolchildren. In any case, I sat in the back with my legs hooked onto the opposite seat and bridging the body of the sick boy on the floor. Then, seated toward the rear, on the least comfortable seats over the back wheels, the two barefoot doctors!

The young man called gently to me from the floor, "What is your name? What is your nation?"

The truck moved. He closed his eyes at this early shock to the suspension, and also in exhaustion.

I was aware that he was going home, to the nation of his desire, that he was attached to his *cause* the way only such time-displaced eighteenth-century survivals as the Poles were. I felt a strange embarrassment as I spoke to him. I would never discover what his name was. Later I asked the girl, Christine, if she'd ascertained it at some stage on the road. She was often attentive to these things. But she hadn't found it out either.

Our track out of Sudan and into Eritrea was at first a flat and unapologetic desert road. Sometimes it looped close to the Red Sea, and you saw a strange border land of vivid green reed beds, and among them a low, clapboard fishing village. These people fished in boats built on a most antique, high-pooped design, some of which could be seen offshore that afternoon. Made sedentary by the plenty of the sea, the fisher people bought their goods from the Beja nomads, who—according to all I've read—pitied them, and whom they despised.

Tecleh, the young Eritrean truck driver, shouting above the noise of the engine, made what sounded like one of his few set speeches, this one on how to behave at the last Sudanese border post, which was still two hours to the south. There were two policemen there, he said, one a sergeant. "Never sees an Englishman, never sees an American, never sees a Frenchman. No wife, nothing to make him happy. When he says, *Where is your passport?* you say you have the movement permit. You go to the border regions, you say. But you do not say, *We are going to Eritrea!*"

There was no single road, only a set of alternating tracks, a series of sandy, treacherous options. Along them that afternoon, as apparently on all other afternoons, the Eritrean trucks plowed, traveling empty up to Port Sudan to collect aid consigned to them—however much against the wish of Addis—and returning south laden. Supposedly, if you had crawled over the backs of these trucks, you would have found sorghum and wheat, Oxfam high-protein biscuit, water pump replacements, canisters of raw pharmaceuticals, and stacks of plastic bags to be filled with Eritrea's own surgical drips in deep sterile caves.

All afternoon we encountered these Mercedes trucks, green-painted, each of them with a number on its flanks, the number the last thing we saw before we raised our shawls over our mouths or clamped our hats or bandannas there against the world of dust.

I couldn't avoid being touched and excited by all this afternoon traffic. The American Henry got enthusiastic, too. He leaned over from the front seat, where he was sitting with Christine, and yelled, "These guys are astounding! Running all this. And you know what? The world hates 'em for it! The world's hooked into the idea of the helpless African!" Even from his dry mouth little globules of spit sprang. And as an Eritrean truck lumbered past, dragging its mountain of dust, Henry resisted the normal courtesies of winding up his window and instead leaned out, choking, from the passenger door.

"Way to go, Africa!" he screamed.

Christine squirmed around in her seat to share a mysterious smile with me.

With all this movement, it came as a surprise to see an occasional nomad standing swathed, all except his eyes covered, in a brilliant jacket and white jellaba and turban, holding his sheathed crusader sword by the handle; a man impenetrable to dust. The owner of this empty quarter.

He drew my eyes inland, toward the beautiful Red Sea hills where, if the dust cleared, you could see strings of camels bearing nomad women through the fumes of the sun toward tents strung along the wadis. Beja people. Muslims, they spoke Arabic only for occasional convenience of trade, keeping instead an ancient hermetic language of their own for more important things. So when they faced east at sunrise and sunset, they exalted Allah in their own, stubborn, aged tongue and—so Stella informed me—watched Egyptian soap operas on battery-operated TVs in their tents.

In better days, one of the most ancient of the pilgrimage routes had run through here, through this quarter vacant on modern maps. The old route, which ran from Shendi on the Nile to Suakin, had depended on the Bejas' blessing once, and for a thousand years every pilgrim had needed their goodwill to make it to the Red Sea. But war and bad government and the mysterious intent of God had spread the Sahara right down here. And, in any case, the jet plane had altered the travel arrangements pilgrims made.

The last Sudanese town—half clapboard houses, half nomad tents—stood for mysterious reasons of its own on a random acreage of sand. It did not even serve as an authentic border post, since it was still many miles before the Eritrean border. Botany had no place there. Botany lay with its seeds deep in the earth, waiting for the rumor of moisture.

The road was fairly level and Henry was able to talk to us without screaming. "These people have it pretty good," he told me. "The Eritreans pay the camel herders thirty dollars to take bags in by the coastal route, through the Sahel. Now and then an Ethiopian MIG shoots one up, gets the driver or the camel. Just the same, thirty dollars is big money here. Danger money. Fat city."

I wondered how he knew all this. And all I remember is that the leanest of people loped through the town.

A wadi divided it in two, and all the goats and camels were along this watercourse, dry as it was. It was as if they had a genetic rumor in their brains that if water were ever to flow, it would be here. They'd discovered long before the Greeks that water finds its own level. They shuffled and groaned in the sage way of desert beasts.

As if by ritual, Tecleh tried to run by the police post, a hut as nondescript as the rest of this town, marked only by the flag of Sudan, pure green in the futile hope of fertility.

A young policeman came running diagonally across our path, hallooing, carrying an old .303 rifle left behind by the British.

"Ai-ai-ai!" said Tecleh, like an Italian, and pulled to a stop.

When the young policeman caught up, he opened the back doors first and inspected the paraplegic who lay on the floor beneath me. "How are you?" he asked the young veteran in English. But then he came round to the front and spoke an argumentative Arabic with Tecleh. Tecleh spoke jovial, languid Arabic back. Two hundred yards out in a mist of sand, aid trucks came and went as if the young cop did not see them. He continued to take our vehicle seriously, however. He paced up and down for a while in front of its grillwork, staring at it, then cast an eye upward at the covered luggage in the rack. Maybe, as Tecleh intimated, this was the only acting fun he'd had for weeks.

Next he put his head in the window and looked severely at Henry and Christine, and then over the back seat at me. The two barefoot doctors were exempt from his professional concern. But he seemed to be confident that the rest of us would fail at least one of the Sudan's proliferating sets of regulations.

"All of you down!" he ordered.

To leave the truck I had to roll my body along the two parallel seats, making sure that my hips didn't fall and injure the paraplegic. At last I jumped through the open door. The young man with the rifle stared at me. You couldn't tell what complicated set of political and tribal creeds, orthodoxies, prescriptions were operating in a man like that—you'd have needed to be Sudanese yourself to work it out.

Henry walked back and forth in front of the young man, muttering one- or two-word complaints in Arabic. Christine murmured to me, "But they will not stop us?"

"No," I told her. "No. They'll just go through the rituals."

The young policeman led us to a clapboard hut. On its shady side a more senior policeman was cooking part of the spine of a goat in a frying pan over a vivid little fire of sticks. His hands were covered with flour, but when he saw us he began to brush the flour off on his khaki pants. The campaign ribbons he wore on his chest may once have been vivid scarlets and emeralds and blues, but now they were reduced to a general umber. All martial meaning had been blasted out of them by the wind and the sun.

He, too, argued a little in Arabic with Tecleh before asking each of us, "You are going to Eritrea? Is that right?"

"We're going to the border area," I kept saying, as Tecleh had instructed me.

The sergeant gave Christine the slowest time of all, checking her features one by one against the photograph.

"There is something wrong with this permit," he said.

"I don't think so, *effendi*," I said.

The sergeant ignored me and spoke in Arabic to Tecleh. Tecleh then reported to us. "He says he must radio Khartoum. Hours and hours. Ai-ai-ai!"

"Come," the sergeant told us in English at last. "You must sit inside. And your luggage. I must see your luggage."

We groaned. Tecleh was arguing strenuously, but I could not understand what he was saying. Henry said to me, "He's not opening my luggage! You know what it is? He wants to have Christine around for a few hours to look at. Probably hasn't seen a European woman for years, if ever. I know it's lonely on the frontier, but for Christ's sake . . ."

He patted the colorful mountaineer's belt-cum-wallet which hung around his waist. He caught up to the sergeant, who was already in the doorway. Beyond the opened door I could see a table with a radio-transmitter, and a suit of lime green pajamas hanging from a rafter. The sergeant had some style!

Henry spoke in a low voice to the sergeant. In contrast to last night, Henry seemed to be operating smoothly; I was sure he would bring the sergeant around. Occasionally the honorific *effendi* could be heard, and the rasp of the zipper on Henry's belt. There was a flash also of highly colored Sudanese pounds.

After more talk, the sergeant turned to us, hitting the Sudanese pounds from Henry's hand onto the ground. "I am a Muslim," he cried. "I am not as dishonest as Christians!"

"Ai-ai-ai!" cried Tecleh.

"You are from everywhere. France, the United States, the last places on earth! How do I know what you are taking to my friends the Eritreans?"

There wasn't any doubting his professional affront. Yet the Sudan was a place where official venality was a tradition, so Henry's assumption that he needed paying off hadn't been unrealistic. Nonetheless, Henry was scrabbling now on the ground for the Sudanese pounds he'd offered the sergeant.

And what this rejection of Henry's offer meant was hard to gauge. Did the Eritreans use the sergeant to process their foreign visitors? It would accord with their idea of politeness. Was he a just man? Did that account for his being here in the last of towns? Or did he so long to spend an hour with Christine's pale European presence that the longing surpassed money considerations?

Behind him now Henry waved the notes in the air, as if offering them to the world. There were no takers though. The sergeant frowned at the girl. "Then it is for just the one month," he told her. "Some people stay longer, some for very long times. But unless I can radio, you are not permitted to remain beyond a month."

She gave the same kind of dangerous, negligent shrug I seemed to remember her giving the night the Norwegian officers told her she could not think of sleeping in the May Gardens. She didn't know if she'd stay in Eritrea for a week or forever. You couldn't tell if she was going to punish or honor her father, or both, or for how long. But obviously it wouldn't depend on a Sudanese permit.

"We have a green cell inside," the sergeant told us all. "You would not like the green cell. It is very hot. When you come out of the south, you must speak to me again."

From an iron bedstead and palliasse standing on the same shady side of the hut as the fire, he fetched an accounts book, a rubber stamp, and an ink pad. Our names were copied from each permit into the accounts book, the dates were filled in. The sergeant consulted his watch at great length, frowning as if he wondered whether it was reliable, and then wrote the time down in Roman numerals. He was a man of some education.

Back at the truck the barefoot doctors were changing a colostomy bag on the paraplegic. They covered him with a shawl. I listened as the patient spoke delicately to his nurses in Tigrinyan.

Sorghum—A Gift

Perhaps an hour later, south of the so-called border post and while we were still within the Sudan, the Sahara ended. We entered subtler, rockier country, the beginnings of Africa's acacias. The sun fell and trees grew abruptly taller. I could see the black shapes of aid trucks in the shadows of these loftier thorn bushes and eucalypts. This was the oasis I'd heard of, Kurburaka.

Tecleh braked and called, "Ai-ai-ai! Here we eat some *injera*."

The barefoot doctors gave the paraplegic an injection, while all the time he spoke softly to them, the patient comforting the physicians. We were led away between trees and into a clearing, to an open-sided hut of clay, clay platforms spread with rugs sofa-like inside it. Some Eritrean drivers were eating here. Others slept, each completely enclosed in his shroudlike cloak.

Lanterns were burning in a square mud brick kitchen, and from inside the earthen oven flashed as the cooks lifted *injera* bread, a kind of immense, flat pancake, off its metal shaping domes. Tecleh pushed us toward a platform in the hut, and soon a plate appeared in front of us, a vast tin dish covered with the brownish bread, a pile of peppers and lentils heaped in the middle. Tecleh tore out a triangular wad of soft pancake and used it to scoop up lentils and peppers. Chewing a mouthful in an exaggerated way, he uttered patriotic gasps and groans of pleasure.

Henry cast his eyes upward at all this overacting. "It tastes like goddam crepes made out of tears," he muttered. "We need to remember to shit before we go." He was eating with his mouth open to let out the heat of the peppers. "This stuff is instant arousal to the average Western bowel."

Henry was accurate. After we'd finished eating, Christine came to me and asked me matter-of-factly but with old-fashioned delicacy if I had tissue paper. In with the recklessness which had brought her here and which sometimes surfaced in her answers to Sudanese officials, there was something staid. You could imagine her face beneath the black hat of a church-going French spinster. And another thing: She didn't use much slang. Perhaps her mother had protected her from movies and television, given the impact these things had had in her own life.

Like a gratified parent anyhow, I went to my kit and tore off an excessive wad of the stuff for her. Henry and I then set off out through the perimeter of supply trucks to the farthest rim of the oasis. We stepped carefully. This was the acre assigned for the comfort of truck drivers.

The moon had brilliantly risen. I could see every nuance of Henry's smile when we remet. We began to stroll back toward the flicker of kerosene lamps, the robust surge of flame from the *injera* oven. While we were still far from all that, though, Henry swung himself up on the rear bumper bar of a truck. He wrestled with the dust-thickened tarpaulin, loosened it, and peered inside at the cargo. He took out a pocket torch and shone it. Even from ground level I could see sacks marked *Sorghum—A Gift of the People of the United States.*

"Sorghum," Henry improvised with a grin, "a gift from the Department of Agriculture, who can't give the stuff away!"

Then he readjusted the cover and switched off the torch.

"I just thought I might stumble on a shipment of another form of aid. Assault rifles, for example. Gift of the PLO."

I felt in a not quite rational way that Henry was betraying the trust of his hosts. I wanted to put him in his place—a strange urge for a supposed journalist when faced with a good rumor.

"A friend of mine," I said, "an English correspondent in Khartoum, has looked into all that. According to her, it's a myth. The West says, 'The PLO supports them.' The idea is that the West can then forget about them. That's my friend's thesis. And she's nobody's fool."

Henry gave a hard-bitten roll of the eyes. "They've been fighting for a quarter of a century. Who do you think does supply them, friend?"

"They're fighting the Ethiopians," I said. "The biggest army in Africa, perhaps the best supplied, and one they have consistently defeated. That's—according to reliable report—their main source."

Henry laughed as if at innocence.

"God, you're such a smug bastard. A hard man to share a goddam desert with. No wonder your wife cleared out!"

I felt an anger that actually transcended the desire to hit him. It was an anger at myself for having mentioned Bernadette to him that night up the coast, in the guest house at Port Sudan. Until I escaped him and went to witness the ambush beyond the front line, he could harry me all the way through Eritrea with my wife's name. He hadn't needed to hear it, I hadn't needed to utter it. Yet I'd paid it out freely to him.

"That's the lowest bloody card to play," I told him.

"I suppose it is," he admitted, suddenly and erratically the disarming midwest boy again.

"My source argues," I persisted, "that they're capturing so much Russian equipment from the Ethiopians that if it were known in Moscow to more than a few self-serving bureaucrats, it could . . ."

"What d'you say? Bring the Russian government down?"

And he chuckled again.

"I think you ought at least suspend judgment," I said irrationally, "till you've seen the bloody place."

"In Africa," he advised me in an enraging big-brother sort of way, "you don't get any marks for going sentimental on people."

Worse still, he seemed to think this was a great aphorism.

"A hard man to share a goddam desert with," Henry had said randomly. But like many random insults it struck accurately. Because once, in Fryer River, that had been my exact conceit. I'd thought I was a wonderful man for deserts; I'd thought I had a gift for them, for the massive and complicated stretches of earth and the rivers in which no visible water ran. Returning to the area around the Kurburaka cookhouse, I seemed to experience the dry, fiery redolence of Fryer River, and I was translated there again, under the same moon, fatally determined to see Bernadette's absolutely untypical Fryer River misery as a phase, a fit, a pet, a chemical spasm, a spate of ego.

The intimate flavor of her unhappiness returned to me there in Kurburaka. Yet I hadn't acknowledged it at the time. Friends of ours, visitors to Fryer River, found themselves sitting through our arguments, which they noticed more acutely than I did. My line was that this was the competent, black-sweatered social worker Bernadette Yang, star of the Legal Service. She must know the tribal women would change as she got closer to them, that she would ovecome what I chose to call "their shyness," that they'd greet her in sisterhood in the end.

One old friend said later that both of us knew what the truth was but were forbidden by our ideas of orthodoxy and heresy from stating it. The easy racist/nonracist division of humanity, which we'd used as a tool in our youth, a sort of adjustable spanner of debate in our work for city Aborigines, wasn't of any use to us here. The clear truth was that both the tribal men and the tribal women did not want her to be Chinese. They had known Europeans close up for only a few generations and had come to accept them as priests of a world scheme mysterious yet parallel to their own. Someone Chinese did not fit this parallel system. The question was: Where was her authority?

Those tribal people who went to Alice Springs knew that the few Chinese there lived on the fringe. So what did Bernadette Yang have to give the Fryer River population; what power could she exercise in the world's mechanics?

Bernadette wanted me to admit all this now, to admit that in Fryer River she was not so much a pariah as someone who lacked a place. It's very likely an admission would have been enough to satisfy her. But out of some strange, naive loyalty to the tribal council, the source of my most wonderful posting—because of some desire to cast them as Western liberals—I avoided saying it. I was scared it would bring me to a choice between Bernadette and this most perfect job, my stature as a desert wonder.

For I was too good a man at deserts to risk being disqualified and sent back home just because my wife didn't fit the desert view. So I managed to believe that they'd make room for her in the end. This mental trick was my first betrayal of her, and probably the decisive one. It *did* go on for a long time, for unhappy months, and all the time it was apparent that we both understood and did not say anything.

Visitors to the settlement recall a dinner with wine. For though Fryer River was dry, the community advisers were allowed to bring in their own small cellars of wines with them. Anyhow, at this crucial dinner, Bernadette began to talk in a hostile way about the women's strange eye movements and modes of walk.

Three miles southeast of the trailer was a gap in the mountains. The lovely, arid peaks either side of it seared the iris of the eye at noon, but in the late afternoon they became a radiant violet. The ordnance map name of the place was Stanley's Gap, but its name on the millennial tribal map was Panitjilda.

Bernadette had learned that the women didn't only never go through that pass. They averted their eyes from the sight of it as well. Their view of the south was limited therefore. But so was their view of the north. For on the north side of the settlement stood a shaly hill, Namjuta, bound together with desert acacias and grevilleas. And women, Bernadette had found, didn't look at that place either. Pressing one of the older women for an answer, she'd been told, "That's a man's place."

"How long have these people lived here?" she asked me at table, in front of the visitors. "At least twenty thousand years. And in all that time women haven't been allowed to look at Namjuta or Stanley's Gap! Half the world's been denied them. And this is somehow an ideal tribal condition!"

I scratched together the sense of pique a spouse feels whenever the marriage fight is frankly declared in front of visitors. Of course I was disappointed in her, but having so badly disappointed her myself I couldn't say so. I began to argue back. The tribal world, I said, was made up of the sacred and forbidden on the one hand, and the sacred and accessible on the other. "If you do away with that system," I argued, "you'll end up with the sort of exiled trash we dealt with in the city."

"Ah, so now our city clients were trash! I'll tell you, they had one bloody thing up on this crowd! They could look to any point of the horizon without fear of dropping dead."

"But you knew!" I accused her. I wished that all the people at table knew how strongly she'd pushed me toward coming here. "You knew that there's this conflict. It isn't news to you that the tribal setup's at odds with some of the usual democratic impulses. For Christ's sake, it's at odds with the law of common bloody assault."

For the tribal law, as I sometimes informed visitors, countenanced occasional bloody punishments and even executions for crimes such as the violation of blood laws—for sex within forbidden relationships, even for the utterance of the secret name of an ancestor. And it *was* true that Bernadette was familiar with all that, that in Melbourne, surrounded by semi-tribal men and women drowning in the European strangeness, she'd yearned for that tribal clarity, that desert sureness.

But now she began to speak like a supreme European. That's what the tribal council and their wives—without knowing it—had forced her to. She used the old-fashioned term *darkness*—to mean darkness of culture. In her city life she would have pitied anyone who spoke like that. "If anyone else lived under the same sort of darkness these people do," she accused me, "you'd feel sorry for them. Yet you go on pretending to envy them."

I kept on insisting that I *did* envy them, the ones who still had a connection to the mysteries.

I think the friends were pleased when it was time for them to leave and return south.

Our video machine was what kept us afloat: video films ordered dozens to the batch from a great warehouse in Alice Springs. Between forbidden Namjuta and proscribed Panitjilda we watched French, American, British, and Australian films. Even with a complicated film like Klaus Maria Brandauer's *Mephisto*, our discussions extended only to *good/bad, enjoyable/not enjoyable*. That most robust and least dangerous form of marital argument, the argument over the merits of a film, had become dangerous for the Darcys.

As friends would discover later, during a bitter and vinous account of events delivered by me at a dinner in a Melbourne restaurant, it was in the desert winter of 1985 that a Pitjantjara man named David Burraptiti got out of jail in the town of Berrima in the tropic north of the Territory and came south to Fryer River in the desert, where his clan lived.

The tribal council, I could see at once, didn't welcome the return of Burraptiti. They considered him a troublemaker. They were very practical about troublemakers; from their harsh desert history they were used to sloughing off those dangerous to the clan. They would have preferred it if Burraptiti had stayed in Alice until his next break-and-enter or car theft took him back to the Territory's jail. But without incurring a blood debt, that is, without taking an expiating wound, they could not deny him access to his tribal ground.

Burraptiti arrived home by truck. He was tall but carried a jail flabbiness around his middle. He flashed a slow, dangerous smile which the Fryer River people seemed to remember well but professed not to like. Yet often, at the sight of him, his kinswomen clustered around him despite themselves. Their tongues shrilled. They sang like birds, shifting the swatches of *pitchuri*, the desert narcotic which they chewed, from one cheek to another.

Burraptiti arrived with half a dozen cases of beer, contrary to the tribal council's anti-liquor ordinance. I noticed the council did not want to talk to Burraptiti about it. I found myself cajoling them into enforcing their own law. They seemed to have a terror of any argument which might come to blows. Every blow had to be repaid by a kinsman of the person struck. Great wars began that way. For that reason the Fryer River police aide had been recruited from far away, in the desert of South Australia, a man who had no kin in the Fryer River area, no blood debts to pay back.

Reluctantly the aide confiscated Burraptiti's six cases. As it was done, Burraptiti whimsically saluted him.

Later, by secret arrangement, the elders got the cans back from the South Australian and helped Burraptiti drink them. It was their concession to him, their placation. They didn't want him to have a grievance. He was dangerous enough without that.

Everyone seemed delighted when Burraptiti went hunting with an uncle of his and came back after three days, a speared red kangaroo carried effortlessly across his shoulders. Yet they all knew this phase of innocence would come to a close. There would be some attack by fist or bludgeon against one of the Pintubi or against one of Burraptiti's kinsmen; it would probably be a fight over a woman. To avoid punishment Burraptiti would then flee to Alice by vehicle and commit a new crime, and the cycle of imprisonment, return, blood, and ejection would commence once more.

About this time, when the tribal council was expecting the worst of Burraptiti, a young anthropologist, one of a team charting tribal sacred sites, arrived at the Fryer River strip by light aircraft. The anthropologist, several of the tribal elders and council, and I all spent three days traveling together in the country to the west of Fryer River, crossing the barely populated ground on the edge of the Gibson Desert where tribal boundaries and mysteries overlapped the administrative border between the Northern Territory and Western Australia.

I was delighted and engrossed by these days. At the very least they were a release from the marriage impasse. But the journey wasn't mere flight. We visited men's mystery caves by dry riverbeds. We came to awesome canyons where the birds and even the sun at its sizzling height seemed to convey an absolute message and call up power from the stones. We stopped at springs concealed by overhanging rock from the heroic evaporation of the sun and populated by the holy and ever returning dead.

At night we camped in more neutral ground, where the gravity of spirits wasn't as fierce as in some of the places the young anthropologist was marking on his map. Under dry, cold stars we slept without tents in comfortable bedrolls called *swags*.

The holy places restored me to my full status as a good man for deserts. I would have been pleased if the work had continued for months. But the elders knew the country so intimately that even over such immense spaces the task was quickly done.

On the way back to Fryer River, the party met up with a Pintubi tribesman and his wife by a broken-down Holden. Freddy Numati, the elder-mechanic, went to work on its carburetor. The Pintubi man began to speak of what had happened in Fryer River while our party was gone. Someone had been arrested and locked up by the police aide, he said—I could not pick up the whole story, and I presumed the old man meant Burraptiti had been locked up. But as the car owner spoke further, the elders' glances began to slew away from me.

As the three trucks of our map-making group reentered the settlement at Fryer River, I noticed an old, near-blind man sitting cross-legged on the ground near the petrol pumps of the settlement store. His mouth was open and gave out a wail. He snatched up handfuls of red dust and threw them into the air, as if—I felt even then—into the eyes of potent, unleashed spirits. I knew at once what had been done in my absence.

I expected to find the trailer empty, and I did, a few half-read books and half-watched videos strewn around the living room.

I felt a frightful panic as I rushed to the settlement lockup, a small prefabricated shed standing like an outhouse behind the council chambers. I did not enter the place. Instead I called for the police aide to come out, and the man emerged, moving with delicacy and with turned-aside eyes. I had been dealing with averted eyes all day and had been undermined by them. Now I understood how Bernadette had been thwarted by averted eyes for months on end.

The police aide told me that one of the Pintubi men, out hunting, had seen Bernadette two miles beyond Stanley's Gap, in the holy ground of Panitjilda. She had been wearing a swimsuit top and shorts and had been sitting in the shade of a boulder outside a cave rendered powerful through the death of a clever man there. They always used that term—clever man. Or else they said *important man, important woman*. They never said when he or she had died, whether it was ten, a hundred, ten thousand years past. For the time of *clever men* was circular; or else it was two parallel snakes of time, the past and the present, and they kept on interweaving, according to the Aboriginal idea of *Tjuparata*, Dreaming.

I had always considered this tribal system enchanting and enriching. I'd believed it had a harsh edge, of course, but only for the initiates. For me it was religion and magic and poetics, and I believed it would not strike back at me.

Bernadette had worked out a way to make it strike back. At me. A good man in a desert! I felt severely and intimately the shock of being alien so soon after, as a brother to the tribal council, I'd visited mystery caves and drunk from holy pools.

I listened to the police aide explain with gentle apology that he'd locked her up to show that he was doing something. "Otherwise the old blokes were so upset they might do something themselves."

The aide was a reasonable fellow despite his few Wild West affectations—a lawman's roll of the hips as he walked, an inverted set of U.S. Army sergeant's chevrons sewn on his shirt. He was worth listening to. He knew perfectly how grievances got started in this sort of place.

I limited my demands therefore to seeing Bernadette. He led me inside. She sat on a cot beyond the bars pretending to read the Heinrich Böll novel she'd taken on her sun-bathing excursion to the *clever man's* cave. By now she'd hung a blouse around her long neck and over her shoulders, but she had not done up the first two buttons: the swimsuit top could be seen. She blinked furiously and looked up at me. She looked shrunken inside her beach clothes; her breasts hung loosely inside the bikini. She looked up fiercely at me; I could tell then, I think, that I wanted some change of soul. But I could not tell what that change of soul might be—unless it was to attack the police aide, take the keys by force, liberate her, and flee the settlement with her. But that was impossible, of course. Good men in deserts didn't behave as erratically as that.

"You're the lawyer," she told me. "How do you think this would stand up under *habeas corpus* in the High Court of Australia?"

I pushed my hand through the bars, cheap comfort which she wouldn't take.

"I would have thought a husband would tear the bars down," she told me lightly, exempting me with irony from that sort of primitive excess. It was no use telling her that was my impulse, and in any case the police aide made it all beside the point by unlocking the door at once.

Bernadette did not move. I asked her to come home, but she sat on stubbornly on the camp bed in the open cell. At last, at her own pace and taking no notice of my coaxing, she got up and walked out of the cell and out of the lockup.

By now the police aide was thoroughly embarrassed for me, for Bernadette Yang had compounded her Chinese face by becoming an unmanageable wife. On the way home she walked about five paces behind me. I looked at the afternoon light and the mauve shadows of trailers, clinic, schoolhouse, desert oaks, and mountains and, frightened as I was, thought it perverse of her not to be happy here. And not only was she unhappy. She was guilty of sacrilege, of ritual vandalism. I knew but hadn't yet acknowledged that she'd invalidated us at Fryer River.

Nearly back to our trailer, she called out a question. "Do you think that that troublemaker, Burraptiti, would be worried by what I've done?"

I was enraged at her for dragging Burraptiti, who—apart from her—was Fryer River's other great problem, into the question. I told her Burraptiti was spoiled, that his opinion did not count tribally.

Bernadette said, "He knows better than to divide the world up into things you're allowed to look at and things you can't!"

I made the speech she probably expected, the only one my status as good desert man would permit me, compassionate and firm. I said I knew exactly why she had done it. She was trying to get them to take her seriously. I pleaded that I had been unthinking. I pledged my concern for her happiness and so on. But I could already see that she was not just chagrined, not just a discontented wife. The desert people and I, between us, had started in her a malignant anger, a sort of inoperable hurt.

Freddy Numati, the elder who was also a mechanic, came to the trailer that evening. The tribal council wanted to speak to Mrs. Darcy, he said. He, too, was apologetic, after the manner of the police aide. The council *had* to have a talk with her, he said.

I asked him to wait at the door and went inside to the bedroom, where she lay with the Böll book, still blinking frantically at the print.

"If you don't want to go, then I'll resign and leave," I said.

I risked touching her arm near the elbow, but it was a creaky gesture, a gesture between strangers. Bernadette became very calm, almost amused.

"So you didn't tell him to get lost?" she asked simply.

I argued lamely that I couldn't tell Numati to go because Numati was still my employer and hers. We could resign, the two of us, and go and tell Numati as much and tell him we would leave at once. Or, of course, she could face a sort of quasi-judicial inquiry of the elders. At which she might be disciplined verbally. But never bodily! I would never permit that! And anyhow, they were worldly enough to know that that was not possible, that that would attract the police.

Secretly, at a basic level, I thought she deserved to face them. Her perversity had earned it for her.

In the end Bernadette consented to face them. She even insisted that it was what she wanted. "It'll be a change to have them actually talking to me," she said, smiling up at me. The smile was strange, but at the time I chose to read it as reconciliation. I repented. I urged her we should tell Numati to go away. But now she wouldn't hear of it. Or maybe I'd stated my loyalty to her too late in the argument.

I sat at the back of the council room. I discovered that someone had spread the instruments of punishment haphazardly around the platform the council sat on. I could see spears, their side-prongs bound onto the main shaft with kangaroo sinew; clubs molded from branches and roots. Freddy Numati began reluctantly explaining in a low voice that a woman who went over to that place, beyond Panitjilda, had to pay a blood debt—otherwise so many bad things would happen the world could not contain them. They did not want a blood debt from her, however. Yet if she did it again, they would have to kill her. Numati pleaded with her please not to do it again, that it half killed the old people. Then he said, "You watch, some of those old people will die now!"

Bernadette began to weep, as if contrite. She stood up and made a formal apology. The council asked her to pay them $250.

"My husband has the money," she told them with a sudden steeliness. "He'll pay you."

I took her home and stayed with her the rest of the next day. I cooked meals and opened a bottle of wine.

In the middle of a meal she said, "They let me off without physical punishment. But you can bet the old men sang me to death. I know the old men do that."

I held her in my arms but she hung limply. There was now a core in her which somehow refused to be protected, at least by me.

That night David Burraptiti stole the clinic sister's four-wheel drive. As would later be discovered, he drove it northeast on tortuous tracks toward the main road to Darwin and the tropic north, where he had spent his prison term. Bernadette, I discovered, waking alone later in the night, appeared to have vanished with him.

Since I was a good man in a desert and she, for reasons of her own, was refusing to honor that fact, I believed that this fantastical escape of hers was like the Panitjilda visit, a gesture of vengeance. Burraptiti would treat her with creaky politeness, and she would call from Alice Springs to ask me to collect her.

The Road to Eritrea:
Meeting Julia

Beyond the oasis where Henry and I had our quarrel about arms supplies, the road was a scarcely perceived rumor. We followed riverbeds clogged with lumps of stone in which you could read, if you had some sort of divine sense, a history of Africa's uncertain rains. The insides of the truck hit us fierce blows on elbows and shoulders, the sides of the head. The paraplegic retched, and I could smell the thin, piteous stench of his bile.

In a depression between hills, an impala, exquisite in the truck lights, danced in front of us. Tecleh braked so that we would not pass it. He and the barefoot doctors began arguing wildly. The barefoot doctors were not impressed by the impact of Tecleh's driving on their patient. Tecleh, I could tell however, was impressed by the presence of meat.

Twenty paces up a defile, the impala stood on its sublime legs waiting for the outcome of the debate between Tecleh and the others. It considered the truck. Its eyes glittered in the diffused light with that tranquil timidity of herbivores, that same level inquiry I'd seen in the eyes of kangaroos who leap away a distance and then can't resist turning to verify their first assessment. If they're being chased by the Pitjantjara or Pintubi, it's the second look that does them in. They perish for the sake of knowledge, as the impala might, too.

Tecleh and one of the two paramedics carried the main weight of the discussion, while the other barefoot doctor passed the information to the sick man on the floor. For the paraplegic was germane to the debate. The impala could not fit where he was, in the back, and the roof was taken up by the equipment of Henry, Christine, and me.

Before the barefoot doctors were ready for a conclusion, Tecleh opened his door, jumped to the ground—a movement which caused the eyes of the impala to flinch yet did not make it run—and withdrew from beneath his seat one of those Russian automatics called AK-47s.

This was exactly the sort of weapon whose provenance Henry and I had been arguing about an hour before. If Stella's judgment was to be believed then somewhere—in some skirmish or in one of the Eritreans' sweeping triumphs over the Ethiopians—it had been captured. Its wooden stock was reinforced with tape. You saw such taping in photographs of rebels bearing AK-47s the world over, but I did not know why it was done, for style or for some technical reason. Tecleh in any case raised this taped stock to his shoulder. Not a wastrel, he set the lever to single shot.

I hated this moment. I felt the unaware blood of the beast swelling in my own throat. I looked at the girl then, the young Parisienne. I half hoped that she, influenced by the vegetarian fashion of her generation, might burst from the truck and protect the lovely creature.

My ears shuddered and I saw Christine Malmédy's body jerk. The impala, lit by the moon and naked under the headlights, showed just one frightful rosette at the side of its neck. Its hind legs were swept sideways from beneath it. It knelt forward and toppled aside with the exact philosophic grace I had seen in the animals native to Fryer River. It was as if they, the kangaroo there and the impala here, subscribed to the same propositions as the flesh-eating hunters.

The barefoot doctors were full of protest. They were clearly asking again where the meat was to be carried. Henry began yelling across the front seat at Tecleh. I suppose he had hunted as a boy and was excited. "Tie it to the goddam hood! You've got rope, don't you?"

Tecleh gathered up the dead animal and toted it back by the pits of its arms and legs, and Henry had already left the truck to join in the joyous business of roping it to the front of our vehicle.

The paraplegic, from his position on the floor beneath my legs, could only have heard what was going on, but he seemed to be greatly cheered. He made some delicately spoken joke which caused the barefoot doctors to laugh as well.

As the road became rockier still, the impala's horns jolted, putting up too late a defense.

The moon had risen, and ahead of us, up a bluely splendid valley, I noticed a stalled truck. Tecleh dimmed our lights and rolled us toward it but at a tangent. From its shadow emerged an African. There was also a pale, elderly European woman there, walking back and forth between the levered-back bonnet of the truck and its tailgate, fetching and carrying tools.

"Ai-ai-ai!" said Tecleh. "Where do these people come from?"

"It depends," said Henry. "Are we in Eritrea yet?"

Tecleh said, "We are in the mountains, and so we are in Eritrea."

The vehicle we drew up beside was small, Japanese, and reliable, mechanically apt for Africa. Yet in another sense it was the very worst for the country. Apart from the driver's cabin the rear was all canvas, cleated down but offering no answer to the dust.

This time everyone except the paraplegic got down. I levered my way painfully once more to the rear doors. I kept murmuring "Excuse me" to the crippled veteran, whose eyes had been bludgeoned by the road into a sort of barely focused muteness. By the time I got the door open and had landed on the stony ground and moved to the front of the truck, Henry, Christine, the un-identified African, and the elderly European woman had already made their introductions.

The woman was robust, square-faced, frankly gray-haired. She stepped forward at once and offered her hand to me.

"I'm Julia Ashmore-Smith from the Anti-Slavery Society," she said in the distrait manner of the well-bred Englishwoman. Her voice had all the exasperated toniness which I, in my colonial soul, identified with British hubris. In *her* empire, though it no longer existed, she was the Amhara, and Henry and I the Somalis.

"I mean," she said distractedly to no one in particular, "we're going to need a new distributor."

Henry winked at me. "Julia's come in from the west." He already knew that much. "From Kassala. The cheek of this girl!" He turned back toward the woman. "I know there's some tough roads out there, ma'am."

"We've had no real trouble till now," said Julia Ashmore-Smith. She seemed to resent Henry's jovial patronage.

"But you were shot at," Henry said, stepping forward and raising his hand to two rents, putative bullet holes, in the canvas at the rear of the truck.

"Well," said the elderly woman, "you must know that those ELF splinter group people are very active over there in the west. I mean, we were lucky the roads weren't *mined*."

Everyone in the party—except perhaps Christine Malmédy—knew about the ELF. They had been the first Eritrean movement of resistance. According to their opponents, however, the Eritrean *People's* Liberation Front—an almost identical name, as if to confuse the outside observer!—they'd been elitist, narrowly Islamic, and had not countenanced rank or power for women. To a European the acronyms ELF and EPLF were simply a series of capital letters for which Africans inexplicably struggled and died in the night. In a savage factional war in the seventies, the ELF had been driven out of their base areas and reduced to a covert existence on the western flanks of Eritrea, near the Sudanese border. The EPLF, by contrast, had gathered the mass of popular support and put the Ethiopians to flight as well. Yet though victorious, the EPLF—whose guests we were—were said to carry uncomfortably the memory of this earlier brotherly mayhem.

Unhappily, to add to the European impression of feverish and fanatic partisan activity, the remnants of the ELF still attacked EPLF work parties and shot up convoys. Saudi agents and even the CIA were said to hang round Kassala, the Sudanese border oasis and city, encouraging the ELF to attack the EPLF. For it was a matter of surprise, as Stella so often remarked, that no one seemed to want the Eritreans to win. Neither the Americans nor the Saudis, who wished to see Mengistu and the Dergue fall and Ethiopia drop ripely back into their camp, nor the Russians, who were supplying military advice and arms. No one wanted an independent Eritrean republic along that stretch of Red Sea shore.

Under the prodding of these foreign agents in Kassala on the Sudanese border, anyhow, the Englishwoman's truck and her gray but remarkably well-ordered hairs had been shot at.

Henry asked, "You said the Anti-Slavery Society?"

"Exactly," said the woman.

This ancient British organization with its strange-sounding name had been one of the first of all kindly bodies to intrude in Africa's bitter affairs. Africans might consider it a relic of empire itself, but I had vaguely heard good things about it.

Christine Malmédy seemed very interested. "Are there slaves in Eritrea?"

The woman gave a small smile and brushed a strand of lustrous gray hair away from her forehead. "It depends, doesn't it, how literally you interpret the word. I would say there were slaves everywhere, my dear. They are called women."

"Oh, I see," said Christine solemnly. I remembered that during her two mornings at Stella's place in Khartoum she had stared down from the living room windows at the masked middle-class women waiting in the garden below to visit the Sudanese doctor who shared the villa with Stella. She had asked hushed questions: "Do the women wear their masks when they are with the doctor?" "When they are grandmothers, can they take the mask off?" She did not make any quick or flippant judgments about the mask—and that was good sense, because she didn't know enough. But I was sure now, as she said, "Oh, I see," to this British campaigner, that an image of the women in the garden had come to her.

Henry groaned. "You're willing to get shot at, Julia? To wave the feminist banner?"

He had a power both to win and lose people in the same breath. In the most dazzling of moonlights, I could see the flicker of Julia Ashmore-Smith's eyebrows. "It is because I am no orthodox feminist that I am here, young man. I have heard wonderful things of Eritrea. How liberated women sit flexing their minds in foxholes and so forth! But I am not as easily impressed as most. I wish to undertake an accurate study, not an impressionistic one. I hope you don't consider *that* too fantastical an aim."

Henry coughed and held his hands out in front of him. "Hey, look, Julia, friend, be my guest!"

I began asking her questions about why she'd come in from the west like that, rather than down the Red Sea coast. She shrugged. She didn't have a lot of patience for such minutiae. She'd been visiting refugee camps in the Sudan, south of the Gezira, she said. Henry joined in the discussion—he'd been running services into a refugee camp in the same region. This seemed to raise his credit a little with the Englishwoman.

"I thought you were a journalist," she said, as if in explanation of her earlier terseness.

"*I'm* the journalist," I admitted.

"Anyhow," she said, "I had the truck, and it didn't seem to make sense for me to double back on my tracks and catch a plane in Khartoum."

Tecleh and one of the barefoot doctors decided to drive back to a workshop which sat, without our having seen it, camouflaged in the bush three miles back. The paraplegic had no choice but to travel with them. It was better than moving him to the ground on his mattress, the surgical infusion still in his arm, and setting him down on the rocky floor of the valley. Before leaving, Tecleh found a rug in the back of the truck and spread it on the stony valley floor by the side of the road. The Englishwoman's driver also found a rug and unfolded it beside Tecleh's.

"Please," Tecleh begged us. "You must all lie down."

He would not leave until we were at least all sitting on the rugs. Henry sighed in an overacted way, as if to satisfy the driver that we were perfectly comfortable. In the end, as Tecleh reversed and turned our truck, he leaned out of the window and yelled, "*Ciao!* All lie down and sleep!"

Before the truck had traveled ten yards, the Englishwoman asked, "What is that thing I see bobbing on the bonnet of the truck?"

Christine Malmédy sat up, prodding herself with an elbow. "It is a deer, madame," she said.

"An impala," said Henry.

"Oh well," said the Englishwoman. "At home I'm a vegetarian, of course. But then when I'm in a place like this, where there's no protein overload . . ." She yawned and covered her mouth with her hand. The moonlight drenched all of us. "Were you aware," she continued in a drowsy voice, "that four-tenths of the world's grain goes to fatten livestock? That's the only reason I forgo meat. In protest. I am not sentimental about animals, like most of my compatriots. And I'm certainly not a hippie."

"They might have killed you," Christine Malmédy, genuinely aghast, said suddenly, as if it had just occurred to her. "These ELF."

The Englishwoman said, "I am a widow. It is appropriate for widows to take risks."

I noticed that her driver, a little distance away from us, rose on his elbow. He was yawning, as she was. He looked around him and reached out for a boulder rendered smooth by thousands of rainy seasons. He dragged the boulder in under the one thickness of blanket. An Eritrean pillow, I thought. He put his head down on the stone and began sleeping rowdily. Very soon I could hear the polite sleep-modulated breathing of the Englishwoman, too. Where had she learned to sleep on stone?

I don't think Henry and the girl slept, though, however keen Christine might have been to adopt Eritrean manners. And neither did I.

Tecleh came back an hour later and woke those who were sleeping with the news that nothing could be done for the Englishwoman's truck. She would have to travel the rest of the way with us and collect her vehicle on the return journey.

I began transferring her military-looking pack from the failed truck. By the moonlight, the address on the airline tag was legible: *Lady J. Ashmore-Smith, Onslow Gardens, Chelsea, SW3.* There was an offhandedness both in the writing and in the lack of a building or flat number. If the airline lost her bag, they could bloody well track *her* down in that square of old and fashionable buildings in Chelsea.

As the paraplegic was being readied for the last stretch of the road, and as Tecleh discussed with Henry the new seating arrangements, I turned to her.

"I notice you have a title. Do you want us to use it?" I can't say what balance of etiquette and colonial mischief lay in the question. I'd prefer to think etiquette was predominant. I liked the woman, and if she wanted to be called Lady in this moonscape, that was all right with me.

She waved her hand dismissively. "Oh no," she said. "It's totally unearned, you know. For some twenty-five years I was wife and lover to a man who rose to become a District Commissioner in Dongala—you know, in the Sudan. These posts used to bring with them an automatic knighthood on retirement, and that's what he wanted, poor old Denis."

It had been decided that she would take my position in the back, sitting with her legs bridging the floor and the paraplegic. She climbed the step in a way that forbade a helping hand, and turned around to me in the doorway. "These days I use the name cynically—actually, I think many people who carry round honorifics with them do the same. I mean, I use it for travel arrangements and hotel bookings. I'm sad to tell you, it *does* make a difference. But since you are not an airlines reservation clerk, I want *you*, Mr. Darcy, to call me Julia."

She passed into the inside of the truck and extended her gracious inquiries to the paraplegic on the floor. I slammed the doors and went and joined the others in the crowded front seat.

In the balance of that night we would suffer a sand bog, and the track tore two tires off the front wheels. In the front seat we would make occasional small kindly adjustments of posture for each other, to allow an extra cubic centimeter of space; I had an idea that Henry was as cooperative as any in these fraternal exercises.

At some time an Eritrean amputee wearing military fatigues, a cloak, a crutch, and an assault rifle blocked the path and took our names down on a list, inquiring things of Tecleh in a polite, dreamy voice. He shone a torch he held by the crook of his neck onto his book of people's exits from and entrance onto "the field." Behind him stood one of the EPLF's strange fuel stations. Lady Julia seemed particularly warmed by the sight of the place, a great tank of petroleum buried there beneath rubble, and two pumps feeding from it and wearing camouflage jackets with slits for reading the quantity of fuel and its price in Sudanese pounds.

Here we all got down from the front seat to stroll around and let our sweat evaporate. Two attendants in white cloaks and military fatigues had crawled out of a hole in the ground nearby to fill our tank and arrange the appropriate paperwork. While they worked I watched Christine bend to look in through the slits of the pumps at the Arabic numbers.

"Do you know if your father filmed this?" I asked her.

She smile briefly but nonetheless with absolute confidence. "I think he would like this, yes. If he saw it, he would film it."

Masihi's *femme particulière*, the EPLF, pumping petrol.

"We must nearly be there," I promised her on little evidence. But we weren't. Under a moon bright as delirium, along the rough tiers of handmade Eritrean road, I took flinching looks over the lip of the trail at drops of rubble a thousand feet in depth. We braked to allow the Eritrean aid trucks going to Port Sudan to make the turns—forwarding, backing, edging, playing with the cliff—and the body of the impala kept jolting. The mountains piled up on my mind, all identical.

The moon set. At the first stain of day across the peaks, Tecleh stopped the truck at no given place I could discern. He stretched, yawned, slapped the wheel. "Ai-ai-ai!" he said. "Okay. We're here." I looked over the back to see the remarkable Lady Julia sleeping with a gracefully tilted head, an old woman who would—I was willing to bet—never know dotage or a slack mouth.

Outside I couldn't see anything signaling arrival, not even a pump in a flak jacket. I had a sudden conviction, though, of having come to the right place.

After we'd climbed down and found our luggage, we all shook hands with the soft-voiced paraplegic who said, "*Ciao!*"

"We'll see you again," I promised him.

"No," Tecleh told me brusquely. "You will not see him again. The hospital here is too big."

"You are taking that poor dead beast with you?" Lady Ashmore-Smith asked Tecleh in her utterly commanding voice.

Tecleh couldn't understand her distaste. "For the sick," he said, as if accused of dishonesty rather than of having shot lovely flesh dead. "At the hospital."

Approaching torchlight wagged at us from the hillside. It proved to be held in the thin hand of an official of perhaps thirty-five years of age, who introduced himself to us as Moka.

I liked this small fussy man on sight. He made earnest greetings, practiced each of our immeasurably foreign names, touched our shoulders, insisted on carrying things.

"Oh, my dear girl," he said in a low, melodic, lullabying voice when he learned that Christine was Masihi's daughter. "He has gone to the front to make his pictures. There are events at the front just now! Great movements. We shall find him. But first you must sleep and eat!"

"Will he be long coming back?" Christine asked plaintively.

"He will come here, or we will send you all along to him. The first step, Miss Christine, we shall send a message to him."

I imagined the stunned Masihi, in some observation trench on the Nacfa Front, frowning over the news of the arrival of his lost child.

As he led us deftly up a ravine, Henry's duffel on his shoulder, Moka gave out a cruel wheezing noise. I found out later that this noise was an after-effect of a chest wound he had suffered in battle.

Gentleman Salim

The "guest house"—just as Stella Harries had already described it to me—stood on the steep slope above the floor of the valley of Orotta. I suppose you could call the structure a semi-bunker. Its back wall was dug into the mountain. A terrace, paved with dry stones and camouflaged with a vine, stood at its front. It was rumored to be protected also by its own medium flak gun and gun crew. We couldn't see them. They were believed to be entrenched under the brow of the mountain higher up.

The guest house possessed three bedrooms, among which were distributed six of Eritrea's rare hospital beds. And in a washhouse by the terrace we took turns to rinse off the sweat of the night journey and to squat over a noisome little porcelain bowl inset in the floor, the only flush toilet in the entire besieged regions of Eritrea. I didn't expect Henry to betray any sign of distaste, nor perhaps even Lady Ashmore-Smith, since she too had long experience of Africa. But again I was intrigued at the lack of complaint from Christine. The truth is that I would have been consoled by any signal of revulsion she gave—I was so close to giving some myself. But there was no flicker as she came out of the washroom, gleaming with soap and with the bandanna she had worn to combat the stench still frankly knotted around her neck.

We were awakened at noon and harried by Moka, our skeletal minder, from our beds and to the dining room. The air had taken on the consistency of an element in its own right—a mix of fire and hot mist. Angles of fierce sunlight fell down the pit

90

of clay in which most of the house sat and sliced across the windowsills, which held no glass and at which giant African wasps played.

The cook placed dishes on the table before us. She had her hair dressed in those long thin strands which Christine Malmédy had so admired in Bufta, the cook in Port Sudan. Moka sat beside Christine. He spoke with that bent overearnestness of his, his legs crossed and ending in army boots which looked immense on his narrow frame, his shoulders jerking for emphasis inside his shirt.

"There is no news yet of where your father is. He has trained six cameramen, but they are all busy all the time, up and down that front trench on both sides. And they do not only the front. They film the motor pool in Hishkub, and the road building in Upper Senhit and the agriculture at Agrae, and the great food dump at Jani. I might send you to A to meet him, but he might already be in B. Or might already be back in Orotta . . ."

Moka looked at the other guests as if a meeting with Masihi was also their chief reason for coming into Eritrea. "You will be very safe. We will keep you safe from the MIGs."

The girl gave her normal half-smile of dazed expectation. She began to eat heartily of what was at table—the *injera* bread with the strangeness of dhurra grain in it, the bowl of scalding lentils and peppers, and the goat ribs.

"I wouldn't touch that goat, missie," Henry advised her. "The goat meat does for *me*, every time!"

"Don't be mischievous, Mr. Henry!" said Lady Julia, deliberately selecting a rib and biting into it. "You must be aware that goat meat is the highest delicacy here. A food for weddings, as you know, and for victories!"

"Well, I'm sad to report that my life's a little short on weddings and victories. And my stomach knows it."

Lady Julia composed the lines of her mouth subtly, and I knew she was genuinely annoyed. "It doesn't behoove us to ignore the significance of goat meat here, at this table. The Ethiopian army confiscated half Eritrea's herds, and even when it didn't, drought killed nearly all the rest. People with sixty goats lost fifty, people with a hundred lost eighty-five. The one we are eating now must have come through the drought of 1985. It may have seen the poor tribes of the Bani Amir wasting away, it may have seen Mensa children die, and young girls of the Saho tribe. And here we are making an ungracious fuss and lavatorial jokes about being fed the ribs of such a goat! The flesh of an animal hero! As if we were being fed leavings!"

She swallowed and adjusted her chin.

Henry said in a lazy, small voice, "Feel free to indulge yourself on my share."

But it *was* true that Henry *had* spent all those years in Ethiopia and must have been aware of the festive meaning of goat meat. His feverish, bad-child table manners had some other meaning than ignorance.

Moka kept on urging everyone to attack the bowl. Lady Ashmore-Smith and myself set to in a tentative sort of way. Christine chewed the meat calmly, experimentally, again familiarizing herself with a taste from her father's chosen world. After we'd been eating for some time, or—like Henry—had shown we didn't wish to touch the meat, Moka himself tucked in, gnawing the bones with an African voracity.

At this stage of our uneasy meal a tall, portly, Arab-looking man entered the room. He was dressed like an old-fashioned Arabian businessman, in a turban, a painfully clean white shirt and tie, the coat of a gray business suit. Instead of trousers, a swath of white linen was tied around his waist and hung to his calves. You couldn't have picked him as a rebel except for Eritrean plastic sandals on his feet. His large features were far lighter than the complexions of most Eritreans. Only later did I think about the oddity of his dressing European from neck to waist and Arab for the rest. No other Eritrean I had seen dressed this way, so I wondered if the man was a visitor from Saudi Arabia, a dealer of some kind?

"Good afternoon, good afternoon," he said in English, the English of older Africans who once had lived in British colonies. His voice was melodious and breathy. "Ah, I had heard there was goat!"

You couldn't guess what series of Red Sea genetic contingencies had made his face; what balance of Semitic, Hamitic, Cushitic, Turkish, European was represented there. He was about sixty years old, an age most Eritreans didn't manage to achieve, and had an old-fashioned gravity.

"May I introduce myself? My name is Salim Genete. I am an Eritrean, but I live in Saudi Arabia, in Medina, where I do business and help—as far as I can—the cause of my Eritrean brothers and sisters." He eyed the bowl of meat. "Ai-ai-ai! How remarkable!"

He, too, set to work on the *injera* and the bluish goat flesh-and-bone left in the bowl.

We introduced ourselves. When it was the Englishwoman's turn, she used her unadorned name. Henry said, maybe to embarrass her, "Julia's a Lady or a Dame or some such."

The question of what Lady Ashmore-Smith should be called all at once seemed to dominate. But I didn't even know how Henry had found out about it. I hadn't told him.

"Please," said the Englishwoman. "I am not a Dame. I do hope this business is not going to become an issue!" Then she uttered her real name.

"Oh," said Salim Genete, considering the wad of goat meat he held in his hand, "so your husband was a baronet? Or a life peer?"

The question caused Henry and me to exchange grins and a few archings of the eyebrows. It wasn't the sort of matter you'd expect rebels generally to involve themselves in.

"My husband," Lady Julia told Salim Genete, "was a District Commissioner in the Sudan. He was first knighted. But after retirement he was involved in Foreign Office work in what was then Rhodesia, and was made a life peer. So I have been both Lady Julia and Lady Ashmore-Smith, and since my poor husband, Denis, died seven years ago, and since I have little right to any title myself, I suggest, Mr. Genete, that you call me Julia."

"Not at all," said Salim, a stickler. "I know from my youth, when Massawa on the Red Sea was a British port and when my father entertained distinguished guests, that *Lady Julia* is the correct mode of address for the wife or relict of a life peer. And that if you were simply the wife of a knight, the proper mode would instead be *Lady Ashmore-Smith*. I'm not incorrect in my memory of these forms, am I?"

Lady Julia herself seemed amused.

"You have it absolutely exactly," she told him. "Though it *is* strange to hear such a rundown on the protocols of address from a member of the Eritrean People's Liberation Front."

I tried to memorize these nuances of title Salim Genete had acquainted us with, for my future dealings with the English-woman. I could see the girl smiling faintly but engaged in the same effort.

"And so," said Salim, eating energetically, copiously, but giving an impression of restraint, of appetite under control, "you have found our corner of the globe and our struggle. Do you think our guest house a little impoverished?"

Lady Julia denied it.

"Let me tell you," Salim Genete continued, "that sadly this is an Eritrean palace. One day we will enter our holy and much desired city of Asmara. There, evening prayer will be called from the Eritrean mosque, and benedictions from the cathedral. And you will see better things then. But for the moment . . . I am afraid this is the best. Yet I trust you will discover we are not an uncultivated people. Politics have done this to us. The politics of *other* folk. Imagine then what politics do to the defenseless seed in the earth. Ai-ai-ai! But come, eat these delicious lentils and the goat meat!"

Moka and Salim Genete continued to eat after the rest of us had stopped. Soon they noticed, however, that for the visitors the meal was over.

"Ai," said Salim. "The meat is good for my friend Moka. It builds him up against malaria, which is very dangerous in his case because of his wounds. Shall we drink our tea in the open?"

Outside, on stone benches draped with colored cloth and un-derstuffed cushions, we drank from a thermos of frighteningly sweet tea. Salim squinted at the sun through the camouflaging trellis covered with some flowering plant. "From Khartoum to Kuwait the just are asleep," he murmured. "Because it is so very hot . . ."

It was at the height of this African heat that I noticed particular Eritreans—*bureaucrats*, I suppose you'd call them—in the defile below the guest house. In oddments of Western clothing, often paramilitary in appearance, they would emerge singly now and then from a particular hole in the ground and move toward another. For the first time I began to spot the cunningly tucked away windows and air vents of these places. There was, for example, a bunker high up on the slope to our right, and another below us. From it I could hear an occasional burst of conversation, a groan, a snore.

One official who moved toward us up the defile was a lean woman with a turban loosely tied around her dark neck-length hair. She wore an Arab-style shawl around her neck, a striped shirt and jeans. At the large drums of fresh water just below the guest house she paused. She found an empty milk can and filled it from the drum on her left, the one intended for washing rather than drinking.

Carrying the can of water in both hands, she climbed to the bunker off to the side of the guest house, the bunker I'd barely discerned ten minutes before but which now seemed obvious, permanent as an apartment block.

I was engrossed by her easy glide. All the people of the Horn are impressive movers, even though they mightn't have stable surfaces to move on. In profile she was exquisite, lean-featured, her skin blue-brown. Her style was what you'd call "Italianate." I don't think this was due to Italian genetic influence—a lot of people in the Horn happen to carry such fine-lined features. It's one of those little ironies of history that the Italians should get a colony called Eritrea in 1889 and see an African echo of their own finest faces staring back at them.

As I watched her move from the drum to the bunker, I thought at first she was very young, perhaps twenty-two or -three years, and then I wondered if she wasn't a mature woman.

Even after she reached the door of the other bunker I didn't lose sight of her. She stayed in the recessed doorway. I noticed now that she was wearing, as if they were items of Milanese *haute couture*, the Eritrean plastic sandals, manufactured in a bunker-factory somewhere near here. She hooked her right leg up on the knee of her left and poured a thin thread of water over both foot and sandal. Having rinsed the day's dust off the right foot, she now washed the left. In posture, in delicacy, the two rinsings were a perfect mirror of each other. I looked at Lady Ashmore-Smith-cum-Julia, but she was talking to Salim Genete and had failed to notice the girl bureaucrat's almost ritual elegance.

The woman used the last of the water on her forearms and hands, thrusting the hands out full length, treating them to no more than a narrow, thrifty flute. Rhythmically, she kneaded the moisture between her fingers. Then she put the can down, raised her hands briefly to the sun to dry them, ran the palm and the back of each hand once across the tail of her shawl, unwound her turban, shook out her hair, and disappeared into the bunker.

Salim was speaking drowsily to Christine Malmédy. "I saw your father two weeks ago in Himbol. He was filming the locusts. A plague, as in the Bible. And as in the Bible brought down upon us by Pharaoh."

"For *Pharaoh*, I suppose," murmured Henry with an edge of cynicism, "read Mengistu."

"Ai-ai-ai," said Salim, "Mengistu. There is a fleet of planes for spraying plagues of insects, but the enemy will not guarantee that the planes will be safe from fire. He does not want us to be saved from this plague; he does not want us to be saved in any way. But let us not be too concerned about that for the moment. Rest now. We must all rest."

In that heat, in the wake of the ablutions of the woman official, I had in fact found Salim's little recital damn near narcotic.

"When it is dark," he continued, as if telling a story to exhausted children, "you will see wonders in the sides of mountains. You have read *Peer Gynt*? You have heard of the Erle King? This is Peer Gynt in Africa, all this. When we have Asmara, we will remember these bunkers as magic caverns."

"*Inshallah,*" murmured Moka, the toothy veteran, and laughed sweetly amongst his white teeth.

Something About Fida

In our room inside, I took out my pack and reread a letter I'd gotten a few months back. It was written in faultless English by a man named Major Paulos Fida, an Ethiopian prisoner of war in the hands of the Eritreans. Stella Harries had befriended him here in Eritrea during her visit and been very impressed by him. Later, at her suggestion, I'd written to him and sent him a few books. He'd felt proudly bound to submit in return a written, mannerly essay, which I now held in my hands.

> *Prisoner of War Camp*
> *She'b*
> *4th February, 1988*

My dear Mr. Timothy Darcy,

> *Thank you for the gift of books you sent me from England. I was particularly fascinated by the copy of the Koran you sent, since I had never acquainted myself with that document before. My mind is attracted by the echoes of the Christian Bible one finds in the Koran. The treatment of the Virgin Mary, for example.*
> *It is not so much that I believe that Mohammed borrowed from the New Testament. I think he took from the same basic set of myths and fables, the same store from which the New*

Testament itself grows. For if he had borrowed from Matthew,
Mark, Luke, and John, the story would be closer to the ones
they told. What in fact one finds is the pattern and the strength
of the myth, which is a higher thing than mere detail.

The fact that Major Fida needed to be introduced to the Koran
by an itinerant journalist like me was, according to Stella Harries,
an index of the hauteur of the Amhara, among whom Fida had—
at least until the day the Eritreans had shattered his plane in the
sky—counted himself a proud member. Given that the Coptic
Christian Amhara looked east to Red Sea Islam, west to desert
Islam, and considered themselves encircled, I wondered why he
didn't bother earlier to inquire into the faith of his Mohammedan
co-nationals.

Major Fida continued:

The American novels confused me, though it is just as well
that I read them. I can see why in my youth at the Harar
Academy we were restricted to Mark Twain's Tom Sawyer.
I had in more recent years read Nathaniel Hawthorne's The
Scarlet Letter. *There is the same spirit in the Updike, the*
Styron, and the Bellow books you sent me. I believe it is called
a "sense of sin." Despite how lecherous the books might be,
everyone is as cruelly punished in them as in Hawthorne.

I found a strange, joyless obsession with some sexual acts—
distracting reading, I might tell you, for a prisoner of war.

But a fixation with sin is no different from a fixation with
virtue. Sex and purity are equally likely to consume the mind
wholly.

I have to confess that I do not like the idea of the world run
by the sort of people who write these books. However, as you
know, I don't desire a world run by the alternative either.

The novels were instructive, though. I seem to hear rever-
berations of them in American foreign policy, at least as that
is interpreted to me by the BBC shortwave news.

Someone let slip that you may be coming to Eritrea. I re-
member my conversations with Miss Stella Harries, and I

*would be delighted to have one with you, so could you please
ask your guide to put a visit to my camp on your schedule.*

*Did you hear about what the Chadians did to the Libyans
in Wadi Dhum? They captured an entire army corps from
Gaddafi. Of course they had logistical help. The Eritreans did
the same thing to us a few years back, but it was not reported
on the BBC World Service. This most enormous victory since
El Alamein did, however, receive some coverage, I believe, on
Voice of America. I, of course, heard nothing of it, since I was
still flying then for my country.*

I returned to that sentence. "Someone let slip that you might be
coming to Eritrea . . ." I wondered how an Ethiopian major, a
prisoner of the Eritreans, knew that.

*There is a rumor again that the Red Cross might succeed
in repatriating us all, might indeed be negotiating secretly
with my leader, the same one who denies our existence here in
Eritrea, denies that we have been captured, denies that our
captors spared us, denies that our wounds were treated, denies
even that we were brave. I suppose that if the International
Committee of the Red Cross did take us home, the Dergue
would be too ashamed to massacre us, though we could never
expect to have a future in the armed forces. Perhaps I could
work as a teacher. In prison I have become more of a scholar.*

*In the meantime, here the air is full of the flap of locusts'
wings, and the fear of poor rainfall possesses everyone.*

*Yours sincerely,
Paulos Fida, Major,
Ethiopian Air Force.*

I was carrying in my pack a letter for Major Fida, given to me
by Stella. It was apparently from Fida's wife in Ethiopia and had
reached Stella indirectly, by way of West Germany. It was pretty

crass of me, but I found myself daydreaming now and then about the impact of the letter on him.

Stella had visited Eritrea in the season in which the Eritreans had swung their right flank around the provincial city of Barentu, captured it by dawn one morning, held it for fifty days, and replenished their armory from the large depots lying around the city. Brave Stella was one of the three Europeans to visit Barentu during the time the Eritreans held it, before the Ethiopian air force inevitably drove them out of town with bombing raids.

It was on the same journey that she had met and talked with Major Fida at the prisoner of war camp in the valley of She'b after dark one night. Stella later played me the tapes of the interview. Later still, of course, these tapes were edited up and played on Radio 4 in Britain.

She had asked the major whether he had ever used napalm on any of his bombing missions. She said that at the question there had been a flicker behind the major's broad, handsome eyes, a flicker which said either, *I'm telling the truth but this woman won't believe me,* or else, *I am not telling the truth and she knows it.*

The interview went thus:

FIDA: I did not carry napalm on any of my missions. Of course, I was new to the Eritrean front, I had previously been down in the Ogaden.

HARRIES: Did the Air Force use napalm against the rebellious Somalis in the Ogaden?

FIDA: My squadron did not use napalm against the Somalis. I had heard rumors of other squadrons . . .

HARRIES: During your time flying on this front, the Eritrean front, were you aware that you were doing much damage to the Eritreans?

FIDA: No. We felt we were hitting nothing but mountain caps and stones. And we wanted to hit more than that. Certainly we knew we were fighting for an imperfect regime. But twenty million Russians perished for an imperfect regime during World War II, and like them we thought we were fighting for the integrity of Ethiopia, for an idea, for the nation's mysterious wholeness. And within that frame of thought, a fighter bomber pilot brings a lifetime of training with him into the cockpit. A MIG-23 pilot has wonderful technology at hand. The West likes to think of Soviet technology as flawed, imperfect, what you call Mickey Mouse. We, who are supplied by the Soviets, and the Eritreans who have armed themselves by plundering our supplies—we both know that Soviet technology is a capable enough affair.

Now, to have all the resources of a MIG-23 at one's command, and to be at war, and to feel that all that force and energy is not being applied—well, it dispirits the pilot. It was a common complaint in our squadron—you heard it daily from all the pilots. Our squadron's Soviet military adviser was always buying such pilots consolation Melotti beers in the officers' club. So sharp was this frustration that my fellow pilots confessed that if they saw a flash of green or blue or golden cloth below, they dived at it and strafed by impulse.

Though not entirely by impulse, of course. We had been told that all the Eritreans were a legitimate target, since all the Eritreans were in revolt and needed convincing. The normal propositions, you see, which are so easy to believe.

Stella's Instamatic photograph of Major Fida showed a broad, brown face, limpid brown eyes, the whites tainted to yellow by bile salts released by recent episodes of malaria.

"After capture," said Major Fida on the tapes, "once I had had a chance to look around, I was astonished at how much damage we had in fact done."

On one of the tapes in Stella's possession, Major Fida talked with a professional self-absorption about his last mission. He had been engaged with a colleague, someone he called a "wingman," to bomb a segment of the foothills of the northeast Sahel, the desert littoral of the sub-Sahara which, since the great tank battle at Mersa Teklai, the Eritreans have securely held. He had been told to bomb Eritrean military bunkers on the edge of a barely inhabited Sahel village. Anti-aircraft, heavy in some areas, was here considered to be light.

The cockpit computer brought Fida exactly to the area. He dropped out of a sky of African purple and came down over the mountains at a height of a few thousand feet. Dropping further, he *could* see bunkers neatly slotted into the mountain side. There were windows inset in them, their sills plastered and painted the cerulean blue the Eritreans liked to use in their interiors. On the flanks of the hills, a flash of yellow, then a grayer and browner movement caught his eyes, as if the stones themselves were taking flight before his awful descent. This was the first time in his flying career that he had sighted the rebels.

By his own confession, he was eager to do them damage. The mistrust of Eritrea, he told Stella Harries, had been taken in with his mother's milk. Compared with Eritrea, the Ogaden was altogether a simpler business. It did not derange the mind the way the very word *Eritrea* deranges the mind of Amhara, the mind of Ethiopia.

At the sight of the cerulean blue windowsills and the movement on the slopes, he released two general purpose bombs. He was not expecting any riposte from the ground, so he was thinking of climbing a little and going back for a look.

He *had* heard that, far on the other side of Eritrea, the Eritrean Peoples' Liberation Front had captured the city of Barentu and held it for a time—captured, too, its four batteries of 23-millimeter cannons, suitable for anti-aircraft defense. It had not been suspected that any of these might have been rushed down here, to the far flank on the Red Sea shore.

But the sky until then so pleasantly vacant all around him was now tarnished with sudden little blue-white clouds. A second after he noticed them, one of his gauges showed a loss of engine power and a falling off in hydraulic pressure. Over his shoulder he saw a banner of flame beneath his wing, and then oil began flooding around his boots. With the one surge of flame he lost two thousand feet. He could hear his wingman screaming to him now over the radio. He pulled his ejection lever. He did it with the unarguable certainty that the Eritreans would torture and execute him when he landed. He didn't like that all his military skills and his laboriously put together mastery of English were about to vanish, sucked up into the sky. On the way out, his left arm caught the canopy and shattered on both sides of the elbow. Vaulting and then falling through a narrow instant of time, he lost all his consciousness.

Under blankets and beneath roof logs in a bunker, he awoke without any of the pain which had been with him when he ejected. The plaster on the walls was painted blue, as was the windowsill, and he presumed in his delirium that this was the very place at which he had aimed his bombs. A large-breasted Eritrean woman in battle fatigues, seated on a grenade box, watched him with maternal amusement. He did not lower himself to ask any questions about their intentions.

As in a blue dusk they carried him down to a wadi where an ambulance was waiting, he said in Amharic, "Why don't you show your hand? When do I see the bastinado and the water torture?"

There was only one person among the Eritrean soldiers and stretcher bearers accompanying him who understood Amharic. To most of them it was the language of the oppressor. Yet the Amharic speaker in this case was a very black young man, probably from Barka province in the west, which bordered on the Sudan and—in a land of great nomadic activity—was virtually Nubian. He also had, this Amharic speaker, three diagonal scars on each cheek—a tribal person therefore, and one wondered why he had ever bothered to learn the imperial tongue.

"Don't be anxious on the score of torture, sir," he smiled darkly. "We do not want to satisfy your arrogance. We'll subject you to something worse than that. We will treat you as if you were a prisoner of war under the Geneva Convention. We will insult you with compassion."

Stella Harries had interviewed the major only a month or two after his capture, and he seemed already pleased that the Eritreans had not satisfied his worst dreams of torture and assassination. There were by now other matters oppressing his mind. He had discovered that his government had renounced him, had denied that he existed.

The Ethiopian conscripts and regulars held by what Addis Ababa called "the bandits" had not died in torture, but were instead held in vast prisoner-of-war camps stretched along valleys, loosely guarded by small squads of Eritrean boys and girls who wore—according to a phrase of Stella's—"the discreet air of victors."

These prisoners had been excited at various stages by visits from Red Cross officials. Negotiations for their release were under way. Fiercely held hopes rose and fell in the p.o.w. camps of Eritrea. But in the end the Ethiopian tyrant Mengistu, a soldier himself, who should have understood how captives felt (or so Fida told Stella), had ordered the Red Cross to stop dealing with the rebels, to stop talking about Ethiopian prisoners under pain of being thrown out of Ethiopia itself.

In the photograph Stella had taken of the major, the man carried in his great, lambent, malaria-yellowed eyes the pain of a man who has been, as a matter of policy, declared a nothing.

The Splendid Bureaucrat

I was awakened much later in the afternoon of that first day in Orotta by Henry's voice advancing in anger toward the door of the bedroom the two of us shared. A series of conciliatory Eritrean murmurs followed it. The door opened and Henry was there, sketch pad and charcoals in his right hand and around his waist his belt, which was also a wallet, made of bright scarlet fabric, the sort of item a mountaineer or skier might use. I could see Moka's face, too, weaving about with anxiety in the corridor.

Henry was saying, "Just hear me out. I'm not going to have fucking guns pointed at me, and I'm not going to be nursemaided."

Moka tried to conciliate him with gentling movements of the hands.

"Don't you think," Henry asked, "it's a reasonable enough initiative to want to go up the goddam hill and see the valley from a height? So that's what I do. And some fucking goatherd comes jabbing at me with a fucking grenade launcher. I come here and get treated like a fucking trespasser!"

Henry's voice reached hysteric pitch and I got up, thinking I might have to stop him from hitting Moka.

He threw his sketch pad and box of charcoals onto the stone floor, dropped the belt-wallet from around his waist, walked to the shuttered window of the room, and jerked the shutters wide. A small hint of coolness played around the windowsill.

Moka spoke soothingly, almost too quietly to be heard. Mr. Henry must understand that the guard up there beneath the summit of the mountain had been thinking of Mr. Henry's safety. The belt was a very bright belt, and in such an exposed place a MIG might see it. The guard knew how important it was to get Mr. Henry off the mountaintop quickly. So by waving his rifle he had not been saying, Mr. Henry, you are unwelcome. He had been saying, Mr. Henry, please for your own welfare find cover.

Henry threw himself on the hard bed. "Another thing, Moka, I don't want my pack carried by other people. It's fucking patronizing. I'm tall and I'm strong, and I don't like seeing my pack toted by some asthmatic runt." From beneath his pillow, he grabbed his diary, with its photographs and mementoes and cards held within it by elastic bands. He turned to the wall with it, as if it were bedtime reading.

"With all due respect," he murmured.

Moka said, his face stricken, "It is Eritrean politeness, that's all."

I smiled at Moka and made a hand gesture to imply that he shouldn't be too distressed at Henry's moods. Perhaps Henry had spent so much time playing the ugly traveler just to test the Eritreans' solicitude for him and his safety.

His mouth gaping with concern as it had never gaped under the stress of carrying our baggage up the defile, Moka left. Across the corridor, in the women's room, I could hear Lady Julia commenting to Christine on the fracas.

"By all I hear," I told Henry now, "they're very competent. What I mean is, their advice on whether someone should be on a mountaintop or not is worth taking."

"Why don't you leave the fucking propaganda to them?" Henry asked.

"If you'll forgive my saying so, I don't think the women and I want you attracting hostile attention. Any more than the soldier up the hill did."

"You're so tight-assed," said Henry. "You talk as if you're auditioning for the part of Lady Puke's butler."

I thought we were close to more shouting and even punches. Henry was at *that* level of unreason, and I felt the centripetal pull of the man's fear—if that was what it was—or the pull of his distress.

Surprisingly, silence fell on the room. Henry flopped and turned his back again. But there was no tautness in his shoulders anymore.

"I thought I was just fed up with the turpitude of events," said

Henry. "So I said, Henry boy, you just need a tonic tour, a journey. But you know what? It hasn't been a tonic. Seeing those goddam brave trucks running through the night, meeting up with the vigilant sentry on the fucking mountaintop . . . I've found all that as melancholy as hell. Because these people are behaving as if nature can be folded back like a carpet. There isn't anything sadder than people who don't know the score."

"Maybe they know the score but decline to accept it."

"Yeah, yeah, yeah," groaned Henry. "Goddam depressing semantics. It reminds me of Ethiopia, too. Am I allowed to say that? How much I miss the place? *They* remind me of the Ethiopians. The same lean, fucking dignity. The same dark questions in the fucking eyes . . ."

I could see Moka still hovering in the corridor. He wasn't certain yet that Henry had subsided. Soon though, Henry was snoring unabashedly, the sort of noise only the very tired make. It seemed to me all at once that it had cost him greatly to get this far, to the threshold of the Eritrean furnace.

That afternoon, there needed to be a coffee ceremony. Moka seemed wary about inviting Henry. But he could not avoid it. It was a debt of tradition which all the besieged Eritreans of Orotta felt they must pay the visitor.

At the hour for the ceremony, I found Lady Julia sitting on the terrace with her camera and notebook. Her mouth was tightly held and her eyebrows arched, as if I somehow shared the blame for Henry's fit.

I watched Moka lead Henry and the girl out of the bunker–guest house, the three of them moving carefully, as if not to interfere with each other's magnetic field. Henry climbed down the embankment to the drum full of washing water, scooped out a powdered-milk canful, bent his head, and poured the water over his skull. There was something self-baptismal, apologetic in this action performed in the sight of Moka and Lady Julia. Drenched, he did not shake his hair vigorously, boyishly. He hung his head, staring at the ground for perhaps two minutes.

"What an absolutely extraordinary man," Lady Julia told me. "I mean, first of all, *Fuck this!* and *Fuck that!* And now he's going on like a Hindu at the Ganges! Are we supposed to be impressed?"

Henry stood up at last, his nostrils curved, fixed on the smell of charcoal from the bunker down the defile. Moka, with a straight face, had described this nearby hole in the ground as the office of the Eritrean Department of Information. There, on flat ground by the door, a woman was building a fire for the serious gestures of coffee-making. The sun, falling quickly behind mountains, diminished by the second the risk of bombing and left the valleys full of a radiant lilac light which, of course, reminded me of Fryer River —what it would have been like to travel maritally here, with tough little Bernadette! Despite Mengistu's air force, she might well have been safer here than where she was now.

Salim Genete, the expert on British honorifics, was familiar with the ceremony and was no new visitor to Orotta in any case. So instead of joining the party, he borrowed a prayer mat from the Department of Information bunker and spread it on rubble off to one side, not far from a camouflaged tent which housed Tecleh and the other drivers. It was a top-of-the-market prayer mat, fringed, with a compass sewn into its leading edge. Spreading the mat in a northeastern alignment, Salim made his obeisance.

I surmised that Salim was probably too sophisticated to pray for specific benefits, such as the safe arrival of his son from the areas where the mobile strike forces operated. And being an engineer, he must have been aware of the iron ore lodes in these mountains, and the influence they might have on the prayer mat compass. But this was an appropriate locale, in any case, in which to praise the God for its very existence, its unspeakable splendor—and to eschew all deals.

The rest of us took seats on stones on the forecourt of the Department of Information bunker. Around a little square metal brazier of charcoal, an Eritrean woman placed the implements for the ceremony on a square of well-washed linen.

Unlike the soldiers and the bureaucrats, she wore a little jewelry, too. Small, silver, conical bells hung from her hair. Around her neck was a necklace of modest slivers of silver. She had very likely brought these treasures with her when she fled the Ethiopians. Silver waiting on the rise of its mother, Africa's moon.

Henry murmured to me, "Those silver tassels! See them? They end in two little balls. They're phalluses, man."

The Eritrean woman placed a square metal brazier full of charcoal on the ground and over it held a pan full of coffee beans. Meanwhile, across on the prayer mat, Salim had joined his large hands so delicately that you got an impression of the layer of air between them. As he bowed his forehead to the earth, a team of EPLF boys and girls, guards and gunners from the hill behind the guest house, included among them perhaps the one who had ordered Henry down from the summit, came skidding along the shaly hillside, crossed the line which held Salim to Mecca, and went on laughing toward their meal of *injera* and *sewa*. Some of them were holding hands.

There had been a time when sexual contact hadn't been countenanced in the trenches and gun emplacements of Eritrea. No love had been permitted among the rubble. But ardent wars, to quote Stella's radio feature, create ardent comrades.

Now Salim opened his hands and touched the lobes of his ears with his thumbs, murmuring, *"Allahu Akbar."* Lowering and folding his hands, the left within the right as prescribed for prayer, he began the *Fatiha*: "Praise belongs to God, Lord of the Worlds . . ." The words could barely be heard, were a mutter. Withdrawn and gracious in our sight and Allah's, he recited his *Suras*.

The woman with the phallic necklace picked out of the roasted beans the ones which had not turned black. Using her cupped left hand as a funnel, she poured the remaining beans into a mortar, ground them, poured the grounds into a strange round coffeepot with a conical spout. The grace and the exactness of the movements absorbed everybody's attention. There was an occasional small flash of Lady Julia's camera, a minute spark in an immense dusk.

The woman plugged the mouth of the spout with a wad of sisal, placed the pot on the charcoal brazier, and sat back on her haunches, her eyes guarded, not intruding at all on the conversational liberty of her guests.

Looking up just then, I saw the Eritrean girl, the bureaucrat I'd noticed washing her feet at the height of the day's heat. She stood behind the stones we were sitting on and wore a shy half-smile, the smile of someone confident that an invitation to join the party will soon be spoken. *"Salaam,"* she said to the coffee-making woman, who covered her grinning face with a web of fingers and murmured,

"*Salaam-at!*" Conventional greetings borrowed from the tongue of the Arabs, uttered now by the Christian coffee-maker and the nameless, magnificent bureaucrat.

Over by the drivers' tent, Salim had reached the point where the believer looks over his right shoulder and murmurs, "Peace be on you, and the mercy of Allah." The coffee foamed up through the sisal. The woman took the pot and, continuing to stare at the bureaucrat, poured off a sludge of undrinkable concentrate and then filled small cups for us from the pot. The brew she had made us was sweet and acrid and strong as malt whisky. It had an ancient taste; commerce, bazaars and the dominance of the sun were there.

In the midst of the pouring, Moka himself noticed the bureaucrat, stood up at once, and greeted her with the full series of Eritrean handshakes and shoulder bumps.

"*Kamilla-hai*," he said to her. *How are you?*

She replied with almost the same Tigrinyan words. Both emphatically laid the bulb of their right shoulder joint into the other's shoulder hollow, working their way up through the comparatives and superlatives of how they felt. "*Suba*," they both said, one after the other. *Good.* "*Lilai.*" *Excellent.* "*Cernai.*" *Superlative.*

Cernai was, I found out, the Tigrinyan word for wheat. In a land blasted by the Sahara's breath, a land in which the rains grew timid, wheat was as much a superlative as Beluga caviar might be in London.

"Please, you must join us," said Moka, with languid movements of the arm urging the bureaucrat to sit on a nearby stone.

The woman obeyed him and drew the tail of her turban deftly across her mouth. It fell away at once, though, as she accepted a cup of the bitter, peppered, gingered coffee. "This is Amna," Moka announced after another cup of coffee had been drunk. "She is from Frankfurt."

What African style she would bring to a Frankfurt February. I thought, Yes, a pretty apparatchik! An operator. You wouldn't expect to find her toting an AK-47 in the front trenches, or operating in heroic squalor beyond the front line. She would be much better suited to some sort of promotional work, perhaps on behalf of her Eritrean sisters, whose destiny was after all a severe one. She'd be the appropriate woman to stimulate the European feminists by detailing the lives Eritrean women lived in their holes in the earth. She was not, I thought, a woman designed for living in a hole herself.

Charged with acrid coffee, I found it too easy also to imagine her with a German boyfriend. I imagined a trade unionist, say, or a provincial politician, a journalist, or an academic. It was impossible to believe that she wouldn't attract that sort of attention. I thought academically, abstractly, about the happiness of such a man.

I had a lot of more licit questions to ask her about her work and her life in West Germany and her reasons for returning to this, "the field." But I had a more immediate duty—to utter praise for the coffee-maker, for the rebel movement which had assigned her the task of grinding and brewing. I attended to that, and when I turned again, the bureaucrat called Amna was gone.

Something About Lady Julia

From the shade outside the guest house, where we drank sickly tea with Moka and Salim Genete, we watched an Ethiopian reconnaissance plane, already a familiar sight to us, wheel above the mountains across the valley. This plane, however, attracted white clouds of shellfire from a dozen or more unseen Eritrean emplacements. Lady Julia tried to photograph this startling sight. While the Ethiopian pilot climbed out of range, Henry and the Englishwoman discussed exposures on the creeper-covered terrace. "Hate to say it, Lady Julia," Henry called above the noise of flak, "but it won't show up on normal film. And even with a zoom, you're not going to be satisfied with the result."

"Every time we fire," Salim told me dolefully, "then we have to move the guns. We are a race who cannot afford to be pinpointed."

Ceremonial coffee brought on the darkness every evening.

I decided to interview Lady Julia.

Lady Julia saw her engagement in the struggle against the mutilation of girl children as in a way an inherited duty. The inheritance came from an aunt.

"My aunt," said Julia, airily it seemed, "became a casualty. And all when I was at an impressionable age."

"A casualty?" I asked.

Lady Julia waved a hand. "A fatal casualty, Mr. Darcy. She was a nurse. African Inland Mission. Kenya. The early 1920s it was. I suppose you think everyone involved in missionary work was a scoundrel."

I denied it. I had a sudden image of Fryer River in the Western Desert. I had once been a sort of secular inland missionary there. Bernadette and I had brought our own strange humanist miscellany of safeguards, kindnesses, embargos, confusions, and clarifications to the Pintubi and Pitjantjara tribes. I wasn't in a position to judge the African Inland Mission.

This aunt Lady Julia had accused me of thinking the worst of had been Julia's mother's younger sister. Even in Eritrea, in 1988, Lady Julia still called her Aunt Chloe, as if she were retired somewhere in the home counties. Unhappily, it wasn't so, and the tale of Aunt Chloe's tragedy was compelling even for me, a stranger. One can only imagine how it compelled the young Julia.

In the first rains of 1929, said Julia, who had researched the matter exactly, two girl children had been rushed to Chloe's medical post in Kenya suffering from blood loss and from the severest form of mutilation, called "pharaonic" from the belief that the ancient Egyptians used it. Both the girl children were members of the Kikuyu tribe. Though Chloe saved their lives, she knew who her rivals were: the traditional midwives and mutilators of Nyeri province, Kenya.

Aunt Chloe had had no compunction about calling on the District Commissioner to arrest both village midwives identified by the girls' mothers as the ones who had performed the ceremony. In a town called Kiambu, the two women stood trial for grievous bodily harm. Throughout the trial, however, a young local politician called Jomo Kenyatta was active on behalf of the accused. The practice was African, he said, and could not be artificially curtailed to make the fussy colonizers feel civilized. He wanted independent Kenyan missions to be formed. It ought to be said—in fact, Lady Julia intends to say it in a book she intends to write—that Kenyatta, who would come in the end to lead his country, wasn't necessarily being stubborn for the sake of it. He believed the practice would die out of its own accord if given a chance, that British law was likely to encourage mutilation simply through its unreality, its lack of connection to tribal life.

The two midwives were given a modest fine in the end, and

Kenyatta's organization, the Kikuyu Chantil Association, met at Nyeri—on whose outskirts Chloe lived in a small clinic—and passed a resolution supporting the genital excision of every Kikuyu girl child.

Just after Christmas that year, Lady Julia's parents in London got a telegram telling them that Chloe had been found murdered in her villa on the edge of Nyeri. Overly traditional people had broken into the place, had held her down, had performed on her the same operation which as district nurse she had opposed. The raw edges of tissue had been fixed together with thorns of the dwarf acacia. Her legs were tied together at the knees and ankles, as were the legs and ankles of all such initiates. The doctrinal and cultural point having been made, she had then been stabbed through the heart.

The record of the coroner's court into the murder of Aunt Chloe managed to bring no one at all to trial. But it convinced Julia, the niece, then barely out of childhood and unsure of why Aunt Chloe had been killed, that the world was somehow full of unnameable injuries—injuries as barbarous as slavery or ritual dismemberment—inflicted on women and counted as normal.

Again, at the time the thing happened and Aunt Chloe's remains were shipped home, Julia had not been told of the circumstances of her aunt's murder. The few British newspapers that mentioned it spoke in cloaked terms, as did the entire family. This ensured the young Julia's fascination with an aunt whom she had barely met. All the indications the teenage Julia could pick up were that Chloe's death had been both unutterable yet somehow suffered on behalf of other women. At a memorial service organized for Aunt Chloe by the Anti-Slavery Society, the parson had said, "She suffered for those whom she considered her sisters under the skin." It was itself an image that penetrated Julia's skin.

Years later, after she'd married what she called "someone's likeable and well-educated younger son named Denis" and they had themselves gone to work in Africa, she as a schoolteacher, he as a district officer, she began to be educated in the extent of this vengeance, this unspoken civil war waged against girl children. Men, she told me dismissively, tend to become fixated at what is thrown at them—the weaponry, its caliber, its explosive power. But all that counts for little beside the masses of the invisibly wounded, the millions of mutilated girls. How does trench foot, she asked (drawing on a common World War I soldier's disease and maybe thereby showing her majestic age), compare with the accumulations of bacteria within the sealed-off urethra of mutilated African woman? For every wound which African man imposes upon African man, said Julia passionately, there are three or four wounds and bleedings which go unrecorded in any newspaper or table of statistics. In every province in Sudan, girl children bled to death, and this was considered a justifiable price! And throughout Africa, throughout Egypt, Sudan, the Horn, Zaire, Kenya, the girl children perished in a war barely declared—a war nonetheless eternal and basic to man's view of woman as a fallen and dangerous enemy.

Lady Julia saw herself as a mediator in that terrible strife. She had come now to inspect the Eritrean flank of that most ancient and perpetual war. She had hopes, she said, from all she'd heard, of finding good omens in these highlands, even in the great hospital in the valley below us.

The Kindness Caves

It was a hospital of night. As we lay all day under the guest house trellis, the doctors and the sick of Orotta sheltered—until the generators came on at dark—in bunkers and under foliage in the hospital valley nearby.

In the bottom of this hospital valley stood the dry stone shelter where the surgeons spent their off-duty hours. There, seated on draped clay platforms, we listened to a stocky little man called Doctor Neroyo, who seemed to be doyen of the cave doctors. He had learned his medicine, he said, "in Addis in the old days" and in Cornell in the sixties. If I'd closed my eyes while he spoke, I could have thought I was listening to a hospital administrator in Philadelphia or Birmingham or Melbourne. "Neurology and neurosurgery," Neroyo told us. "Chest and vascular, orthopedic, dentistry and maxillofacial, maternity, ear, nose and throat, eye, medical and pediatric. Supporting departments: X-ray, pharmacy, operating theaters, central chemical lab, outpatients. And an educational arm: clinics and training!"

Outside, in the last of the light, the jagged flanks of hill seemed to weigh down and deny a place to science. It was therefore hard to believe Neroyo with your eyes open. Lady Julia took calm notes of everything he said, but I wondered—was it possible: literal surgery in a place like this, a place made like Fryer River, out of the rudiments of earth and fire?

Whenever we went back there—Julia, Christine, and I—to the hospital three miles away, whenever we caught a ride at dusk or walked there amid the crowds of soldiers, nomads, and officials who emerged from the valley's bunkers at dusk, we were likely to meet frenetic little Neroyo rushing along the valley floor from one hospital department to another. He would always stop to tell us something new in his Cornell-accented English.

"When our troops go into action," he told us one night, expatiating on the casualty rate (that is, he told the women and me, for as you will see Henry completely reversed his Port Sudan pattern of behavior and visited the hospital only once), "either side of the line, they go with a certain knowledge. No matter how likely it may be they are hit, it is *unlikely* they will die." He had all the figures. The Americans had found in Vietnam, he said, that with abdominal wounds every hour of delay produced a ten percent increase in the chance of death. So he, Neroyo, had organized mobile operation units which worked just behind the rebel troops to treat the wounded within half an hour and bring them out of their shock.

Neroyo would have made a wonderful media hound in the West—he knew how to utter the salient detail and catch the crass journalistic attention. It was a pity so few cameras, other than Masihi's, came to Eritrea to record the jaunty angle he held his head at, his two-handed whimsical gestures, his spirited statements.

"But I will give you a number. In Vietnam, the Americans, using helicopters to move their wounded, reduced their losses to twenty deaths for every thousand soldiers committed to a military operation. Without helicopters, with nothing more than hammocks slung on the flanks of camels or ambulances ballasted with sand, we have reduced our own losses to twenty-five people in every thousand!"

Then he beamed and brushed fatigue from his forehead. "How do you like them onions?" he said like a suburbanite boasting of a new lawnmower.

On the Red Sea plains, Henry had seen the aid trucks moving through the arid zone and beaten the side of our vehicle, applauding the Eritreans.

That had been his last show of zeal for the rebels. His first—and only—visit to the hospital seemed to put paid to his Eritrean fervors.

That first time, after a disarming and graphic harangue from

Neroyo, the four of us were sent—because of Lady Julia's interest in the health of women—to the women's wards near the mouth of the valley. Later in the night I would wonder whether the subtle rebels had deliberately started us not with the headier scenes of their medical arts, but instead with all too normal and frightful African business.

We were led into a long tent supported by hewn logs. Here some thirty women lay on camp cots. They wore dusty but colorful sheaths of cloth. Their most prominent feature was the mouth—all the rest of their flesh seemed to have been sucked down into their eye sockets. Their elbows were prominent, too, where the cloth exposed them; their arms were each a tendon and a bone barely held in a filament of flesh. *Muselmenschen,* they'd called such figures in the Holocaust. Muslims. These women were literal Muslims. Farmers' wives from the south.

Some shared their bed with children: half-naked, aged children, an awful submission in their eyes. There was on each bed room to spare for the scrap of woman, her apostrophe of an infant. Sometimes a child would languidly search in a fold of cloth for a breast, but finding none would not complain.

Christine and Lady Julia passed among these women like physicians in their own right, taking studious notice of them. That girl mystified me with her detachment. It wasn't casual. It wasn't catatonic. It was the dispassion of an older and wiser being than Christine herself could be.

The gynecologist who had care of the tent, herself an Eritrean woman, remarked with a clinical lack of passion that these were survivors of people whose crops had been confiscated and oxen shot by Ethiopian soldiery near the city of Afabet. They'd fled, starving, from the south to what the doctor called "the liberated zone."

"You have seen this sort of thing before, Mr. Henry?" Lady Julia asked in passing.

"Sure I have," said Henry. "You can't even talk about it to people, can you? The fucking adjectives don't fit, do they?"

"Exactly," said Lady Julia.

But her pity was like the woman doctor's. It was no indulgence. It was calm. It was exactly the pity I had tried to achieve in the clinic at Port Sudan and failed.

* * *

After the abiding horrors of the long tent, the four of us, flanked by Moka, moved down the valley's long course for miles, continuing our education. It would be a night whose shocks and exaltations I'd find very hard to absorb. I played at being detached because I had an unfounded, irrational, conceited idea that I had to stay that way for Christine's sake. I was on trial as wise uncle and good man in a desert.

And all the way, fright and exaltation alternated.

Outside the labor ward, made of two sea containers dragged up here by captured Russian two-ton trucks, other women, women who talked and whose mouths had not been deserted by the rest of them, were waiting to see the gynecologist we'd just escaped. We stood back awkwardly in the shadows below the terrace. We listened to Lady Julia speaking in Arabic with the patients.

I found Christine by my side.

"Are you well, Darcy?" she asked me.

Her concern made me peevish. "Some of those girls in the tent are no older than you," I told her, crudely didactic in the panic I felt.

"I know. They look seventy years of age, don't you think?"

Moka also rejoined us. He had left Lady Julia among the women, from the midst of whom her high, honking Arabic could be heard.

Moka had no trouble leading the remaining three of us, the willing and the less willing, off again to another point in the hillside, where he waved us inside through a double screen of curtains. We took off our boots and stood in a long corridor inside the mountain. Peer Gynt, as Salim had promised. Five stretchers were ranged lengthwise along the wall. On four of them, EPLF male soldiers, naked, blankets over them, slept off anesthetics. On the fifth litter, a boy of perhaps six years lay. A surgical net covered his skull.

We squeezed against the wall as surgical teams in green gowns and masks came and went. Christine seemed very capable in this cavern air; Henry and I were the lost ones, Henry's face actually pricked with a kind of redness like embarrassment.

By way of double-glass windows, we could look from the corridor into three operating theaters. Through the window of Operating Room Two, Henry and I gazed together at gowned doctors and nurses and at a fresh-faced girl in army fatigues who sat on the operating table. A nurse unwound the gauze from the girl's ankle wound. As I gagged, I was aware that I heard no sound from Christine. She might well be a brave camera like her father, I thought. Or was she, through some accident of soul, shockproof? If her child had been aborted, had it somehow numbed her too?

In fact, though Henry and I made excuses to leave, Christine kept us there. I watched her inspecting the faces of each of the noisily breathing Eritrean boys on the stretchers. She reminded me of a nurse, trying to match each set of features with a chart.

Outside at last, Henry and I stood for a time, breathing, blinking back nausea.

By midnight, though, when we had visited every bunker, every ward, I felt invigorated. I found myself exercising a politeness toward Henry rather than sharing revulsion. Henry saw the girl with the frightful ankle and the child with the surgical stocking and all the rest as part of the familiar whole cloth of African pain, a continuum with everything he had seen in the Sudan and Ethiopia. I was disarmed by the cunning, by the competence, by all the crafts socketed away in these mountains of shale, in these secret and kindly caves which the MIGs and the Antonovs couldn't find.

By the time Henry and I entered the X-ray Department therefore, we were poles removed. Down the steps and between the painted plaster walls, yellow and brown this time like a hospital room from my own childhood, a technician introduced us to the Siemens X-ray machine, the Liberation Front's first, captured in battle in 1977 outside Asmara. Belgians had given a more modern and glittering device—it gleamed by its own screen and table in the farther depths of the X-ray bunker. It matched the immaculate quality of the room, but it lacked the aura of the older machine.

Divided in our response, Henry and I watched the radiographer's favorite plates: A femur fracture, the lump of shrapnel embedded in the bone. A bullet lying in the shattered radius of an arm. A bullet in somebody's colon. A machine gun round which had entered a neck, struck the spinal column, somersaulted to face puzzlingly back in the direction from which it came. "This man's spine is wonderful," the technician told us cheerily. "He instructs in the training camp, and he runs like he wants."

Always, free from extremes of emotion, Christine Malmédy was beside us, but again she wasn't engaged in the same argument as

Henry and I. No expletives, no gurgles of revulsion or approval escaped her. It was as if all this served as education for her reunion.

And then the dental surgery: Henry and I, and the girl for a rudder. The surgeon an Eritrean graduate of Sofia in Bulgaria! A woman of perhaps forty years. I imagined her moving with equatorial composure among the Eastern snows, tormenting the young Bulgarian dentists with her Red Sea style.

She owned a photographic album of plastic sleeves, almost identical to the one in which my mother had once slotted photographs of my marriage to Bernadette. This woman's album, however, was packed with *befores* and *afters* of the most inglorious wounds, wounds of the kind which are somehow never advertised on the war memorials: the bearing away of the features, the shearing-off of the maxilla, the facial bones.

The *afters* were superb—humanity restored because human features had been restored. She was a palpably happy woman, this cosmetic dentist. There was no remaker of people in Beverly Hills—to name the supposed center for the surgical revision of humans—as happy as this woman. For if you could judge by her pictures, she had made the absolute difference. In Eritrea, the jaw wounds of the seventies had gone unreconstructed as she studied in Bulgaria. But now she was here, the defaced were restored. How terrible and astounding it would be to come from the battlefield, having lost your face, and have it given back to you carefully over months by this woman!

That wasn't the end of the wonders inside the caves. They accumulated further. After the maxillofacial, it was the pathology lab with its kerosene-refrigerated blood bank, its kerosene incubator, its bacteriological section! And then, like a final statement of rebel unrepentance, the three-sea-container bunker where, behind glass, water was sterilized in an autoclave and dextrose and salt solutions were prepared. Four hundred liters every night (someone boasted to us, the dazed visitors) more or less straight from the infusion room, the demineralizer, into the veins of the wounded and the ill, into the remaining tendons of the Afabet women.

I noticed that, as if she intended to return home one day, Christine souvenired one of the plastic bags marked in green lettering MAN-UFACTURED BY THE PHARMACEUTICAL DEPARTMENT OF THE EPLF.

She led us to a bay in a bunker where we met an antibiotic capsule machine from Bologna punching out its forty thousand capsules per shift. She soberly watched it extrude its particolored product, but Henry hung back and seemed defeated. He lingered at the door and did not want to know anything. He made pointed suggestions, again and again, about going back to the guest house.

We did not meet Lady Julia again until we were nearly back to our truck. I managed to fall behind the others with her. I wanted to hear her balanced answers.

"Impressive," she said. I was disappointed at first. She'd used the adjective in a measured way, like a dowager visiting a private school for an art show. I wanted an enthusiast. Then, all at once, she became one. She stopped and considered me. "I don't wish to be quoted, Darcy. I'm under their influence, and I have to get away from the enchantment before I can speak reliably. That aside, let me say I get the impression that these people have taken flight! I mean, *flight*. They are jumping a gulf which no other race has jumped, Darcy. You get the impression therefore that these people are *it*! The link! A new level of moral being! Very disturbing, Mr. Darcy. Especially since outsiders, hearing a person speak like this, might think one had less than the full weight between the ears."

"Not me," I told her. "I think it's all absolutely bloody startling."

"Oh yes," she murmured.

Waiting by the truck, Henry gave me a particular kind of look. "Excitement's cheap, Darcy!" he warned me.

He paused and leaned against the trunk of one of the African pines growing in the valley bottom.

For the rest of the night I couldn't sleep or rid myself of a childlike exhilaration. To me the valley of Orotta *was* like a carnival park of the moralities. As Lady Julia had implied, there the greatest human fantasy, the fantasy of perfectability, displayed its glittering, supremely complex and supremely simple wheels. And dazed and giddied the spectator! Lady Julia and me, anyhow.

"It is not only the hospital," announced Lady Julia Ashmore-Smith the next morning on the terrace.

Salim Genete, the middle-aged and turbanned Eritrean in the business jacket, was there. His son had again failed to arrive during the night.

Lady Julia had been in the small hours into the bunker in the valley where the exercise books were manufactured by a woolly-haired girl who had lost a leg on the Hallal Front. Now she held up an exercise-book cover Moka had given her, a memento to go with Christine's plastic infusion bag.

This was over breakfast—wheat and unleavened bread and sweet tea—on the terrace. She spoke low. She had already detected the bewilderment in Henry and could not utterly forgive it. I could see in the way she spoke the stubbornness with which she must have hunted down the mind of poor Sir Denis, her District Commissioner husband.

Henry, an edge to his voice, said, "So the Memsahib is pleased at all the Sambo cleverness?"

Lady Julia surprised me by not taking offense. She raised her eyebrows and smiled. "Yes, I suppose I must sound like an old-fashioned imperialist. But there you are! That's the world I was raised in."

Henry hurled out the remnants of his tea onto the stones. The morning sun sucked it up almost instantly.

Salim stood up, craned his neck for a view across the valley, and sang, "Ah, my poor kinswoman."

For a time I thought he meant Lady Julia. His mind had certainly been on her. He had watched Christine and the Englishwoman as they rinsed out their soiled shirts at the washing drum beneath the terrace. "Two generations of women talking together," he had sighed. "Ai, a fine sight!"

But he wasn't speaking of Lady Julia now. We followed his eyes, which were fixed on a point down the defile. Three figures had emerged from the Department of Information bunker. Two tall men were supporting between them a hobbling figure in turban and shawl and jeans. I guessed they were making for the clinic. I recognized the figure in the middle as the woman called Amna, who had sat with us so tranquilly and without saying much at the coffee ceremony.

"Is she ill?" Lady Julia asked Salim.

Salim said, "Milady, oh yes. She gets swellings of the legs and joint pains. The Ethiopians treated her badly, you know. Afan, the Ethiopian police. She should be in Frankfurt with her physiotherapist, but she is very stubborn."

I found it hard to identify the hobbling being I could now see with the Italianate elegance I'd admired the day before.

Salim told us, "Neroyo will give her injections of vitamins. *Ciao,* Amna!" He returned to his seat again. "She is in fact a kind of niece of mine, the daughter of my cousin the pharmacist from Asmara."

The nonappearance of his son now seemed to leave him all the less composed at seeing his relative stumbling among the shale, being eased along in the daylight at an hour when, wide open to the bomb sights of the MIGs, the Eritreans did not normally go looking for vitamins.

Something About Salim

Salim's habits of mind were not those of the revolutionary. We could all tell that by his Empire loyalist interest in the correct mode of address for Lady Julia. He was instead a kind of Jefferson figure, a man who'd rather do business and be a Rotarian than join a liberation front.

He was frank in confessing all this to me. His ancestry derived from a particular coastal Cushitic tribe who had always done jovial business and tried to avert their eyes from history's great steamroller. His grandparents had spoken Saho and Arabic and some Italian, and dealt in shells, salt, bone meal. His father was a civil engineer engaged in the construction of piers and warehouses in the great port of Massawa. The family had lived offshore in a villa on the handsome island named Talud. Only the poorest of folk lived over the causeway in the mainland suburbs of Massawa, said Salim, beneath the hot brow of the coastal massif.

From these mountains above the port, however, snaked down a trade road as old as the kingdom of Axum and much appreciated by whoever ruled the Red Sea coast. Salim's family, said Salim himself, had a traditional skill for getting on with the manifold administrations which either came ashore with the tide or descended down the road from the massif. There was a tradition of offering accommodation, of finding your new niche, of adapting your ways adequately though not crucially.

"If you live like us on the Red Sea, right at its neck, the Babel Mandeb, the mouth of the bottle, then you've done business with everyone. You have sold and bought from the Coptic highlanders. You have sold salt and lentils to Christopher da Gama as he landed to help the Massawa garrison against the Imam of Harar, the grand Mohammed Ibrahim. You have certainly done business with the Turks, who held fast to Massawa until the Italians came. I suppose, if the truth be told, our lives were like those of Jews in Russia or Poland, or of Jews in the Yemen, for that matter. There weren't grounds for us to work up any national fervor, whether in favor of the occupiers or against them."

His grandparents, for example, saw the Italians become interested in Massawa Island and the Gulf of Zula, then watched without regret as the Turks marched off. After four hundred years of doing business!

Salim was a child of eleven when he beheld the Red Sea Eritrean port of Massawa fill up with Italian naval vessels, with the sort of ferries whose bows come down and from which drive forth battalions of armored vehicles. From Massawa the Italians would invade in 1935 the empire of the Ethiopians, the kingdom of the Negus, the squat Chosen One, the Lion of Judah, Haile Selassie.

Let me make an abstract of Salim's subsequent history, drawing both on his superior whimsy and my lesser brand. The Italians lost Eritrea and Ethiopia very quickly in 1941 to British forces operating from the Sudan. Salim's family was content enough, even though some of the highland intellectuals were agitating for independence. Salim's father, another kind of Eritrean altogether, became mayor of Massawa during the British occupation. The port in those days was host to countless British naval vessels, on all of which father and son had been welcomed to drinks parties. Salim and his father were both, according to the Prophet's command, abstainers—but politely and discreetly so, no fanatics. They knew that human beings from the larger world answered in their behavior a quite exotic and farfetched range of imperatives, desires, prohibitions, and commandments, and that it was gentlemanly to be cool about these things.

Eritrea was federated by vote of the UN with the Emperor's Ethiopia six or seven years after the end of the World War. There had been no referendum to get the approval of the Eritreans to this forced twining of the two nations, and in Asmara and even on the coast Eritrean intellectuals and agitators seemed aggrieved by the new federal arrangement. The young engineer Salim took it with traditional calm. With his wife and two young sons, he moved down the coast to the extreme southern zone of Eritrea, the province called Danakil, after the tribe who inhabited it. His new job was in the bay of Aseb, a rainless and scorching zone, the least rained-on port on earth. In the face of a glittering Red Sea, the great energetic sun was impotent to produce a rainfall of any meaning, a dew, a tentative shower. Yet the Emperor and the West had large plans for Aseb. Bunkering, oil refineries, berths, a bitumen road to feed into the highway from Addis to Asmara. The young engineer Salim became a town councilor, then mayor. He was president, too, of the Chamber of Commerce, which had grown out of the old Italian *Società di Navigazione Rubattino*.

He expected to have to swallow certain items of Ethiopian hubris. After the Emperor canceled the federation and simply took Eritrea over as a fiefdom, all public examinations were conducted in Amharic. But his sons were sufficiently clever to take that language to memory as well. Sometimes the Ethiopian garrison behaved savagely and on various pretexts—searches for weapons, Arabist agitators, or contraband—slaughtered encampments of the Afar tribespeople who shared the zone. Salim was driven to conclude that these slaughters were countenanced by the Emperor's government.

The Ethiopian forces in the hinterland of Aseb, in breathless and rainless Danakil, were largely Coptic Christians, like the highland Eritreans. The coastal Muslims therefore came to believe that the massacres along the dry wadis of Danakil were somehow inspired by their Eritrean brothers and sisters in the highlands. Killings and the burning of tents and villages were good policy, Salim could see. They stopped an Eritrean common cause from forming.

Salim Genete found himself a functionary of the Ethiopian government now, a civilian administrator likely to be appointed anywhere. Already the sons and daughters of old colleagues from Aseb and Massawa were slipping away northwestward over the massif to join this faction or that of Eritrean rebels. His own sons, however, were admitted to the University of Addis. There, he hoped, they avoided political groups, particularly Eritrean ones.

"As the Emperor got weaker," Salim said, "he retreated in time. From being an imitation of a modern head of state, he began to take on the appearances and utter the edicts of another time, of the time of, say, Charlemagne. There were agents everywhere—in every city, in Aseb itself—and all of them straining to find the news which could feed the Emperor's failing ear, feed its appetite for hearing the worst. Did the empire fall? No, it performed the disappearing trick. Instead of breathing the air of *this* century, it tried to breathe the vanished air of some other. It choked in a vacuum."

In the Emperor's last days, Salim was anxious because now he knew his sons had grown political and so—in police-ridden Addis—endangered. When the Emperor was deposed, however, and driven away from the New Palace in a Volkswagen, Salim rejoiced. Now his sons were safe. With other brilliant boys and girls they were laughing in the streets of the racy suburb of Mercato, laughing up at the hills where the Menelik Palace stood and where the Lion of Judah occupied a few rooms under the guard of the aggrieved officers who had now taken command.

Salim says with touching emphasis that he was ready to pretend to be a Marxist if that was what the new Ethiopian government, the Dergue, required; if that was the banner under which the people were fed, the children educated, the tongues of the Eritreans liberated, the nomads and villagers of Danakil left to their traditional devices.

Of course, both he and his sons were to be disappointed. For Mengistu, chairman of the Dergue, vested all the prestige of Ethiopia in the extinction not only of the Eritrean languages but, with them, of the Eritrean mouths.

It was suddenly more, not less, horrifying; more, not less, risky; more, not less, erratic a business to work as a civil administrator hand-in-hand with an uncontrolled military. Salim told, for example, of a friend and fellow member of the Aseb Chamber of Commerce, Doctor Berhai, owner of a Mercedes 380SE. Three members of the Aseb garrison coveted it. They had Berhai arrested for conspiracy and encouraged some of their NCOs to shoot him through the head in a poor Muslim cemetery inland. The Mercedes was backed into the belly of an Antonov transport for transfer to Addis. The transport, however, could not take off because of engine trouble, and while the air force waited for spare parts to be flown north, the back hatch of the plane stayed unabashedly open. Berhai's 380SE could be seen glimmering headlights first across the tarmac. Air force officers saw it; the military administrator of Aseb saw it;

Salim, the mayor of Aseb, saw it when he passed the airport fence on official business or when he visited the terminal to greet an undersecretary of the Dergue's Department of Public Administration. No one protested or complained about Berhai's car, and at last it was flown to Addis.

The children of many of Salim's cousins had been arrested and proved hard for him to find in Ethiopia's chaotic prison system. And everywhere there were violations of equity, sanity, the principles of service, of honorable commerce. The hacked-off arms of young Eritrean agitators—agents, writers and printers of underground newspapers—were permitted to lie in the streets; it was no use talking to the military administrator or the police about that, no use invoking either humanity or aspects of hygiene. At the power plant the big transformers were shipped away to Addis; at the water works the pumping system was permitted to stay antique. Yet that was all that was required of Salim—the supply of water and electricity to the port town. The Ethiopians didn't want to talk to him about much else.

"I had to travel with the military governor everywhere he went. That was to protect the man. He had his offices next door to mine. A parable for the people to see: the civil and the military hand in hand. And camouflage and a shield for the military ruler, too! For the mayor was usually a man with friends and relatives among the Eritreans, even among the rebels. And rebels knew that bombs and volleys of fire intended for the general would also finish the mayor. Ai-ai-ai, what a situation this was!"

After protecting the military governor of Aseb in this way for some months, Salim was all at once transferred to the western city of Keren. This was a time when the Eritrean rebels, many of them children of his old business associates, were descending from the north with captured Kalashnikovs. Keren was threatened, and with it the road and the railway to Asmara. The Ethiopian military garrison, under a Brigadier Wossef, was in a confused, uninformed, reckless state of mind. Driving to his offices in the city, Salim could hear the large 122-millimeter cannon of both sides speaking out in the plains to the west and the mountains to the north. The Ethiopian conscripts were in a terrible panic: farm boys and goatherds from Harar, Gondar, Ethiopian Somalia who did not know what in God's name they were doing here, listening to shellfire in a threatened town.

Salim says Brigadier Wossef, their commander, was a joke-teller, but his humor had a frightened and savage edge which Salim didn't like. And so the journeys they undertook together and the official ceremonies within the sound of guns were tedious to Salim. The brigadier became depressed on discovering that the town was full of Eritrean rebel agents, most of them under twenty-five years of age. But because Salim's own sons were involved in the rebel movement, the Eritrean People's Liberation Front local cells took pains not to attack garrisons which he might perforce be visiting with the brigadier.

"For my life I was dependent on my sons," Salim admitted with a shrug.

A summons to Asmara separated him from Brigadier Wossef. The Dergue wanted civilian authorities from throughout Eritrea to meet in the capital, to discuss the blowing-up of power stations and water reservoirs in the face of the rebel advance. Salim left for Asmara from the market square of Keren, outside the ditch and the double wall of razor wire behind which, in a two-story building, he and the brigadier had ruled the city.

The convoy Salim joined was long, and the drivers were tentative. As they entered the mountains, firing could be heard ahead and behind. All night the lead trucks came under hit-and-run attack, the wreckage needing to be pushed over the mountainside to make way for the vehicles behind. Among the civilian administrators gathered in Asmara, the word was that none of them would get back to their provincial seats, that the rebels were about to take everything.

Without Salim for cover, Brigadier Wossef was himself ambushed and shot dead while escaping Keren.

It was apparent now that all of Eritrea was about to fall to the rebels. They were in the foothills of the massif outside Massawa. They threatened the whole string of cities which lay along the old Italian railway line from Massawa to Agordat. The beaten Ethiopians, so the Eritrean administrators whispered to each other during their Asmara meetings, would now have to come to settlement with the Eritreans.

In fact, what happened then was that the Soviets decided, for the sake of control of the Babel Mandeb and of the Dhalak Islands out in the Red Sea, to intrude mightily and in terms which would be recorded on film by Masihi.

Eritrean rebels began to withdraw from their positions threatening the string of cities, the railway line, the central east-west road which filleted Eritrea. From his hotel in Asmara, Salim used a relative—perhaps, I surmised, even Amna, his Asmaran "niece"—to contact the secret Eritrean cells. For the first time in history one of his tribe had been forced to identify himself with the retreating cause. All the barbarities of the past five centuries had not caused one of his mercantile clan to do what he was now doing. "And they speak as if the twentieth century were the high point of the human soul!" he told me.

On the same night that the agents of the Eritrean People's Liberation Front took him out of Asmara disguised as a peasant and bearing false papers, his wife and two sons escaped Keren. It was the desolation of the northern mountains which now became the portion of this consummate townsman.

The townless maze of brown peaks.

Casualties and the Heart

Moka the stringy veteran brought the news up the stone steps of the terrace, two at a time, that Masihi had been definitely located. The cameraman was known to be on his way to Himbol, a dry riverbed half a night's drive south, where he intended to film a locust plague.

"It is hot and dusty," Moka told us, "but there is a bush shower there. And then the daughter meets the father!"

"Merci bien, Monsieur Moka," Christine told him, and she closed her eyes and covered them with her hands, reminding me—strangely—of a woman whose son has been found. I had an impulse to go up and congratulate her, but her manner was very private and I decided against it.

"Merci bien," he repeated, hitting his skeletal chest with his fist, as if she'd told him a joke.

Henry, Lady Julia, Salim Genete, and I were all on the terrace drinking tea. The news of coming moves sobered us. Salim coughed. "Ai-ai-ai, if I could but travel with you . . . but there are certain questions of health."

It was the first time he had mentioned anything to do with health. But it did explain why he didn't go afield searching for his son, the way Christine intended to hunt down her father the cameraman.

Any other travel purpose I had was now subsumed into getting the daughter to the father. I didn't think that could have been Tessfaha's idea. I wondered if I should take Moka aside, mention

132

Tessfaha's name. I would have liked reassurance, the sense of traveling on rails.

Later I overheard Moka assuring Lady Julia that around Himbol she would find many peasant refugee women to speak to. It sounded as if Lady Julia had expressed the same doubts I felt.

After midnight in the guest house, in the room I shared with Henry, I was shaken awake by Salim, who was fully dressed in turban, white shirt, upper half of business suit, jellaba. A switched-on torch shone in his hand.

I forced myself painfully awake from dreams of the Eritreans' relentless bunker technology. The handsome dental surgeon and her picture album had figured in the dreams, as had Salim's guerrilla son. I thought that this was what Salim was waking me for, a celebration party for the arrival of the boy. So there'd be more of the bitter liquor called *sewa* to be drunk—except, of course, by Salim, who was saved from that duty by being an orthodox Muslim.

In fact, I could hear music outside and a sort of party in progress.

But Salim looked wan and not celebratory. "I wonder could you help me?" he asked. "I don't like to ask one of my fellow Eritreans, since they might make too much of it."

He pushed into my hand a little vial of white tablets. "Would you come with me to the hospital? There has been a great battle. Wounded are arriving in front of the operating theaters. I have been told that one of them is my niece."

"The girl?" I asked, thinking of the remarkable bureaucrat I'd seen being helped down the defile toward an injection of vitamins.

"No, not that one, not Amna Nurhussein. Another one. My dead sister's girl." Salim seemed to emit a mist of grief which I thought I could very nearly see in the light of the torch.

"These tablets are for the girl?" I asked, still in a half-daze.

"Not for the girl. For me." He had dropped his voice. "Kindly watch me, my friend. Should you see my face contorting, give me one of those. Angina is my grief, you see. If they knew that it was severe, as indeed it is, they would not have let me travel here."

He rehearsed me in what symptoms I should look for: sudden halting of his speech, a blueness around his mouth and eye sockets.

Across the room, Henry was sitting on his bed barefooted and yawning. He apparently feared he might be asked to join us, though he could have overheard very little of what Salim and I were saying.

"Sorry," he said perfunctorily. "I declare I can't move. I'm struck down with the big D."

It was clear he wanted to avoid the hospital, its poignant competence which made his African blues deeper.

I sat up and pulled my boots on. From beyond the window came a drumming, the thrum of a stringed instrument, and a woman's voice following the jerky line of some Eritrean song of triumph.

"Oh Jesus, boys, here she comes again," said Henry, lunging upright and grabbing a wad of toilet paper. It was an authentic performance. I repented of my earlier doubts.

Salim and I followed the American into the corridor. More sedately than Henry, the two of us made for the door. In the dining room, Eritrean soldiers and officials, using their unwound turbans or their shawls in the two-handed manner of English football crowds flexing team scarves, swayed to the music outside and passed among them two powdered-milk cans of *sewa*. Moka was in this group. He came up to me, his eyes shining. He looked feverish. Because of his chest troubles, he'd told me earlier, he wasn't supposed to drink *sewa*. Now, briskly, he wound his shawl around his neck, taking on his official stature again.

"Oh, this is so big, Mr. Darcy. If there were cameras in Eritrea, this would be headlines. They would know about us in every place. Two Ethiopian brigades! Two! A total destruction! On the Nacfa Front."

In the West, I liked to play the pacifist. Being militant didn't seem an option. But here I felt the pull of Moka's primitive martial excitement. With a flush of blood I remembered that the Ethiopians had promised to drive the Eritreans "into the Red Sea." "Into the sands of the Sudan," Mengistu had put it once. This grievous intention of the Dergue's had made the Eritreans into just warriors, a corps of the righteous. To feel an association with warriors was a new experience for me, but I suppose that what the news had unleashed in Moka, and even in me, was the African equivalent of a good old 1942-style post–El Alamein, post–Stalingrad joy at battles won.

Moka noticed Salim, the sober face the older man carried. He reached out his hand. "Your niece will be cured," he said. "Doctor

Neroyo will see to it. And your son will come, my friend! One morning he will be here in the guest house when you wake up!"

Moka led us at once to the door and, on this night of victory, swept both blackout curtains aside at once. His minute torchlight hit the rock walls as he bounded down the defile toward the truck he had waiting. For the moment his wounds meant nothing to him. Salim, uttering small slow noises of Islamic resignation, was far more unsteady on his feet. "There have been too many of my tribe," I heard him murmur elliptically, as if to himself.

Our truck, when we reached it, rolled off between bands of singing and dancing Eritreans. They were the same kind of woolly-haired, piercing-eyed youths Tessfaha had shown me photographs of in that London restaurant.

"Your son wasn't in this battle?" I yelled over the noise of the road.

"No," Salim called back. "Though God knows. No, he was on his way to me. Perhaps. We shall see."

Moka himself joined in the loud talk. From him we heard a somewhat florid account of what had happened. The EPLF had attacked two small towns to the south of what he called "holy Asmara": Areza to the southeast of the city, Maidema to the south-west, each garrisoned by an entrenched Ethiopian brigade! The assault on the wire and the trench lines had begun three hours before dawn, and both towns were entirely in the hands of the rebels hours before noon.

"The sun," said Moka, achieving a bardic overview of the battle, "shone not caring on the bodies of the poor conscripts of the Dergue!"

I privately reflected that it must have shone, too, on the tightly curled heads and the British-gaitered legs of certain fallen Eritreans, veterans and novices, for whom one day sad fanfares might sound in Asmara.

And above all, even to an intermittent journalist like me, the figures seemed high. "You say two brigades, Moka?" I asked.

Moka went on in his sing-song, poetic-martial voice. "Four thousand Ethiopians are fallen or are prisoners, are scathed or are unscathed. But there has been also a relief column from Adi Igra. Our village militias and our volunteers turned it around at midmorning. So, four thousand and more!"

From a hole at the side of the road, Salim's bureaucrat kins-woman, the glorious rinser named Amna, emerged all at once. She moved nimbly, whereas last time I'd seen her she'd been limping and needed Neroyo's vitamins. She waved to the truck. When we stopped I got down from the cabin to make room for her, but she refused to take it. She climbed into the back. Reboarded, I strained around in my seat to see if she was comfortable. She looked at me for only a second with limpid irony, like one of those omniscient girls who saw through your crookedest advances when you were fourteen.

Although the unconcluded business of Bernadette (which I couldn't accept as *finished* even though Bernadette thought it was) lay like a filter over all I saw, I found with a strange excitement that I thought of this Eritrean woman Amna as a kind of kinswoman, too. All her features, her flowing gestures (so I thought in the heat and ardor of that peculiar night) seemed to have lain a long time unidentified in my imagination, waiting on this woman, on Amna Nurhussein, to assume them and give them a focus.

Salim, too, took up an uncomfortably crooked position so that he could speak to her as we went along. The conversation seemed to be in Tigrinyan. She answered her uncle/cousin liquidly. Now and then there would again be an instant of ironic apology in her face.

Moka had now produced a communiqué from the pocket of his khaki battle jacket. The poetry was over. He was giving us the figures. The noise of the vehicle on the stony road was enormous, but his damaged, exultant lungs overrode it.

"Twenty vehicles—that's value fifty thousand dollars each. Five T-55 tanks—their values so hard to guess. Four one-hundred-twenty-two-millimeter and eight seventy-six-millimeter heavy artil-lery. Each of them stands for a hospital Mengistu might have given the Somalis or the Oromos or even the people of Addis themselves! Eight fuel and ammunition depots! Three light weapons magazines! Twelve supply stores! Thousands of the AK-47s which were theirs, but which in our hands they fear!"

"Oh dear, the ambulances," called Salim, breaking into Moka's bardic rundown.

I saw that black ambulances, inching slowly along ahead of us, occupied most of the valley floor now. Moka, Salim, the kinswoman

Amna, and I abandoned the truck and began walking toward the terraces outside the operating theater, where the stones were covered with wounded on stretchers.

I found myself shivering at the sight. I flexed my jaw to keep my teeth from giving away my condition of terror. As a reporter of fact, I counted perhaps fifty litters set down there. It was all reminiscent, I thought, as the trembling spasm gave out, of the tent of the Afabet women. There was a notable lack of protest, of moaning. I thought at first that this was because the wounded must all have been sedated for their ambulance journey. But then I noticed certain signs of the usual mannerliness of the Horn. For example: A boy lowered from the back of one of the ambulances onto the stone terrace insisted on reaching his thin arm up and shaking hands with each of his stretcher bearers. The next soldier lifted down did exactly the same.

"Why do they all shake hands?" I asked Moka.

But it was Salim who answered absently. His eyes were darting for a sight of his wounded niece. "Pride. They don't wish to die without having thanked everyone they should."

By a stone bench where on quieter nights surgeons might have sat to drink their tea, a young peasant—leaning on a crutch—held a surgical drip upright in his left hand. There was a marvelous stillness about him. The drip bag did not shake, the peasant did not alter his stature by a millimeter. The feed line on the drip ran down into the arm of a thin-faced girl. She was not as pale as Salim in spite of her wounds. Someone, I could see, had introduced a Nilotic darkness into both Amna's face and hers. A blanket covered her up to her chin, and around her neck was a plastic plaque on which Tigrinyan script proclaimed what I guessed to be *Nil by mouth*.

Even before Salim and Amna spotted her, I had decided she was Salim's niece purely through resemblance, particularly to the exquisite Amna. I pointed her out.

"Ai-ai-ai!" said Salim.

An extraordinary sort of feral hiss escaped Amna.

Salim knelt agilely beside the wounded girl. But Amna the bureaucrat half-crouched in a far more awkward manner. Perhaps Doctor Neroyo's injections of vitamins had not quite brought her back to full suppleness.

The eyes of the girl on the stretcher opened. They settled on me but then mercifully moved to her uncle Salim. She began speaking at once to Salim, hindered it seemed only by a dryness in her throat.

"Ah-ah!" said Salim, with little breathy groans. "Say nothing. Say nothing."

She kept speaking just the same in a thin musical voice. When she had finished, Salim seemed to feel bound by tradition to translate for me, the foreigner. "She tells me my son is okay, waiting in Nacfa for a truck. But it might be days. Even the Russian buses we captured last year, they're using them to carry the wounded and prisoners. So he cannot catch a bus."

The girl continued talking, like a child wanting to clear her toll of messages before sleeping. "She says he was not in the battle," Salim further murmured.

"Though she was," said Amna.

Even there, beside the litter, I was taken by the way Amna used her English, as though she'd learned it in the abstract and loved it purely for its building blocks. Each word was well marked in her mouth by sharp consonants and by the deft sibilance of such words as *she* and *was*.

A young surgeon in a green coat came to the stretcher, knelt, conversed somberly with Salim. I watched Salim's face for possible symptoms, but none displayed themselves. The surgeon drew the blankets down from the girl's body. In the instant before I looked away I saw she was dressed only in the remnants of a khaki shirt. Her thighs and her legs were bare. Gauze and cotton wadding ran from her navel down to her pelvis and then, like the head of an inverted T, across it. "Ai-ai-ai!" said Salim.

As two orderlies lifted the girl to take her away, I noticed that her eyes were quite sharply focused yet somehow suspended. They had that same quality of pernicious independence that I'd seen in the mouths of the children of the Afabet women. They were waiting for the surgeons. They had suspended judgment.

We suddenly had more space now on the terrace to stand and debate our next moves. Amna suggested to me that she might stay with her uncle Salim, and Salim with her. That I should go back to the guest house to rest. With Salim's angina tablets jiggling in my pocket, I knew I shouldn't give in to her. Yet she seemed to know our party was meant to leave before dawn, looking for Masihi.

I could not consider sleep now in any case. I was sharply awake. I had suffered from some of the massed expectancy of the fifty or so stunned presences on the stretchers on the stone terrace. I was for the time being as brave and as shocked as they were. I yearned for the Eritreans to permit me to keep watch.

The surgeons worked, the terrace began to empty a little further, the night grew icy. I did not have much chance to talk with Amna, who moved here and there about the terrace, insinuating herself into spaces between stretchers, talking to nurses and drip-holders and doctors, murmuring at the wounded. I could tell I lacked probable cause to walk beside her.

Amna returned at last to the space from which her wounded cousin had been lifted. An orderly brought the three of us blankets. I watched as Amna sat on a stone bench and wrapped herself leanly into hers. To my embarrassment, the best bench had been vacated for me, and Salim kept pointing me to it.

"Are you well?" I asked him.

"I am well. Don't worry. *Ciao* and goodnight."

I showed him which of my pockets his tablets were in, but he dismissed this information with a flapping of his hand. Shaping my bush hat into a pillow, I flopped. I would lie down among the heroes, I told myself, but there would be no sleep. Nor would there be the sort of futile, self-pitying tears which had incapacitated me in Port Sudan.

Despite everything, maybe because of everything—the strain of behaving well and of all the terrace sights—a chilled sleep took me whole. Even in the midst of it I could feel the night through the thin blanket and the denim pants.

I woke a little time later when the moon was high. I could see the plump surgeon Neroyo standing talking to Salim and Amna. I was ashamed to have been sleeping while they were in such busy discourse. Around Salim's shoulders his blanket was still draped, and over the terrace could be heard a multiple gurgling and rasping, the snoring of the post-operative.

Neroyo finished his conversation with Salim and Amna, noticed me, nodded, smiled briefly, then went inside.

I stood up. I could not stop myself from quivering with the cold. I knew, too, that when this spasm of shivering passed, Salim would tell me something I might want to postpone hearing.

Salim murmured, "Internal bleeding, Doctor Neroyo said. Too much damage. They needed so much blood and the supplies are low."

I wanted at first to ask why they had not roused me and taken mine. I did not say anything, because the unnegotiable nature of his niece's passing, the fact it couldn't be argued with, seemed to be a comfort to him.

"It's Allah's will," he murmured, and the trite line had somehow great power in his mouth.

Amna argued that Salim and I should *both* go back to the guest house now. It was as if she didn't want me there for the mourning phase. Did she want to weep and keen, and would my presence inhibit her? As she spoke, in any case, stretcher bearers appeared with what must have been Salim's niece wrapped in a blanket.

"Oh dear," murmured Salim. "We need to bury her before daylight."

Having his tablets, I was forced to stumble into an informal procession behind the litter. We had gone maybe a hundred paces when Salim halted, grabbed my arm and looked out at me through a suddenly twisted face with profound and solemn meaning. If the situation had been different, I could have yelled with the pain of his grip. But he was drowning and I was his single contact with the earth. One-handed, I got his tablets out, opened the lid with my teeth, clumsily poured a couple of pills into the palm of my hand, brought it up to his mouth. I think that I managed to get both of them in without asking myself whether this was an overdose or not.

We both remained still and he leaned on me. I could smell his sweat and it was strangely pungent, like the smell of a father. I could see Amna, the four stretcher bearers, and the dead niece receding before us. I wondered if I should call to them.

After half a minute Salim's grip eased. The hand on my arm became more independent. The fingers retracted from the pits they'd made in my arm.

"Ai," he sighed at last. "We can catch them." And, too fast for his own good, he dragged me off toward the others.

The graveyard at Orotta was unmarked and indistinguishable from the surrounding terrain. A few modest superstructures of clay and stone, oval in shape, randomly studded with lumps of a white marblelike stone taken from the hillsides, marked the place. Even the funerary arts of Eritrea were geared to be invisible from the air.

Among these plain memorials lay a wide grave which caught the moon, now at its zenith. There were few shadows. One other blanketed shape had been seated in the pit, though there was space for a dozen.

The diggers, a party of boys and girls in khaki, perhaps artillerists from the mountaintops around, stood quietly to one side with their shovels. The stretcher bearers crouched, lifted Salim's niece in her blanket off the litter, and lowered her down to two soldiers who had jumped into the pit to receive her.

The boys handled her with delicacy, I thought—I expected them on a night like this to be more offhand.

But then, contrary to my earlier suspicions, there was no ceremony to speak of. I was the one who suffered an urgent desire for everyone to begin keening, perhaps to cover some of my own potentially grievous cries.

I watched the seated dead in the pit, leaning over toward each other, supple shapes still, so recent was their tragedy. No one made a sound. I thought the struggle to strangle my own plaints would choke me. I heard Salim at my side intoning something in Arabic. The artillerists, including the two who had now climbed out of the hole, were moving off so soon to other work. The stretcher bearers were already on their way back toward the operating theaters.

Amna turned away from the grave and toward Salim and me. If I expected to find tears in her eyes, there were none. She said authoritatively, in her sharp-edged English, "It is *certainly* time for you to go now."

I did not want to—I wanted to wait out the balance of the night on the terrace. I felt irrationally it was a contribution I could make. Salim, however, took me aside and asked for his pills back; so he, too, was dismissing me. He would not have another attack now, he explained gratefully. I'd ensured that by double-feeding him his pills.

"Your other niece . . . Amna . . . she's very strong," I told him. "She doesn't weep at all."

"Oh," he said, "there are reasons why she doesn't."

I wanted to say something further to her, but she stood with her back preventively to me.

"You may see my son," said Salim airily, as if the pill had tranquilized him as well as opening his heart. Shaking hands with him had a feel of finality.

In the moon's aqueous blue, I went looking for the truck.

Himbol

Crossing Himbol's empty river the next morning, my boots filled with warm sand. It was only eight o'clock, but I felt that the air was already so perilously hot that it would take just one spark of panic from any of our party for it to catch fire. Ahead of us, by the door of a low-slung dry stone house hidden under a network of thorn trees, three women, hair braided and Coptic crosses tattooed on their foreheads, sat on stones. Moka spoke to them but shrugged dismally at their answers and looked away.

"Jesus H.," I heard Henry murmur behind me. "The son-of-a-bitch isn't here either."

One of the women called a name, and a young official dressed in jeans and a fawn shirt—a deliberate renunciation, it seemed, of the usual paramilitary uniform of rebel officials—appeared from the doorway of the house and spoke to us in English.

"But he's gone on to Senhit province now," he told us. Senhit was to the west. "He was here but he isn't here now."

We all looked at Christine. She flinched, of course, looked away and then—apparently reconciled to going on—back. The journey from Orotta had been a bruising, unsettling one, and it would not have surprised me if even she showed wilder feelings and cried now or got peevish. I would in fact have welcomed it, since it would have made her a more intelligible companion. But she composed her body. It was now Lady Julia who seemed wan. For in that superheated day, it appeared even more obvious than ever that none of us might be allowed to attend to our own journeys until the reunion had taken place.

I was promised an interview by the young official who'd spoken to us—from this little dry stone hut he directed the sharing of food among three million Eritreans, and I thought there was a story to that. With this small consolation, I turned back toward the Himbol guest house, a small wooden shed dug into the riverbank and shrouded in foliage. Moka pointed to the shadows under trees.

"There is the Economic Planning Commission. There is the Department of Public Administration. There is the Department of Agriculture."

An open-sided brush shelter stood outside the hut we were all to share. In its shade a small girl, perhaps four or five years of age, waited for us. She was dressed Western style—tracksuit pants and a T-shirt with German writing on it.

"The daughter of one of the officials," said Moka.

In her hand a strange toy hung—it was a live bird, black and yellow, and she held it by a harness of string some adult had made for her. The bird flapped limply and again and again. Its residual tension passed into the child's arm and somehow soothed her. Moka explained, "The fathers catch them for them."

Henry shrugged. A small whimper came from Christine, though. I watched, not quite believing it as she broke away, left the cover of the trees, ran—at a half-lope varying back to a fast walk—wide open to the sun, across the gritty riverbed.

It was curious the way Lady Julia and Henry and I looked at each other then, as if we were holding an election to choose by barely visible gestures a comforter for this suddenly demented Christine who had at last complained. All the odds said that the task should have been Lady Julia's. Sisterhood and shared toiletries should have ensured that. Yet somehow, almost instantly, perhaps because of the exhaustion of the others, I was aware of having been elected myself.

I stepped out of the shade of the trees and made after her. She had reached a clump of African oaks which grew in the middle of the empty riverbed. As I ran after her, strangely delighted to have the task of saving her from Himbol's excessive light and disappointments, the ferocious air struck me, tumbling over my lips like beads of fire. This Himbol, home of the bird-catching officials of the Economic Planning Commission, etc., etc., was a terrible place, already uninhabitable so early in the day.

When I arrived beside her, Christine wasn't making any sound apart from the rasp of her breath. Her mouth was agape and her eyes swept across my face. She looked like one of those scrawny distance runners from some European republic. Then she stared down at the roots of the desert oaks.

"We *will* catch up with him," I said. "He can't be far off." Though, of course, he might well be.

She said nothing.

"It's because you're tired that you feel it's impossible."

My tiredness was certainly the reason I felt it was impossible.

I reached out my hand to her wrist, but she brushed it aside and began to shiver. We continued to stand in mid-river, among the notional waters and the burning air, and still she wouldn't answer.

In the silence I felt a frightening shift in the atmosphere, both a movement and a profound, unnatural vibration in the sky and within my own chest. This is a MIG, I thought, the one I've been fearing from the start, and so close that I can't even hear it. The air grew dense and fell on me like a weight. The impact! I thought. The sky, what I could see of it, was speckled. I was sure combustion was imminent. Christine and I had an instant in which to cling to each other for life, and we did.

It was locusts, I understood then. I knew it from the wings and antennae beating against the cringing flesh of my face. A plague of them had come down on us. I had, as if seen through snow, an image of a branch by my shoulder stripped of its foliage between blinks of the eye. I didn't want to watch the obscene voracity, even though I understood it would leave me untouched. Christine had closed her eyes and was hunched in my arms. We fell to our knees and made a tent of ourselves. So—for perhaps ten minutes—we huddled together, while all around the earth was stripped of its last sap. After a little time, as long as I kept my eyes locked shut and held Christine, I felt strangely safe at the heart of all that devouring. Holding Christine, I felt in the simplest way brave and fatherly and sexual at the same time. Hard up against each other we were arrant, fragile, assured survivors. We'd occupied a state where even the day's heat had become an irrelevance.

When I looked at last, the air was tranquil and had returned to me like a mother with a clear but ambiguous face. The plague had lifted and vanished. We knelt among bare sticks. Moka was hobbling toward us.

"All the camouflage has been eaten," he said. "Come, we must get you into a cave."

"I am very stupid, Darcy," the girl murmured to me.

"No," I said. "No."

Later that day, waking on our air mattresses in a fiery noon in a bunker roofed with logs, we discovered that Masihi was reported to have gone to Jani, a great food dump in Senhit province to the southwest, to film the distribution of aid.

No one argued about it. We would go to Jani.

She'b

At least the chase to Jani after Masihi took us through the valley of She'b, where I could, sooner rather than later, pass the letter I was holding on to Major Fida. I would enjoy a conversation with a man who had intrigued me from the first time I heard his melancholy voice on the BBC.

I had, of course, heard the numbers of Ethiopian p.o.w.s quoted, not least in Stella's radio pieces. Yet I was still taken by surprise by the mere sight of the huge population of prisoners of She'b. Before us as we walked in through the narrow neck of a ravine in early morning, the valley was crowded with Ethiopian privates and NCOs. They walked in the open more freely than the Eritreans themselves. I presumed their keepers must have some early warning system against air raid.

As if to explain the crowd of prisoners and all that movement, Moka told us, wheezing, "It is Thursday. They have no classes on Thursday."

He gestured toward the two volleyball games which were in frantic contest on a level patch of dust in a ravine to our left. "An Olympic sport!" he said.

Some of the players were notably muscular and broad-shouldered—they came from a husky tribe. Others were more characteristically wiry. Quantities of nonplayers sat on rocks at the sides of the valley, writing in booklets made out of brown paper taken from aid packages and stapled with string. Math homework, I discovered, or else Tigrinyan grammar.

There were no guards visible, though we had seen a few EPLF girls and boys patrolling the outer entrance of the valley, carrying weapons and grammar books.

Before dawn, the truck which had brought us to Eritrea, the green one with *Deutsche Arbeiter Bund* written on its side, *our* truck, rendered familiar with our sweat, had broken its drive shaft. Tecleh, after working on the engine, stood dolefully for a while with pieces of shattered metal in his hands. Then, after covering the truck with brush, he began walking—exactly as he had the night we'd met Lady Julia—back to a camouflaged mechanics shop we had passed some five or six miles earlier.

Moka told us we were then still miles from the camp at She'b. He led us off south, or more or less so, along the bottom of the valley. He carried the girl's pack. Occasionally Lady Julia would call on everyone to pause while Christine retched cruelly. She had become ill after the locusts and disappointments of Himbol.

When the sun rose there were still a few miles left to travel. We stood still, according to the accepted Eritrean wisdom, while an Antonov ground away across the gap in the mountains—so high in its path, though, so languid, that we felt no great threat, no nakedness, but listened instead to Christine Malmédy panting in our wake. By signals I still did not understand, we all knew that now it was Lady Julia who should help her along and hold her by the shoulders.

In Africa's erratic way it had rained here, and little ankle-deep pools lay in our path. An Eritrean soldier, the same sharp-eyed, pointedly handsome boy you saw everywhere among the rebels, was washing his shirt in one of the puddles. Soon after, and more remarkably still, we noticed a woman sitting bare-headed on a rock and giving suck to a baby swaddled in a shawl. She called musically and waved to Moka.

The veteran climbed up to where she was sitting with the baby. He and the woman exchanged a knuckle-wringing handshake— the baby attached to her right nipple prevented the normal full-shouldered Eritrean greetings. After more conversation, Moka waved for us to join him. "It is my friend Askulu," he called to us.

We began to climb toward the woman. She'd brought an un-expected air of bounty to the morning. As the baby continued to feed, she extended her right hand to each of us. She wondered would we like breakfast, sweet tea and *injera*. Lady Julia explained that her friend Christine was too ill to eat. "Oh yes," said Askulu. "If she does not get better soon, she should take some of our tetracycline."

They all said that: "*our* tetracycline," as if Dow and Pfizer and Bayer produced a cruder version.

"Of course," said Askulu when she heard we were going to the camp. "But the womenfolk should stay with me. Perhaps they do not need to see the Ethiopian men in such quantities. And I have a fine shack here." She laughed and sat the baby upright, trying to clear its wind.

"This is my beloved little Beret," she explained. The baby's mouth emitted a bubble of milk as the woman began to speak in that voice mothers seem to use universally when they talk on behalf of a speechless baby. "Beret does not like Himbol, with its nasty dust and its heat which gives her a rash. She is happy to be here where the climate is more pleasant. Indeed she is."

Askulu tucked and wriggled her breasts back inside her jungle-green shirt, and buttoned it one-handed. Standing, she then led us down a few steps in the mountainside to the standard Eritrean hut half-submerged in stony earth. I noticed a plastic-coated rattan carry-cot sitting on a table made of ammunition cases. Askulu lowered the baby onto a blanket on the table, unfastened its loincloth and began to change it. Singing in Tigrinyan, she spread Johnson's Baby Oil on its cherub thighs. I wondered what her source of supply was for that stuff.

When the child had been put down mewling in its basket and a mosquito net placed over it, Askulu went to sit with the two women where they were, on the clay platform in front of the plates of wheaten bread and the pump thermos of sweetened tea. "Sit down," she ordered the three of us men, who still stood by the door, hesitant to intrude on the rituals of motherhood. With a sigh she sat down herself beside Lady Julia.

Lady Julia said, "Of course we've met, Madame Askulu. We were on morning television together at the BBC!"

Askulu laughed delightedly. "But you have changed a little."

"I took off some weight," Lady Julia admitted, making a mouth. I couldn't imagine her as a plump woman, bereft of her lean authority. I realized I'd seen Askulu, too. During the great famine of '85 she'd been very visible on all English-speaking television. It developed that she had now been elected to the Central Committee of the rebel movement. Even now, as she attended to her infant in She'b, she was an emissary of the General Secretary, a man called Issayas, a military veteran and an intellectual.

I knew the name of this nearly invisible leader Issayas. By choice, he remained inaccessible. I hoped that after my return from the ambush I might be able to use my service to the Eritreans as a lever to get an interview with him. His second name was Afewerki. He was believed to be—by such partisans as Stella—the world's most successful rebel leader. If he made, said Stella, half a gesture toward the world press, ravenous for personalities as much as for news, he would become what she called "an international glamour-puss."

Rising from the bench, Askulu looked into the baby cot again to check on the repose of the baby Beret. Her voice softened appropriately as she inspected the child. "The latest rumors are that Issayas once gunned down two Ethiopian judges and poisoned the food of a political rival. I mean the man *has* been a rebel and engaged in rebel business, never gentle on either side. But I know him. These are the libels of both the Saudi and Israeli secret services. *N'est-ce pas*, Beret?" She laid a finger interrogatively on her daughter's cheek.

As Askulu and Lady Julia continued to speak of British media figures—the special emissary still occasionally checking on the now sleeping infant—Christine Malmédy leaned back on the clay bench, her eyes half-closed.

"She should stay here and rest, at least two days," said Askulu.

Christine opened her eyes for a moment. "We have to keep going," she said. "My friends have things of their own they want to attend to."

"Masihi is always hard to locate," said Askulu unnecessarily. "As I am, too. My husband is back in Orotta. His letters can take three weeks to reach me—I am always one step further down or up the road than he thinks." She chuckled at this idea of conjugal messages chasing her among the mountains.

Lady Julia moved away from the now somnolent Christine to give the girl's body more room to subside. Askulu sipped from her tea. She did not drink from the cup in the usual, more audible, full-blooded Eritrean way. Nonetheless she gave the normal gasp of pleasure after each mouthful. Tea was the greatest luxury even members of the Central Committee had.

"There is so much activity, too," she murmured. "Especially after our victories near Asmara. I mean, just down there . . ." She gestured with her thumb toward the bunker's southerly wall. " . . . just beyond the Nacfa Front."

I remembered these were the successes for which Salim's niece had perished.

"We all have to be careful," she continued. "Our agents tell us there was a panic in the Ethiopian command. Our friend Haile Mariam Mengistu visited the city after the military debacle and summoned his chiefs of staff and his commanders from along the front. I speak of just last week! He accused them of treachery and of being incompetent, and he used profanities, filthy words. All the people on our general staff who knew him when he was an officer, they all say that of him—he has a profane tongue. But one of the generals speaks out, answers him in the same terms! Mengistu orders that the man be taken out at once and shot. Three other officers at the table protest very strongly. They tell Mengistu there have been too many summary executions. They will not stand for summary executions among their own. Mengistu begins to bluster and then walks out of the room. Within a day, two of those generals have been shot, five have been removed from command and stripped of all rank and sent home. We are now facing a very nervous corps of generals and—may I say?—a very nervous Mengistu."

She lowered her voice even further, as if she did not want the apparently sleeping Beret to overhear. "It makes us worry about chemical warfare. We know our friend has stocks of the stuff left from the days of the Emperor. American chemicals. What chemicals he has from Russia we do not know. I have a gas mask, but how does one fit a gas mask on an infant?"

For a while, as we sustained a horrified silence, she considered the ceiling of logs, reading omens in the patterns there.

It was by Central Committee member Askulu's fiat that Lady Julia was persuaded to stay in that cool, matriarchal bunker. Even though I had interviews to do and Major Fida to meet, I wanted to stay there, too, in this ambience of straight talk, mother's milk, baby oil, within the wholesome animal redolence of baby Beret.

But Moka led us off to our own hut first—a more traditional, conical thatched affair, yet recessed enough into the hillside so that only the bravest bomber pilot could have come low enough to see that it was distinct from its mountain. Henry chose to stay there, watching two emerald lizards, splay-footed like geckos, that ran up and down the mud brick wall and climbed lingeringly over each other's bodies, barking with a *yip* sound.

Moka knew I had my mind on reaching the commandant, whose hut was somewhere in this valley. I don't think he deliberately delayed me on our way there that morning. By now the sun was high and most of the prisoners sat beneath brush shelters, away from its full glare. The volleyball games were over. Some men, however, played skittles with a small rounded stone and spent short-wave radio batteries.

When we reached the commandant's home and office, we found him sitting under a tree—in a pit lined with sandstone seats—conferring with a number of Ethiopian prisoners, some sort of prison committee. The commandant was that same lean Eritrean official we saw everywhere throughout the country, from the same gene pool as Tessfaha. Seeing us, he stood and began to shake hands in the exhaustive manner of the Horn with each of the committee. They trailed away back into the camp, speculating with a mild flicker of the eye, but not too energetically, on what my being there might mean. I can't have looked much like a repatriation official from the International Committee of the Red Cross, and that was above all the man they were waiting for.

The commandant led us into his bunker. He poured me tea from his pump thermos. That and the flowered *injera* dish seemed to be the staples of Eritrean kitchenware. The sugar in the tea, instead of livening me up, brought on a sort of blunt exhaustion. Moka explained in Tigrinyan that I wanted to see Major Paulos Fida in the officers' camp. The man gave an answer—judicious, polite, and firm.

When he finished, Moka turned to me with a kind of pleading in his eyes. "Major Fida isn't here. He's gone away."

I asked him if I could be told where Major Fida had gone to. I said that I had a friend, Stella, who was in contact with Fida's family in Addis.

Moka passed this on to the commandant, even though I could

tell from his face that he already knew what the answer would be. After the commandant had spoken, Moka turned back to me.

"He doesn't know where Major Fida is. Major Fida was moved. He doesn't know where."

I began to grow rebellious. They had no right to deny me this meeting with Fida, or to stonewall me if something had happened to him.

"Is he dead?" I asked. "If he's dead, his widow is entitled to know. So are his children."

There was a discussion between Moka and the commandant. At last Moka said, "Major Fida isn't dead. His health is good."

"Then I can see him," I argued.

There was more discussion. "I'm afraid that that is not possible," Moka conveyed to me at last, pleading, his eyes enormously yellow and desperate in his thinned-down face.

"Major Fida is one of your most famous prisoners. Some very well-known journalists have interviewed him. You can't use him as you've used him and then just say he's not on tap any more. You can't use me either . . ." I felt the undue weight of the journey I'd made to see Major Fida's melancholy face. I'd believed that however hard it might be to find Masihi, the reputedly reasonable Eritreans would present me to Fida without argument.

The commandant kept earnestly explaining things in Tigrinyan. He was being very concessive, and I felt a little sorry for him—he was clearly a man defending received orders.

The discussion was interrupted by the squealing arrival of a small camouflaged truck outside. I could see through the doorway its canvas-flap sides. It was the sort of vehicle in which Lady Julia had come from the west the night we had first met her. Out of the vehicle stepped yet another rangy Eritrean officer. You could tell him not by any insignia but by his long trousers and his hard-bitten, mid-thirties look. He carried a sketch pad in his hand and, yes, it had to be Henry's, a guess which was instantly verified, since the officer held the door open and Henry himself got down from the vehicle. His Scandinavian features came through pinkly under his tan. Whatever had happened, we stood to hear a good rant from him.

From the back of the truck jumped two armed soldiers, very

young, with that peculiar unmarred glitter you saw in the eyes of Eritrea's child-military.

The officer ushered Henry first down the bunker steps but then pushed ahead to knock soundlessly on the door jamb. He entered, making space for Henry to pass into the middle of the room. The two young soldiers waited outside on the stairs.

The Henry I now saw had a faint, nauseated smile on his face.

"You're not under arrest, are you?" I asked him.

"Don't be fucking stupid," he said tightly.

The officer had taken the sketchbook to the commandant. It lay open at a panoramic charcoal which was apparently Henry's work. A Tigrinyan discussion went on for some time—perhaps no more than twenty seconds, but it seemed too long to me. I began to feel that the Eritreans were turning mean-minded, that the bureaucrats had suddenly developed their occupational disease, the one which raged everywhere else in the world but from which, until today, the highland rebels had seemed free. I watched them now pawing over Henry's inane sketch as if it had significance.

"What's the trouble?" I asked, loudly enough to bring a silence. I'd hoped that by now Henry would have been profaning and— to use the American idiom—*kicking ass*. But he remained standing with that half-smile of sickly anger and said nothing at all.

My outcry caused Moka to join the conference at the commandant's desk. The commandant pointed out certain aspects of the picture to him. I was about to go and join them, a critic on equal terms, when Moka picked the sketchbook out of the commandant's hands and brought it to me.

Moka said pleadingly, "It is a very wide drawing. It is very . . ."

"Panoramic?" Henry suddenly suggested.

Moka gave a small affirmative gurgle in his throat. "We don't let people take photographs from such angles. The Ethiopians wait for such pictures, panoramas, to appear in magazines."

Then, without any of his normal apology, he tore the sketch out and gave it back to the commandant. All the while, Henry looked him in the eye but said nothing. I could all at once imagine the three of them—the officer, the commandant, Moka—as functionaries in a future tyrannous state. There was now an increased redolence of high-handed bureaucracy. I was tired enough to resent it, to add it to the denial of access to Major Fida, and so to make an ardent demonstration.

"I hope you remember," I told them, "I'll be writing for *The Times*. They'll be only too willing to hear about this sort of bullying." Indeed they would. It would balance their picture.

Moka held his hand up as if asking me not to crowd in on him with threats of international chagrin and so on. He spoke briefly to the commandant and then brought the sketch pad back to Henry.

"You keep it, Moka, you little asshole," Henry said in his tight, quiet voice.

"I'm sorry, Mr. Henry," said Moka. But it was without any of that ceremoniousness that normally marked him. When Henry refused to move, Moka slotted the sketch pad in under the American's arm, where tension and perhaps sweat caused it to stick.

Then Moka turned to me. "Darcy," he said familiarly, the old Moka again. "Major Fida is farther south now. Perhaps we will meet him. I cannot make promises about it. But cannot you see from this valley that we do not devour our prisoners?"

I was unhappy and disenchanted. I had perhaps the proprietary idea that *my* rebels had let me down. Outside, as we skirted the edge of the valley back toward the bunker of Askulu the politician, tripping on the sharp-edged, burning stones, Henry turned to me. He had on his face the same pained, stiff smile he'd worn inside, a smile like that of someone who has had cosmetic surgery and does not have the flesh left to grin broadly.

"Listen, Darcy, it isn't your affair. I can make my own statements to the sons-of-bitches. Understand?"

"I could understand better if I could also understand what in the bloody hell you're doing here. All I know is you break all the rules and you're still not enjoying yourself."

"I expected to hang together on this trip and . . . behold . . . I've come unstuck. The unpredictability of the human beast, what?" He uttered the last sentence in parody of the Englishwoman. "I don't even have a proper job description. I leave the exactly defined projects to people like Lady Julia. God, what a fierce old tart!"

I said, "Do you like any of us at all?"

"I like you fine," he said. "It's just that I don't think your little civil liberties act in there did anyone any good. I mean, these guys are playing for keeps. I respect them for that."

"Then why bother breaking their rules?"

"Why not? I think they're fucking doomed. You know what I think? They're brave to the point of folly and they're clever to the point of being dumb. No one, absolutely no one, from Washington to Moscow, wants them to succeed. No one. If the Americans wanted them to, these hills would bristle with Stinger missiles. God's even taken the rains away from them, for Christ's sake. Even he thinks they're wrong-headed. The sin of pride, Darcy, the sin of being sharp when no one wants them to be. Their presumption, Darcy, that organization can save them. *That . . . that* won't easily be forgiven."

I was surprised to find this outburst made me feel very partisan in spite of my recent disappointments, raised the temperature of the debate.

"The world doesn't want to lose this Red Sea coast to them, that's all," I said. "But the world will bloody well have to. *They* won't give up."

Henry sounded very calm. "After fifteen years here, I know what will be allowed to happen and what won't. This whole Eritrean operation smells of *what won't.*"

Moka had caught up with us by now. I didn't like the sound of his chest—things were pooling there which had no place. Henry and I walked on in silence and in mutual rancor.

The two of us didn't speak again until we got back to our hut. We lay on the clay benches. The sun breathed in the window and the joyous emerald lizards yipped and barked from the wall. Moka went down to a field kitchen dug in halfway down the slope. A young EPLF goatherd took his company's flock up the shaley hillside—I could see him from my bed, how comfortably he moved in his heavy military boots. I could hear Henry gasping for air as he lay on his inflatable mattress. I said idly that outside he'd mentioned "job description." I said I hadn't known what he'd meant.

"Well," he murmured, "*I* thought of it as a job description when they first talked to me. I mean, I thought it was serious business. Then I find we're sharing a truck with that French kid and with a goddam geriatric feminist! I think they could have given us a truck to ourselves."

"Us?"

"Us. Maybe they think the girls will give us protective coloring."

I considered this awhile. "You're saying that we're going somewhere together? Somewhere more than the normal traps they take aid workers and the occasional journalist to?"

He said, "Don't play dumb, Darcy. We're both going to the big convoy bonfire. You on behalf of what's loosely called *the press*, me on behalf of what's called—with maybe an equal lack of accuracy —the aid organizations!"

I stared at the thatched ceiling, so studiously made. I'd expected the plans for the ambush would have been made with equal study. I tried not to grimace or show any anger. For as a casual traveling companion, Henry had his charms. I have to admit that one of them was that the more he showed the strain in the way he himself talked and acted, the more he made the rest of us feel better and braver journeyers. Also, both Lady Julia and I were so solemnly *taken* with the Eritreans that without his irreverence and whimsy we would have become bores.

But now that I knew he was yoked with me on this mission, I felt more alarmed. Tessfaha should have told me. When I met Tessfaha I'd complain savagely, etc., etc. I spent some seconds making myself promises of that nature.

Henry said, in an imitation of my accent, "You sound abso-bloody-lutely delighted about it, cobber."

I asked him who had invited him—I wondered if it was Tessfaha. But it was some of their aid people! Maybe Tessfaha had decided to let them into the plan, too, to achieve maximum coverage. Even so, I could not feel happy about this expedition, which had now been reconstituted in purpose and scope and more or less in front of my eyes.

"You may not believe it, Darcy," Henry told me, "but I'm very popular in the Gezira. I behave myself and I run down the Ethiopian bastards with a passion you can cut with a knife. I would joyfully, Darcy, I swear *joyfully*, eat the bastards' livers."

It didn't sound too promising.

"These aid people?" I asked. "Did they give you my name as well?"

"They mentioned there might be others. When I found out you were a journalist, I presumed from the start you were the other party to the excursion. I could tell Lady Julia wasn't. It wasn't what you'd call her primary area of interest!"

I took thought. I wanted to find an Eritrean official and harangue him. Across the hut, Henry fell asleep—I could tell by his breathing. In that solid heat, I was not so fortunate. The lizards on the wall yipped and caressed and celebrated their luminous green pigmentation. I felt solitary and neglected at the bottom of Africa's pit of isolation. Even in the worst of countries, in Poland say, I could attempt to call Stella or one of my London friends, even one of the Melbourne people, the old friends who thought that because of what happened with Bernadette I was something of a joke. Even in Mogadishu or Khartoum I could at least cheer myself up with the attempt to telephone companions in far places. Among the Eritreans, however, that glib therapy was not available.

Editor's Interjection:
Recruiting Fida

We are forced to interrupt Darcy's account to explain Fida's absence from She'b. There is a need, too, to clarify the arrangement achieved between Colonel Tessfaha, the Eritrean intelligence officer, and Major Fida, prisoner of war and ejected MIG pilot, and to see how Fida became involved in a course parallel to the one Darcy committed himself to.

Tessfaha's approach to both men was a little out of character for the Eritreans. In their quarter of a century or more of war against the Ethiopians, these rebels had never begged much of foreign powers. At one stage they were believed to have approached the Americans and indicated that as a people subject to bombing they would appreciate Stinger ground-to-air missiles. But if so, the Americans didn't oblige. Nor would the EPLF have shown much surprise at America's rebuff. Perhaps they were not willing to give enough in return.

In any case, it was a rare occasion when the Eritreans asked outside people for help, apart, of course, from the obvious mercies of grain and cheese and powdered milk.

Colonel Tessfaha must therefore have won some argument among the Eritrean military leadership—an argument which took account of and paid reverence to the Eritrean dogma of nonalignment—and on the basis of that successful appeal, been enabled to approach both foreigners, Major Fida and the Western journalist Timothy Darcy.

On the afternoon of his recruitment, Major Paulos Fida—according to his own taped account to Stella—sat listening to the BBC African news in his bunker in the She'b officers' camp. On a packing-case table in the middle of the bunker sat his bunker mate's, Captain Berezhani's, shortwave radio. Berezhani had been captured together with the radio at the great slaughter of Mersa Teklai, which had left, within the space of little more than twenty-four hours, the bare Red Sea plains of the Sahel strewn with the corpses of four thousand Ethiopian tankmen.

Fida thought it very civilized of the Eritreans to let Berezhani keep his radio. For they themselves were so short of them. In the mountains they had a workshop where shortwave radios captured from Ethiopian soldiers were repaired and then distributed throughout the Eritrean population. They ran a similar workshop near the first one, where they repaired watches, alarm clocks, and the large Russian wall clocks which ordinary Ethiopian soldiers lugged to the front with them as if such an item, the edges of the face glass often frosted and etched with scenes from Russian winters, were essential for the peasant conscript going into battle.

In any case the Eritreans, whose officers did not wear any badges of rank themselves or seem to the outsider to assume any privileges, let Berezhani keep his shortwave and his alarm clock because he was a company commander. Both possessions were great supports to him and his fellow prisoner, Major Paulos Fida, who, having ejected from his plane, had brought no possessions with him into captivity.

Captain Berezhani listened to the daily African news in English with all the pent-up hope of a gambler waiting for an unlikely number to come up. He was almost daily disappointed in his yearning for news of Ethiopian change, for BBC speculation that the Ethiopian prisoners of the Eritreans might be repatriated. For there was rarely a mention.

Every day the two prisoners, the broadly built Fida and lanky Berezhani, huddled over the ammunition-box table and listened to the calm voice of BBC African news speaking of government clinics shot up by guerrillas in Mozambique, of Zaire's deplorable economy, of half-reliable rumors of some terminal illness afflicting Colonel Gaddafi of Libya. The stooping intentness of Captain Berezhani, his almost pleading demeanor toward the shortwave radio, were those of a man who had lost faith in military postures.

It was during such an afternoon broadcast some months ago, well before Darcy's disappearance and Stella's investigatory visit—well before, in fact, Tessfaha made his approach to Darcy in London—that the Eritrean intelligence officer called unexpectedly at She'b for Fida. Tessfaha, entering the bunker of the two Ethiopian officers, was already wearing a padded jacket to prepare for the evening chill but, as was again customary among the rebels, he wore no badge of rank. As both Fida and Darcy described him, he had a moustache, a slow smile, and an extremely polite manner. He shook the hands of both Fida and Berezhani that afternoon, for he had debriefed each of them after their capture.

For a while the three of them discussed the African news of the day, whether Gaddafi of Libya had gone pathological, for example, though of course Berezhani would have preferred to talk of things closer to his own concerns. They discussed the book Major Fida was reading, a volume of Henry Kissinger's memoirs loaned to him by the political officer in She'b camp.

Tessfaha all at once told him to bring the book with him. "Where?" asked Fida. "You are going on a journey with me," said Tessfaha. "Bring your cloak and your blanket and water thermos. We'll leave at one in the morning."

"My friend Captain Berezhani also?" asked Major Fida.

"You alone," said Tessfaha.

Suspecting that Tessfaha might have some novel purpose in mind, though he couldn't guess what, Fida reminded him that while the rebels were not bound by the Geneva Convention, they had chosen until now to observe it. It was wise policy and would give the Eritreans great moral standing on the day the Ethiopian prisoners were at last repatriated.

Tessfaha raised his hand in a wry, dismissive way. "Of course, of course," he said.

The Eritrean then sat with the two of them during a radio reading of a novel by the English writer Melvyn Bragg. Eritrean soldiers all along the front line would be trying to listen on their unit shortwaves, to figure out the usages and grunt in triumph whenever they heard a word they already knew. An army berserkly devoted to learning foreign languages and mathematics! Perhaps, Fida thought, the Eritreans were winning because there was a lower level of boredom in their front trenches than in the Ethiopian ones.

After ten minutes Tessfaha looked at his watch, rose with apparent regret, nodded gracefully but without saying anything, not wanting to interrupt their enjoyment of the radio, and loped out of the bunker, allowing himself to lean a little against the dry stone wall of the entryway in what Fida took to be partially faked fatigue.

✶ ✶ ✶

In the middle of the night, Colonel Tessfaha woke him in his mother language, Amharic, the tongue of Ethiopia's dominating tribe. Tessfaha's Toyota and its driver were waiting outside under a drench of moonlight.

Once they had climbed aboard, the truck stopped for no one. High officers in the Eritrean People's Liberation Front army frequently halted on the road to pick up other travelers—private soldiers, village militiamen, nomad women and their children. This was, Fida knew, deliberate policy, a studied denial of Amharic arrogance, of the caste system of the enemy. But this truck was under orders to dash through knots of waving Eritreans who rose from the undergrowth or out of holes in the ground or from behind boulders. Everyone seemed heavily armed with the captured weapons of the Dergue.

When they have their way and their nationhood, Fida wondered, what would they do with this thirst for weaponry?

Major Fida spent the night journey studying the alignment of the mountains to one another and sorting out directions. After four o'clock, the morning star rose like a carbuncle. When the light came they kept going, however. They kept going, too, when the light turned brazen. Fida knew what an easy target a vehicle traveling in the open presented to a MIG pilot, but he said nothing.

After half an hour of such naked travel, the driver veered hectically off the road and into the shade of thorn and oak and eucalyptus trees. He must have been good, an old soldier, a man with his senses arrayed. For an instant later two jets came searching at great speed down the valley. Squinting out from beneath the metal framework of the truck's window, Fida watched them go with great curiosity. That used to be me, he thought. Watching them circle toward the east, he thought, They'll be debriefed by lunchtime and have the rest of the day to spend in idleness.

The two planes banked south and were gone in seconds. Tessfaha tapped the driver's shoulder. They were to roll out again into the morning.

For the next hour Major Fida, who did not wish to be hit by cannon fire or cluster bombs from home, found it necessary to match Colonel Tessfaha's composure. But then he began to detect, through the opened window of the truck, the chemical smell of napalm. (Though he claims never to have dropped napalm himself, he says he once visited a burned-out Somali village where that unmistakable redolence prevailed.)

From behind a boulder along the road three village militiamen in their white jellabas, dyed jackets, and turbans rose. Behind and above the road stretched a natural platform, terraced, dotted now with burned and uprooted thorn bushes and shade trees. There were seared uprights, too, of what had been brush houses, and a number of unroofed, tumbled, napalm-oily drystone walls.

The truck braked and one of the militiamen leaned in the window. He spoke quietly in Tigrean, a language with which since his imprisonment Major Fida had achieved a little familiarity. The name of the village, said the militiaman, was Moshkub. Three MIGs had dropped napalm and fragmentation bombs on it the afternoon before. There had been deaths. The surgeon from the regional hospital at Zara had not arrived until two o'clock that morning. He had been operating ever since in the mosque.

The militiaman advised them to get the truck under cover. He waited till they had done this, till it was tucked in among oaks and eucalypts. The other two peasant militiamen returned to the cover of the boulders, but as Tessfaha and Fida dismounted, the third man strode off across the middle of the scorched place, leading them. They followed, walking gingerly. The ground seemed full of black shapes into which one did not closely inquire. The earth had been fused to an evil glaze.

Even beyond, among the trees and brush shelters which had not been burned, boughs had been stripped and lopped and roofs and walls torn away to show the rudiments of the refugee life—a plastic cup or bucket, a crumpled quilt with blood on it. This part of the village was built entirely of boughs and therefore was its own camouflage. The village militiaman led them to the largest of these shelters. From within could be heard the piercing weeping of a child.

This place, the militiaman explained in Tigrean, was the village mosque, built to hold a hundred worshipers at a time. It lacked a minaret, he told them in his limpid tongue, since that would attract bombers. What had attracted the bombers yesterday was ill fortune. A hygiene class had been in progress in the wadi just below them, and the pilots had seen the women running for shelter in their bright-dyed clothes.

Today, however, before dawn, all the women and children and the aged had been moved up the mountainside and into caves. In the village there were left only a few members of the assembly, the village militia, the surgeon from Zara, the village barefoot doctor, and her two young health workers, together with those who were too damaged to be moved and the dead, whom he and his colleagues had already buried.

Tessfaha said to Fida, "Do you wish to look inside?" His tone allowed for the possibility that, of course, Fida would not wish to, and there was no question of forcing him.

They had to crouch to enter the mosque's low door. They did not bother to take their shoes off. Neither piety nor the desire for a sterile operating theater seemed relevant. The smell of disinfectant and ether dominated here over the napalm stench from outside. Perhaps it is for that reason, Fida thought, that I was willing to come in.

By the near wall a surgeon and his assistant, both masked and wearing modern green surgical gear, were operating on the shaven head of a naked girl child of about ten years. Deeper in the shadow of the bush mosque, Fida could see the barefoot doctor in her revolutionary fatigues, a woman in her early thirties, lifting burnt flesh from the back of the complaining child. Two young health workers, neither of them more than twenty, each dressed in the traditional manner, the boy like the militiamen, the girl in unrepentant emerald, held the child down by its unburned shoulders and ankles. On their restraining hands they wore surgical gloves.

There was a woman, the militiaman told them, whose delivery had been brought on by the bombing. They had helped her up the hillside before the contractions became too bad, and she had given birth on a stone before dawn to a boy. The village militiaman laughed quietly. The mother was probably a kinswoman of his.

Fida made a frank survey of the mosque. From cleats in the roof supports, surgical drips hung and fed into the arms of half a dozen burned children, into three thin women who, half-naked and part-swaddled in bloody gauze, snored off their anesthetics and their shock. Near the operating table, an aged woman with bandaged chest and shoulders lay, grayly snuffling.

"This is my aunt," said the militiaman. She had shell fragments in her chest, he said. "She gave birth to eleven children, but now the surgeon from Zara says she will not live the day."

Fida watched Tessfaha walk among the cots but desisted from walking with him. At the far end of the mosque, where in grander structures the pulpit might be, the Eritrean turned and strolled back toward the major.

The major called on his Amharic pride. The tears which come from shock were close, and he thought that to shed them would be inappropriate both to the damage he saw before him and to his curious status as a traveling p.o.w.

"I never saw napalm loaded aboard or dropped by any squadron with which I served," he murmured, so that only Tessfaha could hear.

"Ai!" said Tessfaha. He raised his hand palm upward, slowly, and gestured toward the interior of the mosque. "You do not think, though, that this is a little of our propaganda, surely, do you?"

"Of course not," said the major.

"We should go and have some tea," said Tessfaha, not turning to look at the wounded again.

He led Fida up a defile. The earth grew steep and the village changed from bough shelters to bunkers. A typical flat-roofed, dry stone hut, half dug into the mountain, revealed itself. It could have been the place farther south which he and Captain Berezhani shared. They entered it. The militiaman was already there, his rifle still over his shoulder. He had covered a stone platform with a cloth and placed on it a thermos of sweet tea and a plate of unleavened wheat bread.

"Breakfast," sighed Tessfaha.

Fida wanted no breakfast but ate out of his officer corps pride. These old habits of arrogance, which he did not know he still retained, were handy tools now in this valley of tears and damage.

After eating, the Eritrean colonel yawned and stretched himself out on the clay platform.

"Let us take the rest of our sleep, major," he suggested.

Perhaps he wanted Fida to say, "But won't they be back?" As surely as *they* had seen those two MIGs this morning, anyone who stayed here would see the MIGs return. The surgeon from Zara was, of course, hoping that it would not be today, so that he could move out the less serious cases from the mosque to the caves tonight. Fida shared that hope, too. Tessfaha may have wanted a sign of fear from this pilot who claimed never to have flown with napalm, never to have released it, may have sought a suggestion from Fida that they might find safer places to sleep further up the hillside. But Fida was determined not to offer one.

* * *

In the sweats of early afternoon, Fida woke to the expected scream of MIGs. He rolled straight from a usual dream of Addis off the clay platform on which he was sleeping and onto the ground. Already on his knees, he stopped himself dropping flat to the floor. For across the bunker Tessfaha stood in the doorway, squinting out at the afternoon's activities. He turned and shouted to Fida. "They've sent four this time." At the end of its great crackling descent, ripping the air as it fell, a fragmentation bomb hit the far hillside. Fida fell on his face, Tessfaha threw himself against the inner wall. There was a jolt, then a vacuum. All the air in the pores of his lungs was sucked forth, returning only just in time to prevent him from choking.

As the atmosphere grew normal again, Fida heard anti-aircraft fire among the hills. The Eritreans had moved their light flak guns into place overnight, though the Ethiopian briefing officers would not have warned the pilots of this, were not permitted to let the pilots know that such guns had been captured in quantity and deployed by the mere banditti of Eritrea.

Colonel Tessfaha and Major Fida now seemed in the one instant consumed by the same curiosity. They both rose and ran to the deep-set entrance of the bunker. They stared as the second MIG unleashed a string of cluster bombs at the already burned earth from which yesterday's victims had been taken. What sort of pilot was this man? Fida wondered. Was he a fool, or was he practicing euthanasia, seeking to end the sufferings of the humanoid shapes he detected among the burned sector? Misreading burned and tumbled uprights as men and women.

The aircraft banked to avoid the end of the ravine in which Fida and Tessfaha had been sleeping and was struck in one wing by one of the anti-aircraft shells the rebels were firing. The jet began to pitch upside down. But at the last moment of possible vertical ejection, the pilot pressed his button and flew barely skyward into that same seamless sky which had received Fida months before. Fida was, of course, riveted by the sight of the aviator in his seat tumbling through one of the sky's lower quadrants, by the blossom of silk, by the seat in descent, the pilot immobile, his hands clasping either elbow rest, sedate beneath his lovely canopy as a Coptic metropolitan on his throne.

Below him the third plane had now begun its run at a time when the anti-aircraft crews in the hills around had been disordered by their sudden success with the second. Fida turned away from watching the descent of the parachute to see this new attacker land a canister of napalm exactly into the laneway outside the mosque. The outer wave of bursting heat felled Tessfaha and Fida, pitching the Eritrean in a tangle of limbs on top of the Amhara.

The chemical stench and the shock wave kept them locked together on the floor, and they would both later consider this fortunate, since the fourth plane's cluster bombs came down just across their narrow ravine. It was largely geology which this bomber had assaulted, but demi-boulders and discs of steel bounced across the ravine, thunking against the dry stone walls of the bunker, clattering on the roof. As Fida and Tessfaha lay clasping their ears, clouds of dust swept in the windows and doors and settled on their shoulders, and vicious little blades of stone whizzed in though the windows, one of them hitting Fida on the buttocks as stingingly as any fragment of shrapnel.

Then the raid was finished. Into the purely industrial redolence of napalm had crept the odor of human sacrifice, that appalling and obscene savor. Tessfaha and Fida made their way in clouds of dust out into the ravine. Fida was astounded by the uncertainty of purpose in Tessfaha's movements, as if he were simply another panicky bystander on the edge of the conflagration. There was a black column of smoke from the crashed MIG beyond the end of the defile, and a parallel one from the blazing mosque and its surrounding brush huts. Fida remembers that Tessfaha said, "Ai! We have lost the surgeon from Zara."

Fida remembered the surgeon from the brush mosque. Could he really have been consumed? Yet how could he not have been?

In the Eritrean scheme, surgeons were quite irreplaceable.

Fida could see the militiamen futilely circling the blazing village at whose core the mosque had by now been consumed. From the hill behind Tessfaha and Fida came contradictory noises, the wailing of children and the cheers of gunners.

Later in the afternoon, Tessfaha himself went down to the smoking environs of the mosque, but he did not insist that Fida come with him. The colonel's behavior remained very correct, therefore, both in terms of international law and of the obsessive etiquette the Eritreans seemed to practice. This politeness rose from the Eritreans' historic function as a conduit of trade between the Red Sea and the upper Nile. The line of major Eritrean cities presently held by the Ethiopian army ran east to west, demarking this ancient line of commerce. Massawa, Asmara,

Agordat, Keren, Tessenai, Barentu. Trade maketh manners, Fida believed.

Tessfaha returned to the bunker at dusk. He seemed reflective, and his clothes reeked of napalm. The militiaman with the limpid Tigrean voice brought them more tea and the same unleavened bread they had had at dawn. Pensively slurping his tea, Tessfaha remarked, "They tell me the pilot is dead."

Fida wondered what that meant but did not want to discuss pilots or planes. It was a difficult subject in this reeking air.

"I think we will spend the night beyond Moshkub," Tessfaha suggested.

"Will I see the pilot?" Fida asked him.

"If you wish," said Tessfaha.

The terrible, assertively industrial smell pursued them all the way up the defile and into the mountains beyond. They reached a mountaintop where young gunners lolled in cloaks and shorts and British-style gaiters. Beyond the summit a long valley stretched away obliquely, full of blue light. Along its slopes Fida saw chattering and chirruping squads of Eritrean gunners, men and women. The girl artillerists chuckled liquidly through their white teeth. Descending to the bottom of the valley, leaping from one unsteady platform to another, Tessfaha and Fida joined them around a large bonfire. The air was celebratory, and the gunners were passing round a powdered-milk can full of the opaque liquor called *sewa*. Half-embarrassed, an Eritrean girl, full-breasted within her khaki shirt, gave the can to Fida, and as he drank he saw a few of the other young rebels stealing glimpses at him. Yet no one uttered accusations.

A certain 56-millimeter crew had been credited with destroying the MIG. One by one they were forced to their feet and were tunefully applauded in something just short of full-fledged song. Then a soldier produced the *kirir* and began to sing a favorite martial Eritrean song.

> *Hail the heroes of Sahel,*
> *Who feast on song and dance*
> *After a hard day's fight,*
> *Carousing in the wilderness*
> *With Kalashin and Bren in the pledge's solemn*
> *celebration.*

Hail the Red Flowers and the Vanguards,
Being forged in the fire of Sahel!
Performing the chain of the sentinel's vigil,
To guard the front in the people's war.
In their hands our dignity is safe . . .

Tessfaha and Fida left the bonfire and moved farther down the valley. The Ethiopian pilot, Tessfaha said, had died during ejection. He must have struck his head on the canopy, yet when he landed he looked so perfectly composed the gunners had not been able to understand what had befallen him. There were no visible marks of injury.

At each bonfire they passed on their way to visit the Ethiopian pilot they were forced to drink *sewa*, and Fida drank it gratefully until his senses began to hum, to vibrate sweetly. It took a mile of libations before they reached the bunker where the pilot lay. When Tessfaha threw torchlight over the man's face, he did indeed look composed and uninjured. Fida noticed particularly his officer corps moustache, which was, in imitation of Mengistu the demagogue, neatly clipped. His name was stenciled on his jacket—Captain Kebede. When struck by the shell, he had not had the same height of sky Fida had—in similar circumstances—enjoyed. He had been unlucky in his body alignment as well. Yet only a slight dislodging of the forehead and a bruising under the eyes indicated it.

As Kebede would no doubt have wanted, Fida made small crosses with his right thumb on the man's eyelids, nostrils, lips, and on the lobes of his ears.

They urinated on the slope behind the bunker. In the midst of his flow, Tessfaha spoke in his normal reflective way. "Did you notice one of them attacked the garden at Moshkub? Turned it into two craters. Do the pilots know what they are doing?" The question had no venom to it. "Do their superiors tell them that if you bomb an acre of the sub-Sahara, you turn it into Sahara? You do the desert's own work and spread dust all the way to the Red Sea! Do they tell them that?"

Fida had his back half-turned to Tessfaha. "Of course no one ever talks like that. Briefings are not such philosophic affairs."

"I suppose not," said Tessfaha.

Tessfaha finished first and buttoned up. The Eritreans did not favor zippers, which they considered susceptible to dust and rust and other low comedies. "We have only one answer to this fire from the air.

Years back we entered Asmara airport and blew up more than thirty aircraft."

Fida had, of course, heard of that occasion but said nothing.

"We have been preparing for another such raid, but our agent in matters to do with the Asmara field has been arrested. I regret very much dragging you around from mountain to mountain; as you say, it is not according to the letter of the international convention. But we believe that we need a true Amhara, a supreme Ethiopian familiar with the premises, to take us there once more."

Fida, buttoning up, felt giddy. The mountains spun around his head as they must have by daylight for Captain Kebede in the instant of his ejection.

Tessfaha said, "We have never asked anything of Ethiopian prisoners except that they attend Eritrean history classes. This is larger, I confess. But consider what an economic blow it would be now. Not simply a military affair. Something with economic, political, *diplomatic* results. Replacement costs alone could bring Mengistu down, coud cause the Soviets and the Ethiopian generals to cry *'Enough!'* And, of course, you realize that none of your colleagues are likely to see their families until *'enough'* is cried. Another consideration perhaps."

Fida was both excited and drunkenly angry at the idea. He saw his fury vaporize above him in the mountain air, and he began to shiver. "I cannot do it to my country," he told Tessfaha, "and it can't be asked of me."

"We would intercept and seize a military supply column outside of Asmara. Then you could lead it into the perimeter for us. Only you know where everything *is* behind the security wall they erected after our last raid. Only you know where are the hangars, the fuel and bomb dumps, even the napalm."

"They were not using napalm when I was stationed there," Fida insisted.

Tessfaha considered him, seeming—worst of all—to believe him.

"Well," Tessfaha conceded, "let us forget napalm for the moment. You know where the Soviet military men are billeted. Imagine the value to us of holding a Russian officer! The Soviets would need then to negotiate with us directly!"

And so that most important debate of Major Fida's life, one he could not even have imagined a year before, continued on the slope outside the bunker where Captain Kebede lay.

At last Tessfaha caressed Fida's shoulders and began to lead him back toward the campfires and the liquor and the girl soldiers with gleaming mouths and white cloaks. As they walked, the Eritrean said, "Forget everything for the moment. But I know napalm appalls you. The Sahara appalls you. They are a blot on your honor."

Fida yearned to deny it. The noise of the young carousers, however, consumed him before he could frame words.

The Groves of Jani

I knew that the Eritrean front line was divided into the Nacfa Front at the eastern end, the Hallal Front at the western. At Himbol and She'b we were far from the Hallal, and it was toward Jani, behind the Hallal, that Masihi had fled—or at least *fleeing* was how I irrationally saw it.

We who had experienced together the descent of the locusts and who had, through the drift of events, taken on the stature of attendants at the reunion of father and daughter, now began to suffer even more intense discomforts. Leaving the p.o.w. camp in She'b, still unreconciled—at least in my case—to all that happened there, we spent two nights lurching toward Jani, where Masihi was rumored to be. In the high, gritty hills beyond Himbol we bogged in sand too many times. In the jungle swamp of Zara we stuck in the mud. It seemed as dawn neared that we would have to abandon the truck, hide for the day, wait until some heavier machinery arrived to haul it loose. I saw Henry apply his shoulder to the back wall of the vehicle, strain against it when Moka and Tecleh, the driver, gave the order, and then stagger off into the bush. Christine was still stricken as well. Conversation was rudimentary and likely to be broken off halfway through short sentences.

In jungly Zara we slept on a hospital verandah, surrounded by fever patients wrapped in their cloaks. Wheezing but undefeated, Moka shuffled around like a duty nurse, checking our mute faces. As he swung his torch, I saw mosquitoes in a mist around Lady Julia.

"A fucking Sheraton of mosquitoes," growled Henry as we suffered Zara's day, waiting for another night. Yet he took time to sketch some of the patients, their comatose faces as they slept off their malaria. I liked the idea that he hadn't been chastened into giving up his sketching.

As we arrived in Jani at first light the next day, Christine forgot her nausea and peered through the red film of dust on the truck window as if she expected to spot her father's camera crew at work under the shade trees. Jani looked sublime, a meeting of rivers among enormous granite peaks. Unlike the river at Himbol, water ran here, broad slow strands among boulders.

But the climate was savage. Lady Julia had a watch which told the temperature and the humidity. She pointed out to me what it said. Ninety-eight degrees, it read, and ninety-three percent. Lady Julia's fair skin had taken on a stewed look here at the bottom of Jani's deep valley.

I would have been happy to see Masihi, too. But all I could see in the undergrowth were peasant wives hiding their faces—their noses, too, with the gilded marriage bands in them—behind brilliant shawls. Young goatherds watered their goats in the river, but they did it with the look of people who would soon take shelter. On the edges of the scrub, a few farmers were persuading their camels in under the cover of trees.

When the truck could not go any farther, we covered it with a tarpaulin and piny branches from the river oaks just as we had with our earlier vehicle outside She'b, the green one with *Deutsche Arbeiter Bund* on its side. I was cowed by the energy with which Moka worked at this—the rest of us were sapped and broken. Lady Julia helped Christine up to a bunker on the banks of the stream. It looked exposed to me, and I was concerned for them. Yet the place was entirely covered with thorn bushes, botany's chief gift to the Eritrean cause. Locusts had not been here to strip the foliage.

Christine's arms hung limp as she walked in Julia's embrace. The price of being Masihi's daughter, I thought, my imagination broiling away.

"EPLF tetracycline for your stomach," Moka had called after her, echoing Askulu in She'b. "We shall get you some here!"

He had great confidence that a barefoot doctor in the Eritrean wilderness was worth two or three physicians anywhere else.

At last, after going away to make inquiries, he led Henry and me into the bunker's second room. Through an open door into the back of the hut we could hear Christine still retching. Still observing Henry's demand that he shouldn't tote other people's gear, Moka watched us lay our packs on the clay benches where we were meant to sleep. A box of Soviet grenades sat at the base of my bench. I wondered how volatile they might be in this inflamed air.

Moka said, "This time they say Masihi is sleeping in the bunker of the Eritrean food official across the river." But even he seemed to be getting skeptical about reports of Masihi.

"You meaning to sleep?" Henry asked me.

I said no. I was very angry with Masihi, the delinquent father whose abandoned child was groaning in the next room. "We might as well go and find the bastard," I said, "and be done with it!"

"I might join you," Henry said. "No son-of-a-bitch can sleep in this place. What a fucking sex aid! A box of grenades!"

Henry and I wanted to go across the river at once, and Moka was willing to lead us. Traversing the river boulders we could see among the trees on the far shore a birdlike flash of green or gold in the undergrowth where peasant wives were socializing. Village militiamen sat by camels and nursed their Kalashnikovs in the shade and laughed with each other. They had such leisure only every so many months, on the recurrent date that the Eritrean Relief gave out the food ration to their particular village.

But from the gods' eye of the MIGs, there would have been nothing to see now except a wide valley in which the sun reverberated and, of course, three fools crossing the riverbed.

Moka filled the time telling us the granite peak above us was dedicated to the Prophet. During Mohammed's exile from Arabia, the Prophet's horse had jumped from this mountain, totally bypassing Jani, landing among the tangle of mountains beyond, toward the Hallal Front.

"The fucking horse knew what it was doing," Henry said.

We passed over the last river boulders into the cover of river oaks. I saw at the heart of the grove orderly mounds of aid bags, of sorghum, rice, powdered milk, beans. Moka led us down the avenues of these squared-off stockpiles. Each bag boasted discreetly of the generosity of this or that democracy.

The bunker of the Eritrean official who minded the food dump was dug profoundly into the ground. We entered it down earth stairs. The heat had pooled unspeakably in there. I could see two figures: a prone one on a bench, completely encased in a cloak, who might have been Masihi, and at the desk an Eritrean, a ledger covered with Tigrinyan script opened in front of him. Light came in through a breezeway between the props of the walls and the log roof. It struck the official in the face as he rose to meet us.

"*Salaam,*" he murmured to Moka, and the two of them exchanged as much formal handshaking as they could manage in the heat. The official seemed exhausted from issuing food all night—his eyes kept rolling up; the whole business of focus evaded him. In the deeper reaches of the bunker I saw a small cache of bags, stacked neatly—his own ration of food. It was a scanty reward for working here, in this pit of treacly air.

The man kept shaking his head in answer to Moka.

"Oh God!" said Henry. "The son-of-a-bitch ain't here either!"

At last Moka admitted us to the conversation.

"This is not Masihi," he said, pointing to the shrouded figure who did not move. "Masihi was here but is gone—into the mountains near the Hallal Front to escape the heat."

"Oh shit!" Henry said.

Moka, sheepish, led us back to our hut by a quicker route, over the river, along the boulder-strewn shoulder of granite, beneath the peak sacred to the Prophet's nag. Great marbles of stone had been tilted against each other here, and wherever they made a cave or anything as minor as a niche, children were sitting, chanting lessons with an energy my airless brain couldn't even aspire to.

"Who can write the *t*?" I heard a teacher cry. And then, "Is he right? Is he right?"

"A regional school," said Moka, almost apologetically. "They live here among the rocks and they learn here."

In shadows cast by two tilted megaliths lay a shaven-headed boy, wrapped in his blue cloak but with his face showing. He seemed comatose. Moka deftly bent, barely breaking stride, and raised the boy's eyelid.

"Malaria," he told us.

Above our heads, in thorn bushes among the boulders, hung

small nests of blanket and wooden lath. Here the students slept. "It is a boarding school," Moka couldn't stop himself explaining, even though he knew Henry would mysteriously curse the news.

We found Lady Julia sitting on a stone bench just inside the door of our billet. She stood up when she saw us and showed no particular tiredness.

"I could tell he wouldn't be here," she said when we broke the news.

"How could you tell that?" I asked her.

"An instinct. I mean, you don't go missing for fourteen years and then let yourself be found too easily."

"But he doesn't know Christine's coming for him."

"Maybe he's got agents," said Lady Julia, closing her eyes.

She was working in a notebook and had already checked what hour the patients would begin to attend clinic in the groves of Jani—4:30 that afternoon. Her mind was on that, and on her survey of the trauma which African tradition imposed on women.

Moka started to wheeze. "I know the exact village Masihi has gone to. It is high up and the air is dry. The Ethiopians burned it during the Silent Offensive, but it has been ours since then."

Lady Julia asked, "Could we go there then after clinic hours? This heat is not very helpful to Christine."

"Before dawn tomorrow," said Moka. It seemed to be a message we were hearing all the time these days.

"Why not dusk today?" asked Henry, sinking onto his bench, lolling sideways without bothering to take his boots off.

"Before dawn," Moka pleaded, wary of an outburst from Henry. "Otherwise you cannot see anything of Jani at night."

Henry did not react. He may already have been asleep.

But I did not sleep. My back burned beneath me on the air mattress. The most beautiful African wasps, gold and black, full of subtle poison, carried on their trade between the bunker window and their nest high in the wall. I began to get near-hallucinations of the new child's face, the one obviously Bernadette's and just as obviously not mine. I had laid eyes on this baby just once, but that sighting came potently back to me now. She was *my* abandoned daughter, *my* Christine. Whose name I didn't know.

With a feverish exactness I saw Bernadette driving the child, in the paintless Holden I had once seen them in, down tropic roads outside the city of Darwin, past the crocodile plantation. The Berrima prison lay down that road. So what did this vision of mine mean, with its reptiles and prisons, car, and mother and child?

It seemed to me in some strange way, not borne out by the statistics, that the baby's destiny was more pitiable than that of the malaria sufferer in the blue cloak we'd seen in the area of boulders earlier in the morning.

By mid-afternoon I was in a level state of sleeplessness and wondered if I, too, had malaria. I felt my brain as a hot wad pressing down on my eyes. Late in the day I was childishly pleased to trail along behind Lady Julia, who was more or less the only one of our party left standing and coherent. She'd tell me what moves to make, I thought. With her as an example, almost connected to her by a filament of need like a child on a restraining strap, I attended the afternoon clinic.

On the earthen floor of the mud brick infirmary Julia led me to, we found a peasant woman on a litter. Various males of her clan would carry her to the regional hospital at Zara at dusk. "But nothing stays in her stomach," said the barefoot doctor. "Everything flows. She is a reed."

I yearned to be as admirable as Lady Julia, dropping so competently on one knee and speaking to the woman in Arabic. The woman was beyond replies, though, and offered just one birdlike consonant back, a barely palpable, fluting sound. Lady Julia's hand didn't stray in the direction of stroking the woman's brow. She was very functional, very fact-finding. She probably knew that that was the only real compassion available in a place like Jani, beneath Allah's savage knuckle of granite.

At dusk we went outside and, for some reason I didn't have the strength to argue with, knelt on the ground like acolytes beside the barefoot doctor who had seated herself on the clinic's one folding camp chair. Lady Julia made notes about the ill who presented themselves. The line of forty or fifty patients squatted on the ground—the same kind of people Moka and I had seen earlier: wives with gilt bangles in their nostrils, militiamen nursing their assault rifles, camel owners with wands in their hands, all hunkered down in a gracious, curving line across the grove. From the record the barefoot doctor kept in an open account book on her lap, Lady Julia copied down the names, ages, symptoms, and dosages of each patient. I found myself occasionally and confusedly copying the same figures into my own notebook.

"Kidija Adam," I wrote, "thirty-five years, malarial fever with cold, 50 milliliters chloroquine syrup . . ." Later I would see these details in my notebook and barely remember having put them there. I would have liked to pitch forward and sleep, but I had this idea that the heat condemned me to go on being vertical. And if not the air, the string which connected me to Julia.

And so, trailing the movements of the unbeatable Englishwoman and copying them, I found myself on the edge of darkness in a natural amphitheater across the river, in a circle of granite crowded with Eritrean men and women. This was some sort of graduation ceremony for the regional school, the event for whose sake Moka had insisted we remain in Jani this evening. We sat among the stones. I remember stray details. There was a speech from a member of the Central Committee, who wore traditional clothing, a white ankle-length gown, a blue jacket, a skullcap. People were called up to receive certificates as barefoot veterinarians, blacksmiths, motor mechanics. Dark-eyed women in vivid cloth and full of a glinting, antique beauty improbably received certificates as village account- ants or legal advisers. Their gliding movements were so strange, the lines of their faces so unexpected, that it gave me the delirious sense of being a traveler in the old way, of being an eighteenth- or nineteenth-century trekker, previous to empire, lost profoundly in Africa.

Lady Julia sat beside me and energetically applauded each grad- uate. On my other side sat a lean farmer, yet another village mili- tiaman out of the same genetic stable as the looked-for Colonel Tessfaha. The man cradled one of those snub-nosed rifles used for launching grenades. Its blunt barrel rose from the cloth around his shoulder and armpit. I believed myself safe between him and Lady Julia.

Now it was full dark and a bonfire surged in the middle of the amphitheater. From a four-sided enclosure of cloth, dancers and drummers appeared. I liked the contour of the song they sang. I laughed and clapped without quite knowing why. It had something to do with a small Eritrean child who broke from the audience, somersaulted among the dancers, and returned again to his graduate parents in the fringes of the crowd.

I was suddenly aware that nature, in Africa as in Fryer River, had its mercies. In some previous flood the river had carried sand up here into this bowl of rock. Beneath my hips its feel was luxurious. I slept. The laughter of Lady Julia and the patriots woke me fully only once, to the confusing sight of a comic scene enacted by two graduates and concerned with the grinding of coffee.

At the same time I was aware, too, for an instant of Moka, a little distance away, seated beside a perfect, small woman in jeans, a minute bureaucrat, an apparatchik with teeth whiter than the moon.

I felt at first a pulse of anger and then of pity. This was the woman, I understood at once, for whom Moka was delaying our journey to the cooler mountains, our pursuit of Masihi as well, until just before dawn.

When I woke properly I was on my side in sand which still kept the day's warmth. From behind my back I could hear a woman's voice speaking one of the Eritrean languages with that familiar cadence. It was a rich, full-lipped, sensual sound. For some time I didn't dare to turn around. All I knew was that close to me an Eritrean woman was in passionate voice.

After a lot of planning of the movement I was to make, I looked over my shoulder. The little bureaucrat with the dazzling teeth sat by Moka against a log in the now empty oval of stone. They were severely distant from each other. Moka's gaze was fixed abstractedly across the river, in the direction the Prophet's horse had fled in the seventh century. Now and then he'd punctuate the flurries of language from the girl with a languid "Ai!"

As I turned my back again and began to drowse, the little bureaucrat's Tigrinyan explanations ran strongly in my sleep. They were points of light in a drugged night, a film across the brain. They prevented me from the full-bodied coma of exhausted sleep and they pricked my fairly deprived flesh. Waking regularly, each time I would think that Moka and the little apparatchik must by now be in each other's arms. Somehow the gravid intonations of the girl demanded it. Yet whenever I gave in to the urge to check, they were still apart. Moka seemed dazed by the rising moon and by the girl's hypnotic chatter.

It was still hot and the mosquitoes had come up from the river, the lives and deaths of both emperors and peasants written in their snouts. One day, probably in a suburb where doctors don't often see the disease, I'd get a sudden fever. It would be the price of lying there uncovered in the sand, listening in on this gorgeous voice.

The next instant, it seemed, Moka was waking me. I sat up. The veteran's small vocal companion, who was probably an AK-47–toting veteran herself, was asleep now on the ground, five paces away, lying on a cloak, her head wrapped in a shawl. Moka said, half-embarrassed, "The wife of my friend. He is far away, beyond the lines, near Massawa."

"She likes to talk," I said.

"Ai!" Moka laughed toothily. "She likes to talk."

We left her sleeping. Across the river, under the trees, we could see lights jolting and camels and asses sending up their ancient complaints as bags of American sorghum, Australian rice, and Canadian wheat were strapped to their flanks.

"Some of those people can still reach home by dawn," said Moka. "If they start out now."

Masihi Surprised

The road that went up to the high village near the Hallal Front where Masihi, according to rumor, was sleeping had been till two years ago a camel track. Moka said that two captured Russian bull-dozers had been thrown into the effort to make space up these bare cliffsides so that trucks could pass. Though he showed a certain enthusiasm for the difference his brothers and sisters had made to this cliffside, he seemed wistful to me and may have felt wistful at leaving the perfect little speaker behind.

The coolness of the high plateau we were grinding up toward at last began to enter the truck. People sighed and smiled at each other wanly.

But in a defile at the top, Tecleh needed to brake. A series of logs had been thrown across the track. No one spoke as we sat still, the engine stuttering away, wondering what the logs meant. In an instant the road was full of men in white robes and blue jackets, men belted with ammunition and stick grenades and carrying assault rifles in their leisurely grasp. Moka wound down his window, and one of the armed men stuck his head into the vehicle and began explaining himself in that same indolent, hypnotic way that had marked Moka's small friend far below in Jani.

Moka seemed happy with the conversation and with the men. They were guarding the front, they said, against occasional sabotage from those old, bypassed Eritrean factions who did business with the Saudis and knew no righteousness. Moonlight fell on the tribal slashes on the faces of these militiamen. Lady Julia dismounted and began to speak to some of them in Arabic. She used a delay in the conversation to fetch the ghost-white Christine down from the front seat and take her off on a little stagger among the rocks and cactus.

In the first crisp, enormous light we rolled between the unroofed buildings of the promised cool village. Above the higher mountains some ten miles south, amid tattered cloud, the last flashes of a night artillery barrage on the Hallal Front could be seen. Wherever the shells struck down there, great columns of dust rose and walked across the sky.

The truck slotted itself in under some stunted pines. Moka led us off to yet another Eritrean hut/bunker outside which, into a terrace of beaten earth, the casings of 122-millimeter shells had been hammered mouth first. Their flanged bases, with numerals and Cyrillic script clearly legible on them, provided a seat for the traveler. This ironic use of whatever was thrown at them was absolutely typical of the Eritreans, yet Lady Julia and I had stopped exclaiming about it for fear of setting Henry off.

We sat down and savored the cool morning air. Christine kept her eyes closed and let the faint breeze rinse her face. No one dared mention Masihi. Moka did not even utter his name as he staggered off to make inquiries, to seek out the barefoot doctor or the official of the Department of Public Administration who might know where the Frenchman was.

While we waited, pot-bellied and shaven-headed children in dust-laden gowns straggled past us on their way to school in some cave. Their transience was just about palpable—you could taste it on the tongue, in this high, dry country, where a delay in rain or an upgrading of an Ethiopian offensive could cancel them. It was nearly beyond bearing to think of them learning their math in holes in the earth or behind the negligible walls of scrub shelters—7/8 > 3/4, True or False? Training in a pocket of dust for the computer age. *This is the goat of Osman* changed through their schooling to *This is Osman's goat*. Language for a future of commerce with the West, the hard and fast curriculum of the Eritreans! Even the children with the swollen and misshapen skulls, even those who could not credibly expect to see twenty, even those whom one delay of rain or one small enteric fever could be expected to do for, even they were made to sit in class.

We watched the two village teachers, each with his assault rifle and his belt of grenades, boys of eighteen or twenty, saunter along chattering.

It was cool, as everyone kept saying again and again.

Moka returned. He had a berserk grin scarcely under control. He may even have forgotten the divine little chatterer.

"He is here," he told us, looked away and smiled. "He is asleep." He began to laugh. "He cannot escape!"

I watched Christine stand up. There was no hint of expectation or fear on her face. She settled her body firmly on her feet. Moka led and we all followed across bare ground. It was sown with tarnished machine gun cartridges and with shell craters from the Silent Offensive, which can't have been too silent.

I'd only think afterward how curious it was, the way Lady Julia and Henry and myself felt entitled to trail along behind Christine now, to share in the intimacies and the dangers of the reunion.

Moka led us to a hut, half of which was of wattle panels plastered with mud, the other half of latticework. Since there were no mountainsides here to bury dwellings in, a whole range of alternative, plateau kinds of camouflage existed.

Through the latticework we saw two figures on the dirt floor, both of them entirely shrouded in those white cloaks which soldiers of the EPLF wore. Around the human shapes lay a number of notebooks neatly fastened up with elastic bands, and what even a layman could tell were video cameras, sound gear, video film cartridges, all zippered up in dusty but fashionable waterproof bags of their own.

There was a noise of snoring from one of the shapes. For some reason it caused Christine to turn to Lady Julia and smile delightedly.

Moka whispered, "I know Masihi. He will wish to be awakened."

Moka brushed through the burlap door curtain and into the crude verandah-room where the two sheeted figures lay. One of them roused at once, swatting the white cloak away from his face. But it wasn't Roland Malmédy the cameraman, I could see. It was his Eritrean assistant, a thin boy so exhausted still that his flesh did not seem brown but blue.

I saw Moka hold a whispered conversation with him and then,

instead of waking the second man, creeping back out to us. "It *is*," he whispered. "It is Masihi. It is your father, Miss Malmédy."

He seemed to acquire a certain authority by this brief visit to Christine. Now he returned to the remaining shrouded shape, bent down, and began jiggling the white cloak round about where the cameraman's face should have been. Staring unabashedly in through the lattice while the sleeper fought the cloth away from his face, I watched the emerging features. They seemed blurred by tiredness, by the upside-down business of filming a night war by day. The broad face growled. Perhaps still unaware of what it was doing, the body sat up. Its eyes stared without focus at the four European faces gazing in upon it, all of them utter strangers yet all of them seeming to be exercising rights of familiarity.

Masihi was wearing a brown sweat- and dust-stained shirt. He reached for a swath of orange cloth lying beside him on his blanket and, like a statement and a defence, began to wind it round his head until it was a turban.

"*Ciao,* Monsieur Masihi!" sang Moka.

"*Ciao,*" muttered Masihi, unreconciled. "What in the hell . . . ?"

"We have your daughter here," Moka told him.

"Daughter?" asked Masihi. The brown eyes opened enormously in the handsome face. His whites, too, were stained with malaria.

Only later would I reflect on the stunning impact of this particular awakening on Roland Malmédy. In a place like this, how safe—beyond ever having to think about it—he must have felt from the business and the intrusions of family. High on the Hallal Front, in a demi-village marked by the rubbish of war, lost children from another place could be depended on not to materialize.

The shock of Moka's announcement made him stand. He wore loose khaki trousers, his feet were bare. The standard pair of scuffed plastic sandals waited for him in the corner. All of us at the lattice expected him to reach for them. We would have reached for *our* shoes even under the attack of MIGs, because we knew how dangerous the earth of Africa was, how bestrewn with thorns and scalding stones—not a terrain for the unschooled heel.

Masihi, however, who in the past eleven years had learned to walk on this earth of scorpions, came forward through the open door. *"Poupi?"* he asked.

Christine stepped forward, drawn by the pet name and tripping on a stone. *"C'est moi,"* she said. The word and the voice, barely louder than the breeze, seemed to come direct from old French melodrama.

"Mama mia!" said Masihi. He considered his daughter with a crooked, apologetic smile. "It is you."

She grinned at the ground. "Oh yes," she said, and it sounded both a piteous and relentless sentiment.

"Oh God," said Masihi, his eyes darting. *"Excuse-moi, j'ai besoin de pisser. Ton père légendaire, Poupi, en fait il est comme tout le monde. Un instant!"*

And the man we'd all pined to see disappeared around the edge of the bunker, looking for a crater in which to relieve himself. Christine pursed her lips and stared after him. She did not believe his need was as pressing as that, and neither did I.

Just the same, we all seemed to realize at once that we were intruding on this remarkable reunion, that we could be the element which was making it ridiculous. We would have liked to have remained there and stared, but we understood that it would have been somehow improper.

Lady Julia murmured, "I should leave you to it, Christine. Be firm with him . . ." She walked away toward the hut Moka had pointed out as hers.

But I was determined not to be led off to the bunker Henry and I were assigned to share. I found myself suddenly declaring, swearing in a mumble that I, too, had a full bladder. I ducked behind the cameraman's dry stone shack. I wanted to make sure he did not escape or try to evade the girl.

Up to his knees in a crater, Masihi was pissing reflectively on earth that was all grit, goat droppings, cartridge cases. Hearing me, he looked sharply over his shoulder but showed no recognition. I didn't speak until he'd finished and had buttoned so slowly that you got the impression that his plea of nature was a mere delaying tactic.

He turned and nodded at me cursorily in a way which said, *What in the hell are you doing here when you have the whole of Eritrea to choose from?*

"You mightn't remember me," I said unnecessarily. "My name's Tim Darcy, and I met you at Stella Harries' place in Khartoum. You showed us footage of the famine and of the battle of Mersa Teklai."

"Oh yes," said Masihi, being polite and clearly not remembering me. "You didn't bring in any brandy, did you?"

"Sorry. The Sudanese aren't big on brandy."

"Oh, well. *Sewa*'s nice. I made my bed . . ."

He still had trouble working out why strangers were following him around this morning. He didn't know the power of his pale daughter to draw the rest of us in.

"Is that really my daughter?" he asked.

"Her passport indicates she is," I told him.

"Ah! I must have a look at her passport."

"It's back in Port Sudan, I'm sorry."

Masihi reflectively felt his stomach through the ragged brown cloth of his shirt. "But you saw it?" he asked.

I must have laughed at that, reprovingly, as if I suspected him of trying to avoid all claims of parenthood.

"Consider this!" he said. "I am aware of the cult of personality in the West. Who isn't? Would it be possible that some impressionable kid saw one of my films in one of the unfashionable places they're shown in Europe and *decided* to come and claim me as a father? Is that possible?"

I actually felt anger. He was wriggling to avoid what we'd all traveled so far to establish.

"You ought to accept it with grace. The girl's your daughter. Who'd have a motive to do the sort of thing you describe?"

After all, you're not Robert Redford, I wanted to tell him.

He laughed, but was still willing to argue. "Oh, motives are everywhere. Who would have thought anyone could have a motive to perish for such a plateau as this?"

I was merciless. "This is definitely your daughter," I told him with a smile.

He made a face. "How is Stella?"

"She's in England."

"Ah, England," said Masihi with a Gallic grin, as if an English return were forgivable in Stella's case. "That scrawny man? He is not my daughter's lover, is he?"

It was an extraordinary question, but of course he was still sorting us out.

"She doesn't have one." Though I did remember the story Henry claimed to have been told on the roof in Port Sudan. "Certainly not at the moment, anyhow."

He reflected and then let out his breath so that his shoulders collapsed. "So she's my daughter, that thin little girl?"

"Seems so."

"The accent's right, my friend Darcy. There's a family resemblance. She's like her mother. And like a grandmother of mine—a thin, miserable old bitch."

I could imagine Christine in those terms if she suffered a lifetime's thwarting. I began to laugh and he misinterpreted it.

"I know I must seem a comic person. I mean, it is hard to imagine that many French girls would forge a passport and an identity just to chase me to the Hallal Front and yell *Papa!*"

"It's a bit farfetched," I confessed.

Now he walked energetically toward me, studied my face and frowned. "I suppose I'll have to go and see little *Poupi*. But what in God's name will we talk about?" He laughed helplessly and musically, with the charm I remembered. "I feel ashamed, let me tell you. To be caught out here. There's a rumor they'll use nerve gas. And my child arrives at such a time, in such a place?" Under his turban, he raised one eyebrow. A music-hall Frenchman couldn't have done better. "I'm a little tired, I suppose. But I suppose I must see what I can do to renovate my fatherhood. You'll excuse me . . ."

He moved back in the direction of the place where Moka and the girl were waiting. Then, struck by a thought, he turned around to me again. "By the way, what sort of traveling companion is she?"

"Quiet," I told him. "Not a natural tourist. But she never complains. She has a generous streak, too." I was thinking of the Malinta cola she'd bought for the cripples and amputees in Port Sudan. "She's a strange kid, but she's not malicious."

"Strange?"

"Detached. And she never complains. That's strange in someone as young as that."

"Her mother was like that. Uncomplaining. But you couldn't tell whether it was courage or a certain dumbness." He devoted a few seconds' thought to his remote marriage.

"That Englishwoman," I said. "She and Christine seem to get on well. She trusts other women."

He laughed. "She's learned so much already then?" he rumbled. "Poor little *Poupi*. And please forgive me, but perhaps I *do* need some sort of briefing. Did she say why she came looking for me now of all times? It is, after all, springtime in Europe."

"Something happened to her," I said. "Nothing massive—not an accident or trouble with the police. Some emotional business. But I don't know what it is. A boyfriend maybe."

"Motherhood?" asked Masihi, arching his eyebrows.

"I just don't know, Roland."

He lowered his voice. "Her mother is a frightful woman. Maybe I made her so. I married her too young. It was my stupid idea as well. A sullen beauty, and I went for that then. I should have seen the signs. She loved modernist furniture, the stuff you can't sit in, as if she'd discovered it herself!"

The irony was, I thought, that Masihi had now found a nation without furniture.

"Don't you think it's a cruel business?" he asked. "Here am I, all at once again the father of the child, asking a stranger for hints."

"Well, you've been very busy," I conceded.

"That does not seem an excuse. Thank you, Mr. Darcy, for the guidance."

He finally left me standing by the crater. From the far side of the bunker I could hear Masihi's voice, falsely hearty, and then Moka's running away into laughter, and then Christine's level and relentless speech. I admit that I still felt a proprietary right in this reunion, but the bunker or hut or whatever it was blocked my view. "But I can use sound equipment," I heard Christine say. "Good, good," yelled Masihi with creaky jollity, warding off his strange child.

I began to move toward the guest bunker, to which Henry and Lady Julia had very decently gone earlier. Lady Julia was still sitting on its highest step, as if surveying the scenery, the continuing wafts of detonation and dust from the front.

I was going to speak to her about my fears for Christine, the almost certain disappointments of this reunion. But I heard a noise behind me and, looking over my shoulder, was astounded to see, as the cameraman gestured and no doubt raised his eyebrows beneath his turban, the girl laughing in a full-throated way I'd never seen in her before. She showed no sign of the illness which had taken all her attention for days past. The sight of her parent, this abashed and uneasy hero, had achieved that much.

The Camel Races

From outside, up the stairs of the bunker room Henry and I had been given, I heard a camel's frightful groan, that awesome, existentially discontented noise. The souls of the damned, the Armenian metropolitan in Khartoum maintains, speak through the throat of the camel. The camel debates life's misery with the sun. Etc. Etc.

Both Henry and I had been drinking tea. I was feeling a certain hollowness—I had been the girl's guardian since Khartoum and had become accustomed to it. In the new vacancy I spent the afternoon transmuting all my notes into two features—*The Times* might ultimately take them on the strength of what I would write about the coming ambush, if it ever occurred. The work cheered me. I felt fresh and sweatless and energetic in the bunker's dry air. Even Henry seemed calmer than he had at any other Eritrean place.

Hearing the camel lamentations, we both went to the door and looked up the dug-in steps to the ground level.

"Come out, gentlemen!" I heard Christine call, and then I saw her. She was sitting astride the neck and forequarters of a skittish one-humped beast she must have borrowed from a villager. She managed the thing well as it tried to wheel and went on lamenting. This was flamboyant business, her onboard-camel manner, entirely different from her usual style.

Coming farther up the stairs, I got a sight of her father, turbanned and shaven, sitting astride a second camel and holding two others by the reins. "Come, comrades!" he yelled. "It is the Hallal Front camel races!"

The light was still bright. "What about MIGs?" I asked.

"The MIG pilots are all in their mess back in Asmara, drinking Militta beer."

I saw Christine laugh again. Masihi must have behaved well, like a papa, because she looked happy, a child diverted and enlivened.

Henry and I looked at each other and began laughing. This is the best day, I thought. The best day we've had in Eritrea. We had been rehabilitated by the reunion and the low humidity. We grabbed our bush hats and came out of the bunker to join *père, fille,* and the dromedaries.

The cameraman instructed us how to haul the beasts down onto their knees by their necks, how to mount them, where to kick them to make them rise. As I mounted mine, the camel uttered complaints and threats which filled the earth. I couldn't hear Masihi's jovial advice. Henry, however, handled his animal expertly, taking it for a canter among the shell craters. The skeletal children of this zone, whom earlier in the day we'd seen trailing to class, appeared in the shade of thorn bushes, hooted and placed splayed fingers across their faces. Christine rocked in her saddle and yelled, "Long-champs!"

Under Masihi's direction, I tried to steer my camel to the un-roofed houses at the south end of the village. They marked the starting line in the proposed camel derby. The other three were all in position before me; my beast veered off on triangulations among the craters and the huts and bunkers and occasionally half knelt as if to throw me. Partly by my wrenching at his reins and partly by his own consent to joining his fellows, I got him in line for the start.

"Is everybody ready?" asked Masihi, grinning with the full breadth of his scoundrel charm. "Christine?"

"Partez!" yelled Christine, and we were all racing, my camel as much through his willingness to run along beside the others as through any control I had over him. The other three were, of course, ahead of me; I could see Henry crouched forward on his camel's neck like an authentic jockey. Masihi was screaming, and Christine's head jiggled in gales of unusual laughter—she wasn't so much racing as stating her simple joy. I began to gain on her. But I saw Henry throwing his elbows wide now, kicking berserkly, urging his animal out in front. Masihi screamed certain joyous Gallic threats after

him, but as far as I could see from my risky purchase aboard my camel's shoulders, Henry drew farther away.

I started to understand that Masihi hadn't nominated any limit to this race. Where did it end? Maybe at the escarpment which fell away down to the ravines above Jani where the militia had stopped us the previous night.

Ahead, near the edge of the scarp, two startling events occurred at once. Henry's galloping camel seemed to pitch willfully forward onto its knees, throwing Henry over its neck. Above its hump, above the pain and the comedy, the camel's knees seeming to splay, its bizarre joints shooting its limbs in a number of directions at once, a MIG appeared, and instantly another. In less than a second they roared on down over the rim of the plateau and were lost in the valley. The edge of the cliff cut their noise off like a knife, and all at once you could again hear the competitive eloquence of the camels. Henry's tried to rise, Masihi's screamed at being reined in. Christine had succeeded in dragging hers back to a canter. But mine seemed to declare an intention not to stop of its own will.

I got the impression that the finish line had now been reached. But my camel kept on, bearing me down the desolate road. At last the thing propped, bowed, and slid me with amazing gentleness out of my seat and forward into an aloe bush. Snuffling, it began to graze on a patch of gravel by the trail.

When I stood up, I saw Masihi and the girl trying to raise the stunned Henry to his feet. I looked then into the valley, where gobbets and surges of flame had begun to rise. The two MIGs maneuvered for space against Mohammed's granite mountain and shot across its western face still golden from the vanishing sun.

I glanced around to see if the others saw what I did. I thought of running to them and forming a primal huddle. Henry was still lolling on the ground. Masihi dragged him upright, at last put one hand on his brow, the other on his shoulders, and frowned. Christine stood still by her now docile camel. The MIGs wheeled easefully between the granite peaks and then made second runs nearly faster than the eye could account for. We had a wide view, though Henry wavered on his legs and couldn't focus.

"Fragmentation bombs," Masihi yelled dispassionately.

We stared down fixedly through the slightly distorting lens of Jani's hot, rising dusk. Its river ran mainly rock, but loose and separate strands of water glimmered. Both arms were fed by a similar fall of boulders and strings of water flowing—like the stem of the letter Y—out of the south. These waters, which I think race away ultimately, fighting evaporation all the way, into the Blue Nile, were fringed with scrub where all day villagers had been waiting for the nighttime food share-out. Even from that distance and height, I could see along the edges of this foliage a flurry of gold and emerald cloth, a serpentine, panicked movement made subtle by distance. At the core of each disaster in the valley of Jani was a pulse of flame out of which climbed white smoke, fragments of foliage, and an outer nimbus of orange dust. Balls of white smoke rose from the Eritrean artillery placed in the mountains around. It struck me that these two MIG pilots must be true gauchos to have come in so late in the day, so low, confusing the defenses.

Later Masihi would utter the opinion that they were hotshots (his term) transferred from a career of rough, low flying above the heads of Somalis. On the Eritrean front they were new brooms sweeping clean. They were like Major Fida, who'd come to the Eritrean front from Western Somalia and who'd similarly struck low—and been struck in return. But these two were getting away with it.

Though our view was so complete, from that distance everything seemed to have a leisurely effect. Both aircraft turned away from the flak now, acquired height within seconds, flashed away southeast. We watched until their black outlines were lost in the night rising up from the Red Sea.

Henry had managed to stand and was shaking his head, trying to clear his vision. "Son-of-a-bitch camel!" he was muttering. "What's happening here?"

His vision cleared and he apparently saw smoke and the glint of a dozen fires in the valley below him. He pointed. "Holy shit!" he said. Perhaps his bruised brain was suggesting to him that all this had been brought on by his fall from the camel's back.

Masihi remarked, "The Ethiopians hit the place eighteen months ago. Killed thirty people. I filmed it."

"Son-of-a-bitch!" yelled Henry. It was a scream of amazing volume. We knew he wasn't talking about the camel and its lesser malice now. "Those barbarians!" he screamed. "Those fucking barbarians!"

Masihi didn't take much notice of him. "Come, Christine," he ordered his daughter. He dragged his camel around by the reins, back toward the village, and so did she. It was as if they had been together, yanking camels over plateaus, for eleven years instead of eleven hours. "I have to get a camera down there," he called in cursory explanation.

I had an argument with Moka about going to Jani myself. His plan was to travel on, parallel to the front, till we reached Nacfa, a bombed and ruined city, second in holiness only to Asmara, toward the eastern end of the Eritrean highlands. He had planned to begin the move before dawn the next morning. If I went back to Jani with Masihi, his assistant, and Christine, I wouldn't be able to return to the plateau here before tomorrow night. It was difficult to know whether Moka's insistence that Henry and I move on was based on some timetable I was ignorant of but which Tessfaha had set for him. But I still felt rebellious: If Tessfaha wanted me, let him tell *me*. Let him bloody well appear!

Christine was loading a tripod and sound gear into the back of her father's truck. She did it with an easy grace, with an air of custom. Perhaps for his own protection, Masihi had given her what she hadn't had while traveling with us: a job.

Lady Julia had also made it clear she wanted to go down to Jani with the cameraman and his new assistant, so that Moka had little choice but to give in to us. The agitated Henry could not be moved, however. A barefoot doctor in military fatigues looked at his pupils and an elected village health worker called Mohammed Mohammed, in turban and blue jacket, fed him dosages of EPLF paracetamol. By Masihi's truck, when I took my kit there to load it aboard, the camel which had thrown Henry was grazing with soft prehensile lips on the savage two- or three-inch thorns of an African acacia. Masihi himself was also waiting there for the driver.

"It's a heartbreak," he confided in me, "I won't be able to get any footage till the morning. If these awful things are to be filmed, they should be filmed in their rawest state, before the wounds are dressed." He hauled a Betacam in its snazzy fabric bag into the back of the truck. "What I film by the time we get down there, or in the morning, won't have any distinction to it. It will resemble some *chi-chi* documentary segment by CBS or French television."

* * *

On our way back down into the valley after dark, Moka kept hailing the drivers of other trucks ascending to the plateau, six-tonners loaded with supplies, a captured Russian bus taking soldiers from Zara to the Hallal Front. The figures from the bombing varied. Their inexactitude caused distress to Lady Julia. During a toilet stop called by Masihi, she surmised whether the women we had seen queuing at the clinic the day before had been harmed in the bombing. As Lady Julia got tireder that night, she became more agitated. She took on more of the feverishness and bewilderment which till this morning had marked Christine.

When we arrived, village militiamen were digging a large pit on the edge of the groves of Jani. By the clinic, which was still intact, shrouded figures—thirty, it was said—could be seen surrounded by a circle of keening women. Closer to the food dump were placed the blankets on which wounded lay. Pot-bellied children seemed to make up half the figure, though I lacked the hard journalistic concentration actually to count. I saw Masihi, his Eritrean technician, and Christine walking among the trees, discussing the advisability of trying to light the scene. Men and women on the edges of the clearing lamented loudly and in compelling tune.

At last I risked looking full-on at one of the victims, a girl of perhaps thirteen, bare-headed and naked except for bandages which ran tinted with blood or disinfectant from her ribcage to her hips. Her face seemed empty—she had withdrawn from it. She was waiting somewhere within herself, exactly as Salim Genete's niece had on the terrace at Orotta.

At the sight of her, a gush of the tea I had drunk up on the plateau an hour or so before ran out over my lips. I looked around, obscurely ashamed, to see if anyone had noticed. Lady Julia was staring at me levelly.

"I'm sorry," I told her, spitting. "I can't get used to this."

"People are permitted not to be used to it," Julia told me.

Some of the head wounds Jani's barefoot doctor wisely did not dare to touch. She was waiting for a surgeon to arrive from Zara.

In the meantime, everyone, I noticed, the wounded and the attendants, seemed to suffer from a strange pallor.

"Why is everyone so white?" Lady Julia asked me *sotto voce.* She believed some chemical agent had been dropped. But I pointed out to her that even the river oaks and the thorn bushes had taken on a white complexion.

Masihi, bustling past with Christine and his assistant, explained the phenomenon: A fragmentation bomb had hit the powdered-milk dump, over beyond the sorghum. An Etna of powder had been thrown into the air, had been sieved up through the branches of the trees. The gift of the EEC had blanched all the shocked and upturned faces and had come down even on the wounded.

Now and then, I matter-of-factly embraced this tree or that; I muttered primitively against the trunks of river oaks. Lady Julia, a genuine veteran, did not seem to be as troubled now that she was here at the site. She knew the way of the world better.

At some stage we all ended holding up surgical drips, me over a young farmer who told me his name was Mohammed Mohammed, the same name as the health worker who had been dosing Henry's headache on the plateau above us.

Throughout the night, as we took an occasional rest on a blanket or drank some sweet tea, Moka and Masihi returned to the aspect everyone unscarred seemed to be discussing. "They were accurate," Masihi said. He meant the bombers. "More accurate than normally. The casualty list is very high."

Toward dawn, while Lady Julia and I rested against the trunks of river oaks, a young surgeon and three nurses turned up from Zara with a portable operating theater. The dead had already been buried. To mark the arrival of the surgeon with his old-fashioned anesthetics—he lacked compressed oxygen and respirators—the mourning under Jani's white, blasted trees fell off to an occasional shrill, an intermittent yell of maternal incomprehension among the oaks by the river.

Julia in Endilal

It was late in the afternoon that I said goodbye to Masihi and the girl. This was on the banks of Jani's river, in the awful torpid air. She and her father, both of them hollow-eyed, were sitting on the back tray of their truck, sharing water from the canteen Christine and I had bought together in the market in Khartoum. They would stay here one more day, Masihi said. Perhaps there would be another raid. Of course, of course they would be all right if that happened. He was a veteran in these matters! Anyhow, it was unlikely, since more anti-aircraft guns were being moved in, and the Ethiopians weren't in the economic position to throw planes and pilots away.

So then Masihi and his daughter would run their footage back to Orotta for editing, before replenishing their film stock and taking to the road again.

Christine and I made hurried goodbyes while Julia was speaking to Masihi.

"You have been very kind, Darcy," she told me formally.

"Not at all," I said hollowly. But in spite of myself, I felt under-rewarded by this farewell. "So, you're happy now?"

She gestured over her shoulder at the jumble of equipment in the truck. "I am very busy, anyhow."

But again there was the stupid sense of being owed more.

"What is it, Christine? Why do you seem dazed?"

"Dazed?" she asked. But she didn't try to define what I meant.

I was already regretting my rashness but I was, of course, committed now.

"Something started you off on the road. Something happened. Anyone can tell that."

Her eyes narrowed. She didn't like it. This drove me to the greatest, the crassest mistake.

"Henry says you mentioned an abortion."

Her face went red and she dropped her head. "Please, Darcy," she said. "I told him that to send him away."

I could see Masihi frowning at me over Lady Julia's shoulder and was at once repentant.

"Forgive me," I murmured. "You'll tell me one day."

"Yes," she said, not lifting her eyes to mine.

The group farewells were hearty, lots of laughter and gruffness from Masihi and me. Yet it was all melancholy to me. I was aware that we would soon lose Lady Julia, too, and then it would be simply Henry and I on our own with Moka. I did not know if Henry and I between us had enough composure to go around.

So Moka and Julia and I fetched the concussed Henry from the plateau and traveled all night again, parallel to the front line, to a high village called Endilal far to the east, behind the Nacfa Front. I was still dazed from the flour-white horrors of Jani when we arrived there, and trailed behind Lady Julia like a bewildered nephew just as I had in Jani.

Endilal, revealed by daylight, stood close to the sun, was high and dry and plagued by wind. Julia, quit of her responsibility for the girl, was looking very tired, as you would have thought a woman of her age had a right to be. But one look at a place like Endilal told you it was the perfect village for the sorts of questions Lady Julia wanted answered: for matters to do with the health and well-being of peasant wives.

Some time during that coming night, Moka said, Henry and I were to go on to the Nacfa Front. We'd spent the afternoon with Julia, and she and Henry very nearly got on together now that they were assured of a parting. We sat together in a hut of logs chatting, by way of Moka's Tigrinyan and Julia's Arabic, with four of the local women and a man who appeared to be an out-of-work farmer. Most of his goats had died of thirst and hunger in '85, and some livestock disease accounted for the remaining fifteen a year later. He was therefore Job, but whimsical about it. He waved his hands and his eyes sparkled darkly. He was ready for any catastrophe, trimmed down for it—it was obvious by his bearing. Death was a mean joke, but a day of *injera* and adequate water and no bombing seemed cause for euphoria or even hilarity.

One of the women, the most forthright one, shared the same name as that bureaucrat cousin of Salim's. I wondered how long past it was since the women of the clan of Salim's Amna, of Amna Nurhussein, had dressed and looked like this Amna, had carried in their faces both the painful coyness and the earthiness of the peasant, the pastoral nomad.

This Amna was the elected birth attendant in Endilal, and I could imagine women in labor getting some comfort from her businesslike way of speaking and moving.

All the women wore the golden bangle of marriage in their nostrils—even the one who did not know where her husband was. Masihi had told me that when the Ethiopian army massacred Eritreans, the soldiers walked among the fallen plucking these nose bands as if they were gathering fruit.

Coughing from the day's dust, Henry and I ate a quiet meal with Moka—*injera* and the ground-up chickpeas called *shiru*. The dust sounded heavy on Moka's chest. This place used to be heavily treed, only seventy years past, the engineer had told us earlier in the day. But peasants had cut the trees for firewood, and now the MIGs made the planting of new ones impossible. He'd shrugged, smiling. "Dead peasants and live bombs! They made this desolation."

Lady Julia had already moved into the clinic with the barefoot doctor. That's where she would spend her time and conduct her inquiries. Early in the night she came from the clinic to ask me to join her over there for a farewell drink. She did not ask Henry, who in any case was already cold and tired enough to be in his sleeping bag thumbing through his diary, looking at photographs of his days in Addis and rearranging the elastic bands around the mass of his memories.

As we walked together among the desolate black hills, I thought Lady Julia restrained. I knew she'd sat through that afternoon's clinic hour, and I wondered if she'd found that depressing. But when I mentioned the clinic, she brightened.

"Nothing conclusive," she told me. "Only indications. But—on top of what we saw in the great hospital in Orotta—the indications are astounding. As I said then, Darcy, the chance of a great shift in history! No less, I assure you. No less."

She led me down into the bunker of the barefoot doctor, whose name was Ferreweine, a chunky woman of about thirty-eight, dressed in the usual military fatigues. Ferreweine had a bucket of *sewa*, which she covered with a cloth to prevent it going off. She filled three plastic mugs with the opaque liquor, and we sat around the ammunition-box table. Lady Julia performed her usual trick, telling me things in English, then breaking off to tell Ferreweine in Arabic what she had told me; and Ferreweine would smile but make adjusting gestures with her hand, as if in a way she wanted to tone Lady Julia down.

As Lady Julia spoke I, too, found myself giving room to the possibility that the world might in fact be more habitable than it had seemed to be since Jani. Perhaps this shift was made more possible by the *sewa*, by drinking it with two wise women. In any case, I let myself all at once experience an excitement parallel to Julia's, a normal enthusiasm of the type I'd been keeping in check since my foolish upbraiding of trees after the Jani bombing.

But there was still an ambiguous, overbright sparkle in Lady Julia's eyes. The exaltation seemed to be fighting its way out of her through a thin but obvious skin of loss, of ice-calm grief.

"I wish my late husband, Denis," she cried out, "was here to see this with me. What an education! Even more perhaps for my Aunt Chloe. Aunt Chloe would understand the significance, where poor dear Denis might need it explained to him."

I wondered about her choice of words. *An education for Aunt Chloe?* Yet Chloe was a martyr and therefore needed no education.

"I must tell you, Darcy," said Julia, "that I've never been anywhere in the African world where I've felt so sharply the hope that millennia of foul practice have been reversed. But by the people themselves! You see, old Denis had something when he said, 'We can't push things too hard, Julie. The whole business is just part of the fabric of things!' Now curiously, Ferreweine keeps on saying the same thing. But it's obvious to me. They *are* defeating it here. And in a way that I could never defeat it in Sudan! Oh, there was nothing wrong with Aunt Chloe and me. We just weren't Africans, that's all."

I saw tears spill down her cheeks. They lasted so briefly that I don't think chunky Ferreweine saw them. Julia dashed them aside and began again on some solid quaffing. "This positive demon of male clitoris envy!" she announced. "Do we ever encounter a reference to it among the psychoanalysts? I should say not! Yet there it is, present in our own society. Why, even in this very century doctors have used it as a treatment for hysteria! But who confronts it, this monster with the knife in its hand long before the Christian era and the coming of Islam? A stone knife before there was a steel one."

"Imagine, if you will," Lady Julia invited me after we'd drunk yet more of Ferreweine's hard, acrid brew, "a heavily treed Eden —an Eden such as Endilal once was. There Adam looks upon the being of perfection and hears—even in the first embrace—the unsettling cries of *her* desire. And so he takes to her with a knife. Because he fears the whole world will be unbalanced by her honest sensuality. And there, in that first touch, is the root cause of all this savagery, Darcy! The first caress was a caress of the hand. The second was of the knife!"

I began shivering, perhaps from the drink. I suffered a sensation, this no doubt from Ferreweine's harsh liquor, that there was some sort of alliance of thought and grief between Bernadette and Julia. This was *déjà vu* of the sharpest kind, and my shivering grew to a ridiculous extent. I feared Ferreweine might try to diagnose me. I was aware of my face flushing and sweat all over my brow and under my eyes.

In the high, barren village called Endilal, Lady Julia explained, she'd expected the barbarity to be at its worst—hard times, a population of refugees from the south, conservative and frightened people who might, as the whole world turned to fire and grit, fall back on old practices as a means of balancing out the cosmos.

But that night, she said, some forty people—three quarters of them women and children—had been presented at Ferreweine's mud brick clinic, and she, Lady Julia, had seen the immaculate girl children untouched by the knife, children as "traditional" as any in the Sudan. And every one of them had lived through the famine of 1985, when, according to the engineer's report, the people here had had to walk out for their water, bringing back little cans of it from a well fifteen miles away.

"What pitiable little pannikins of fluid these children lived on," said Lady Julia, "and yet they came through! And their mothers? Even in the fury of the famine, whatever it portended—the anger of Brezhnev, the anger of Mengistu, or the anger of Allah—whatever happened, Darcy, and however small grew the drops of water in the groins of the tin cups, their mothers had not let the knives come near them!"

Ferreweine again intruded. The barefoot doctor felt bound to point out that cases were still brought in from the remoter hills where the traditional excisors had been at work. It was only when a child began to hemorrhage beyond control that the grandmothers let them be rushed to the clinic. But once such a practice as this began to die, Ferreweine explained, then it died quickly. Because it was obvious the world did not fall apart when girl children were no longer mutilated. Here—it was obvious again—the world had already fallen apart in any case. And so for the knife, for the sharp stone or the razor, there was no excuse!

When—after midnight—it was time for me to find the truck for Nacfa, Lady Julia and I hugged each other and she walked outside with me. Even after the lantern light of Ferreweine's clinic, the stars were vivid. The dust still blew.

"I am sad to see you left to the company of the unspeakable Henry," she told me. She belched slightly. "Give the scoundrel my best wishes."

Half gone with the *sewa*, I could still tell she wanted to speak to me out of the barefoot doctor's hearing. The feverishness I'd seen in her inside, which had fed her slightly disordered eloquence, still sat in her undissipated.

"I had the sharpest experience this afternoon," she told me. "Speaking of knives, it was the equivalent of a knife. I was talking to a peasant woman, a girl of about twenty-seven. Not a well woman at all. Anemic, and so on. She was holding a four-year-old daughter on her lap, a child of quite satisfactory health. Now, the operation is generally done about the age of five, but this woman promises it won't be done. I had no guarantees, yet I was suddenly convinced the woman was telling me the truth. This woman, who would still be called *a girl* in the West, though here she's already middle-aged. And the suspicion I've had for some years—a merely notional suspicion up until now—that Aunt Chloe needn't have died, that *all that* might indeed have been the way Denis saw it—a needless intrusion—struck me so fiercely that I couldn't find my breath. And I saw that all the years of argument were futile. I am a witness to this question, Darcy. No more. I had never actually seen myself in those terms. I mean, I'd thought of myself as a doer. Quite a shock, I can tell you. Quite a shock . . ."

I heard her voice break off into tears.

"Henry is right. I am an old imperialist dragon, and we old empire types want to make the great alterations ourselves. I'm sorry. I'm being very silly."

There was more choking. I put my arm around her. What spare yet comfortable, round, *inhabited* shoulders they were.

"Perhaps I should just concentrate on visiting my grandchildren," she murmured.

And then she had vanished. Back to Ferreweine, back to the large question, without allowing me to mutter any prosaic comfort at all.

I felt bereft and considered following her inside again. For some time I stood in Endilal's night looking at the hint of light through the clinic blackout. There were two sage women in there, conversing in Arabic, and I yearned to be back with them.

I knew that if Lady Julia were quick to publish the articles she meant to write about her Eritrean findings, they would steal some of my chances of freelance publication. It didn't seem very important here, with the sleep of the swollen-headed children rising all around me in the dark.

Nacfa

The loss of Julia and Christine seemed suddenly compensated for when Salim Genete's beautiful cousin Amna Nurhussein rose out of a hole in the ground outside Nacfa, under a waning moon.

This apparition took place by one of those EPLF filling stations. Seeing the truck appear in the half light, other people had risen as if from the earth along with Amna. It was the sort of crowd I was getting used to—soulful-looking Eritrean soldiers with shawls wrapped around their heads against the night chill; mechanics from the regional garages, traveling on business or visiting relatives; militiamen—like the ones on the plateau above Jani—in peasant clothes. Apart from her paramilitary drab, Amna was still wearing the striped Italianate shirt she'd worn when I first saw her, and it still looked freshly put on.

Moka had Tecleh stop. Between Amna and him there was the predictable shoulder-bumping, the normal greetings about wheat and health. Teeth—hers and Moka's—scrupulously cleaned with olive twigs, glittered in the dark. Her eyes flickered upward toward the cabin of the truck and saw Henry and me there.

"Good night," she said to us in her sharp-edged, penetrating English.

Henry, nodding back, whispered to me, "Great-looking girl."

"Has Salim's son arrived in Orotta yet?" I asked her.

"Not yet," she said. I could hear the click of her tongue against those little stonelike syllables.

She'd confused my image of her by turning up here. Despite what

I'd seen of her in Orotta, when she'd hitched a ride to the hospital, I hadn't expected her to stick round in this high barren land waiting in holes in the ground for the chance of transport. I crawled into the back of the truck, so that she could sit in the front beside Henry. He carried on a brief, practical conversation about the roads and the weather and the Jani bombing and how he hadn't expected to see her again so soon—all of this before the truck started up again.

She was on her way to visit friends in Nacfa, or so she said.

I watched her turbanned head jolting as we entered the bombed town, and my first sight of it was framed by the gap between the slope of her head and shoulder on one hand, and Henry's body on the other.

I wondered if Henry was thinking the same, embarrassing, pa-perback kind of thoughts I was: *Thrown together on a dangerous frontier,* etc., etc. Yet in view of Fryer River, I knew it was childish to give space to any feeling for a woman like Amna, whose life was so *essentially* removed from me, essentially beyond my imagining.

The city of Nacfa, holy in the Eritrean perception as Guernica, Coventry, Jerusalem might be in the perception of others, had in spite of all its wreckage the look of one of those places where, given a chance, civilization would pitch. It stood in a high bowl among the kind of mountains which seemed to guarantee a rainfall. Through it a good, clear mountain river ran. You crossed its stones as you came into town through a northern suburb of wrecked and formerly substantial villas, all quite roofless. Roofed, they were probably Italian in style. What a polished life Eritrean traders and officials of the Italian empire must once have lived here, in this town which marked a boundary between the Islamic plains of the Red Sea and the Coptic Christian highlands.

What was left of plaster on the ruined walls of all the town indicated that its color was once golden—golden schools, yellow offices, yellow rows of shops, a golden mosque whose minaret still stood (a symbol, of course, since it had survived the MIGs). In the late afternoon the minaret glowed with what you could fancifully call a golden assertiveness against the brown western hills.

Our bunker in Nacfa (since I always seem to start with whatever warren we occupy): It stood on the edge of a large garden pocked with bomb craters. Eritreans who lived in the ruins grew crops of tree seedlings, black pepper, cabbages, and tomatoes there, kept rabbits from Kenya and California, and raised chickens. Once, judging by remains of walls and ornamental gates, this had been the garden of an aristocrat, one of those Eritrean nobles with whom the Italians entered into a social contract for the control of their sweet Red Sea colony.

Before our door lay an exploded rocket of the type the Eritreans nicknamed "Stalin organs." It had sown lumps of shrapnel round the hillside and the edge of the garden. Moka looked at the body of the rocket, the tassels of steel which grew from it, testimony of the force with which it had landed and done its apparently futile business. He picked it up and hurled it into the undergrowth.

Rats lived there. A leisurely convoy of three appeared atop the garden fence and made off to spend a day among the chickens and the vegetables. They moved like masters in Nacfa.

From the outside the bunker was simply a mound, and the door was deeply recessed in the mound and led by a narrow corridor into a sort of living room lined with clay platforms. The walls had been painted, a design meant to represent the drapes of a nomad tent, tent flaps hanging by rings from poles.

"Nice touch," said Henry. "Poignant!"

Off this living area was a bedroom, bare-floored, where Henry and I were told to put our gear. Amna stood in the doorway, her small kit bag hung on her shoulder. She smiled evenly at us as we disposed our sleeping bags and air mattresses around the floor, Henry expressing his usual desire for privacy by setting his in the far corner.

The light in the living area came from outside, up the deep entrance corridor. But in the room Henry and I shared it entered through a hole in the roof, a shaft lined with planks and perhaps six or eight feet deep.

"You should have this room," I suggested to Ms. Nurhussein with creaky gallantry.

"Not at all," she said in that choppy, melodious voice, before vanishing. "You are the guests."

Henry and I lay on our bedding experimentally and looked at the ceiling, which was canvas and lath suspended from the roof logs. Lizards and rats were busy in the air spaces between the logs.

* * *

There was often shelling in the late afternoons, when the dusk was ennobling the hills to violet. Shells fell outside the bunker with a concussion I could feel in my spine, but all that deep crafty work with soil and logs protected us. Moka, lying on a clay platform, would tell us in a sleepy voice exactly what was happening above our heads. "Seventy-six-millimeter," Moka would say indolently, not bothering to open his eyes. "Stalin organ," he might sigh. These racks of rockets, before firing and in their recumbent state, *did* resemble organ pipes. "One-hundred-and-twenty-two-millimeter," he might say of the basso *crump* of the Ethiopians' biggest Russian-made cannon. The Ethiopians, he said, thought troops moved through the city at night, and the frontline tanks and artillery *were* all around us. The remnants of population, soldiers on leave, and bureaucrats like Amna could be found there, too, on the edges or passing through.

The fact that shelling usually began in the later afternoon was read by Moka as a sign of Ethiopian terror and disorientation. They wanted, he said, to make the night as loud with sound as the day had been with light. Moka would go on reading his novel throughout—it was a book by Han Suyin—and would occasionally ask me about this or that usage of English. A serious student. The Ethiopian artillery was merely a background to his classes in English idiom.

He might look up only to comment, to claim, for example, that in these circumstances of undifferentiated, panicky artillery duels, the rebels replied only with one battery of 76-millimeter, large enough to make a statement, small enough not to waste value. The lessons of the battle of the Somme and of Guadalcanal had not been lost, he would say.

It made my flesh creep the way Amna would arrive from her "friends' places" somewhere in Nacfa during these bombardments. It is too dramatic to say that the town was full of flying shrapnel, but the shrapnel *did* fly and high explosive made craters on the edges of the town. By the light of a kerosene lamp provided by the Department of Public Administration I would see her turbanned head bow to enter our bunker, and I would understand that she had been out among the explosions, which to her, as to most Eritreans, didn't seem to mean more than a hailstorm.

When Amna approached the bunker from the direction of the ruined town and the river, I would see the outline of her large turban and the flash of the oversized, stylishly tinted glasses which she tended to wear in most lights, even the dim light of sunset, as if she were a rock singer affecting a style. She would pass the Public Administration bunker, whose tenants she of course knew. Sometimes she would call to the woman and the child who were sheltering there in the doorway, in a space as narrow and as effective as a slit trench. That four-year-old seemed to take the bombardments with the greatest composure. She had grown up with them. To her they were the traffic of the earth.

After these pleasantries Amna would come on to our entranceway, to our bunker with its mural of tent walls blowing in a gentle breeze—tent walls cleated as if to hold out dust, no matter who might try to raise it.

She always went into the little side room and poured water into a powdered-milk can with a red cow painted on it. This was actually an Australian brand of powdered milk, though I never mentioned the creaky connection to Amna.

Then she would come back to the mouth of the entranceway. Seen from inside she was pure silhouette. Seen from just outside the door she was lit by the storm lantern by which Moka sat, deep in the living area, reading his Han Suyin novel.

Then she would repeat that slow, beautiful, and efficient washing I'd seen outside the bunker in Orotta some weeks past. With that fall of liquid she seemed to rinse away the memory of grit from my mouth as well.

One afternoon when Moka and I were both reading by the light of the storm lantern, I looked up when she arrived and, as she washed herself, saw great nodes of scarring on the sole of one of her feet. This might be the scarring from that original injury Salim had spoken of, the one which still occasionally reduced her to a hobble and forced her to go to Doctor Neroyo for vitamins.

Tentatively, as she went on washing, I drew Henry's attention to her. I was reluctant to do so. But he *did* know Africa. Maybe he could explain the scar tissue.

"This is Africa, my friend. You know that. Jesus, there's thousands of things might scar an African girl. Between the creeds and the goddam tribes and the powers. What do you expect?"

Even by day the bombed and abandoned city had an invisible life. One of the bunkers along the bank of the stream by the garden, for example, was occupied by a husband and wife from the lantern-providing Eritrean Department of Public Administration. The bunker next to that belonged to the horticulturalist. He was a graduate of the University of San Diego. He ran a clandestine school, an agricultural college, on the hill behind our bunker, giving a husbandry and agriculture crash course for Eritrean farmers—some of them sixteen, some of them sixty, brought in from the north and east and west, some of them even smuggled through the lines. During our wait at Nacfa, we occasionally went and visited them in their unofficial, unroofed, shell-pocked polytechnic on the hill.

"Most of my Western friends are experts on grass for golf courses," the horticulturalist told us. "There is enough work in Southern California alone for every one of them." On his blind slope behind the front, he seemed indulgent about the Southern Californians playing their golf.

From these visits and conversations with people like the grass-grower, I found out that Amna was a pharmacist by training, that she had never studied in the West until now. These days she was doing, she said, an undergraduate course in history and politics at a university in Frankfurt.

"But I did not bring my texts with me," she said.

Amna: Networking

Although Amna spent her days going from bunker to bunker, fact-finding, as she said—networking—she would come back across the stones of the river beyond the garden to dine with us. She did not want to make any inroads on her friends' limited rations, but she also liked the pasta the Public Administration woman in the next bunker cooked for us. Pasta was not usual Eritrean rations. It was considered a supreme delicacy, and the woman next door sowed canned mackerel in it to give it greater body still. The bowl came to us carried in the middle of a broad circle of *injera* on a tray.

I was amused by this frankly uttered taste of Amna's, especially since her appetite was so minute. Henry and Moka and Amna and I sat on ammunition boxes, winding up spools of pasta on our forks, sharing from the communal bowl. Of all of us, Moka was the heartiest eater. Amna ate mere strands of the spaghetti, single crumbs of mackerel, and very slowly.

Because the bowl was common, Moka and Amna prepared for the meal with copious washing. And after the washing, it was better for the spirit, even for the stomach, to have two rebel eaters share the pasta like this. Slowly the *injera* bread became patterned with strands of spaghetti. Inhibitions were lost.

Sometimes when Amna turned up in the evenings, Henry and I were already at the door of the bunker, watching the flashes from the Ethiopian lines, feeling the impact in our feet and bones as, from nearby hills, the bombardment picked up drifts of parched topsoil. I suppose we now saw ourselves as veterans, unlikely to be driven underground by anything except intense attack. Earth was being blended with air; disks of shrapnel sought out the arms which planted the reforesting tree or the chives bush, though at this hour all the reforesting arms were deep below ground, tearing fragments of *injera* and scooping up the lentils which were too hot for Henry and me to eat.

Henry would grow feverishly angry as the sky flashed and the earth moved—a different sort of ire than he showed when confronted by rebel skillfulness. "To pay for *that*," he said, pointing, "he makes the peasants grow navy beans. This is fucking coffee and navy beans and tomato paste converted into high explosive!"

I decided late one night, after Henry had gone to the other room, to spring the question on Moka. I interrupted his novel-reading.

"Do you know a man named Tessfaha?"

"There are lots of Tessfahas," he wheezed, holding his book in a way that told me he meant to return to it as soon as he could manage.

I adopted a manner, including a sort of pensive clapping of my clenched fists and a sideways glance, which was meant to let him know he wouldn't get too much peace from me until he had answered properly.

"Are we waiting for Tessfaha? I mean, the man who spoke to me in London."

"Tessfaha isn't coming here," said Moka blankly and, I thought, without much sympathy for my confusion.

"Then what?" I asked, angry. "What will happen?"

"We'll go into the line when our escorts are ready."

"Is Amna in our party?"

Moka suddenly reverted to his breathy, compassionate norm.

"I don't know. She moves on her own. She should not be here. Afan, the Dergue's secret police, treated her so badly. But Amna moves on her own. Her own boss." He tapped the novel he was reading as if he'd gotten this last phrase from it.

"I want to be kept informed," I said, but Moka nodded so genially that I was already, against my best instincts, halfway appeased.

Amna and Moka between them went on keeping us busy while we waited for a sign or an order from Colonel Tessfaha. By day, wearing our dun clothing, we would move over the hill behind the bunker to visit the gunners and the tank people. The front trench itself ran along a high ridge two miles ahead of us. Great sounds and enormous pillars of dust moved across these hills whenever the Ethiopians fired. I found it very fantastical to be traveling with a beautiful bureaucrat in a turban and a wheezy veteran, making social calls in such a landscape. Social they were. All the older soldiers, men and women, seemed to know Amna and Moka and exchanged fraternal shoulder bumps, the third bump, the one that had to do with wheat, slow and emphatic and like an embrace.

It was particularly Amna who attracted intense greetings. Old friends of hers emerged from holes and ran hallooing across earth widely covered with lumps of shrapnel, the scything metal we had heard landing during the past evenings. Across this ground, too, moved lines of young soldiers going to class in brush shelters scattered amid groves of cactus.

Amna's friends would show off their dug-in cannon to us, the Soviet markings, the calibrations and instruction plates in Cyrillic script. We met the 23-millimeter, which had two months past brought down a MIG-23; the 37-millimeter guns, which were murder to tanks; the 78-millimeters draped in their camouflage tarpaulins, their barrels in sleeves of canvas to keep the dust out. Amna never asked any questions. She stood back with a neutral face, neither smiling nor frowning. She always let Henry and I attend to all that.

Behind the batteries, remnants of *injera* bread sat desiccating on the rocks. They would be ground up to make *sewa*, the opaque, sour liquor Ferreweine and Lady Julia and I had drunk so plentifully in Endilal.

We would visit the tanks, too, backed into earth garages hacked into the slopes and covered with logs. When the tank crews saw us coming, they would immediately disappear inside the machines and emerge with their tank helmets on. They made us sit in the things, look through the gun sights, and pay attention to the place, repaired with epoxy resin, where the shell which had killed the Ethiopian crew of the tank during its service with the Dergue had entered the machine's steel apron.

Amna said little throughout all this. It was always Moka who urged us to consider the strange histories of those large beasts called T-55s. Made in the Urals, shipped to Africa, demonstrated to Ethiopian regulars by a Russian expert, captured at Mersa Teklai or Barentu with their heroes dead inside them or already fled, now ready to roll in Nacfa, to probe a flank in Sahel, to defend—if things turned bad—a retreat through this holy, razed city with its unbeaten yellow minaret. And the Russian manual, the key to all the tank's uses, captured intact inside it, translated into the tongue for these lanky boys in their strange helmets.

One afternoon a pensive Henry sketched a gun crew in action. A very good sketch with the distant ridge of trench line exactly rendered. No one seemed to object to this verisimilitude. Moka didn't choose to confiscate the thing. I believe Amna Nurhussein would have laughed at him if he had.

"Where is your wife, Mr. Timothy Darcy?" she asked one afternoon during a bombardment. She was obviously certain I had a wife.

No, she wasn't in England, I told Amna. She was somewhere in tropical Australia. For mysterious reasons I could not myself understand, I'd meant to pretend that the marriage was still alive. Or at least afflicted only with the sort of remoteness found in Eritrean marriages—the marriage, for example, of that superb little speaker who had kept Moka awake and me tormented in Jani.

But I understood that "tropical Australia" was a strange term to use—it gave too much away by its inexactness.

"My wife and I don't live together," I admitted. I amazed myself by blushing. I had the residual vanity not to want her to believe that this was one of those average first-world separations, caused by the pedestrian griefs of suburban marriage. I found I took a shabby moral pride in the idea that my marriage had been singularly cursed. But I couldn't convey that. "My wife lives with someone else now," I confessed.

Amna considered me studiously. It was an unworldly look. It reminded me of Christine. "So your wife left you?"

"Technically," I said, sweating, "she left me. But in real terms, we left each other."

"Isn't it strange that in famine and war there are few marriage problems . . . apart from death itself and the scattering of lovers over the map. Although some of the Muslim peasant girls who join our forces divorce their husbands first."

I didn't know whether to be pleased or not that the chat had so quickly become analytical.

We had agreed to go to a village called Inkema, because there was a poet there, a woman called Mama Xenob. At dawn, when we reached the place ten miles behind the front, we found from people eating their breakfast *injera* and sipping their tea that Xenob had gone. She was visiting the Sudan, where her reputation for revolutionary verse had recently burgeoned.

We were welcome to look at the other wonder of Inkema, its two-hectare garden. "Jesus," Henry told me. "We've seen enough fucking lentil plots in Nacfa!"

But, of course, we needed to be polite.

The gardener was a middle-aged man wearing a dirty smock and a wool cap. He had a quick whimsical smile. He pointed up to the contour of the hill, in which he'd dug some cunning little channels. From the air, he believed, they looked like mere chance drainage.

Henry refused to take up any of the slack when it came to asking the normal questions expected of a visitor. I asked the man the only one I could think of: whether he came from this place so close to the line to start with, or if he was a refugee.

I heard the expected answers: He was a member of a group displaced from a town called Embahara, three days' walk away. He told the by now usual stories of massacre and looting. Good ground, he said with typical nostalgia, better than this; granaries full of sorghum to which the enemy set the torch. He could never understand it, for they needed sorghum, too. The smoke rose for three days, and even as the gardener, a bullet in his hip, was carried away by EPLF soldiers who had turned up there after the Ethiopians left, he could see the smoke of burning grain stores.

So this place here, Inkema, was merely Embahara's shadow.

Then the gardener said something which struck me as less authentic than the rest of the tale. He said that the soldiers of the Dergue had had orders to force the people to learn and speak Amharic, the imperial language. People who refused to learn it, he said, had had their arms cut off.

When we'd left the garden and moved down into the village, I drew level with Amna Nurhussein.

"That story of people having their limbs lopped off?" I asked her. "Surely that's not the truth? I know the Ethiopians are tough. But cutting off people's extremities over a matter of language—that seems fanciful to me."

The other three, including Henry, who was still walking with us, kept a silence. I got the impression I'd been guilty of some sort of gaffe. I listened to our feet clattering on the shards of mountainside.

In fact, it was Henry who surprised me by answering. "They do that," he said. "It's in the tradition."

I was taken by surprise at this new alignment between Moka and Henry. Moka, of course, gave a more expected answer. The Amharas felt outnumbered; even inside Ethiopia they were outnumbered by other races speaking other languages.

I waited for Amna to speak. For some reason I had an idea of her as a reliable witness, less partisan. Moka and Henry were in their ways as questionable as the gardener.

Amna said nothing, however.

At dusk, when the valleys filled with shadow, we headed back for Nacfa. It was a tranquil evening. From the back of the truck, I watched Venus rise. But as we arrived at our bunker, the largest shelling Henry and I had experienced began. Through it the woman from the Public Administration bunker brought our supper as usual. Afterward, in spite of the thunder above ground, Henry took calmly to his air mattress in the bunker's second room with his diary-journal. Moka wrapped himself in a sheet and lost himself in his novel, which soon fell from his hands. In his sleep he snuffled and wheezed like a man running a race.

I was surprised how remote we all felt from the shelling here, deep under our mound of earth. The barrage outside seemed very nearly nothing to do with us. Once or twice concussions close by seemed to jolt us sideways and bring a momentary blackness into our vision. But I was delighted to be here with the exquisite Amna, desultorily discussing German novelists, my shortwave radio on the table between us, and emerging from it, as part of a BBC shortwave transmission able to be heard only intermittently, a professor from Leeds discussing the desirability or otherwise of one-party systems for African nations.

Without warning Amna said, "You know the gardener?"

"The one I didn't exactly believe."

"That one." She gazed at me levelly. "It is true. I saw the arms of children on the street in Asmara. It happens. I would not invent such a thing, Darcy."

She chose not to say any more. I was reminded of something Henry had mentioned once—that they don't relate their personal histories in any intimate way, that they don't put much stock in the subjective. But if I was to believe her, she would have to give me some such subjective tokens.

I think she understood this—the idea passed between us like a contract.

"I saw you being helped to the clinic in Orotta. Did that have anything to do with language?" I dreaded what I might hear. Perhaps the shelling, the enormous occasional thud outside, made me febrile. It was as if the present Amna remained in this cavern of ours on the strength of just one sinew, which even the memory of evil could snap.

"In some way," she said dismissively and with that choppy enunciation.

"The bastinado?" I risked asking, naming one of the oldest tortures and one I knew was favored in the Horn. I was trembling, as if I'd uttered an obscenity. I was also frightened that Moka would wake and overhear. I watched the apparently perfect order of her features, the impeccability of the maxilla behind the flesh. Surely, I thought, surely none of this was touched.

"Oh," she said, "it's well known that in prison I was luckier than most people."

"Just the same, your Uncle Salim says that you were tortured."

"I am here," she said. "And I can walk. That means things aren't as bad as my father's cousin Salim might believe."

She began cautiously, though, some of her sentences broken into by the strangely intimate, strangely remote row from ground level. She bore me gently along, speaking of family history. I was asked, for example, to imagine the family business, a large Asmara pharmacy, which had been founded by her grandfather in the days of the Italians. In the pattern of Asmara's worldliness and energetic commerce, her father, too, had gone on measuring out dosages in his dispensary through all the shifts and turmoils. As Amna described it, it was one of those Continental-style apothecary shops, owing more to the Italian influence than to the British. The medicines lay in enormous varnished cabinets bearing labels in Latin shorthand, and a librarian's ladder on runners put every cure and specific on the highest shelves within the reach of the pharmacist.

I found it easy to envisage those calm, varnished walls where Amna glided along attending to prescriptions, where between the sliding of the ladder in one direction or another, her father might hear of the arrest of the son or daughter of this or that client. The rebel organization in Asmara was called the Committee of Seven. Young nationalists of high school age distributed leaflets for it and wrote little insurgent columns in mimeographed tracts.

Such children suffered the cells of the Gebi barracks, Amna told me. They might be trucked off shackled to Addis or, if things went really wrong, jettisoned dismembered along Asmara's faubourgs. "There are avenues fringed with palms," Amna told me. "There are great roundabouts where yellow flowers bloom all the year. A civilized city! But Afan made it mad in this way. Passing traffic was *meant* to see!"

She explained that her father was a quiet man. He took pains to dissuade his daughter from doing anything flippant enough to land her, trussed up, in a place like Gebi. In high school, though (Amna announced, without seeming to know that the same cliché was uttered in the West), there was a certain fashion to rebellion, to being a member of the old ELF, whose most visible members were certain glamorous intellectuals and various grizzled tough men who had once been NCOs in the Ethiopian or Sudanese armies.

The ELF divided its rebels into five zonal cells, according to racial and religious divisions. Amna's father, a moderate Muslim, like his cousin Salim Genete down on the coast used to doing business with all kinds—the sort of man who belongs to service clubs, said Amna, because he actually *enjoys* doing business with all kinds—saw dangers in this. "We will have war zones like China, he told me. And bandit chieftains! I wanted to be a Sierra Maestran, and he knew it. He knew also that he could prevent me from being one, that I would obey him to that extent."

"Sierra Maestran?" I asked, though I had dimly heard the term from Stella. There were boys and girls who took off with their backpacks to the Ala hills south of Asmara. In revolutionary innocence and in tribute to Fidel, they gave a Cuban name to these hills: the Sierra Maestra.

But though prevented from vanishing into the Sierra Maestra, by the age of sixteen, Amna claimed, she was a runner for an intelligence cell which included schoolteachers and older pupils.

It was the ambushes and other humiliations the Sierra children imposed on the Emperor's forces on the road south of Asmara that helped bring about the fall of Haile Selassie, the Lion of Judah.

"I was very pleased," said Amna primly. "I had reasons of kinship, of family, to be pleased." For after the Emperor vanished, the leadership of what emerged as the new government, the Dergue, belonged at first to an Eritrean, General Aman Andom, "a relative by marriage." Andom knew how bitterly the Eritreans would always contest any foreign possession of Asmara and the highlands. He knew, too, said Amna graphically, the cost of napalm and high explosive—"It is as expensive as gold leaf. If they chose to coat all the highlands with gold leaf, it would be less wasteful than paving them with napalm."

The Dergue and its young Captain Mengistu had Andom shot dead on his doorstep in Addis for recognizing these Eritrean verities. They believed that with their fresh strategies and Marxist probity they could reduce Eritrea to a province by one firm, sharp move.

I watched Amna demonstrating with her hands the movements of the Dergue against the knapsack-toting kids of Sierra Maestra —one blow from the direction of Massawa on the Red Sea, one from Tessenai to the southwest. But the Eritrean rebels met both. The Ethiopian army was as convincingly repulsed as it had been under the Emperor.

But of course the Ethiopians continued to hold Asmara itself, and on the trams of Asmara sat the composed student and intelligence runner Amna Nurhussein, now a pharmacy student in an unsettled but determined nation.

"What was your main work for the rebels?" I asked her.

"I was not working for the rebels," she told me with her concisely edged English. "I *was* a rebel."

"But your main work?"

"Fraternal work."

"Fraternal?"

She was aware—"fraternally"—of the other Ethiopian races who had been forced to serve in the tyrant's army and who had little truck with Amharas, with Addis, or with whatever imperial concept presently possessed it. Together with her physics professor she prepared a weekly newspaper, printed on an illegal Gestetner machine. "Hard news," she said. "From the home regions of the conscripts."

I wondered what an Asmaran undergraduate's concept of "hard" news might be. I also began despite myself to imagine a Frankfurt friend, a British or American journalist, from whom she'd be likely to hear such a term.

Just before her arrest by Afan, the Cubans sent ten thousand regulars to help Mengistu and the Dergue crush Eritrea, and she and her colleagues, chastened, stopped speaking of the Ala hills as Sierra Maestra.

Asmara, she said, had many elegant villas and apartments and looked altogether far more urbane a city than the scattier capital of Ethiopia, Addis Ababa. But Afan, of course, the Ethiopian security police, for the time being set the city's tone. They raided her parents' villa one evening at dusk when her parents were themselves out at some social event. She still considers it fortunate that she was home, for it was known that if the suspect was not on the premises, Afan might take other members of the family as replacements.

She had to wait while the police, in the manner of police in more places than Asmara, casually plundered the place, taking the shortwave radio, the recorder, silverware from the dresser; flicking over the titles in her father's library and confiscating this volume or that.

I noticed she related Western-style, one could say *bourgeois* details. Such as that one policeman emerged from the parental bedroom with her father's best suit and three of her mother's dresses carried over his shoulder. She showed an old-fashioned outrage over that. The business of being a revolutionary had not undermined her sense of a certain holiness in possessions. At some time in the future, I could see by the way she spoke, she wanted her own dresses in her own wardrobe.

While this loot of the clan treasures continued, a young policeman sat at the end of the dining room table, keeping a pistol leveled at her, and with a soft smile continued to refer to her as "a whore from the front!"

After the pillage, she said, she was forced out into the garden and thrown into the back of a Polish Fiat. She was aware of neighbors looking flinchingly from behind the grilles and shutters at their windows.

"I felt a rush of blood and pride up into my head," she said, placing all her fingers to her forehead. "It's very important for prisoners to feel that—a sort of pride in being arrested, the one chosen."

"Pride?" I asked. I could not imagine myself feeling pride at such a moment. Though I did remember then, among the reverberations of the Dergue's artillery, the prideful graffiti in the Pawiak prison in Warsaw, where after torture and before execution by the SS, partisans had written their forthright scrawls on walls of the cells, brave assertions picked out in and honored by luminous paint these days. Perhaps that was what Amna was talking about: a sort of foreshadowing of that future luminosity the Polish graffitists were sustained by in their last hours.

I had by this stage of my interview with Amna begun to take notes. And *pride* was the first word I wrote after her name.

They had taken her across the city, to the old Italian cavalry barracks at Gebi her father had warned her about. Even under the Emperor, Gebi had been the interrogation center. There were grand stables, which had been converted into cells, each stall high-sided and dank. The walls threw groans of other prisoners upward till they became diffused and disembodied among the stylized rafters.

She was willing, for the sake of validating what the gardener had said to us earlier in the day, to throw in further details. She was left overnight without food or water. There was nowhere to urinate except the corner of the cell. But her father had old friends from the days of the Rotary and the Chamber of Commerce, before the Dergue put an end to both institutions. The network still existed. There were Eritreans still retaining influence to whom her father could appeal.

Above all, this strange pride remained. The tyrant had shown how much she had hurt him by throwing her into such a hole.

By the next morning thirst troubled her, as they meant it should. There were other instances of what she called in the bunker "indirect means." They would sometimes lead you along corridors or across small courtyards in which you would see the lolling cadaver of some young Eritrean, hands and eyes bloodily gone. Across a parade ground which must have seen all the exotic uniforms of the Italians, the British, the Emperor's cavalry, they led her to a colonnaded barracks and down a stairwell. In the basement the air stank and was full of groans and whimpers.

They opened a green door. It seems that the term *green door* was uttered by both the Ethiopian police and the rebels as a synonym for torture. In the place she now found herself, a large space with a drain running down the middle of the floor as if to collect the run-off of the torment practiced here, she was made to stand to one side and witness the water torture of a male, a member of her cell, a young economist.

She spoke to me not so much of the economist but of the officer in charge of things, a man named Lieutenant Dawit Wolde. Throughout, Wolde occupied a desk in the corner. He had an in-tray and an out-tray, said Amna, just like a normal civil servant. It was unlikely, she says, that this Wolde had any fear of Amnesty International or of the Geneva Conventions, but nonetheless she doubted that Wolde was his real name, suspecting instead that it was some *nom de guerre*. She set herself to memorize his face and behavior. He was a man of about thirty, often unshaven but always neatly dressed. His manners fascinated Amna. He spoke in a normal, level voice, and though he could get angry, it simply introduced more emphasis into his speech. He never shouted or gesticulated.

Lieutenant Wolde told her in Amharic that the economist had given everything away. They needed her simply for confirmation of some details. "So there's no bravery left to you," Lieutenant Dawit Wolde told her with a shy smile.

What made her fearful, she said, was that he seemed to know about her pride. She'd readied herself to suffer like the economist, but she had not prepared herself to be denied heroic chances. The economist's dulled eyes flashed across her face, and she thought there was accusation in them.

So that was the nature of her torment, to watch water bounce off the economist's head, again encased in an orange plastic bag. Her cell, the EPLF in general, had devised a sort of tactic: when interrogated, you offered first the names of rebels who had just recently, perhaps in the last week, escaped through the lines or had gone to the Sudan, West Germany, the United States, or England. She named a man called Tesfapaulos.

"Everyone starts with Tesfapaulos," Lieutenant Wolde told her. Even the economist, he claimed, had begun with *that* name.

She gave him other names, the recently escaped, and after two hours, the economist being in a coma on the tiled floor, Wolde unexpectedly let her be taken back to her horse stall.

When she was returned to the stables, across a yard in which three women prisoners in foul and tattered dresses were cooking millet soup on an open fire, she was dispirited. "The torturers hadn't punished me as I expected. And they took their time. Unhurried." Their leisureliness seemed to have made an impression on her, the unhurried time they took. They had cured her, she said, of what she called "my young idea"—the idea that she was a special rebel and that they were frantic to torment her. She had to join the line, to wait to be questioned and ground down in Wolde's mill.

She seemed to think it was the prosaic timetable of torture, its bureaucratic slowness, which was the great danger in the end.

By this point of her recital, I was not as preoccupied with the thump of the 122-millimeter shells over the hill and around the bunker as by her long wait—that day in 1978—for water at dusk. Suspended in thirst in the holy city of Asmara, she waited to be drowned, confused, blinded with pain—in the city thrust up eight thousand feet above the Red Sea, urbane in its climate, noted in its scholarship both Coptic and Islamic, and removed in its essential being, its refined avenues, from the Ethiopian tropics of torture.

"I thought it was my city," she confessed. "It was not the city of the torturers. I came to believe it belonged to the prisoners."

I knew I'd lost the gift to be impassioned by a city the way Amna was about Asmara. As the artillery barrage began to diminish outside the bunker, her emphasis was less on imprisonment than on that capital set on the high road from the Red Sea to the Kassala province of Sudan, on the high road, too, to Gondar and Gojjam, Ethiopia's turbulent western reaches. She seemed to have the naive but touching idea that all the invaders wanted it exactly because it was a temperate and civilized home, but that they came to it without the appropriate talents to enjoy it. In her mind, no earthly power could feel happy without the option of a villa in Asmara.

And Asmara never sold itself away. Asmara seemed to be, to her, Eritrea focused on a mountaintop. It never gave over to the ancient kingdom of Axum. It permitted the Turks to build towers in its foothills but never declared itself theirs. It was awarded to the Italians, in the time of the European carve-up of the Horn, but only because it was so resistant to the Ethiopian Emperor. Through the Italian and British years, sixty-two of them, Asmara—in Amna's interpretation of history—kept its clear, high head.

Interpreting the ceremonies of torture for me, who had never known them, Amna spoke of how she became sharply aware of their casual, *ex tempore* nature. One day electrodes, the next the circle of rope in which knots were tied to fit over the eyes. This rope, called "the tear-maker," they tightened from behind when they remembered.

"I wondered if there was a textbook," she confessed. "Something they had from the old Emperor . . . or from the East Germans, who were now advising them. Was there a manual which told the order to work in? Or is it part of the science to work on whim?"

In any case, their manner confused prisoners in a way prisoners didn't expect to be confused. "Even the victim of torture would like to believe that he is in the hands of experts," said Amna with a smile.

During our talks she did not pretend that the bastinado punishment whose effects still occasionally swelled her ankles, as had happened in our defile in Orotta, wasn't frequent or that it was comfortable. It was, however, what she'd expected to have to face. In this one regard, they hadn't taken her by surprise. She began to wonder if the nature of her punishment, less wide-ranging than the torture of other prisoners, less physical than that of others, mightn't be due to the influence of some important friend of her father's.

In our bunker, or later, the next day, sitting in the sun on the rocks by the door, she told me something of the strategies of the political prisoner. How to create a sort of mechanism in your brain so that you suffer in shifts and are numb and unreachable for stretches at a time. How you try to give a Lieutenant Wolde, who is unlikely to be a fool, an occasional sense of a dam breaking, of secrets spilling out without stint. How to space your denials and pleas and cosset the interrogator's secretest desire, which is—according to Amna—"to be in charge of the prisoner by a little margin."

These skills she'd learned from observing other prisoners in their extremes of pain. Meanwhile, her parents brought her weekly food supplies and bribed officials so highly that some of it reached her.

Football

A long time before we could see the playing field itself, we could hear the cheers of the football crowd, above the bleating of goats and the susurrus of blowing sand.

Moka said, with exactly the right mix of tension and excitement a man late for a football match should display, "They are already playing!"

We came over a spur of rock to find before us, on a bowl of dust marked out with white lines, a team dressed in white jerseys and shorts and a team dressed in blue, both of them in full play. Fighting for possession of the soccer ball, they raised dust clouds.

The crowd ran to thousands. All of them were armed. Near us, a clump of rebel men and women on a small hillock threw deep blue ribbons of shade across the field. This was the hour when on other days the Ethiopian shelling had begun. I wondered what signs had enabled the Eritreans to gauge that this afternoon would be free of bombardment, a suitable day for championship football.

The crowd had walked two miles or more out of the trenches for this game. It was, said Moka, a final between the champion division of the Nacfa Front and the champions of Hallal. And there was that atmosphere of a great sporting event—the ambience of a contest which had teased away at people's imaginations and hopes for a week or so. I noticed that Henry was taken by the intense crowd on the hill above the ground and sketched them, along with their thin shadows.

It was a sophisticated game, there in the dust. At the halfway mark stood a truck with a loudspeaker, and someone commentated in Tigrinyan. As moments of crisis arose in offense or defense, his voice took on the sharp acceleration of a professional broadcaster.

The goalkeeper of the Nacfa Front was under recurring attack from the Hallal forwards. Blue Nacfa defenders collided with white attackers in mists of saffron dust. Eritrean infantrywomen along the sidelines dragged their shawls across their mouths and shrilled through the cloth.

Apart from the broadcast truck, the Eritreans had appointed what was clearly one of Masihi's cameramen to the match—he was at the far end of the ground, with a sound assistant. He caught all the action amid the dust columns. As the Hallal champions scored and the Nacfa Front women sitting in front of us let their shawls fall from their faces and uttered guttural moans, he did a panning shot of them.

Through all this, Moka and Amna were off far up the sideline, performing their usual greetings with only half an eye for the action. But the Nacfa Front players had begun to strike back, bringing the ball up the wing, and the cameraman and his sound man followed it down the sideline at the jog.

I could see now that the sound technician was a girl, her head swathed in the standard Arab-style shawl. And from the turban on the cameraman's head, I should have been able to tell at once that it was Masihi. It was quite obvious now, anyhow.

The referee, a soldier in jeans and khaki shirt, awarded the Nacfa Front team a penalty kick. I saw Masihi nodding while filming, urging his daughter in with the mike so that the thunk of the ball as it left the Nacfa Front kicker's foot would be picked up above the wind. Christine obediently moved the black ovoid of the mike to produce the best effect. In the midst of this movement, she saw me and smiled. It was not exactly the smile she had brought to the Sudan, not that watery rictus which I'd found so hard to interpret. It was almost an Eritrean smile, very broad, very subtle, a certain breathlessness to it. But she could not say anything yet. She had her job to do.

The corner kick came to nothing. Some very clever Hallal Front defenders took the ball far upfield after there had been one token attempt at goal by the Nacfa center forward. I found Amna at my side. "They are losing," she said, smiling broadly with a fake regret.

"It's Masihi and Christine," I told her, pointing to the camera crew.

"They will show this film all over Eritrea, wherever there is a video machine," said Amna. "*This* is our civil war."

In her shawl, pushing forward with her mike, Christine suddenly looked like a pretty Palestinian. That was very simply it, I thought. She had the appearance of someone who'd found unexpectedly the ideal job.

"He's making use of his daughter," said Amna. I heard again her extraordinary Eritrean laugh. "You do not talk to Masihi long," she said fondly, "before you become either *sound* or *film*."

The surge at the other end of the field produced a goal for the Hallal division. They embraced each other, plying their shoulders. It struck me that here, in this bowl between hills, were some thousands of disappointed spectators armed with automatic weapons and with stick and round grenades. And yet none of these arms were fired, none of the grenades flourished or thrown. The goal score was absolute and it decided things. It was not like the decision of the UN. It *was* like the decision of God. The Nacfa Front was being beaten, and no armaments could help.

Hallal scored again and the Nacfa crowd groaned rhythmically, like a Biblical race. After a further spate of unconstructive attack by the Nacfa Front, the referee blew a conclusive blast and spread his arms. He must have seen the gesture from tapes the EPLF pirated from British television. On this field above all others, his gesture, palms down, was appropriate, since it seemed to settle both the dust and the gale. Players embraced and the crowd picked up their AK-47s and began to trail back toward their trenches. I saw Masihi doing what I think is called a tracking shot, across the ground and to the sudden single line of EPLF troops sloping home to their bunkers and trenches. He signaled his daughter that she could now stop recording. She muttered something into the mike. It looked like a long-practiced identifying mutter. I remembered she had said she'd done sound for the young filmmakers at her polytechnic.

Soon, still carrying their gear, the Malmédys had crossed the corner of the field and were welcoming us. I noticed a long, close welcome between Amna and Masihi, no more intimate than any she had exchanged along the front line in days past. Yet I found myself spending a childish amount of time worrying what this one might mean. I abominated that feeling, that murderous little proprietary glimmer, the beginning of madness. Masihi finished wishing Amna *"Cernai,"* wheat, and came to me and shook hands with European restraint.

"She is very good," he told me solemnly, nodding toward his daughter. "I didn't know what to expect, and so I thought, *Keep her busy!*" He laughed robustly. "And she is very good."

I said I was delighted to hear it.

His eyes shifted and he lowered his voice. "And you were very kind to her, Darcy."

"Not at all."

But he insisted. "No, no. You *were* very kind."

I must have looked baffled. I wasn't aware of being abnormally kind.

"She was disturbed when you first met her," Masihi whispered. "And you did everything the right way."

I was still working that out when Christine arrived at my side, her sound equipment jiggling on her hip, and kissed me lightly on the cheek. It was a very adult, composed kiss. She began asking me lively questions about our recent journey—Henry's and mine— since we'd last seen each other in the flour-white scrub at Jani. She asked after Lady Julia, who—I told her—was discovering amazing things in Endilal.

I asked if she had been back to Orotta.

"Yes," she said. "And I saw Mr. Salim."

"He's still there?"

"Waiting for his son."

"No, not everyone is as successful at finding people as you are, Christine," I told her. I told her, too, that her father thought she was good at this cinematic stuff. She seemed to flush with pleasure but to take the compliment confidently, like an adult woman. "I might stay a long time," she said. "You will need to give my regards to that Sudanese police sergeant at the border."

"I always expected I might need to," I confessed.

Then she lowered her voice. "I may go through the lines, recording sound for my father. He's been there a hundred times."

"Be very careful," I said. I was still puzzling out what Masihi had meant by 'disturbed.' "

"Darcy," she said suddenly in her most pedantic English. "You should be told. I had a baby girl. Masihi's granddaughter."

I couldn't find anything to say. Christine looked away, and the sound with which she began her next sentence was like the expulsion of breath from a woman who has been hit with a blow.

"She was premature and lived only nineteen days. I barely held her, because she could not breathe without a machine. Her name was Sophie."

"Oh, Christine," I said.

I remembered the story of abortion she'd fed Henry. That was because the truth was more sacred. It was better to make up a chosen loss like abortion than admit to the unchosen one.

"Of course, I did not want to talk about it when I first came to Khartoum. My boyfriend said, 'It's probably a good thing.' I didn't like anyone saying that, Darcy."

For a time she bent her head over the sound machine on her hip. She could have been just another Eritrean bending to rub the grit of the Ethiopian turmoil out of her eye. What intrigued me at that second was the stray suspicion that she had followed her father's pattern. Maybe an unguarded, callow sentence from Madame Malmédy—a sentence not unlike the one the boyfriend had spoken—had provoked Masihi's flight. I reached out and caressed her wrist.

From one side I heard Amna's clipped enunciation. "I should say goodbye for now."

I couldn't believe what I had heard. Without foundation, I'd thought I would go on having unlimited conversations with Amna, in bunkers and under artillery barrages, about tyranny's face.

"I have to visit other friends in the field," she said with a languid, apologetic smile.

As I shook hands with her, I considered trying the intimacies of shoulder-grinding, but I realized you had to be in the club for that, as you needed to be for intimacies of any level.

"Please take care of yourself," she said. "And eat more *injera* than you do."

I watched her say goodbye to the others and then move away with a column of infantry, chatting with a fairly grizzled-looking man in a flak jacket and long khaki trousers, probably an officer.

He seemed delighted to be talking to her, and I wondered if she had some sort of stature, a legendary status, among them. But if she was visiting friends "in the field," why was she walking toward the trenches with the infantry?

I heard Christine laughing, a reasonable, knowing, sisterly laugh. "Never mind," she told me gently. "I am still here."

That night, out of loneliness, I completed the notes I'd taken from Amna's account of her imprisonment.

After some two weeks of interrogation, she was taken from her cell in the stables and put in a large room in the cavalry barracks. Once there had been glass windows in place here—it may well have been the officers' mess. Now there were only bars and both the rich sunlight and the insidious mountain cold could penetrate. Here Amna met an extraordinary woman named Kidanu, a woman of perhaps thirty-eight or so who had, under the Emperor, taught Amharic at Asmara University.

"Kidanu made us all feel fortunate women."

Among the prisoners was a girl of eighteen years, a farmer's wife, pregnant. She had been carrying a liter of kerosene back to her village from Asmara. After all, the hills had been stripped of wood and there was no electricity in the villages. They arrested her as a fire-raiser, an arsonist, an incendiarist. She had received five years before a military court. She was the sort of woman, said Amna, whom Kidanu could cause to feel elected, exalted and lucky.

Not totally lucky, however, since she was soon to give birth.

By the rules, each prisoner had two widths of tile to lie on. This principle had been so long established in the communal cell that Amna did not know whether it had been decreed by the prison authorities or by Kidanu. For when you went into a shared cell you fell among strangers, each with her stench of misery, wearing her remnants of street clothes stained with puke and dust. Some of them had nails missing from one hand or cigarette burns across the napes of their necks. You wondered whether any of them would have cause to make room for you. And you were calmed by the news that they would. There were two widths, and that was inviolate. You could make that part of your world picture. As Africa had two seasons, drought and rain, you had two tiles.

As the farmer's wife swelled, however, Kidanu went quietly

among those in the cell whom she knew to be politicals and not just hapless toters of kerosene. The girl carried the future of Eritrea in her belly, Kidanu argued. Kidanu talked three of the prisoners into occupying a mere five tiles between them.

There were further aspects to this model state of a cell as run by Kidanu. If one prisoner's relatives were wealthy enough to bribe the guards and ensure their beloved received food, another prisoner's relatives were not. Kidanu established without apparent force a sharing of food.

To judge by Amna's account, there, in the midst of the Gebi interrogation center, the perfect sisterly community asserted itself. Everyone there knew that they were being transformed, and were fortified to face the knout and the cigarette ends and the electrical terminals, which again, she kept insisting and almost complaining, she herself, Amna, was not subjected to.

Again, I had been able to see, during our conversations, the fine line of her collarbone inside her blouse, and it did seem unlikely that anyone who had been worked over by the torturers could emerge so perfectly. Her elegance, the way she moved most of the time, seemed to bear out her claim that the bastinado was the extent of what she had suffered.

In Gebi one evening at sunset, the Ethiopians opened the door and threw in among the other women a bloodied girl wearing army shirt and shorts, British-style military gaiters, and plastic sandals. So perfectly was this the Eritrean rebel uniform that the other prisoners might have suspected the girl of being a planted spy if it had not been for an untreated and gaping wound in her left breast. From the wound, said Amna, she and Kidanu spooned the maggots. They washed the injury with dirty cloths and clean water and bandaged it with fragments of unwashed shirt. The chief warden, a Danakil with filed teeth and tribal slashes on his cheeks, saw this crude dressing from the door and ordered the cell unlocked. He screamed accusations at them and asked who had told them they were entitled to treat the wound?

While one of the turnkeys kept the prisoners covered with a rifle, the Danakil knelt and tore the dressing from the girl's wound. He carried the bloodied dressings around the cell, checking them against people's tattered clothing, taking the names of those who had supplied the bandages. Kidanu, of course, became vocal. The inevitable speech of the prisoner they can't bring down: "We're as human as you are, maybe more so. Do what you like to us. We're going to treat that girl."

He told her that more bandaging would cost her her life. Yet after he left the cell he clearly wasn't organized enough to make use of the names he'd collected, and two months later, when Kidanu was taken from the cell and disappeared for good, it was probably the result of a random culling rather than because the Danakil had reported her.

Before Kidanu was taken away, however, the eighteen-year-old peasant wife gave birth. Children who draw their first breath in prisons, said Amna, never grow up to be ordinary people.

It was getting late in the evening when we reached this stage of the tale, and the end of the story-cum-interview became sketchy. Her parents had simply bought her out of prison, she said. She said it as if it were a normal expedient of those parents who had the money. All of them, the Nurhussein clan, parents and brothers and sisters, had then passed behind the rebel lines.

She had not seen Asmara for years. Now, since she'd gone off with the infantry, I wondered if this was the truth and whether she still went to and came from that beloved town in the mountains.

Frontline Grammar

Like most cameramen, Masihi would not let anyone else carry his equipment. He had a hard climb of it though, just before dawn, from the valley of Nacfa up to the high ridge the Eritrean trench line followed. The ground was in fact so steep that Moka kept on telling me to hand over my pack to him, though he avoided the same gesture toward Henry, and—frequently desperate for breath—I would say yes and hand the load over to him until breath and shame revived.

Behind me I could hear Christine gasping for air. But when I made an occasional futile offer to carry her sound gear, she refused. She had taken on her father's professional standards—the carry-your-own-gear ethic of the camera crew.

I had for some reason not been surprised to discover from Moka in the small hours that the Frenchman and his daughter would be coming with us. Christine had foreshadowed this the day before at the soccer game. She had said she was or might be going through the lines. It had seemed apparent to me then: If Tessfaha wanted a journalist there, if the Eritrean Relief wanted Henry, then someone must want Masihi to film it.

"All the way?" I asked. "They'll go with us the whole way?"

"I believe it's so," said Moka, sounding a little harassed. "I am never told everything!"

"Then you're as confused as I am," I suggested. But he looked at me as if I were a foreigner, which I had forgotten I was.

✳   ✳   ✳

Straining up the slope to the front line, we met a string of young soldiers coming lithely down the mountain, carrying plastic jerry cans. They were fetching their sections' water for the day from a well concealed beside the track. The soldiers levered aside a slab of stone which covered the well. One of them jumped into the hole and stood on a subterranean ledge, reaching up to take water cans, reaching down into the earth to fill them. This was a well the Pintubi of Fryer River would have approved of—it lived separate from the sun.

They offered us a drink from a powdered-milk can: sweet water with a faintly smoky taste to it. In Fryer River they would have said you could thereby detect the spirits.

Higher up, we were permitted to make a stop at the little bunker of a signals unit, to eat a bowl of millet porridge for which we had no appetite. Moka rolled his eyes at me and said, "We are soldiers now, who eat to keep up our strengths."

Masihi, spread-eagled by the wall, quickly finished his porridge, lay still, and pulled his shawl over his eyes. I could see Christine trying to imitate his gift for grabbing rest wherever it presented itself, but the knack wasn't native to her yet.

Soon, with the millet porridge pressing on me like a burden, we climbed the last bends and entered, through a stone doorway in the mountainside, the tail end of the trench system. We were in a deep, cool sap. Beneath a roof of logs and earth to our right, a wide compartment was crowded with soldiers. As my eyes got used to the dimness, I could see that here yet another class was in progress! Third grade science, Moka said.

Beyond the science class, a slab of light fell along what I suppose is called "a communication trench." It seemed a scene from the Somme or Gallipoli. Yet the drainage was better and there was no stink either of wet death or excremental mud.

We passed through the class and stood in the communication sap, which was open to the sky. Occasional low doorways presented themselves in its walls and led away down steps into deep chambers decorated with posters and colored cloth. I surmised these were messes. In each, a number of large bomb casings sat upright on their circular tails and brimmed with drinking water.

Pointing negligently toward the south, Moka said, "The front line. There."

"Where?" asked Christine in a whisper.

"There," said her father. "Ten steps away."

But we were to rest in one of these mess bunkers. We would not be moving again until night.

I noticed with a kind of heady amazement that Moka seemed to be addressing everyone. So, almost casually and as if according to an intuitive plan drawn up outside anyone's conscious knowledge, Henry, Masihi, Christine, and I were *all* to cross the lines. I was even a little amazed that Amna wasn't with us, to complete the party.

We dropped down out of the sap into the mess set aside for us. Panting and looking for an argument, Henry asked Masihi, "Aren't you going to film the classroom? Education in the goddam front line!"

Masihi, disposing his gear, sighed. "I've got footage. Ai-ai-ai, I have footage! Twelve years' worth of classes. No one believes it in the West. They think each class I film has been specially staged for the filming. I found out too late in life that the camera is a very inconclusive argument."

In this comfortable place underground it was cool and dry. The water in the bomb casings spread its influence calmly over us.

Henry seemed exhausted. We helped him spread his sleeping bag on a bench and he fell on it. The bunker next door to us, connected to ours by a tunnel, was full of yet another class of infantrymen and -women, this one muscularly chanting English grammar.

I wondered if Henry wasn't ill as much as overwhelmed by his surroundings. I was, in any case. We had already had a glimpse of the extent of this trench line. We were acquainted with the fact that it ran for three hundred kilometers. We knew this long scar of trench could be seen from space and was sometimes— so everyone believed—photographed by Russian satellites. But now that we were in the line itself, these concepts had reality for us.

At last, leaving Henry behind to the heedless grammatic valor of the rebel troops resonating through our bunker, we went outside—just a few paces along the communication sap—and were all at once in the trench line. A bearded officer met us and told us to bend low. Stooping, we came to a long covered stretch where two boys were on watch. The ground of the trench and all the stones that lined it were strewn with cartridges. One of the boys removed a stone from the wall in front of him so that we could see the ribbon of Ethiopian trench sixty yards down the hill. I saw a head—Oromo, Somali, Amharic—rise for an instant above the line of the opposing trench and then disappear. The sight was electric and spun me back down the fire step.

At Moka's urging we admired the frequent bays, covered with logs and earth, where infantry caught by shelling could shelter. In one such stretch five soldiers were languidly discussing a map, while one of them, a robust girl of about twenty years, casually changed her shirt and sat bare-breasted on a stone for a time, rubbing her eyes.

"Here," said Moka after we'd passed beyond the map party, "you will see both the enemy and the path you will take. But look no more than a second."

I raised my head above the parapet for the allowed instant and stretched it to two. I had the impression of seeing clear downhill into the enemy trenches, which seemed almost as deserted as the Eritrean line, as if all the Dergue's conscripts were under cover. To our left front a road and a river ran south, the riverbed streaked with alkali and largely vacant of water. Closer, perhaps twenty paces from me, unburied and sun-mummied Ethiopian corpses lay in shreds of uniform. Again I dropped back down the parapet, breathless. I felt their terror, the anguish, the scalding loss of breath of stunned conscripts, solidified there on the slope. Full of hope and desperation and madness, they'd been driven this far uphill from their own trenches, and then the Eritreans had ended their surge.

"We have offered a truce for burying the dead," Moka told me, wheezing. He seemed to understand that I was outraged. "But the Ethiopians will not acknowledge us. They bury only the officers at the best of times. The ordinary men they leave to the sun and the hyenas."

I felt as hostile as Henry. Moka's relentless tales of Ethiopian unfeeling had begun to weigh on me, too.

"Is that true?" I challenged. "Is that really true?"

He did not answer. I raised my head again and looked sideways down the fall line of the trench to a mess of uniform and bone lying on the slope below. I heard Moka mutter, like a rebellious child, "It is of course true, Darcy. Are we barbarians?"

They pursued, these Eritreans, the ideal of honorable warriorhood. I couldn't quite believe it achievable. And yet the trenches were impeccably maintained, as if intended to be the martial face of the Eritrean educational ferment.

We walked a mile farther along the line in the morning sun, past more English classes and sections of young soldiers on watch. Sometimes Masihi and then Christine would risk another glimpse eastward toward the Red Sea, where the road and the river cut through the Ethiopian line. Christine moved here like a veteran. The jerkiness of limb she'd brought with her to the Sudan was fully gone.

Through this little tour of ours, it was apparent even to uninitiates like me that the Eritreans had the preferred ground. From high points we saw their line snaking to exploit every contour of the ridge. It would be terrible to be sent to take it, to be an Ethiopian child loaded with your assigned weaponry and kit, arriving out of breath to face the massed English grammar of the Eritreans.

Behind the ridge, in a low hut out of sight of the Ethiopian line, we met our escorts. We were shown to seats on benches, while the soldiers we had been brought to meet sat loose-limbed on the floor. That's where Masihi chose to sit too, though he directed his daughter to a bench. Their officer was a gangling man with the gentle eyes of this ferocious region. There was a streak of veteran gray in his hair. He could have been the same man Amna greeted and bumped shoulders with at the football match, but he probably wasn't. His name was Johanes. I suppose the Greek-speaking early Christians of Egypt brought such names— Petros, Georgis, Paulos, Johanes—to the highlands of Ethiopia and Eritrea.

Johanes kept referring to a smaller man, perhaps a sort of NCO or—I wondered—a political officer. This man knew Masihi well, so perhaps his main task in life was to escort people across into occupied Eritrea. His name was Ismail. He appeared to be about the same age as Johanes, in his early thirties. There were traditional slashes on his face, and he said he came from the lowlands, over in Barka, close to the Sudanese border.

I found all this out because of the competent English he spoke. While he talked, in a low, authoritative voice, a sort of uneasy glitter entered his eyes—a deep and wary casualness. Masihi drew him out and he told his strange but not atypical story as if only to the Frenchman. Masihi would sometimes put in asides as if Ismail weren't there.

At the age of fourteen Ismail had joined up with the ELF. They'd come through the villages of Barka holding seminars in his own language, Barya. He had heard for the first time in his own tongue that there were reasons other than God's will for death and hunger. The idea, this mother and siren of revolutions, took him by storm and changed him for good.

He had fought in the end in bloody, fraternal battles between the ELF and EPLF. "These days the Eritreans are a little embarrassed that it happened," Masihi told us in a loud whisper, as if no rebels were present, as if his own interest in the question was academic. "It was terrible, but sometimes you have to fight to get control of a revolution so that it won't grow up to be crippled—or maybe become the same beast in different form, another brand of tyranny."

Ismail had been wounded during the crazy strife. He admitted as much and casually touched the upper quadrant of his right chest. He didn't reflect on what would have seemed a pretty massive irony for someone like me: that he was now fighting beside the old enemy. With the mass of ordinary ELF soldiers he had decided some years back to join up with the EPLF on the Hallal Front. I might ponder what extraordinary beasts revolutions were, with their initials and shades of faction. But Ismail didn't waste words on observations like that. Compared to me, Ismail was brisk with history. Perhaps that was the only way to treat it.

He did tell me one thing directly, toward the end of the conversation: "Before I'm fifty I expect to see it. The end." I wondered what he'd do when the time came, when Asmara was entered and the equitable republic proclaimed. And there he would be with nothing but his AK-47 and his memory of a Barka village remoter than the rumor of Egyptian dynasties.

For he had been a combatant for twenty years.

Henry had joined us now, and he and I listened avidly when we found out Ismail had been operating behind the lines for the last year. Henry wanted to know whether the rebels held villages in a permanent way, or did they flit in and out? And when they traveled in occupied Eritrea, he asked, did they stick to remoter tracks, or could they travel by vehicle?

You could travel with your headlights on, he told us, within a few kilometers of some of the garrison towns. He sounded boastful in a muted kind of way.

Because they could depend only on a certain level of valor from their conscripts, the Ethiopians cleared only those villages where there were no EPLF. Ismail, still speaking mainly to Masihi, went into a comedic routine, explaining in a deliberately deep, over-serious voice how the Ethiopians moved in Eritrea. First they cleared the road with infantry and tanks, a terrible peril to goats. And only after that did the convoy creep along behind. They moved at just sufficient pace to avoid being shot by their officers, but not so fast as to present a banzai image.

"Did you say *banzai*?" I asked.

"They see all those American war movies," Masihi explained to us, again as if the rebels weren't actually present. "Someone brings in a generator and video gear, and they watch *The Dirty Dozen!*"

A small woman in military fatigues came into the hut. She sat by the door, beside Johanes. Her hair was cropped and she looked a wiry, competent little woman. She and Masihi greeted each other in an indolent, familiar way with waves of the hands. The two of them had a detailed, genial conversation in Tigri-nyan. At last Masihi turned to his daughter and then to us and explained who she was.

"She's the medic for our little tour," Masihi said. "Her name is Genet."

We all exchanged nods and waves. For me, of course, she brought into the hut the idea of both potential succor and in-jury.

Then Masihi turned to our new paramedic and continued growling and teasing in Tigrinyan. It was a conversation in which we could hear the shared experience, the code of whimsy and in-jokes.

I watched Christine, who was herself engrossed in this exchange. She seemed so calmly exhilarated by her father's Tigrinyan performance with this little rebel paramedic that I began to speculate that perhaps it's the fathers who stay home who really attract their daughters' contempt.

Above all, I tried to imagine her in Paris, wanly holding a small daughter.

Among the other boys and girls we were meeting now, our escorts, our reliable warriors, was a pleasant-looking twenty-two-year-old who said he was from Danakil, far down in the south. His name was that universal one, Mohammed. The others began to tell us that he was taking an officers' course—military technique, science, compass map-reading. He let us know that his father spoke English but that his own was halting. In fact, he uttered his well-formed English sentences with exactly the delicacy, that equal weight on each consonant, which reminded me of Amna.

He, too, like Ismail, had been a guerrilla fish in that sea beyond the front. Tonight or tomorrow night, depending on Henry's stomach, they would do the trick again, taking us with them. I watched Masihi discussing all this. He wasn't very fussed about this prospect so unspeakable, indefinable, startling to me, and his daughter—unfussed likewise, since that was her filial duty—sat by him with her hands folded together and locked between her knees.

Despite accounts given us of life on the south side of the lines by the young veteran Mohammed and by Ismail, I thought of the far side, the "unliberated zone," the way I used to think about the underwater when I was a child. You could not prepare yourself for it. You could not rehearse in your mind the sensation. It wasn't normal until you got there, and then it was too normal, and the danger was that you'd stay.

Henry waited on his air mattress, his dusty diary still and above all now at his side. He had the air of a man stripped down to the essentials for a large effort.

"But we have time, Mr. Henry," Moka confided to him. "We can wait another day."

"No," said Henry. "No. To hell with it."

"But if you are overcome with diarrhea in the middle of the crossing?" Moka asked.

Henry stared at him and would not answer.

I was pleased that Henry declared himself ready to go that evening. After the discussions with our barefoot doctor Genet and the boys, I would have found it difficult to sit contemplating the plunge for another day and night.

At sunset I was too stimulated to eat, even to satisfy the idea Moka seemed to have of the heroic Western appetite. At our rudimentary meal of *injera* and beans, Masihi ate slowly and functionally, and Christine seemed to imitate that style exactly. Just the same, I didn't get the impression that this was an infant imitating a grown-up. It was more that, in the company of her father, she'd discovered her own peculiar manners. I remembered how we'd clung together in Himbol under the attack of the locusts. She'd been a child without ideas in that gale of insects. I was still a child without ideas, but she'd changed.

Without any ill will, Henry asked Masihi the question I'd been too evasive to raise.

"Aren't you anxious this time? I mean, taking your daughter over there?"

Masihi drank his tea with little Eritrean sighs and considered an answer.

"If she were not here," he said at last, obviously offended, "she would be in New York or someplace, wouldn't she? With people who don't know what they're doing!"

He flashed a brisk smile at his daughter, in case she picked up and was hurt by any apparent callousness in this reply. Far from it, Christine grinned unambiguously back. Masihi seemed very relieved. He began telling us further tales about his strange profession.

"Thank God," he said, neatly hijacking the topic, bearing it away from the dangerous zone of the paternal and filial, "that I don't have the sixteen-millimeter camera to carry any more. I'm getting too old for that circus act. I've spent a lifetime climbing mountains at night to witness battles taking place in darkness. I say *witness* rather than *film*, because you need light to film. One night, five years ago or so, when we were crossing the front, I talked the officer around to waiting for the first light, and I got some footage, ghostly stuff, of our party slipping by the Ethiopian outposts. Not very good *technically*, but important for the archive. The grandchildren of these people, they should be able to look and say, 'That's how our grandparents lived.' Though I don't know that grandchildren always do that if the film is technically bad. They look at poorly shot stuff and say, 'Who are those strange people? They don't have reality!' Will there be anyone to say to them, 'That's old Roland Malmédy, nicknamed Masihi, and it was the best the poor old man could do at the time.' That's the puzzle of being a cameraman. The better the polemics, the worse the footage. The better the footage, the weaker the contact between the filmmaker and his material."

He drank still more tea, as if storing up moisture. I began to do the same. After all, he'd been *there*; he was worth imitating.

As if he noticed my intentness, he said, "Anyhow, no one comes to harm beyond the front. The worst I did was get tennis elbow from hauling that brute of a camera. The invention of the portable videocam saved my life. But one thing we're wise to remember: Beyond the front, there is not always a lot to eat and there is not always a lot to drink."

"Thank Christ!" said Henry, belching slightly.

By lantern light, we sat through nearly three hours of shelling. It seemed merely prelude to me; it did not worry me. Christine fell asleep and Masihi moved across the bunker toward me with apparent casualness and then dropped at my side.

"You must think I was rude to Henry," he said.

I denied it, though I did think Masihi had at least sounded defensive.

"Christine has been in a psychiatric hospital. Yes, I know it's astounding, but it makes sense, doesn't it? Her baby died and her boyfriend lost interest, so what do girls do in the West? They go into hospitals. They had filled her with drugs and were promising her shock treatment. So she walked out and came to the Sudan! I mean, that's why she seems a little strange. She walked away from her medication. If she was to get electric shocks, she thought, she might as well come here. Christ! What I mean, Darcy, is that in Asmara and Addis electricity is torture. In Paris it's a treatment!"

And Christine had had exactly that air, a woman who'd renounced opiates and was relearning the world, including its strangest portions.

"I'm pleased to have an explanation," I told him.

"Me too," he said, shrugging.

He left me. We drowsed. Sometimes I saw Christine neatly sleeping in a corner, and sometimes again loud fire would wake me suddenly and I would see the surface of the water in the bomb casings jolting with each concussion. Yet most of the bombardment was pitched over our heads and beyond this front trench. I imagined a hail of shrapnel across that arena of churned dust where the day before the Hallal Front had trounced the Nacfa Front, 2–nil.

Moka wasn't sleeping. He kept studying his Han Suyin novel— I knew it was about an Asian girl who marries a Westerner and was bittersweet and involved the renunciation of love. It had him in. He was no longer interested simply in improving his English usage—you could see he wanted to get to the denouement before the shelling stopped and we started out.

By nine, the barrage—if that was the name for it—grew more irregular. I began to prepare my tape recorder for the journey. Moka was not distracted from his book, however. Occasionally he would pause to ask a question. For example, "What does *Hobson's choice* mean?"

Conversation began again. People stirred. Christine began to ask her father about Issayas, the leader whose representative, Askulu, we had met in She'b.

"Issayas," said Masihi, "is impossible! They all are! Camera-shy every one. You met Askulu? The one with the baby? She is better. She did a lot of television in the West. But Issayas is terrified that the Muslims of Barka or Danakil will be disaffected if he appears on their communal video screens all the time. 'Who does he think he is?' he fears they will ask themselves. A highlander and a Coptic Christian and an intellectual, as he is! He knows that the camera deifies, and he doesn't want to be deified, the way Mao was. He disapproves of the god Mao. Issayas is a puritan when it comes to film. He believes the camera corrupts everyone, the one behind the viewfinder, the one in focus, the one who watches. Everyone!"

And he laughed broadly. I imagined him trying to persuade the reluctant Issayas into focus on a camouflaged terrace somewhere in the mountains.

Ten minutes later, the young veteran from Danakil, Mohammed, appeared on the steps of our bunker and in his musical voice called us up to the trench.

Making No Shadows

It turned out that I had a false and highly colored idea of the kind of stealth we might need for crossing through the Ethiopian lines. The prosaic feel of it all took me by surprise. We stepped from a sap behind a great knob of rock and strolled out from behind it into the middle ground between the two trench lines. We made no shadows; the moon had not risen and the spur on which the front line ran cast its darkness across us. That aspect, at least, was the way I'd foreseen it in my melodramatic imagining.

I had no idea of the direction we took, but after five minutes I was sure we were near the road I had seen this morning, the one which came down from the Red Sea coast and passed through the Ethiopian lines. I wondered about mines but was greatly comforted by what I could see of the easy gait of our escorts, the familiar way they loped across this steep ground.

"You will hear them talking all around you," Johanes had told us. But we were not to take any notice of that. And now I *did* hear them speaking all around, though I could see nothing—the soldiers of the Dergue speaking in casual or prosaically heightened tones. Very soon we seemed to arrive in the midst of a sort of military bazaar. Trucks passed us and we ignored them. I retained a portion of my breath, not because fear demanded it but rather because a kind of wonderment overcame me. What a cunning transit we were making. We passed within ten paces of men unloading undefined supplies by torchlight from the back of a vehicle. Henry and Christine and I, with our white faces and our barely paramilitary clothing!

245

Yet no one took notice of us. Sometimes there would be a light, momentarily revealed from the doorway of a bunker, and a burst of shortwave radio transmitting ecstatic stringed instruments from Addis. I watched the young veteran ahead of us—the one named Mohammed. I got a glimpse of Ismail, the veteran of the ELF who'd been fighting since the age of fourteen. Genet, the medic, walked at my side; her eyes seemed to be fixed on the ground. None of these people swayed. They kept the roll of their shoulders within a restricted arc. The idea was that a normally careful gait would prevent your enemies from paying attention!

In a clump of trees in front of us, a number of trucks were starting up their engines after sheltering all day from the Eritrean observers high up on their lethal spur. One of the trucks flashed its lights. I watched, believing and unbelieving with equal ease, as Johanes walked up to its cabin. We stood about meekly as he chatted with the driver. Some other trucks gave off flashes of cabin light and snatches of shortwave music and Amharic announcements.

Johanes returned to us.

"This is our truck," he told us, smiling slowly.

I hadn't known there would be one.

We crawled into the back—it was a large Ural. I remember how Masihi handed the camera up to his daughter, who was already standing on the truck tray. Definitely two professionals on their way to a shoot, casually transferring their gear. What would her French psychiatrists think of this, the refugee from shock treatment operating without opiates behind the Dergue's lines?

The truck started up and there was a lot of rowdy gear-changing, nothing subtle or tentative, and then we began to move south, passing other vehicles arriving at the front with military plenty. I saw, in a hiatus between dust, assorted command vehicles full of Ethiopian officers dressed Cuban style in Castro caps, bandannas around their mouths. Music surged forth from their shortwave radios for a second or two. Then our cumulative dust choked it.

In a broad river plain we swung away from the established road, cutting our own swath across the banks of grit and boulders. Soon we'll be on our own, I told myself, and I can start to breathe again. Yet then we rejoined a line of trucks. My chest began to pain dully. I had lost my calm for some reason. Was there air at the bottom of this Amharic sea? A young, disconsolate Ethiopian soldier indolently waved us through a checkpoint. I heard a small bark of laughter from Masihi, who had been craning his neck over the sides to watch the road ahead. This was a new procedure, he told me later, this ploy of joining in the mêlée. The other times he had crossed the line, he said, there had been a lot more creeping. Whereas this was a bus run. This was pure fish-in-the-water stuff.

Throughout this phase, Henry seemed to lie comatose. His head was propped against his great duffel bag. When I regained my breath, I lay down parallel to him. Christine, I noticed, was deeply asleep, her head jolting. I felt a moment's parental smugness, seeing her get her rest like this. She would need adequate sleep. And yes, her manner in Khartoum and Port Sudan, her dazed, mute manner, was exactly that of a child who has come out of a profound fever and is relearning the world, studying its mechanisms. But now where will she go, I wondered, if she quarrels with Masihi, if he stops filming—or, these days, videotaping—for half an hour and she begins to look at him merely as a lost middle-aged Frenchman in a desert?

On this question, this late-night, strange-place anxiety, I let the stars numb me. Now and then I was aware that the traffic had diminished all around us. It became obvious that we'd taken to a rough mountain road. The truck pummeled me, but I did not come out of my daze until I felt it slowing. Looking over the edge of the tray, I saw we were surrounded by some twenty men in peasant clothing. All of them carried arms.

"It's the Ethiopian wheat militia," Masihi told me. "They serve the Dergue for handouts of wheat."

Johanes and Moka had stepped down from the truck cabin and seemed to be engaged in jovial talk with these men. Masihi himself vaulted off the back of the truck and joined the conversation. It seemed to be in Arabic. There was laughter. Masihi mimed filming them, and they laughed again and held up preventive hands. It wasn't hard to get the joke. He must have said something like, *What if I make a film of you gentlemen and send it to Mengistu?*

Joking over, they waved us goodbye. Later in the night, when the half moon had come up over this beautiful, arid high country, a more strenuous roadblock all at once stood in our way. At first I presumed it was manned by Ethiopians or wheat militia, and it was only after staring over the side for some time that I saw a girl holding an assault rifle and understood that these were soldiers of the EPLF. Under the moonlight they talked loudly and confidently. Their hand gestures weren't stealthy. They behaved like owners.

Two of them, a girl and a boy, climbed aboard with us. I smelled their somehow pleasant musk of sweat and antique dust.

Before dawn we came with them to a village of standing mud brick houses. There may have been bunkers round about, but this town—unlike Orotta and Jani and Himbol—had an identity above ground as well. Perhaps an Ethiopian would say of a place like this, *There you are! Stop resisting and we'll let you live in the open air.*

In the hut we were shown to, a beautiful peasant woman, very young, swathed in emerald and bearing a marriage bangle through her nose, brought us sweet tea. Henry had little to say and seemed sullen. I thought of Lady Julia in Endilal. I would have enjoyed her company here, a few *I would have thought*s and *I mean*s over the numbingly sweet morning tea. As it was, this Eritrean girl was alien and silent within flamboyant cloth, within her set of peasant modesties, and nothing was said.

Letter Drop

We were there five days. Every morning I expected Colonel Tessfaha, who had gone to such eloquent pains to recruit me, to appear with instructions. He didn't. There was much tedium. We were asked or perhaps ordered—with the Eritreans you couldn't always tell the difference—to stay indoors during the day, when reconnaissance planes appeared in the sky. If we weren't already so, both Henry and I grew dull from the tedium.

In the evenings, however, we were allowed to socialize with the soldiers who had brought us through the lines, and with their more numerous comrades. I presumed that all of them waited in this village, as I did, for Tessfaha's instructions. They always drank some opaque and bitter *sewa* in the evenings, but their talk wasn't simply pub or party talk. They'd quiz Henry and me about every aspect of life, politics, and opinion in the United States and Europe— their interests extended as far as the Australian federal system. There would be pauses while those rebels who understood English translated what we had said into Tigrinyan or Arabic, and further sober questions would arise and need to be answered. We were chastened and stimulated a little by the seriousness with which we were accepted.

Moka came into our hut very early on the fourth day. Henry was still asleep, and the Eritrean sat by the bench on which my air mattress had been spread and murmured for fear of waking him. "The letter you wanted to give to Major Fida. You still have it?"

"Of course," I said. "Do you think I would have thrown it away?"

He told me to get it. I rooted through my backpack, among dwindling rolls of toilet paper, tubes of suntan lotion, and shirts and underwear reeking of sweat.

"We do not have time for tea," Moka said apologetically when I produced the letter. (It is an Eritrean axiom that nothing serious can be undertaken without tea.) I had also found the letter Stella had written and wanted passed to Fida, and I added it to the first. There was no need to tell Moka.

"And do you have any books you have finished?" he asked.

I was a little confused by the question, but then understood he was soliciting books for Fida. I had finished a novel called *World's Fair* by E. L. Doctorow. It might well fruitfully add to Fida's bemusement in the face of American culture, politics, and morality.

I wondered if Moka wanted both the book and the letter handed to him at once. That wouldn't be acceptable to me.

"You can have the book, Moka. But I have to keep his wife's letter with me and give it to Fida in person."

He wheezed. "Ai-ai-ai! You can keep them, you can keep them," he sighed.

I followed him out into the early morning light. Two reconnaissance planes, one in the northeast, another in the southwest, quartered the sky, keeping an eye on the occupied province, the rebel nation.

We walked for five minutes. We passed one guard resting under a tree, who called a lazy greeting to us, and then another positioned under the eaves of a hut. Neither of these men would normally have let me move freely by daylight.

We reached the farthest and most isolated house in the village. Moka paused by the door jamb and began to knock.

"*Salaam*," someone called briskly from inside. Beneath the thatched eaves, Moka ushered me through into the interior of the place. A tall and very muscular man in military fatigues, a man not as pared down as most of the Eritreans, was waiting there, standing by a table. I believed that he must have been an intelligence officer, a friend of Tessfaha's, who would try to get Fida's letter out of me.

"Mr. Darcy," he said.

I nodded. As he smiled at me I tried to convey wariness and strict professional standards.

"You are a friend of my friend Stella?"

"Stella Harries. Yes. I am a friend."

I thought he was going to base an appeal for trust on our mutual friendship: Give me Fida's letter, because no friend of Stella's could be a barbarian! Later I was a little astounded that I had not known straightaway that this was Fida himself. And now he introduced himself, and I recognized him at once from Stella's photograph, recognized even his voice from the tapes she had made.

The three of us sat down. Tea was brought now and drunk. I put the letters beside his cup. "There is something from Stella, and a longer letter from your wife. I suppose that's the more important one."

He behaved like what they used to call "a man of breeding." He did not tear open the envelopes and devour what lay inside. He glanced at them almost as if they were ambiguous, like examination results or a medical report. He would save them to read in privacy.

He smiled at me. "And the book?" he asked.

"Yes," I said. "Another American." He *did* turn that over, read the quotes on the back cover, went searching for details of the author in the first couple of pages. "I shall be an expert in American writers when poor Ethiopia alters its allegiance and falls in again with the Americans . . ."

Moka growled. "They say on the African news of the BBC that the Russians might throw the Ethiopians out of bed—not the other way around. The Russians are so tired of Mengistu!"

"Ai, yes," said the major.

I had my mouth open to ask the question: Why was he, a p.o.w., on this side of the lines? But he turned to me and began talking before I could begin. "I insisted on seeing you, Mr. Darcy. I was in a position where I could do that. But we all hope that you won't say you met me here. The Eritreans hope that, and so do I. Not even to tell Stella. I trust you don't mind that?"

I gave them both my assurances. Moka wheezed joyously once I'd uttered them.

Fida rose and went across the room to where a burlap bag lay in the corner. He took from it a letter of his own, brought it back, and placed it on the table in front of me. "That is a letter for my wife. If I go to God in the next week or two, you'll hear of it, and you'll send the letter to that West German address on the envelope, and they will get it to her."

"What does *go to God* mean?" I asked him. "Are you under some sort of sentence?"

For there were rumors that the Eritrean military dealt with offences fairly summarily. In a confused way I wondered, Had he been condemned by one of their military courts?

He raised a hand. "No, it isn't anything like that. My fellow prisoner, my cellmate you could call him—Captain Berezhani, whom Stella met—may have thought he was under sentence, for he hanged himself six weeks past. He gave way to the purest despair and condemned himself. That, too, is in strictest confidence, since Berezhani's family are Christian and would be demented to find the poor fellow had done that. But me? No, I am not under sentence. But I am sure you don't have to be told the whole situation here is dangerous. Not for you, of course. But *I* am already out of the zone where prisoners are normally kept; I am already back in my own zone, the occupied one. So by all means use your imagination now or afterward, but say nothing.

"This letter, though . . . if you have heard nothing one way or another about me by the time you leave Eritrea, then there will be no need for you to send it, and you can tear it up."

"Literally?" I asked. "Rip it to pieces?"

"Please do. It is just that certain motivations of mine might worry my wife if I am not present on earth to explain them to her." (I noticed how theological his English was: *Go to God* had now been followed by the oddity of *present on earth*.) "I needed to meet someone of whom I could say with certainty, *he* will post the letter. He will not decide that it is unwise or inexpedient to post it, as perhaps one of my captors might. He will post it."

"But how will I *know* whether to post it or rip it up?"

"If I go to God, it will be well known in this region. The cameraman will tell you, for example. It may . . . well, let us say it will be news."

He reached across and put his hands on top of mine.

"I thank you for your service to me."

I had an urge to ask him about Tessfaha's proposed ambush—was he engaged in that in some way? But I knew I wouldn't get a proper answer, so instead I let a normal conversation start. We talked about Reagan's Strategic Defense Initiative and about the meaning of *perestroika* and *glasnost*. We talked about the Poles. He listened to me speak of crime and homelessness in New York. Like everyone who has been to that city for a week or two, I was expert on that. I can't remember how it came up, but he showed me his arm, the one which had been broken when he ejected. He put it through some basic exercises and praised the pin job the Eritrean surgeons had done.

By certain subtle gestures of command, he ended the interview when he was ready, a man accustomed to authority. It was the way that, during my limited journalistic career, I had seen politicians dismiss the press. That didn't mean that at the end he didn't express his gratitude to me a little fulsomely, at least by Western standards.

"I won't be seeing you again while we're here," I said, almost as a statement of fact.

"I regret that," he said mysteriously.

Outside, the bite of the sun penetrated the fabric of my shirt. It seemed hard to stay upright under the heat's gravity. I passed back gratefully into the hut I shared with Henry and hid the major's letter away in the same nest of squalid clothing from which I had taken the one from his wife.

Kirir Music

I had not during my wait in this town forgotten Amna Nurhussein in the least. Her casual goodbye on the afternoon of the game of football still caused me some bemusement. My mind returned habitually to it. I liked to think I was very wary about taking these impulses of memory at their own self-declared value. Again, Bernadette and the Pitjantjara and Pintubi tribes as a group had educated me pretty adequately on the limits of the sort of enthusiasm I felt for Amna. In Fryer River I had chosen to be happy just because I was besotted by elder-magic, by Panitjilda and its mystery rites and the embargos it put on people's sight. I'd thought that because I was passionate about something as alien to me as the tribal cosmos, everything would be forgiven me.

Believing I was twice shy these days, I'd tried when I remembered to fight the charm of the rebels, or at least have doubts about it. But while we waited for Tessfaha's word, I found myself making arguments for some sort of *friendship* with Amna. Masihi had managed it. Having done badly as a husband, he had found his *femme particulière* in the Eritrean mountains.

Sometimes I even went so far as to consider that, if you had to *be* a revolutionary to *love* a revolutionary, then I'd stay here, take a job teaching in one of their bunker schools, or write English textbooks for the Department of Information. I would be a noncinematic Masihi. I'd drink *sewa* and eat *injera* in Orotta's bitter valleys, and so I'd qualify!

But in the day's withering light, I knew that wasn't a possibility.

I wouldn't convince myself, I wouldn't convince the EPLF. Certainly, I wouldn't convince Amna Nurhussein. It would be like my efforts to be counted in among the brotherhood of the Pitjantjara holy places, that time I went off with Freddy Numati and the young anthropologist, mapping the mysteries. The Pitjantjara had been polite to me, and the Eritreans would be similarly polite. But it didn't mean for a second that you occupied the same earth.

Then, I thought, I could go to Frankfurt—as soon as I had the fare—and I would have it if I could make something out of my Eritrean notes. And then when she returned there, I could pay a proper, sustained, righteous, impeccable courtship, one which wouldn't offend her old-fashioned revolutionary sensibility.

That project, too, seemed real only in certain lights. I was again too well educated by the masters of Panitjilda to believe it. I was aware of and defeated by everything that was mysterious in Amna—mysterious in the sense of being African, of having been proud in prison, of having known the bastinado and witnessed the electrodes. Again, I lacked grounds and qualifications to commune with her.

Just the same, the longer Tessfaha failed to show up, the more febrile I got about Amna, and the more these banal and—in their way—fully realized scenes flickered across my overheated brain.

The night of the day I'd met Fida, I was sitting on a stone by a bonfire among a crowd of soldiery who included the medic Genet, the officer Johanes, the veteran Ismail from Barka, the officer-trainee Mohammed, when the fantasy seemed to take flesh.

Henry had come to like these evening events and to get a taste for *sewa*. By morning, when I woke near him, I could always smell the sourmash exhalations the digested liquor gave off through his pores and on his breath. For the sake of fraternity and to soothe the boredom of our long days in the hut, I'd begun heavy evening drinking, too. Once my blood alcohol achieved the right level for folly, I would find myself letting my eyes skim round the edges of the fire, searching the features of the infantrywomen, looking for echoes of Amna's.

That night I did see a woman—turbanned in the style of Amna, the tail of the turban hanging so that it could be used to cover nose and mouth against dust—sitting between a veteran of about thirty-five years and a very young woman perhaps no more than nineteen or twenty. I spent a long time looking at this woman with the turban, gauging the value of my Frankfurt, Amna-courting fantasies against the Amna-image on the edge of the fire.

Masihi meanwhile attempted to enliven the evening. He talked the Eritreans into producing musical instruments—pipes, the guitarlike instrument called a *kirir*, and a harmonica or two. Dancing soon began; I found myself on my feet, gyrating as well as I could to music of surpassing strangeness. I saw spinning past me by firelight the scarred features of nomads and goatherds rendered political by some act of savagery, nameless and unrecorded to everyone but them. I saw the smooth-shaven faces of the town-bred intellectuals like Mohammed, who now lived in holes in the earth. I saw Christine Malmédy with her right arm slung around the shoulders of a veteran—Ismail, I think, the former soldier of the ELF. Her mouth was avidly, uncharacteristically parted and she seemed ecstatic. A dancing woman. A woman who might even take a lover among the warriors.

Here in this village she and her father had been filming interviews with soldiers and villagers every day—they did not have lights for indoor work, but they had placed a chair and fixed the camera and the sound gear in position under a wide-spreading thorn tree. Technically, these were challenging enough conditions to rule out intimate conversation between father and daughter and the sort of uncomfortable hours of proximity which Henry and I spent together. But if distracting Christine was Masihi's only tactic, it seemed to satisfy both of them.

Very few soldiers sat out of the dance that night, but I noticed after a time, when I was dancing myself—somehow, and without any feeling in my legs—that the woman in the turban who looked like Amna stayed seated on her slab of stone. Occasionally she smiled the Amna smile, but you came across that particular form of the divine rictus in many of the Eritrean rebels. What, according to my drunken logic, convinced me joyously that it *was* Amna was that this woman stayed fixed to her rock when absolutely everyone else had risen. The Ethiopian bastinado in her past had, of course, made dancing unwise or impossible now.

I disengaged from the circle of dancers. When I reached Amna I dropped on my knees in front of her. I was astounded at myself, but also delighted. I thought, *You've become a wild man, Darcy. At last!* The *sewa*, which is informally brewed, more potent in some batches than in others and fiercer when made from rice, as was the stuff we were drinking now, had done all that for me, made me unfamiliar to myself.

I said, "You were supposed to be visiting friends in Nacfa."

She gave her complicated smile. "I visited friends in Nacfa. Now I am here."

I imagined her walking through the lines on ankles which could suddenly bloat again and turn on her. "You shouldn't be here. What if you got sick?"

"What if *you* got sick?" she asked.

"I don't know. I wasn't ever a prisoner of Afan. You're a great worry to me, Amna."

"Why is that?" she asked, each word separate as an artifact.

"Because I don't bloody well know where to fit you. Here or there, I mean. If I came to Frankfurt, for example, would you let me take you to dinner?"

"You could come to dinner at our apartment. *Injera* and lentils." The idea made her laugh.

"Your apartment?" I felt that this was progress.

"We live in two apartments. One is the office and the other is our living quarters."

"Listen, Amna, I don't want to have dinner with the whole bloody EPLF Frankfurt branch. And I certainly don't want to eat bloody *injera*, if you'll forgive me for saying so. And as for *sewa*, I don't care if I never see any more, even if it is a drink of heroic stature. I want to eat and drink something sensual, like pork knuckles and beer, *spätzle* and Moselle. Then I want to go to the movies with you. If you'll eat pork knuckles with me, I'll even sit through a Wim Wenders movie, which is my criterion of true friendship. And even if it might be a bit unrevolutionary of me, I want to be your friend."

"I am a Muslim woman by culture still and have never eaten pork. Besides, you are my friend already, Darcy." She said it in that universally infuriating, ambiguous manner of impossibly desired women. *That*, I acknowledged, crossed the culture line. *That* was standard from Lapland to Tasmania.

"Come off it, Miss Nurhussein. *Fraulein* Nurhussein. You know what I bloody well mean!"

I knew that I was getting what used to be called "importunate" and, scared of the results of that, to prevent myself from going further, I stood up. "I am coming to Frankfurt to eat blood sausage with you. To go to patisseries for Vienna coffee and disgusting big Bavarian tortes. Cream will come gushing out of our mouths."

She was still smiling. "That sounds very enjoyable," she told me.

"Believe me, Fraulein Nurhussein, it bloody well *will* be. Believe me."

The officer-trainee Mohammed came spinning out of the dance and landed on his knees in front of Amna. He slapped her wrist familiarly.

"This is my cousin," Amna explained.

"Everyone's your cousin. Salim was your cousin."

"This is Salim's son."

I stared at the boy and saw Salim's features. "Your father is waiting in Orotta," I said. I remembered Salim's panic about heart tablets.

"I will be allowed," said the boy in painful English, "to go to my father after this."

There was Salim, on the sentimental screen in my head, praying on the mat with the compass sewn into its hem.

Amna and her cousin began to speak in Tigrinyan. I stumbled away to my hut, uncertain about what had been achieved. I believed I could hear her laughing—without any definable cruelty—behind my back. Only when I was lying queasily on my air mattress did I begin to wonder why she was here at all, whether she, too, had been co-opted or had by stubbornness forced herself into the party to be another witness to Tessfaha's proposed attack on an aid convoy.

Little Black Boxes

In that village the goats were scrawny but always more or less vocal. They were noisy above all early in the morning and generally woke us. But before the first bleat or cluck was heard the next day, I was awakened not by the animals but by intense, hushed discussions inside the hut. These augmented the alcoholic bewilderment—*where am I and what have I done to cause this stale anxiety I feel?*—as my brain pulsed and stretched for the first daily crumbs of place and time, the familiar mercies which show a person that he is leading a sequential life and is not in hell.

Once that was settled, I looked out from the bench I slept on. I could see that just beyond the doorway, under the eaves, the soldiers Mohammed and Ismail knelt by Henry's giant duffel bag and its strewn contents. Moka stood inside, looking out, mournfully regarding the mess which had been made of Henry's effects. Dolorously, he watched Ismail pick this or that item out of the mess of clothing and possessions and bring it inside for inspection by a tall man who sat on one of our stools near the foot of Henry's sleeping bench. Sketchbooks and small notebooks were delivered in this way. I noticed, however, that Henry's beloved diary, with its memories retained inside it still with elastic bands, lay on his sleeping bench within reach of his hand, but also within reach—at a stretch—of the tall man. The tall man on the stool was Tessfaha, whom I had last seen in an Eritrean restaurant in London and had yearned to see frequently since.

By the small bag stuffed with clothing which he used as a

pillow, Henry himself sat barefoot, both feet still up on his air mattress.

I levered myself upright and began putting on my boots—I don't know why. To signify my willingness to defend my friend, be prepared to go to the convoy perhaps, to show my suitability for that sort of journey. I believed I'd said stupid things to Amna, things which might have disqualified me from being taken seriously. At the same time I felt that Henry needed support in the face of these ransacking rebels.

Tessfaha turned to me and said familiarly, as if he'd been with me for weeks past, "Mr. Darcy, please do not concern yourself. Your property is sacred to us."

I noticed some already inspected sketchbooks of Henry's strewn across the floor. The same nonsense as at the commandant's office in She'b. I looked to Henry, willing to urge him to rebel, promising him solidarity. But he merely winked at me.

"They're back to thinking my artwork is dangerous," he told me in that brittle voice. His eyes bulged and were too bright for the morning after the night we'd both had. "Just like that prick at the prison camp."

Tessfaha shook his head. "It is not so much your artwork, Mr. Henry. It is your more sophisticated possessions."

I noticed that Tessfaha was reaching over from the stool and pushing certain little black plaques of plastic, as if they were dominoes, around the hut's small ammunition-box table. He held one firmly with his left hand and extracted from it a silver wand with his right. An aerial. "This is one of Mr. Henry's high-frequency transmitters," Tessfaha told me. "Given to him by other parties. When set out on mountaintops by experts, these are capable of conversing in frequency with satellites, of sending them pinpoint bearings. First Jani was bombed, and then the prisoners' camp. Yes, the camp in She'b has been bombed with heavy loss, reducing the embarrassment the Dergue feels over the Ethiopian prisoners we hold. And as for Jani, Moka tells me that—but for an accident—your party would have been in that area of the food dump at Jani." He turned back to Henry. "I hope this conveys something of the ordinary, let us say *daily* duplicity of those who employ you."

"Look, friend," said Henry in his strangest, thinnest voice, "don't talk about duplicity. I've lived with the sons-of-bitches."

Again Tessfaha turned and issued an instruction to Ismail and Mohammed, Salim's son, at the door. They began repacking Henry's clothing. I noticed that the attention of both Henry and Tessfaha was fixed on the American's diary-journal, yet they both pretended not to be fussed about it. When Tessfaha casually reached for it, Henry pounced forward on all fours to cover it with his body. Tessfaha pushed him sideways, though, very adroitly and— it seemed to me—without undue force. Henry landed on his side, fetally hunched. Tessfaha took the journal and began to remove its elastic bands.

A howl came from Henry, part rage and part plaint. He knelt upright to wrench the journal out of Tessfaha's hands from behind. Tessfaha avoided him by standing up.

If Tessfaha's argument was right, if the small black boxes were what he improbably claimed them to be, then I should have been enraged at Henry, who'd been an awkward companion and was now under suspicion of being a treacherous one. All I felt was that Tessfaha was about to commit a sacrilege against Henry's external soul, his compendium of memories in which I'd never seen him write anything, from which he drew only an occasional old letter or an iconic photograph of his lost girl, Petra, but whose value to him was obviously supreme. His howling now, as Tessfaha removed another elastic band and mementoes began to fall from the mauled pages onto the floor, was pitiable. From the oppressed cities and violated villages of his childhood, Tessfaha must have heard, been familiar with such shrieks. I felt a peculiar anger at him for not recognizing a cry so much more common in his world than in mine.

I got up from the bed. "Those are Henry's treasures," I told Tessfaha. "There's nothing in there that you need to look at."

I believed it then, though later I wondered if the noted-down instructions for deploying the plastic plaques—if you could believe Henry had deployed any—were in there. In any case, Tessfaha removed the last band and prepared carefully, like a man used to reading books whose binding was gone, to open the diary.

Henry was sobbing, his face already so dirty with dust and tears that he could have been weeping for hours. His cries were terrible, worse cries than a man ought to have to utter, unlikely noises to come from such a tough African honcho.

I got up from my bed. I was aware I was spitting with anger. I could see the droplets issuing from my mouth.

"If you open that book," I told Tessfaha, "I'm finished with you." I meant it. I had thought the acid test of their revolution was the grammar classes, the food dumps at Jani, the surgical caves in Orotta. But now, I told myself, full of a primitive care for Henry, I didn't want them if they plundered his little book of mementoes. What I would afterward recognize as astounding was that the Jani scenes, the ones I had been sure would never be forgotten, the strewn wounded blanched with powdered milk, did not at once come to my mind, that I did not bay for Henry to be punished merely on suspicion.

Then it struck me that my championship of Henry had to do with respect for the size of his act. How could you balance Petra Barre's release, even if it happened, against the thirty shrouded dead of Jani. Yet Henry had, and there was a *size* to that. It was all wrong and I should hate and curse him. Yet somehow it reflected well; it was human, it was love.

"You're *finished* with us?" asked Tessfaha. I thought at first there was sarcasm there. But no. The stressed *finished* wasn't matched by any mockery in his face.

"It's only a few souvenirs of his Somali girl," I said.

Henry had stopped weeping and collapsed sideways against the wall, his back to all of us, his face to the corner.

"Yes," Tessfaha murmured. "Those Eritreans who invited Mr. Henry to come here should have remembered her."

He did the book up again with elastic bands and put it back on Henry's bench. "Your diary, Mr. Henry," he murmured.

Next he reached down from the stool on which he was sitting and fetched first one and then another sketchbook up to table level. He began inspecting the drawings one by one, tearing some pages out, ripping them further into fragments of paper. I still wasn't appeased, and I didn't like the cool, omnipotent, enemy-of-culture way he did this.

Henry, wiping his face, straightened himself, swung his legs off the bed-bench, reached for his journal and stuffed it into his make-shift pillow, and stood up. With a mad suddenness the panic had gone from him. "You can always fucking shoot me," he told Tess-faha with a sick smile. I looked at him. His journal safely retrieved, he didn't really care what they did now.

Still I did not concentrate on the small black plaques on the table and their meaning. I saw Henry instead as a fellow who knows that only a strict and narrow acreage of happiness is allotted, and that it has to be fought for on any terms. On those grounds he was a compatriot.

Tessfaha, however, began to play with one of the aerials again. "Jani and then the p.o.w. camp. They told you that if you spread your gadgets around the mountaintops, if you made your sketches, they'd let your fiancée go. Ai! It's all so stupid!"

"You think so?" asked Henry. He spoke in a strangely muted, explaining voice. "You don't have to tell me anything about them—whether they're efficient, whether they couldn't run a man-ure factory, etc., etc. I know as much about them as you do. But if they wanted those fucking boxes placed, I was ready to go along with it. I wanted just to put the fucking things down and forget them. I don't know if they work or not, but it's my guess they probably don't. A few sketches and a few little beepers left on mountains. Big fucking emergency! Do you know what the emergency really is? Tessfaha, Moka? You want to hear about the really big emergency? The emergency is that if you guys suc-ceed, you'll be an embarrassment to Africa. Who wants a setup like yours? There aren't many governments on this continent that do. There aren't many governments in Europe. Colored folk who can look after themselves? It isn't viable. It upsets the world pic-ture. Don't you know the West has to believe famine's an act of God? If they believe that, they only have to make a donation. But if they believe it's an act of bloody politics, they have to *really* do something, and that's too, too complicated. So what's the story? The story is you guys will fall on your own fucking swords, because you've got this crazy idea that the world will allow you to be perfect!"

"We aren't perfect to start with," Tessfaha told him, but he was ignored. For Henry was still in midspate.

"No one wants a perfect world, my friend. All I want is my girl to get an exit visa. That's the universe goddam perfected, in my book. But your book's different. I know that. So come on, what in the hell are you going to do with me?"

Tessfaha sat on the edge of the table. "The Dergue detains your fiancée. But it's us you hate for that. Maybe you think that if we didn't create so many problems for the Dergue, your Somali woman would not be in prison and—"

"She isn't in prison. She's under house arrest. Pending an exit visa. O.K., if the Ethiopians had a bombing success at She'b, so much the better. They'll let the poor little bitch go!"

Tessfaha did not say anything. He looked at Ismail and Mohammed and gave them subtle orders with a slight shift of face and hands. They began packing Henry's bag again. Salim's son Mohammed came indoors and fetched the two strewn sketchbooks, tenderly reassembling the drawings and putting them on the table. When everything was in place, he lifted the duffel, brought it to the foot of Henry's bench, and propped it there.

"Get your boots on," Tessfaha told him.

Henry didn't obey and remained barefoot. "I admit I flicked the switch on the one I left at the p.o.w. camp," he said. "Those guys were soldiers and had to take their chances. The one I left in Jani, I broke the aerial off. But they found Jani just the same. I don't know how they did that. If I was worth anything to them, I'd say they were trying to show me that they can find me anyhow and punish me. But that's not the case. They're not so nifty as that. That's kind of *deft* barbarity, and they're barbarians in a dull, relentless sort of way."

Tessfaha went, picked up Henry's boots, handed them to him. "Have you set up one here, in this place?" he asked.

"No," Henry said, very casually. "I don't think they knew I was coming this far." He didn't give a damn whether Tessfaha believed him or not. His manner was so reckless now that I felt I had to rush in to corroborate, to give him a suspended sentence. "We've been here a week," I said, exaggerating a little. "Nothing's happened."

While Henry tied the laces of his boots, I started to speak in the same vein as I had in the commandant's office at She'b. For example, I reminded Tessfaha that I was present as witness. For I could imagine Henry before a severe Eritrean military court. I could imagine them shooting him without too much sentiment, and—in this clearcut struggle of theirs—being justified in doing it.

Henry cut me off, as I expected he would. "Shut up, Darcy, for Christ's sake. Who do you fucking think you are? Amnesty International or some other set of faggots?"

Throughout these exchanges, and while Henry dressed and packed his belongings, Tessfaha went on pondering Henry for a time and then turned and came up to my bench. He stood above me, staring confidentially at the log ceiling. "We may need to send you home, too," he whispered. "I don't know what this means . . ." He gestured toward Henry, who continued to dress with a fake leisureliness, pretty much like a man under arrest. The scene—the little black rectangles, the idea of Henry deploying them, pitiably sneaking to hilltops—all of it seemed fantastical and at the same time banal and fatuous villainy and utter self-immolation, unworthy of belief yet possessed of a sort of gritty probability.

"What will you do to him?" I asked.

Tessfaha sat beside me. "We'll return him to the Sudan. Once in Port Sudan, we won't want or need to know him anymore. You can verify his good health when you meet him in Khartoum."

Henry was packed up now and Moka reached out and, wheezing ironically, lifted the duffel bag. *You can let me carry it*, his manner said. *You've got nothing more to hide.*

I stood up and intercepted Henry before he got to the door. Contradictorily, I didn't feel like shaking his hand.

"Sorry, matey," he told me, winking. "If I get unlucky with stray Eritrean fire, you can tell the world what happened. If you like. I don't give a damn."

"You won't get any more unlucky than you already are," called Tessfaha, who was still standing by my bench. "You should continue to take your malaria pills and expect a long life."

"And long memories, I suppose."

"Exactly," Tessfaha murmured.

"To hell with the lot of you," said Henry, and stepped out into the daylight. I heard him being walked away. I could hear Moka's steps, too, the gait thrown off by the weight of the duffel.

Sometime very soon, I became convinced as the party disappeared through the village, they would tell him Petra Barre was dead. They might even be able to evince witnesses, agents from Addis, say. Documents? Less likely. But *that* would be their summary punishment. After that, they would have no cause to shoot him.

I was still so astonished by the substance of Henry's crime that I barely remembered it might have practical results for us, for Tessfaha and me.

"The ambush is canceled then?" I managed to ask Tessfaha after Henry had vanished.

"Perhaps . . . though he doesn't seem a very energetic agent. But he may be in contact with some other representative of the Dergue."

"I don't think you should call Henry an agent," I protested. I didn't want terms like *agent* and *representative of the Dergue* used in front of some Eritrean military court.

Tessfaha shrugged. "I don't quite know what other term to use. And as for his possible contacts, you've seen the people come and go here. The area around the village is full of wheat militiamen, supposedly loyal to the Dergue, apparently loyal to us. There are no hard margins of loyalty, though, and no doubt the Dergue may have a claim on some of them—as it does on Henry himself." He looked extremely depressed for a time. "About the business of the convoy, Darcy, I don't know. What do you think? Would you still go?"

I said I would, though it was in some ways the promise I least wanted to make. For one thing, I wanted time to reflect on the nature of Henry's business with the little electronic plaques. I believed there were enormous questions to be asked. Nodding briskly, though, Tessfaha got up from the bench to go.

"You'll be lonely here," he said. "But tonight you can drink with Masihi." His eyes were nearly closed as he spoke. He seemed a little distracted. Then they sprang open. "You know, Henry's girl is dead, or wishes she was."

"You're sure about that?"

"I'm sure about the Dergue," he said. "Those devices they gave him . . . they're playing with him. Certainly those little things give off some sort of signal, but the technology is shaky. God knows if they had a part in what happened. But that question isn't necessarily meaningful to *them*, to the ones who decided to employ Henry. Using people, that's what they find meaningful. A hundred years ago they would have sent him in with amulets designed to bring on drought and plagues!"

He yawned and stretched, as if he'd been up all night. So he probably had, traveling.

"Perhaps someone should tell him that his woman has no hope. He is a barbarian if ever I saw one. But to some people he would be a hero, I suppose. Selling p.o.w.s for love, I imagine he calls it. A romantic in the truest sense! A sentimentalist. When you see him in Khartoum, he'll probably have a picture of the two of you on his office wall."

The colonel left me to a desolate day. I slept in a slick of sweat and woke from a dream of Henry and a court-martial to find that the noise which had interrupted the dream was the yapping of one of the pert vermilion lizards who lived in the thatch of the roof. I thought, Tonight, unless she's moved again, I'll see Amna. But I couldn't look forward unambiguously to that. It wasn't only because in last night's *sewa* exuberance I'd embarrassed myself and her. It was a lack of daring in me. And Henry had had it—the terrible Henry, the man whose gestures you couldn't predict. His massive intentions toward the Eritreans had misshapen his character, twisted him to madness and sickness. But he had daring. And if it *was* true, as Tessfaha said, that Henry would have a picture of us both on his office wall, that itself was madness. There wasn't any warmth between us to justify a picture. And yet he had daring, and that seemed the most significant thing to me.

And I returned to the vast fact: Henry being willing not only to sell villages and prisoners by the valleyful, but also to put himself in a position where no one, himself included, could be certain he'd actually done it, the technology being—as Tessfaha said—unreliable.

I somehow wanted that degree of venturousness. I actually felt chastened not to have it. And I felt desperate, since its lack accounted for the loss of Bernadette—accounted, too, for my helplessness with Amna. A better man than Henry, of course! A man who had risked no one, especially not himself.

Henry wouldn't have lost Bernadette, I assured myself. Henry wouldn't have behaved judiciously, wouldn't have balanced love and vengeance as, in the pattern of my bank manager father, I had.

All that day in the village near Asmara I rehearsed the disconnected scenes of my morally impeccable and wise search for Bernadette. How I had gone to so much trouble, but never the right kind!

I can scarcely remember the Darcy of the day after Bernadette vanished. I suppose a little shock was justified. I remember Freddy Numati, the Pitjantjara elder, reassuring me on the question of whether Burraptiti might misuse her in some way and leave her beside the road without water.

That was in a way the reassurance I wanted. For the moment, I was looking for reasons not to go straight off in pursuit. For Bernadette to run away with Burraptiti was, I told myself, a temporary act of vengeance against the tribal council and against me. I thought it almost too stupid and foolish to be taken seriously. She was *trying* to make me believe she and Burraptiti were lovers. But I was sure they hadn't been—not in Fryer River anyhow—though I couldn't swear to what was happening now.

On that matter, it wasn't just the hubris of a bad husband that made me believe Burraptiti and Bernadette weren't in some sort of affair. The nature of the fight between us, between Bernadette and the council, the whole balance of behavior would have been different, that's all, if Burraptiti had been an early element in it.

As vengeance anyhow, her escape worked well. In a way, I let it work well. Perhaps I wanted to be able to go to her and say, "Look, you made me give up the best job I've ever had."

To describe the decline briefly, I found my credit had gone in the eyes of the tribal men. Questions to do with land title, petrol-sniffing, police liaison were not brought to me any more.

Within a week of the disappearance, I drove to Alice and then flew to Darwin, searching for her in both places, but she and Burraptiti, if together, were not in the main towns. Her parents and friends in Melbourne had not seen her either, and I would find out later that the Yangs hired an investigator to find her. If he had any success or not, they didn't tell me.

I concluded that, apart or together, Bernadette and Burraptiti must be on the remoter roads somewhere, perhaps in the northwest, traversing some immensity of dust and spinifex grass. Even though Burraptiti had committed car theft, the nursing sister wanted to leave it to the tribal council and the loosely structured Aboriginal bureaucracies in Alice and Darwin to sort out the return of the truck Burraptiti had taken from her.

As for me, I believed the police might be heavy-handed with a Chinese girl who traveled the country with a Pitjantjara jailbird. Besides, I sensed that Bernadette, whatever she might forgive me, wouldn't forgive that.

At the end of six weeks, however, about the time I resigned my job at Fryer River, I decided to bring the police into the search. They thought it very strange I had waited so long, and even suspected me of foul play against my wife and her "lover." Interviews with Freddie Numati and others reassured them on that point.

And then they found Bernadette but would not tell me where. She had asked them not to, had implied there'd be violent scenes if I appeared on her doorstep. I could tell by the way they counseled me that it was very likely to be a doorstep she shared with Burraptiti.

I had good contacts among both tribal people and sundry whites up in the north, in Darwin, where I was somehow sure she was now. Because if she'd been in Alice Springs, I would have known. Alice is not big enough to hide in. But Burraptiti had contacts in Darwin, a group of loyal "brothers." Although they would have been from different tribes than his, their brotherhood had been fused by experience of the police and of jail.

I flew to Darwin but had no success tracking her. Then I went back home to Melbourne and began to scratch a living as a freelance journalist, particularly on Aboriginal matters. I had already done pieces for *The Times* in London and become a sort of tribal correspondent. The British press were very interested in such material: the wash-up of empire, if you like. Some of my old Melbourne friends, less radical and more nationalist than when I'd last seen them, complained that *The Times* liked to take every opportunity to cast Australia as a junior South Africa. They complained about a British middle-class taste for tales of neocolonial oppression in picturesque surroundings, such as the rich desert Fryer River stood in. I found myself defending my small journalistic output. I thought, "I'm not paid enough, I'm not happy enough, to have to do this!"

For a while I contemplated a lawsuit to make the police tell me where they'd found her. But from contacts in the Aboriginal Affairs Department and from journalists returning from the north I heard that these days she *was* sometimes sighted in the streets and shopping malls of Darwin. One journalist reported that she was pregnant. The question was, of course, whether it was my child or Burraptiti's.

As soon as I could manage to do so, I took the long flight to Darwin once again. By now, close on a year had passed since Burraptiti and Bernadette had fled Fryer River. If this journey showed any daring, it was of a very measured kind.

In the bunker in Eritrea in which I recollected it, Darwin seemed more fabulous and strange than the caves of Orotta. You flew to it across absolute desert and discovered it all at once on its low, mangrove-bordered harbor. In its small history it had been destroyed three times by cyclones and once by the Japanese, who bombed it for some months in the 1940s. Its destruction marked their southernmost triumph, a flimsy triumph to match the flimsy town.

These days the city liked to adopt a suburban air. But the most startling antipodean events could still take place there. *Kaditja* men, punishers of tribal violations, might pursue a wrongdoer to town and, adapting to modern ways, find plausible methods to punish him, running him down with a vehicle or—in a case of which I had knowledge—tailing him from a hotel to a vacant plot of land and setting the grass ablaze there as he slept. And so the city's assumptions about itself—that it's a modern city with suburbs— don't really convince people. Everyone knows that the forces of ancient law or of ancient air turbulence might carry it away in an instant.

Her name was not in the telephone book, though there were other Yangs in town, merchants and restaurateurs. I could tell when I called in to the Northern Land Council, staffed by Arnhem Land Aborigines, that they knew where she was living, where she kept house for Burraptiti. One of them, whose cousin had been in jail with Burraptiti, admitted to knowing the address. "But you know there'll be a fight if you visit them," he said.

"I won't start any fight," I pledged.

"Not you. That bloody Burraptiti bloke might."

I explained that I wished only to see that she was well looked after, and the Arnhemlander said that he was sure Burraptiti *did* treat her well, a bloody sight better than he'd treated his black wife down in the desert.

"Is he drinking a lot?" I asked.

"He's the sort of bloke always drinks too much."

The Arnhemlander pointed to a poster on the wall of the Land Council office, a photograph of tribal men and women bloated and bleary with liquor. The legend read, "Don't Let Booze Destroy Our Culture!" Before the European coming, an Iwiaja man like this Arnhemlander and a Pitjantjara like Burraptiti would have been remoter from each other than Venus from Mars. Booze, like the law, had imposed a shared fraternal grief on both the tropic north and the desert.

Ultimately though, the Arnhemlander relented. He was a compassionate man who could see how badly the *business*, as he called it, oppressed me. On the promise that I wouldn't call in the Northern Territory police in their wide brown hats, even if Burraptiti attacked me, the Arnhemlander wrote down the address.

"I'll take some wine there."

"If it's for Bernadette," the man said, "take a bottle. If it's for that bugger Burraptiti, take a gallon."

I drove to a shopping mall, a branch of that true faith of Californian mercantilism you find in every tropic and temperate zone. I wanted to buy her a particular South Australian chardonnay of her liking. It was more than I could afford in this new era of living entirely by my writing. I took it from the liquor store freezer ready for drinking, even though there was a risk that the tropic day outside would turn it tepid too quickly and spoil the taste. I wanted to give it to her ready for the palate. A perfectly chilled memory.

Walking down the mall's central aisle, however, I saw Bernadette emerge from a supermarket. She was pushing a stroller in which sat her beautiful but very young child, its eyes Cantonese and, of course, a desert brooding in them. Bernadette saw me, stopped an instant, nodded, smiled indulgently, and then pushed the stroller away. I hobbled after her. Condensation from the chilled wine had wet the paper bag through. It split and the bottle fell, landed and shattered on the floor. People stopped, stared an instant, but then misread the whole event as a small shopping accident and went back to their ruminating movement along the shopping arcades.

The accident halted Bernadette, too. She turned and slotted her hips between the handles of the stroller. I would later consider it significant that she did not give her baby a sight of me.

"Oh, for God's sake, go away, Darcy," she said.

"Your color isn't good," I said stupidly. But she wouldn't answer me. "I wanted to know whether you were well, and if he hit you."

"I'm happy," she said, tossing her head. "I have a reasonable life."

I thought this an extraordinary phrase. I was fighting a delusion that the cure was only a touch away. I reached a hand out for her wrist.

"Come back," I said. "I'm finished with Fryer River. Or it's finished with me. I know more now."

"Please," she said gently. "Don't try it."

"Would you consider . . . I mean, I'd look after the baby like my own."

"Oh Jesus," said Bernadette, casting her eyes upward. "Do you want a scene?"

And of course, even at this limit of pleading, I didn't.

"Well, do you need any money?" I asked. Of course, if she had said *yes*, I would have been hard put to find any.

"We do very well. The government looks after us. And there are Pitjantjara mineral royalties. *He* has his share of those."

She stared at the glass on the tiled floor. I noticed for the first time the dress she was wearing—floral and not very elegant. It must have come from a secondhand shop or else from the St. Vincent de Paul Society. I wondered if her natty parents, who'd plumbed hills of gold to make a Cantonese princess of her, had ever seen her like this. "You were going to bring me some wine, were you?"

I shrugged. I began to clean the jagged fragments away with my boot, pushing them under a bench. *You see*, my gesture meant, *I don't want anyone hurt.*

"It was an ill-fated little present, Darcy. Wasn't it?"

I admitted that perhaps it was.

"So maybe you should piss off!" she told me.

It was the pungency of that phrase which affronted me. As I blinked, she began to wheel the stroller away again, and I found myself walking helplessly behind her. By one of those circular seats placed around a potted palm for the comfort of shoppers, for the wives of Jabiru uranium miners come to Darwin for a day's spending, she halted a moment.

"You know, there are plenty of precedents for the intermarriage of the Chinese and the Arnhemlanders," she said, very solemn in her explanation, "and so Burraptiti doesn't feel out of it all up here, even though he's a desert native. They feel superior to *us*. So it doesn't have the same dangers as getting in with a white girl."

For an instant, a morbid determination toward self-punishment, the certainty that the ill will of the tribal council had worked, was in her face. I moved up and thrust a piece of paper with my Melbourne telephone number into her hand, and this time she let me.

"Just as well the wine bottle broke," Bernadette told me. "We don't drink vintages, David and I."

So something was rich and right between Burraptiti and her. Because it had a conjugal ring, the way she said "David and I."

"Listen, Darcy," she said. "Don't dare follow me."

And I didn't. I lacked the daring.

The beautiful child, with the double burden and glory of its races lying coiled in it, clucked a little as she pushed it away and out through the doors. I watched them until they paused in the parking area by a riotously dented and discolored Holden. The body of the car had been scraped back for a new paint job it was unlikely ever to receive. I realized that she had not told me the child's name.

I used my visit to Darwin to write a few spiritless articles about the supposed exotic north for *The Melbourne Age*. Then I returned to the more staid and permanent south.

I would wait somewhere else than in my hometown for Bernadette's eventual call. In the meantime I wanted to find a place where my tribal credit had not been withdrawn. I wanted to go—perhaps—to Africa.

All I did at the campfire that night was stay sober and offer Amna the normal apologies of a man who'd behaved badly. Amna was kind enough to tell me she'd heard on the BBC shortwave African news that a party of Australian Aborigines had been to see Colonel Gaddafi seeking recognition for a sovereign Aboriginal state. I doubted that anyone from Fryer River was with them, but I expressed the normal level of interest in this news, and was grateful the item hadn't been there for her to tell the night before. Drunk, I might have said something like, "But they've got their own sovereignties," and then, of course, I might have told her about Bernadette and Burraptiti.

I wonder what she would have made of such a love story. And the idea of daring hung over the night. That's how I could find Amna and arrest her attention. By a sort of daring. It didn't have to involve the bombing of prisoners or peasants—for sweet Christ's sake, no. Hadn't I held infusion bags and keened against trees in the groves of Jani? But it had to be something of that scale, something galvanizing. And I could not find what it was.

Quite early in the night then, I was thinking of going back to the hut which was now exclusively mine when Masihi sat beside me. He was wearing sandals and seemed to contemplate his dusty feet by campfire light.

"Our friend is gone!" he stated.

I said, "That's right."

I could not tell if he knew anything.

"I did not like him," said Masihi. "He had a dangerous bitterness. What was wrong with him, would you say?"

"It was his woman," I said at once. "She's under house arrest in Addis." I did not give him Tessfaha's version: that she was dead.

"That would explain it." He looked directly at me. "Except . . . is there any such thing as house arrest in Addis?"

"I hope so. There's no doubt Henry loves her."

He groaned. I wondered if he had a woman among the ranks of the EPLF. Were they, he and Christine, on the road so that he could get his daughter acclimatized before introducing her to some elegant Eritrean bureaucrat in battle dress? Christine's Eritrean step-mother!

I did not even get angry with Henry, except in dreams. I spent all of one fitful night reverting to the same dream. In those parts of the dream when I *knew* I was dreaming, I thought, this is good, I'll keep this anger when I wake up. But as soon as I did wake, I felt the accusations draining out of me. By the time I was fully alert, I'd be witlessly thinking, *Poor Henry!* Or else, *Great Henry.*

I remembered the appalled face he'd shown as we stood on the escarpment with our more or less ruly camels and looked down on the flame and blast below us, below Mohammed's granite mountain.

It did not seem that Tessfaha considered at any great length abandoning his program with the convoy. At his order, we were moved at midnight by truck to the vicinity of the old Italian railway, the one which filleted Italian Eritrea from Massawa on the Red Sea to Agordat in the west. The rail line was abandoned now—the EPLF had made it unusable to the Ethiopians.

It was here, as we dismounted, that I became aware that Tessfaha himself was not in our immediate party. "He has many concerns," Moka told me reprovingly when I mentioned this. I watched Masihi, who seemed so calm about the circumstances and was checking his video gear and issuing instructions to his daughter.

We crossed the ruined line on foot. By moonlight, I saw that sections of track were bent awry and led off in erratic directions. I didn't know whether this was due to guerrilla energy or to heat and neglect. Amid the sleepers, small spiky suckers and cacti grew. We walked for the rest of the night on shifting, stony ground. It was so hard and so breathless that I was pleased to be able to straighten occasionally and see that Masihi and Christine were with me, to take comfort in rediscovering them. When Christine stumbled, she would say "Ai-ai-ai!" just like an Eritrean.

By now I expected to find Amna somewhere in the line, too, though I could not see her.

When Africa's enormously large and bright pole star came up over the rim of mountains, we reached a hillside on which sat two low goatherd's huts. Masihi and Christine and I were told to sleep in one. When I went down the hill to urinate, I kept an eye out, among all the settling and digging in of the rebels, for a glimpse of Moka and Amna. I felt certain she was with the party. And if she needed vitamin injections and physiotherapy to keep her ankles from swelling, how had this cruel hike treated her? Had she fallen out far back along the trail, where she would spend the day in hiding and join us at night?

Unless, of course, I had more or less collided in the dark with Amna, the state of her ankles couldn't be any of my business.

The Malmédy cinematic family and I slept deeply for an hour or two, until the heat of full day woke us. Masihi sat on his bench yawning and groaning and saying what a life this was and questioning his own sanity. His daughter smiled back at him. A mental patient in enviable control.

I stood up, swigged from my water bottle, and for a while stood at the door, looking out at the hillside. The EPLF were all under cover, sleeping in nests of acacia thorn. In the shade of a scrubby African conifer, however, Amna stood languidly cleaning her teeth with a sprig of olive. I wondered if Amna kept a typical obsolescent Western toothbrush in the Eritrean apartment in Frankfurt, or even there sought a supplier of olive twigs.

From Tessfaha before we left and Johanes before we slept, we had the strictest orders about showing ourselves by day, so even at the risk of waking some of the soldiers who lay strewn in their cloaks around the hillside, I stayed in the doorway and called, "Amna!"

I could think of nothing else to say to her, but I was frightened that the utterance of a mere name, without any prosaic message attached to it, would alert everyone, that they'd all be nudging each other, or whatever Eritreans do when they're joking about people like me. If I was to achieve daring though, I couldn't give a bugger about that!

"Mr. Darcy," she called in her inflected manner. "Are you tired?"

I shook my head. She pointed downhill, and in a V among mountains I saw, palely sketched in haze, a road. She was as good as saying, *That's it. That's where it will happen.* Then she hooked two or three fingers loosely across her lips—this must have been her version of asking for silence. I inspected the road again through the layers of haze. When I turned back to say something to her, or at least to think about composing something to say to her, she had disappeared among the sparse foliage. She must have been living and sleeping and performing her rhythmic toilet rituals in some warren there which I couldn't see.

For the rest of our day, watching out from cover, I did not sight her.

Editor's Interjection:
Fida in Asmara

We know now that, some thirty miles to the east of the encampment from which Darcy had his attention drawn to the old Italian road, another battalion of Eritrean commandos, the soldiers they called "Mobile Strike Forces," were in operation on the afternoon and evening of that day. With the Eritrean Tessfaha and the Ethiopian Fida watching from a hillside nearby, they overran a purely military convoy made up of some twenty trucks belonging to the Ethiopian air force. These were bound from the Red Sea port of Massawa to Asmara airport in the mountains.

Fida later indicated to Stella Harries that a ten-minute skirmish raged, during which the convoy's armed escorts, confused, far from home and—as Darcy would have it—"lacking in grammar lessons," fired in panic at the surrounding rebels and then surrendered to them. The marching of prisoners back through the lines would begin that very evening, the Eritreans again apparently proving themselves scrupulous in this matter of prisoners, even though, in a season of famine, the captives took *injera* which might better go to Eritrean peasants.

The convoy's papers had been captured intact along with its commanding officer. Fida, employing the aristocratic Amharic authority which was his second nature, interviewed the commander and then, that night, made use of the documents to lead Tessfaha and the trucks laden with rebels on through the three rings of security the Ethiopians had put around the military airport of Asmara. He would report that this was shamefully easy, for he was helped by the not unreasonable Ethiopian belief that no force would try to strike Asmara airport, especially given the security measures which had been taken. But of course, as Fida remarks, security measures could be a narcotic.

He remembers rolling—at the head of the line of trucks—past these three mounds, each of them defended by anti-tank and machine guns, behind which young Ethiopians talked, passed cigarettes, and listened to radio music.

Tessfaha had hoped that, again lulled by their new measure of security, the Ethiopians would have parked or hangared their squadrons of MIGs and Antonovs close together. He was delighted to find that it was so—four squadrons distributed around the northwest perimeter of the airfield, close to the officers' mess where Fida himself had lived for a time. So that no one could approach them by stealth, they were bathed in bright yellow light. Some of them were fueled and armed for their missions the next day.

Fida simply took up a position on the edge of the tarmac with Tessfaha—"directing traffic," he would later call it. "There are the Antonov hangars, there is the fuel dump, there is the rocket store, down there, that bunker second on the left."

It was all so quick, so stunningly loud and complete. Within five minutes more than forty MIGs were burning or had exploded on the airport apron. The fire and the column of smoke could be seen from Eritrean positions thirty miles away. Everyone moved automatically, Fida said, bludgeoned by the sound. He noticed some of the Eritreans fall and abstractly surmised that there must be firing from the officers' or soldiers' messes.

At a point when Fida had finished his traffic controlling and the further execution of the damage was in the hands of the rebels themselves, Fida led Tessfaha to the barracks, to the officers' quarters on the top floor. Their objective was the large bay at the end where the Russian military advisers stayed while in camp. Tessfaha and Fida were escorted and protected by a small body of young EPLF soldiers. These men and women fought a swift, terrible engagement with armed officers in the bar halfway along this landing. During it, Tessfaha pinned Fida to the outer wall, shielding him or perhaps stopping him from mediating. Fida trembled and protested as pilots he probably knew perished in there. But he understood no protest was feasible. He had—beforehand—believed that casualties would be on the Eritrean side and that the likely Ethiopian casualty would be himself.

Fida had looked forward to taking prisoner the squadron military advisers he had known—he had named them prosaically by their first names: a colonel named Oleg, a captain named Alexander, a lieutenant named Sergei. If one of them were out in the town, at least two of them should be in the base. But, after the shambles in the bar, Fida's Eritrean escort broke down one locked bedroom door and then another, finding both rooms empty. A third proved equally empty. It seemed sad to Fida, but not absolutely improbable, that all three officers should be in the city dining and drinking with the Soviet engineers of all stripes who lived in Eritrea.

To be thorough, the rebels broke down a fourth door. There was a shot from within which hit the wooden door jamb and bounced off it into Tessfaha's body. Fida presumed Tessfaha's injury was minor, a few wood splinters. In fact, the inventive Eritrean rebel would fall dead from the wound within seconds.

For his two large plans for that night he would posthumously attract frank criticism from his colleagues in the EPLF, for the fact that he went perhaps unnecessarily to Asmara himself, for the way the food convoy ambush involving Darcy and Masihi and the rest turned out. The random Russian shot from within that fourth room delivered him from having to explain himself.

Fida entered, passing Tessfaha as he staggered, and turned the light on. If the shot had come from an officer he knew, he could pacify and reassure the man. But the young man he saw standing by a bed was an absolute stranger, brown-haired, freckled, very thin. There was a bottle of vodka and a drained glass on a table in front of him, as if he had been having a nostalgic Slavic time, downing liquor in the dark. He had a Russian pistol in his hand.

Fida prepared himself to utter something soothing, but in the instant his mouth opened and before a word could emerge the young man sat on the bed and toppled sideways onto the pillow.

So that was it. The poor boy, believing too well the Dergue's stories about the rebels, about the way they tortured and dismembered prisoners, had taken his poison pill. With him perished, Fida can remember having thought irrationally among all the noise, an encyclopedic knowledge of the MIG-23 and all its ways.

By all accounts of this astoundingly effective strike, the Eritreans simply drove out of Asmara airport again, taking Tessfaha's body with them to save it from mutilation. Fida noticed that the guns at the third and second mounds had been silenced and the guard box was empty. Telephone lines had been cut and false messages had been broadcast throughout the city to police and army units.

Once beyond the airport itself, Fida was able therefore to talk the convoy through two city checkpoints and out into the open country.

The figures—the accounting if you like, for this Eritrean ploy—are well established now. Reputable articles have appeared on the subject. The more than forty MIG jets and three Antonovs destroyed that night must have cost the Dergue some three quarters of a billion dollars. The economic and military aspects of the Eritrean attack were so egregious that they were reported as an item in the BBC African News, and throughout Eritrea people in bunkers listened, celebrated with *sewa*, and felt safer.

Two months ago, Major Fida's wife was able to leave Ethiopia due to the special kindness of certain influential West German officials and politicians who were friendly to Eritrea. She lives in Munich, and there is a rumor that her husband will soon be permitted to leave the prison camp in the valley of She'b and join her there.

Darcy's Last Word:
Leave It All For Frankfurt

On the way down to the old Italian road after dark, I kept—like Christine—close to the experienced presence of Masihi. In Jani I had once felt profoundly lost in Africa, but now I walked at the bottom of the sea which had once, a pulse of time ago, two hundred million years gone, used these mountains as shoals and nurseries.

It was impossible in that dark, moving column to see Amna, but I had no illusions about her falling out and staying in shelter. Why should she? She was traveling homeward, toward holy Asmara, while I was awash in the alien and at a loss. Her homecoming was my exotic journalistic experience. I kept advising myself to leave it all for Frankfurt, where we'd be, if not exactly on my home ground, a damn sight closer to it. But I couldn't avoid the suspicion that some other wild option, an option of daring, was open to me.

We were in place above the road by midnight. Johanes first inspected and then pointed out to Masihi and Christine and me some ground in a nest of boulders. He spread rugs there, which one of these soldiers must have had to carry here. Christine and I opened up our sleeping bags on top of the rugs. It was a warm night, and we lay together with our boots on, looking up into a limitless pit of stars.

"Are you well, Darcy?" asked Christine Malmédy, flagrantly well herself, waggling her shoulders and her hips, confidently working the earth beneath the rugs and the sleeping bags into something like her own contours, her new home.

Without grounds, I said I was well.

"And Miss Nurhussein has appeared again," she said archly, and I almost heard her laughing.

I went to answer but then found she had turned on her side and seemed very soon to be asleep. In her father's mansion! Among the hard stones of Eritrea.

Masihi and I were left to deal with our insomnia. I could hear him sighing a great deal.

At last he said, "Darcy?"

I was astonished by his percipience. "How did you know I was awake?" I asked.

He did not answer that. "I think I should say something to you about Amna. In the spirit of what you would call fraternity."

"Oh yes?"

I was, of course, avidly awake now.

"I can recognize what is happening. I have been on that ground before you," he said solemnly. He swallowed rowdily. "I have been enchanted, too, by Ms. Amna Nurhussein."

My face prickled in the dark. "Am I as obvious as that?" I asked.

"Only when you have had too much *sewa*," he conceded. "It is too cruel. In the first place, she is an obsessed woman. And in the second, she is a cripple who does not appear to be one. On neither of those grounds is either of us fit to mix with her."

"She doesn't strike me as a cripple."

"No," murmured Masihi. "The will, you see. Stubbornness, of which she has a plentiful supply, my friend. But you have to realize everything has been done to her! Everything, I repeat. Everything they could think of. Afan. The Dergue."

"That's not what I hear," I protested. "She told me herself. She suffered the bastinado. But otherwise she was a witness. You know, to the torture of others."

"The bastinado is not a picnic," he said, yawning. "But in any case, what she told you is in the usual Eritrean spirit. If you wrote about her torture, she would feel embarrassed in front of her peers, her brothers and sisters." He made a sudden, dry noise of grieving in his throat. "They did everything to her, Darcy. Everything you could imagine."

"It doesn't matter," I said in a panic, "what they've done to her. It doesn't diminish her in my eyes."

"No. Do you know, I tried to marry her! But we to whom nothing has happened have no common conversation with people like her. They did *everything* to her. She cannot weep because they crushed her tear ducts with a circle of rope."

"With knots tied in it?" I asked.

"That's right."

Salim Genete had said something about that. The night his niece had died. There were reasons, he'd said, Amna couldn't cry.

"They did everything to her," said Masihi.

I was getting petulant at this repetition. "You keep saying that," I complained.

"Not even I," he told me, "know everything that was done. God knows what unnameable things! But about the nameable ones, I can tell you."

And he started to do it. She had suffered electric shocks. She had been stretched across a stone, four-cornered and immutable, with ropes. They had destroyed her womb that way. She could not have children and so she considered herself a woman more in a political sense, said Masihi, than any other. All her teeth had been pulled, and all her nails. There were burns everywhere on her body. Decency, said Masihi, prevented everyone except the surgeons she went to these days, and maybe her Frankfurt physiotherapist, from knowing the extent of her violation. However, she had been to extreme limits.

I was in terror now of what else I would hear.

There was an infamous trapdoor in Gebi interrogation center, Masihi told me. It was known by repute to all the EPLF. Opened, the trapdoor gave onto a narrow stone stairwell which descended into a cellar where first the Italian cavalrymen and then, during World War II, the British officers' mess had stored their vintages. They trussed her, her legs bent up her back, her arms behind her, wrists to ankles. They stood on her neck to do it. Trampling on her they dislocated her shoulder so that she had gone into a faint, said Masihi; and without her knowing it, they hurled her roped up down the stairwell. She was there for three days, every bone broken, drifting in and out of awareness.

"And her father bought her out?" I asked him, grasping at a detail she'd given me.

"No," he said. "They released her to a hospital in a coma. They were sure she was dead. They told the surgeon she'd stepped on a mine."

He called on me to envisage Amna in splints and traction, suppurating holes in the soles of her feet plugged with gauze soaked in antibiotic and applied by a doctor who had been a Rotarian friend of her father's. I could see all at once too keenly the desecrated girl, her joints bloated, every bone plastered or splinted, displaying the twenty angry gashes where her nails had been. And those extraordinary lengths of gauze growing from the stigmata in her feet! Had anyone ever been punished as she was punished?

Agents of the EPLF visited her in the hospital, said Masihi, boys and girls she had known. They arranged for her name to be attached to the body of a peasant girl who was brought there after an authentic mine blast outside Asmara.

That was how, in something like the way she'd told me, after four months of recuperation, she escaped with her parents and her six siblings through the cordons of Ethiopian security which ringed the outer suburbs of the city, to a village controlled by the Eritreans.

"They knew," said Masihi, "that very night. The refinements of Asmara were finished with.

"You should be told about this," said Masihi, when he'd finished his account. He said nothing more. His breathing grew steadier, perhaps like someone sleeping, or at least like someone delivered of a burden.

I remembered now my daydreams of a vigorous, sensual meal of sausages and cabbage and beer shared with Amna Nur-hussein in Frankfurt. It was not simply outside the reasonable odds. It was beyond Amna's capacity to digest. Afan had cru-cified her, and my distance from such a height of anguish dis-qualified me.

We could not share the same table. That—simply—was it.

The truth so dispirited me that I fell instantly asleep like someone concussed and did not wake until after midnight. There was much running around and considerable noise. Johanes and his raiders were pointing to a column of flame miles to the southeast.

Editor's Last Word About Darcy

Darcy's account of his Eritrean journey ends here. We know that early in the morning, a little after nine o'clock, a food convoy led by three tanks and two truckloads of infantry appeared on that stretch of road, traveling northeast over a ridge toward the city of Tessenai. The aid trucks themselves carried the flag of the UN.

From the nest of boulders where they had spent the night, Masihi and his daughter were already running tape of the convoy's approach. Echoing Fida from the night before, Masihi would later recount how astonished he was at the ease with which things were accomplished here. The first tank was jolted and untracked by a mine Johanes and his soldiers had planted in the road before dawn. The machine settled on the road crookedly, its barrel pointed downward. Another swung off the road, its turret seeking the rebels, but then stalled and was overrun. The third loosed one round from its cannon before it too was swarmed upon by guerrillas. Masihi, being a veteran, said of this one round, which landed high on the ridge, that it gave him an average jolt.

"And your daughter?" he was asked.

"Oh, my daughter ignored it," he said. "She is a natural."

"A natural guerrilla?"

"Exactly. She is. She has found her place in the world."

The confused Ethiopian infantry were quickly taken prisoner. All this, said Masihi, would be a sign of battles to come: the then future and now past battle of Agordat, for example, where eighteen thousand Ethiopians would be captured in one of the most massive battles since the

Second World War, one which went totally unrecorded in most of the world's press.

On the day of the convoy ambush, and simultaneously with the capture of tanks and the surrender of infantry, rebels flanking the road received the surrender of the conscript drivers of the aid convoy. Then, confidently, they fired grenades into five trucks along the lines. At this stage it was believed that the scope of the explosions would prove the trucks to be full of armaments.

As the witnesses—Masihi, Christine, Darcy, and Amna—now emerged from cover to have the Eritrean proposition proved to them, they became aware of Johanes running down the length of the string of trucks yelling in Tigrinyan and English, "Stop! It was a ruse. The trucks are all aid."

Masihi says that Darcy wondered aloud if Henry had been able to achieve this much.

The Eritrean position has ever since been that the Dergue somehow knew of Tessfaha's plan to capture a disguised arms convoy—that they committed the aid trucks and their inadequate military escorts deliberately to capture or destruction by the rebels.

Masihi does not pretend that everyone came to instant and simultaneous knowledge of the fact. But there was suddenly a conviction around that the undamaged trucks should now be saved. This was an urgency which seems to have touched Amna. For she was the one who would have to explain this destruction not only in Africa but also to the women of Europe. She is reported to have broken from the cover of the rocks and run to the cabin of the leading truck. Its cargo was burning slowly and there was smoke emerging from its engine. But it was still capable of being driven.

On the side of its door was the legend *With Love from Worldbeat*.

Masihi and Christine would later tell Stella Harries that they saw Darcy, running, join her in the cabin. The burning truck circled the stalled Russian tank and headed across rough country before rolling into a depression. When Masihi could no longer see it, he heard it blow up. It burned blackly.

Amna, blown clear with burns around her neck, was found close by. But not Darcy. It was presumed he was thrown very wide. If so, perhaps he wandered away among the thorn acacias, jolted by what must have been an enormous detonation; jerked back perhaps, away from the familiarity of Eritrea to the familiarity of Fryer River. He may have wandered, looking for holy pools and potent caves. The Ethiopians, whom not everyone believes, say they have not seen him and have gone to lengths to assure the world that they are not holding him. Did he wander into the arms of Ethiopian infantrymen fleeing the ambush site, who might understandably have shot him and perhaps even covered him with stones?

The Eritreans, too, have not been able to find him, though their mobile forces have searched for him and perpetually keep watch.

When Stella Harries saw Christine Malmédy some time after the incident, the girl was working the night shift in a bunker in Orotta, learning to edit—on an old videotape desk—some of the mass of her father's film material, covering both the war and the famine, as well even as the football match between one division of Eritreans and another. "The child," Stella thought, knowing that that was what Darcy had called the French girl.

It was a curious phrase, Stella thought, for him to have used of a quite interesting girl of twenty-one or -two. Both Darcy's former wife, Bernadette Yang, and Stella herself knew that Darcy was a normal male. It reflected well on him, she says, on the sort of man he was and still might be, that while he traveled with Christine he didn't see himself as journeying at the side of a woman of independent desires.

It is not yet established if he needs or should appropriately be given a monument—but if he does, this passes for one.

The BBC shortwave news indicated correctly that he had vanished during a separate incident from the one at Asmara airport, though the misconception that he was engaged in blowing up planes persists. There were some vaguely hostile comments in the British press about the value of journalists attaching themselves to palpably illicit guerrilla activities. There were one or two panels convened on British television about journalistic ethics. Darcy, in fact, came out not too badly from this.

For the truth is that the famine has worsened, and the world knows it cannot be entirely because Darcy witnessed the blowing up of a few trucks. The Dergue suffers one military disaster after another. The numbers of Ethiopian prisoners in Eritrea have increased threefold. The Dergue is punished by its own economic fatuity, though not as fiercely as are its people.

The July rains in Eritrea are erratic and the people starve in Endilal where Lady Julia saw the seeds of her revolution.

On the Nacfa Front, the grammar classes continue. And all the incidents fail to be separate.